GENOCIDAL ORGAN
PROJECT ITOH

GENOCIDAL ORGAN
PROJECT ITOH

TRANSLATED BY EDWIN HAWKES

HAIKA SORU

SAN FRANCISCO

Genocidal Organ
© 2007 Project Itoh
Originally published in Japan by Hayakawa Publishing, Inc.

English translation © 2012 VIZ Media, LLC
Cover design by Sam Elzway
All rights reserved.

HAIKASORU
Published by VIZ Media, LLC
295 Bay Street
San Francisco, CA 94133

www.haikasoru.com

Library of Congress Cataloging-in-Publication Data

Itoh, Project, 1974–2009.
  [Gyakusatsu kikan. English]
  Genocidal organ / Project Itoh ; translated by Edwin Hawkes.
      p. cm.
  Summary: "The war on terror exploded, literally, the day Sarajevo was destroyed by a homemade nuclear device. The leading democracies transformed into total surveillance states, and the developing world has drowned under a wave of genocides. The mysterious American John Paul seems to be behind the collapse of the world system, and it's up to intelligence agent Clavis Shepherd to track John Paul across the wreckage of civilizations, and to find the true heart of darkness—a genocidal organ"— Provided by publisher.
    ISBN 978-1-4215-4272-0 (pbk.)
    I. Hawkes, Edwin.   II. Title.
    PL871.5.T64G9313 2012
    895.6'36—dc23
                    2012023460

The rights of the author of the work in this publication to be so identified have been asserted in accordance with the Copyright, Designs and Patents Act 1988. A CIP catalogue record for this book is available from the British Library.

Printed in the U.S.A.
First printing, August 2012
Second printing, October 2023

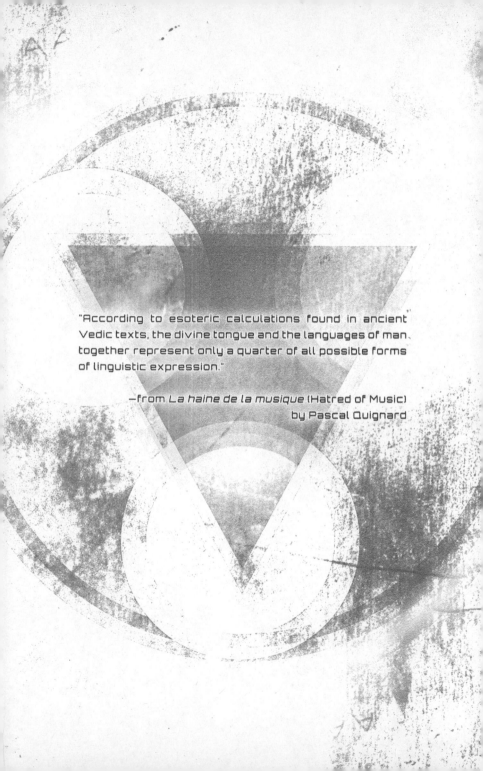

"According to esoteric calculations found in ancient Vedic texts, the divine tongue and the languages of man, together represent only a quarter of all possible forms of linguistic expression."

—from *La haine de la musique* (Hatred of Music) by Pascal Quignard

CHAPTER

ONE

So, there was this little girl's head shoved face first into the tire tracks in the mud.

It looked almost like a scene from *Alice in Wonderland*—it was as though the girl were trying to enter the magical kingdom through the deep furrows in the mud left by truck tires. Only I don't remember the back of Alice's head being shot clean open or the contents of Alice's skull glistening under the sky like a crimson flower in full bloom.

The next thing I laid my eyes on was a kid sprawled on his side in the mud. Less than ten feet away from the girl. Bullets had ripped his back open and had spun their way through his guts before exiting his body somewhere around his belly. His intestines flopped out, washed pink by the rainfall that had just stopped a couple of hours ago. His mouth was open a little, just enough for me to see he had an almost goofy-looking little overbite. It was as if there'd been something he had wanted to say before he died but never had the chance.

We followed the tire tracks and arrived at a small village, maybe twenty or so families in size.

A large pit had been dug in the area that could have been called the village green. At the bottom of the pit was a pile of bodies, charred and smoldering, all heaped on top of one another. There was the smell of singed hair and the smell of burning flesh. The heat had caused the muscles of the half-cooked bodies to contract violently, so the corpses were spread out in a whirlwind. Many of the bones were broken, defeated by the contracting muscles, and limbs were folded over and twisted in ways that no limb would or could ever bend naturally. A tangled web of bodies.

Everyone's dead.
Everyone's dead. I open the door to see my mom, whose body has just been treated with the cocktail of preservatives, sanitizers, disinfectants, and additives as mandated by law in Washington. The embalmer has made her face up good and pretty, and she's ready for her eternal sleep.

"Take a good look behind you, darling. You'll see all the dead pass by," my mom says to me, so I do as she says and turn around. I see a vast landscape of dead people, grinning and waving at me. Some of the dead are fully intact, others have virtually disintegrated. Don't ask me how I know that even the headless ones are somehow smiling at me—I just know, I can tell, and as I look on at them they casually fiddle around with their guts that are spilling from their bellies.

"Everyone's dead, aren't they?" I ask, turning back to my mom.

Mom nods and then gestures to me. "Of course they are, darling. Just take a look at your own body."

I look down and notice that I'm starting to rot away. That's when it clicks that I'm also dead.

Up in the distance I see a stream of dead bodies—everyone who has ever lived and died—flowing gently and inexorably toward their destination, wherever that is.

I ask Mom whether we're now in the underworld. But Mom just shakes her head gently. Just like when she used to correct me when I was a boy.

"No, darling. This is just the regular world. The world you and I have always lived in. The world that's always been here right beside us."

Oh, I see, I say. Tears of relief are streaming down my face. I can now recognize some faces in the distance. Benjamin, who died of cancer as a child. My dad, who blew his own head off.

Mom takes me by the hand. "Ready to go?" she asks. I nod, and we start walking toward the line of dead people in the distance. This is a bit like how it was the first day of school, I seem to remember. My tears turn into tears of nostalgia. And then I realize that they're all here beside me—the girl in the tire tracks who had the back of her head blown off, the boy who had his guts blown out, the villagers who were burnt up in a seething mass in the pit. They're walking alongside us, and we head on over to join the column of the dead.

2

I killed my mother with my own words.

I've killed plenty of people in my time, using all sorts of guns and every caliber of ammo. But I didn't need any of that stuff to kill my mother. Just a couple of little phrases: "yes" and my name. Put the two of them together and my mom died.

Yes, I've killed plenty of people in my time. Mainly using a gun.

Sure, I've killed using the blade as well, but truth be told I'm not so keen on that as a method. Quite a number of my colleagues do swear by it, though. They make it a point of honor to specialize in the blade for "professional purposes." These are the guys who can approach you from behind in absolute silence, slice your windpipe clean open, slit your jugular, sever your aorta, and then go on to pierce your heart, all in less than three seconds flat.

I'm not quite at that level myself, although I'm pretty confident I could acquit myself well enough on this front if I needed to. But guns and ammo are what I know best, and I guess they're what I'm going to carry on using to do my killing for the foreseeable future. All because a couple of airplanes plowed into two buildings standing side by side in New York, back during one fine morning in the year 2001.

Before that day, no matter how much of a bastard you were, the United States of America wouldn't sanction an assassination attempt on you. Not officially, at least. Late last century,

Executive Order 12333 reiterated President Gerald Ford's original proscription of assassination or any government involvement in assassination. Even the Public Enemy Number One of the day— say the drug lord Pablo Escobar who flooded the US with South American drugs, or the US's pet thorn-in-the-side dictator Saddam Hussein—however much the US might have wanted them dead, there was never any official attempt to actually assassinate them.

"No person employed by or acting on behalf of the United States Government shall engage in, or conspire to engage in, assassination." That's how the executive order was worded. Just words, maybe, but each president in his turn—Reagan, then Bush, then Clinton—found himself increasingly bound by their power. That's not to say that assassinations never took place, of course, but the executive order was respected. Assassination had become a risky move politically. More trouble than it was worth. Easier and cleaner all around simply to face the enemy down: engage in formal negotiations or have a war. As a political tool, assassination just didn't have the *priority* it used to. Unless it could be guaranteed top secret, it just wasn't worth it anymore.

After all, couldn't the US start a war with anyone they wanted to? All they needed to do was find some pretext. The bar was much lower than assassination. Far easier to convince the media that we should kill large numbers of people "fair and square" than it would be to try and explain away a botched assassination attempt. Who was it who said that a single death was a tragedy but that a million deaths was a statistic? Well, either way, it was easier to paint yourselves as the "good guys" when you killed tens of thousands—who *must* therefore have been bad—than when you killed an individual person. This was what the world used to be like anyway.

Everything changed the day we were attacked on home ground. Things started heating up. I wouldn't go as far as to say that assassination was now back in as the flavor of the month, but within the halls of power in Washington it was at least back on the table as an option. A worthy contender. A necessary evil in the war against terror, in the fight for humanity. That's how they've explained it. The dark arts that EO 12333 were supposed to have suppressed forever reemerged into the light of day.

And that, more or less, is how I ended up as an assassin.

Not because I'd particularly wanted to—it was just that my job seemed to involve increasing work of that sort. I had duties besides killing, of course. But we in Special Operations I Detachment had sole responsibility for all the assassination jobs parceled out by USSOCOM—the Unified Combatant Command that oversaw the various Special Operations Commands for the US Army, Air force, Navy, Marines, and Intelligence. Back last century the Green Berets sometimes used to get involved in that sort of work, as did that US Army detachment called Delta Force. But now, in the twenty-first century, it's basically taken care of by us "Snake Eaters" in Intelligence. So much so, in fact, that the guys from the LRRP in the Marines and the Navy SEALS had contemptuously started referring to us as "wet boys"—a nickname derived from "wet work," the Cold War–era euphemism for assassination. Novelists like Graham Greene and John le Carré used the term a lot.

Think of that famous poster for the film *Carrie*. Poor, abused Sissy Spacek, standing petrified, doused from head to toe in pig blood. Same for us, only in our case it was human blood we were drenched in. The official headhunters of the United States of America. Or, as Intelligence had named us, Special Operations I Detachment.

And that's pretty much how I've come to be sitting here in the belly of this Flying Seaweed Craft, double-checking the files on our next target.

The face, name, movement patterns, household setup, political leanings of our target were all here, collected in a single file. The next person we were going to kill. We had all sorts of observation techniques drummed into us during our Special Forces training. After all, we aren't just about blowing things up. No more wham, bam, thank you Uncle Sam. These days, we were usually tasked with jobs along the lines of training allied forces in developing countries or winning the hearts and minds of locals through medical care, education, and propaganda. In other words, this job was a lot about the "soft skills" and not as suited to the cliché of the grizzled, misanthropic lone wolf as is often imagined. Those sorts usually became mercs instead—although in all honesty, mercenaries often ended up as tactical advisors for the armies in these Third World countries as well, so their job wasn't all that different from ours.

In addition, we in Special Operations I Detachment had to undergo a rigorous program of psychological training to enable us to grasp a person's character based on a cold reading of their psychometric graphs. You see, the assassination game was still a particularly delicate business—even though the level of political risk, *ethical bias* if you will, had grown more manageable. The world may have moved on from EO 12333, but there were still a shitload of CIA operations that had failed miserably. No, this was no gig for amateurs.

Bungled CIA ops were referred to as "paramilitary operations," but really they were just playing Cowboys and Indians. And so it came to pass that a new category of forces was formed—Intelligence, specifically the Special Operations Branch with its Special Operations I Detachment. A military department that took over the CIA's former remit in intelligence gathering. A sort of soldier-sailor-tinker-spy hybrid. The way the twenty-first century was panning out, intelligence activity was much more relevant in a military context than a civilian one anyway. Military intelligence is a moveable feast, and anywhere and everywhere was a theater of war these days.

Things just ain't what they used to be, you see. There's always that element of uncertainty that needs to be factored in. And because the name of the game was now all about trying to predict and manage that uncertainty on the one hand, and to adapt when that uncertainty did rear its ugly head on the other, it made sense for Special Forces personnel to have a clear mental image of the sort of person their target was.

In other words we needed to be able to apprehend, down to the last vivid detail, the personality of the person we were about to kill: what he was like, how he led his life. We had to walk a mile in the other person's shoes, building our empathy with them to a crescendo—and then kill them. A task fit for a sadist. The stuff a Nazi's wet dreams are made of. So why did this sort of work not cause us to go mad with psychological trauma of our own? One reason, and one reason only: Battle Emotion Adaptive

Regulation. A powerful combination of pre-combat counseling and mind treatment that would "configure" our emotions, our morality. This allowed us to draw a clear dividing line between our personal ethics and our duty. Orwell's "doublethink" made a banal reality by technology.

So: when I looked down at the data of my next target, I wasn't doing so with any trace of pity or compassion for him. Rather, I was thinking about the last person I killed. My mother.

The land of the dead. It came to call on me, to pay a visit, to scratch away at the surface of my heart—only to fade away again as I opened my eyes.

In the land of the dead, there were a number of variations on a theme.

The version that haunted me incessantly was that of the hordes of decomposing dead trundling across an endless plain in a line stretching out for all eternity. There were others too: the grave-yard that seemed to sprawl out forever, each former inhabitant sitting atop its grave, waiting in endless tedium. Then there was the version I experienced regularly just after my mother died: the almost comical scene of a hospital ward populated entirely by patients who were already dead. This was the one that hit home the most. I guess because it was a direct projection of my emotional state the moment after my mother died.

Well, I'm a soldier, Special Forces, and an assassin. So I've seen my fair share of dead bodies. There was one time I saw more corpses than a regular Joe would ever have the opportunity to see in an entire lifetime. It was just after a massacre had taken place in a country in Central Asia. I was an assassin back then too, part of an I Detachment mission to infiltrate the country by way of Afghanistan and assassinate the former chief of secret police who had been fanning the flames of ethnic cleansing. We finally caught up with him in this village.

The man died, of course. I know this because I was the one who pumped an entire magazine of rifle rounds into his head at close quarters. But the man's regiment had already managed to "cleanse" the entire village by that point. Oh, I saw plenty of corpses that day, all right. The rain stopped, and there was the girl with her face embedded in tire tracks in the mud, the back of her head shot to shit, with what was left of her brains exposed to the elements. There was the boy whose back had been ripped apart by the hail of bullets that forced his guts to spill out of his belly. And there was the pile of bodies of women and children who had been thrown into the makeshift pit in the village green, doused with gasoline, and set alight.

Finally there was the man who had orchestrated it all. After I shot him, his corpse seemed to twist into a gruesome parody of the hordes of dead that were his own handiwork.

Returning from my memories of that scene in Asia, I found myself back with my mother. She was being kept alive by a cocktail of drugs and nanomachines, intravenous tubes everywhere, and I was being asked by the doctor whether I wanted to continue the course of treatment. To look at her, there was nothing outwardly wrong with my mother as she lay there all neat and orderly in her pristine bed, silently awaiting my judgment. She even looked alive—an illusion maintained by the nanomachines that coursed through her veins, no doubt. Machines not unlike the ones pumped into us as part of our PIC conditioning (Persistence in Combat, they called it).

I stood there, in the pure silence of that pristine hospital, and the paperwork was passed to me: official consent to pull the plug. The confirmation they needed, proof that I had understood and agreed to the termination of life-support treatment. The consent having been given, the army of life-giving nanomachines sped forth from her body, never to return, and my mother segued into a smooth, quick death.

Having said that—could it really have been said that my mother was *now* dead? How could I really know that she wasn't already dead at the so-called *moment* I gave the order to end treatment?

That ambiguous fine line between life and death had become increasingly blurred due to medical advances in the latter half of the twentieth century, but humankind seemed to be content to close their eyes to this increasingly delicate problem, just as we did for other difficult problems. *Let's deal with that tomorrow* seemed to be our attitude.

How like us, really. Such is human nature, and what can you

do other than shrug your shoulders and accept it? And so I did accept it, and so my mother was embalmed and placed neatly in her little casket. Embalmed according to the statutes of the District of Columbia. After that, she was past the point of no return—no more ambiguity as to whether she was dead or not.

She was the last person to die by my own hands.

"Captain Shepherd. Come in, Captain Shepherd."

I was awoken by a voice calling my name. I must have nodded off while trying to review the file in front of me. I touched my cheek instinctively before I even realized why I was doing so: because I didn't like the idea that the loadmaster who woke me might have seen me crying in my sleep, as I always did when I visited the land of the dead.

"Time to wake up, sir. Fifteen minutes until blastoff."

Having said what he needed to say, the loadmaster left me to my thoughts.

Blastoff. No kidding—that was the right term. These days HALO-style anachronistic parachute maneuvers have been superseded by Intruder Pods: sleek, high-speed pods that kept electromagnetic waves down to a minimum, making detection by enemy radar virtually impossible. The cargo hold in which I sat was lined with a row of black cylinders, like giant ballpoint pens, and the maintenance staff were primed and ready to go. I looked around at my surroundings in the belly of the Flying Seaweed Craft to see the other guys from my unit hustling and bustling all around me.

"Dude, how the hell do you sleep in the middle of this giant pneumatic drill?" Williams shouted as he approached me. "That turbulence back there bashed the hell out of us."

I told him I hadn't noticed.

"Jesus Christ. I've never seen anyone who could zone out like you can. I bet you can't even feel your own dick when you have a boner."

It wasn't surprising that the Flying Seaweed Craft was shaking so much; it was a warplane after all. It wasn't set up to be a luxury passenger liner. The actual technology involved in these craft might have improved by leaps and bounds, but amenities for the comfort of the poor infantry who actually had to ride on the bloody things remained rock-bottom priority. Welcome to my world.

The Flying Seaweed Craft were a weird oblong shape in order to reduce their electromagnetic footprint to an absolute minimum. It was only because of the sophisticated piloting software that they were even able to fly at all. And when it was almost a miracle that they could even take off, let alone not crash, there wasn't a lot of time left to worry about how smooth the ride was.

"I don't know about me feeling my dick, but I've never had any complaints from your mom," I fired back at Williams. "Anyhow, don't you have other things to worry about, like getting ready for the drop?"

"Nice one. And speak for yourself, dude. I'm all set. I'm just hoping you're not going to fuck anything up too badly."

"Funny, your mom also said *that* last time I saw her..." I answered, as Williams sat down next to me. Truth be told, Williams wasn't so much a trash-talker as a shit-stirrer. He'd gossip about anything, trying to take you into his confidence over the stupidest things. Who'd picked up a new piece of ass, what perversions so-and-so was into lately—the more banal the gossip, the more likely he was to be there whispering it in your ear like a girl.

"By the way, Clavis, what's your honest opinion about our orders on this mission?" he asked me.

Now, this was actually a question that had been troubling all of us. Not that anyone had voiced it publicly, of course. *Theirs not to reason why, theirs but to do and die,* such was our unwritten law. For most of us anyway. Considering he was supposed to be elite Special Forces, Williams had this abnormal fascination with trivia and an unusually loose tongue and casual manner to go with it. As a result, we were always being treated to gems such as "Did you know that Charlize Theron witnessed her own mother shoot her father dead when she was fifteen years old? Actually saw it happen right in front of her own eyes?"

"Who knows," I said, noncommittal. "It's going to be tight.

Taking two targets out simultaneously isn't easy at the best of times. Unless they both arrive at the appointed rendezvous spot at exactly the right time, there are a lot of variables that could mess things up."

"No, dude, I'm not talking about the *logistics*," said Williams, who was somewhat antsy now. "I'm talking about Target B. The American?"

"Well, there are Americans all over the world," I said, and then I looked at him and sighed. "Or are you trying to say you have no problem killing the little brown people of the world, but that your conscience troubles you when it's a fellow countryman's neck on the line? Is—"

"Hell, no. He's one evil twisted sonofabitch of a countryman. My conscience is just fine," Williams said, cutting me off. "It's just there's something about his profile that's bothering me. It's like there's some vital clue that's been whitewashed out of the report that we were given. I'm not the only one saying this either—the other guys think the same, that it's impossible to work out what sort of person he is. We just can't get a mental image of *who he is*."

"Other than being one evil twisted sonofabitch of a countryman, you mean."

Williams shrugged his shoulders. "Well, that part's not hard to figure out, is it? Our job is to go after the bad guys. If this guy is our target, it stands to reason that he *must* be evil, right?"

A nice, simple worldview. Williams still believed, after everything, that his country could do no wrong. Of course, this sort of tunnel vision was fostered by the job. Demanded, even. Without it, how would one be able to face strangers, look them in the eye, and kill, kill, and kill again?

The easiest way to make sure that you could sleep at night with a clear mind and an unburdened conscience was simply not to think too hard on things. A simple ideology for a simple mind.

When you're standing at an ethical crossroads, sometimes it's easier not to look before you leap.

To be thick-skinned is to be enlightened. So aim to develop a thicker skin than the next man.

Embrace the tautology: *we're right because we're right*.

An ordinary soldier has to kill that undefined, undifferenti-ated mass called "the enemy" in order to protect himself. And although in Special Forces we might have seemed more like high-tech, elite assassins, in many ways our role was closer to that of the ordinary soldier. The only difference was that it was our job to go one step further, to define and to differentiate that enemy for operational purposes. But it was still easier all around if, emotionally, we treated them as that same undifferentiated mass that the common soldier was firing at, so that the weight of all the individual lives we snuffed out didn't rest too heavily on our shoulders.

Some soldiers still broke down, of course. Think back to the time when the US drafted in counselors by the hundreds in order to try and rehabilitate their troops stationed in Iraq before sending them home for reintegration into society. They set up repatriation camps where those on deck to return to the States would be able to experience a simulated version of American society. That's how Baghdad came to be one big US-themed summer camp.

The soldiers who had been living in the parallel universe that is war now had to try and remember what it was like to go shopping at K-Mart. *How much does a Snickers bar cost again?* And so it came to pass that the men and women warped by the battlefields of Iraq wouldn't be allowed to return to the real America without passing through the virtual one first.

The human psyche is a fragile thing. The more you dwelt on the people that you've killed, imagining the lives that they led and would have continued to lead had you not killed them, the more likely it was that you'd suffer emotional scarring. Which meant that we in Special Forces were particularly susceptible to this sort of thing—after all, unlike the ordinary soldier who fired into the crowds, we killed individuals, face to face. So much more stressful for us.

Or maybe the likes of Williams and I only thought this way because we were Americans, cosseted and wrapped up in our little Western ethnocentric bubbles. There were plenty of places still left in the world where life was cheap or even completely without value. I knew this. I'd been to them.

In fact we were entering just such a hellish place right now, penetrating the darkness in our sleek black aircraft. We were hurtling down toward the badlands below, and when we emerged we knew we would be entering pandemonium. A scene of un-imaginable tragedy that was somehow tinged with manic glee.

A scene right out of a Hieronymus Bosch painting, in other words.

The intercom from the cockpit sounded inside my ear: "*We're five minutes into enemy airspace, but no sign of antiaircraft fire and no response from their missile systems. We're proceeding smoothly, and all signs are we'll avoid enemy detection. Looks like we've caught them napping, gentlemen.*"

All operatives on this sort of secret mission had internal transmitters and hands-free receivers built into our bodies. Other high-tech devices too: software to pick up and decipher the faintest of murmurs, so that what's imperceptible to our surroundings is decoded and transmitted to the rest of the team. This reconstructed speech sounded nothing like your real speech of course. It was an artificial representation of what you would have sounded like, an imaginary construct that existed somewhere between your voice box and the speakers that it was relayed to.

"Our Stealth Paint strikes again. It's absorbing all the radar," Williams said nonchalantly. "If it weren't for our IFF telling our guys back on the ground our position, I doubt they'd be able to spot us either."

"*Ten minutes till drop. Start wrapping yourselves up, boys. And good luck.*"

"Here we go." I patted Williams on the back. He headed into his pod without another word. The reason the pods were matte black was not to block detection by electromagnetic rays, but rather to block infrared. The loadmaster blasted out "Voodoo Child (Slight Return)" by Jimi Hendrix over the speakers. Psyching us up for battle.

I thought what I always thought when I watched the men around me climbing into their pods: *they're getting inside their coffins.*

The dead who crawl back into their coffins. With their faces painted for camouflage they looked just like zombies. As if they were corpses reanimated by a voodoo spell and only now finally returning to their caskets where they belonged. As I watched the guys all around me lumber into their pods I couldn't help but notice their glazed expressions, blank like so many dead fish.

Voodoo Child. I guess the loadmaster must have been thinking the same thing? I glanced over at him to see if I could read his expression, but his face was obscured by the oxygen mask he was now wearing to cope with the increased g-forces.

I decided to join the others and stood up to head to my pod. The rest of the unit were already ensconced in their own pods, arms folded across their chests, braced for impact. From my vantage directly above they looked more like real corpses than ever.

A scene from a movie flitted into my head. *2001: A Space Odyssey.* The scene in which the astronauts in suspended animation were silently killed off by the computer, one by one.

I entered my pod and adopted the posture of a dead man. I crossed my arms across my chest like the Pharaohs of old. I looked up through the hatch to see the ceiling of the cargo bay, lights shining down on me. I could hear my own breathing resonating in the casket. I was a corpse. A corpse and a horseman of the apocalypse, ready to wreak a trail of death and destruction on the unsuspecting lands below.

Then out of nowhere I was overwhelmed by a bizarre wave of emotions.

"Pressurization in the hold commenced. Five minutes until guided ejection. Prepare for blastoff."

Complicated emotions. Something like sadness, but I couldn't quite put my finger on them.

I saw my mom in her hospital bed, lying sideways, eyes closed. Embalmed, ready for her eternal sleep, and smiling.

The hatch door to my pod slid shut silently and smoothly, and the moment it sealed me off from the outside world I felt the reverberating thud of pressurization. Sound disappeared from the world, and all was darkness. This was what it was like to be buried.

Yes. I was now experiencing my mom's death for myself. *That's* why I was suddenly so overcome with emotion, I realized. That was why this high-altitude drop, normally so routine for people in my line of work, had taken on monumental significance.

There was a high-pitched creaking sound from the outside of the pod. The cargo bay was starting to lose pressure.

"The cargo bay is now fully decompressed. Three minutes until blastoff. Release rear hatches."

Motors roared into action, and shortly afterward the locks were opened. The Seaweed's belly opened up. The loadmaster was buffeted this way and that by the air currents streaming in through the open hatch, but those of us inside our pods heard and felt nothing.

"One minute until blastoff. Commence countdown."

I wondered if this was how my mom went too. Being shut off from the light as the casket finally closed, then sealed into place with nails. On the journey to who-knows-where, trapped shut inside a box, buried for all eternity. Is that what happened to Mom—to all people, anywhere, since time immemorial when people first started sealing their dead in caskets?

The countdown continued inside my mind, but I wasn't feeling the exhilaration I usually did just before a drop.

"We have blastoff. Godspeed to you all."

I heard the thud that came with release: both heavy and gentle at the same time. Then gravity disappeared.

I was at the mercy of the laws of physics. Specifically, the law of gravity.

3

My coffin hurtled through the empty skies.

For a few seconds my equipment seemed to float all around me. Then the computer-guided descent kicked in, ending the free-fall section of the flight. The pods we were in had no propulsion mechanism. They were equipped with neither fuel nor engine. The trajectory could only be modified by external stability wings, on the same principle as hang gliders. They were piloted by changing the angles of fins on the wings—somewhere between a glider and a smart bomb. A smart bomb with a human stuffed inside where the explosives usually go.

The flying coffin wove its way through the currents, the wings skillfully guiding it toward its destination. The wings were made of living muscle tissue. In fact, the flying coffin that I was currently riding in—the Intruder Pod, to give it its official name—hardly contained any mechanical parts at all. Or rather, it was maybe easier to say that it was made almost entirely of living flesh. Not only could the pod control the wings, it was covered with cysts that were able to contract at will, causing the actual shape of the pod to warp so that it could adapt to and cut smoothly across the turbulent air currents.

The vibrations and the noise from the air hitting the pod started to die down. The angle of descent was growing less steep, and I could sense how the trajectory was being fine-tuned by the way the center of gravity started to shift. It looked like the pod was entering the final stage of its guidance mode.

I heard another thud, and suddenly my body weight was pressing down on my legs again. The drogue chute had opened up and absorbed most of the propulsive force. We were probably only a few meters from the earth by now. I braced myself for impact. That was about all you could do in one of these caskets. The pod's speed completely killed, it was now falling to the ground.

Most of the shock on landing was absorbed by the drogue chute and the living tissue of the hull. The pod descended as gently as a falling dandelion spore. It was a bit like attaching a parachute to a ballpoint pen. The cylindrical pod hit the ground and then fell over to one side. The way the hull was built meant that it was weighted to one side, so there was not too much chance of it rolling on and on—and screwing up the soldier's sense of balance in the process—unless its occupant was unlucky enough to land on one hell of a slope.

I hadn't been unlucky, and it looked like my pod was now at rest. I released the lock and placed my hand on the hatch. I pushed the square door gently outward. Last time I had looked out it was at the ceiling of the Flying Seaweed Craft. Now I found myself looking up at a starry night sky.

After emerging from our pods and confirming that our positions were secure, we got to work in silence. Williams's pod had landed not forty feet away. The other two guys were both within a four-hundred-foot radius. With smart bombs guided by GPS or laser or drones, you'd expect at least half of them to fall within the target radius; we were working at a level above all that. *We never miss* could have been our motto, even if it sounded a bit corny. But it was true that our technology for guided descent was about as good as it gets.

We put the pods into self-destruct mode, and the living tissue cultures had their supply of special enzymes cut off, resulting in quick cell death and rapid disintegration. The desiccated pods were like ancient Egyptian mummies, keratinized like ancient skin. We could now leave the husks to crumble, safe in the knowledge that before long they would be nothing more than fertilizer for the grassy plains on which they now lay.

All there was left for us to do was to get rid of the handful of mechanical parts not integrated into the pods' biological structures. Even these parts were fully modularized though, and the clean-up operation was simple. We were finished in less than ten minutes. We were like teenagers dutifully tidying up after a campfire, silently removing all traces of clues that we had ever been there.

Only difference was, for us the party was just getting started...

We put our plan into action the second we finished our clean-up.

We needed to have everything finished before dawn broke. Assassination's not really a daytime job. Ideally you want nobody to see you—including the target.

It was a four-man team: Williams, me, and two others. We'd all been in this scenario plenty of times—no greenhorns here. We followed the plan set by SOP: Alex, the skilled tracker, was the forward scout, and Leland, who graduated in the same class as Alex, on rearguard duty. Williams and I pushed through the darkness in the middle, keeping a vigilant lookout on either side.

I make it sound simple now, but truth be told, a nighttime stealth march ain't easy. Easier than it used to be, of course, thanks to the technology that we were blessed with these days.

The snug inner lining of our clothes absorbed the moisture we perspired and wicked it away to be recycled, and the nanolayer surgery coated our eyeballs with a film that not only auto-adjusted ambient light levels so that we could see clearly even on a cloudy midnight such as this one, but also projected useful combat data straight to our retinas.

Even with these developments, it still wouldn't do just to land the Intruder Pods right next to our target and have at them. The basic precepts of special ops remained unchanged: you still needed to land some distance away from the target, replete with guns and explosives and other useful goodies, and then get marching. Considering how varied special ops work was supposed to be, we sure did spend a lot of time walking—at least, that's how it seemed to me. Our job was to walk and walk and walk and then finally, at the end of it all, close in on the target. The first part of selection for joining our outfit involved them strapping a huge Bergen rucksack to your back, filling it with rocks, and sending you on an extended forced march at breakneck speed. This separated the men from the boys, all right—most applicants were weeded out at this stage.

Our team had consulted closely with Intelligence before the drop to decide the very best landing point that took into account all factors. Even so, we were still looking at a brisk four-hour uphill march, and that was assuming no distractions or detours.

Alex was a cut above the rest of us in terms of fitness, so he sped on ahead to scout more effectively whenever there were any contours in the landscape. This was a short mission, in and out within twelve hours, so we didn't need our Bergens stuffed full with food, water, and ammo. This meant that we could set a punishing pace. We marched on the target town as fast as it was possible to walk while still keeping an adequate lookout for indications of enemy presence.

There was a road that led toward the town. No more than a rough dirt footpath, really. But our satellites had shown enough traffic along it that it was never really a viable option for us. Having said that, the Eurasian landscape that we were now in, mostly consisting of fields and forest, was easy enough for us to traverse. Desert or jungle terrain would have been much harder.

The official line was that this country was suffering from the same old story as found the world over: Muslims versus Christians. Of course, conflicts usually have more than one catalyst. After all, there were countries where Islam and Christianity could peacefully coexist, even when right next door. It seemed that this even used to be the case in this country, historically. A former state of the USSR that had declared independence after the disintegration of the old Communist Party, this country had taken the usual course of confrontation with Russia over natural resources, but there had been nothing to suggest that religion was going to be the cause of bitter internecine warfare. Not until a few short years ago.

How had the conflict developed so rapidly? How had the flames of hatred in people's hearts been fanned so quickly that massacres had become commonplace? At such an exponential rate? There wasn't a scholar in the world who had been able to come up with a convincing hypothesis.

We had to avoid an encounter with the enemy at all costs. At least until our targets were safely dead. If we were sighted, it would all be over. They'd radio ahead to our targets, who'd be spirited out of harm's way. With our equipment and training we'd have no problem fighting our way through an enemy company or two until we reached the safety of our pick-up point. But the mission itself would be a failure.

We took a short pit stop after our second hour of marching. We'd virtually been running the whole way, and Williams was on the verge of breathlessness. I couldn't say I wasn't feeling it too. We lay down in a thicket, hidden from view, and our nanocoating sprang into action, blending us in with the colors of the vegetation that swirled around us. A little piece of magic that came in ever so handy when planning an infiltration or ambush.

On this occasion, though, it looked like we had become a little *too* reliant on it.

It turned out there was a pickup truck parked just the other side of the thicket in which we were hiding. Of course, our muscles all sprang into a state of high alert. Breathing silently, we became one with the vegetation around us and watched as three men clambered out of the car brandishing AK rifles. It goes without saying that they were completely oblivious to our presence. They lit a bonfire.

They didn't seem to notice or care about the ammo in their guns. They threw their guns down right beside them, beside the fire, even though the magazines were fully loaded.

"Amateurs," mouthed Williams. I shrugged. In this land, the qualification for being a soldier was the ability to plunder and terrorize a defenseless village when the opportunity presented itself. Training didn't really come into it.

Having said that, we couldn't exactly take off while they remained here, amateurs or not. And we had no time to spare if we were to make our target before dawn. So we had no ethical compunction about deciding to kill these unfortunate patrol troops who bore us no specific ill will, who hadn't tried to harm us, and who were just trying to snatch a moment of warm respite.

The men remained completely unaware of our presence as we silently flanked them. They would also have been completely unaware of the brief flash of steel before their windpipes were slit open with surgical precision. They wouldn't have known what happened, who killed them, or why. Even as their lifeblood poured from their throats, their eyes wouldn't have even caught a glimpse of us. They just flickered orange, reflecting the licking flames from the bonfire in front of them. And so it came to pass that where there had been four men, there were now four corpses.

We frisked the bodies quickly. No sign of any dog tags or other ID. Then I used my knife to open up my guy's sleeve, starting at his already blood-soaked shoulder.

As I expected, there was the slightest of bumps at a point among the muscles of his back. Completely undetectable to the naked eye unless you knew exactly what you were looking for, a bulge about the size of the fingernail on your pinkie.

I used my knife to shave off the chunk of flesh. Inside it, sure enough, was a small disc.

His ID tag.

Williams looked over at me, eyebrows raised. *The usual, huh?* he was asking. As the ranking officer, it was my call.

We were four white men standing there—only whites were chosen for this mission, for obvious reason. The soldiers we had just killed were also white. As were all those in this country who were massacring their fellow countrymen for believing in a different version of a god.

My eyes met Alex's and Leland's. They shrugged their shoulders: *you first, sir.* There was nothing for it. I took the protective gel out of my backpack and used it to coat the blood-soaked dog tag I had extracted from the flesh of the dead man's shoulder, placed the tag in the palm of my hand, and gulped it down like an aspirin.

4

The truck was mounted with a .50 caliber gun, set up so that it could fire while moving. An ordinary Toyota pickup turned into a machine of war by virtue of a simple machine gun grafted onto it. The air force of this country was taken out of action shortly into the civil war, but they had somehow managed to preserve most of their radar and associated antiaircraft batteries. It seemed almost comically imbalanced that a country that managed to fight on with the vestiges of a modern air force was reduced to fielding such amateur DIY efforts in lieu of proper armored vehicles.

And so it came to pass that we were now using an enemy vehicle to speed down the very road that we had been taking pains to avoid. With the exception of our nanolayers, we had to ditch all our fancy equipment. Even our SOPMOD modular assault rifles that, like some kiddie toy with interchangeable parts, could be turned into grenade launchers or laser-guided sniper rifles.

It was better to ditch the gear than to continue on a long-winded night march through unfamiliar terrain. When it came down to it, we pampered Americans had an overprotective attitude toward our equipment that bordered on fetishistic. Our military technology was number one, we knew, and it was great that we were able to get so psyched about how awesome we were—I'll admit I often felt a childish glee myself when faced with our latest fancy gadgets—but sometimes a person needed to forget all about what was fashionable and trendy and get back to basics.

Alex was driving. I was sitting shotgun, keeping an eye out for anything that might be a threat while simultaneously trying to maintain a casual demeanor so that no one looking in at us would suspect anything. The fatigues we'd stripped from the dead soldiers and were now wearing had bloodstains all over them, of course, but they were in such a filthy state to begin with that a bit of water from our canteens was enough to rinse out the worst so that the rest more or less blended in.

"It'll be no time at all to our destination in this baby, sir," said Alex. "I wonder what's written on the side of this pickup, though?"

"It's Japanese," I answered. I'd minored in the language back in college, and as a result I'd once been assigned to train up a section of their army. What was it called? *Ji-eh-tai* or something... Anyway, the lettering on the side of the truck seemed to suggest that it had once been used by a tofu shop called Fujiwara. Would a Japanese tofu shop ever have imagined that their old, beat-up vehicle would have a new lease on life as a makeshift armored vehicle in a civil war in the boondocks of Eastern Europe?

"They're called *kanji*, aren't they, the letters, sir? Pretty cool language," Alex said.

"Sure, when you can't read them they're more like a work of art than lettering, I suppose."

"So you're saying that they seem cool only because I can't read them?"

"You could say that, yeah," I said. "In the same way that it's easy to reject a foreign culture you don't understand, you can also end up putting it on a pedestal. Using words such as 'exotic' and 'oriental' to describe something as being cool, when really all you are talking about is a cultural code for some sort of 'other' compared to what you're used to."

"I think I understand," said Alex. "So a foreign language isn't just another language, it's also *foreign*, is that what you mean, sir? More like a pattern or motif on a textile rather than language as we know it?"

"Something like that. Semantic bleaching, that's what they call it when words lose their meaning—although I suppose it's a little different if the words never *had* any meaning to you in the first place. Imagine a Scrabble board when the game's being played in a language you don't know. The whole board is just going to look like an abstract work of art to you, isn't it?"

We often played Scrabble back at base. Many a long afternoon was made shorter by the spell that magical fifteen-by-fifteen grid cast on us as it filled up with words. Williams, for example, was constantly pestering me to play just one more game. He always lost. And he always went into a snit afterward. His regular lament went something like this:

"Okay. So they say the average American knows forty-five thousand words. Forty-five thousand! So why can't I even think of enough words to fill a pissant board fifteen squares wide?"

Incidentally, the highest-scoring word ever sanctioned in Scrabble once came up in a game between Williams and me. I was the one who played it, of course. *Quixotry*, derived from an old Spanish novel. A furious Williams refused to accept it until it had been double-checked in two different dictionaries. Whether because he genuinely didn't believe it or just didn't want to concede the ridiculous score it gave me—365 points on that single word, was it?—I don't know.

I've never lost a game of Scrabble in my life. Not ever, since my first-ever game against my mother when I was eight years old.

Looks like I've brought up a right little philologist. You and words are just made for each other. I remember my mother saying this to me when I was a teenager. I hadn't thought about it in those terms before, but it was certainly true that I always had a certain affinity for words. I remember thinking it was both strange and hilarious that a few little words could change a person so completely. People could become enraged by words or brought to tears, or have their emotions buffeted this way and that. Words were so *interesting*.

I never saw words as a mere means of communication. What I mean by that is that I didn't just "see" words, but I also felt them, viscerally, their weight pressing down on me as if they were matter. To me, words didn't just connect people, words *bound* people, restricting and regulating their actions in very real and meaningful ways, even if the people using the words were completely oblivious to this fact. I sensed this, just as a mathematician could conceptualize and grasp an imaginary number as clearly as a real one. They say that physicists don't think in terms of words, and that Einstein didn't arrive at his Theory of Relativity just by stringing together words and formulae. Rather, it all just came together in a much simpler place, a primeval space, outside the scope of human language and number systems.

I can sort of relate to this. I perceive words as a sort of landscape. It's hard to explain the feeling to other people. After all, it relates, in a most fundamental way, to how I perceive the world around me. And what people perceive as "real" varies from person to person, mind to mind. The ancient Romans never debated the meaning of taste or color, for example.

Just as I can conceptualize words, there are people who can conceptualize and relate to abstract concepts such as "nationhood" and "race." I could no longer do this myself, probably because I was jaded by a job that essentially came down to killing people for the sake of this very same "nation." Maybe the words were just too overwhelmingly powerful for me, who knows? All I knew was that words such as *nationhood, race,* and *community* were just that, as far as I was concerned—words. And even if I could conceptualize them as words, they weren't concepts that I could relate to my real, everyday existence.

A corollary to this was that people who *did* have their own vivid, holistic idea of what a word like *nationhood* meant could do my thinking for me. These people would be part of the establishment, Langley or Fort Mead or Washington, thinking hard about what *nationhood* meant and ordering me to kill people on its behalf.

I'm sure that the same went for the leaders of the various insurgencies in the country that we were now in. They had the ability to perceive that "their country" and "other countries" were distinct entities, and this enabled them to act accordingly. After all, if you couldn't draw a line between "us" and "them," how could you label anyone the "enemy"? Oh, sure, it was easy enough when someone was physically in front of you, threatening violence, a clear and present danger. But to demarcate clear boundaries along the lines of race or religion, and moreover to label anyone on the wrong side of the "us and them" divide as enemies worthy of being killed? That took some serious will-power, or at least a concerted effort to conceptualize "reality" in a very specific way.

After all, no conflict, anywhere, ever, started by both sides saying "Well, we have our own version of events and they have theirs, and to each their own!"

There was no Holocaust. The lunar landings were faked. Elvis is alive and kicking and runs a thriving little diner in the Yukon.

The very fact that blatant untruths such as these could even be seriously posited was proof, if ever it was needed, that there was no such thing as an objective "history" that the world accepted. And wasn't it that prophet of postmodernism, Baudrillard, who said that the Gulf War never actually took place?

History is written by the victors, of course, but there's more to it than that.

History is an arena of discourse, and discourse is nothing if not subjective. So, while it's certainly true that the victors have more chance of having their views heard, there are still plenty of nooks and crannies and crevices for the vanquished, the weak, and the marginal to slip in their versions of events. History may have been written by the victors, but it wasn't always the victory in the battlefield that mattered more than the victory in discourse.

That's why, as I sat there in the truck driving toward our target, I had no way of telling you which of the forces in this country were right and which were mistaken. I was just another dumb 'Murkin, worldview molded and bent into shape by a diet of CNN and talk shows. Everything I knew about the world I learned from a monitor in my home while I ate my Domino's Pizza. All I knew was that in the last millennium there had been lots of wars, lots of terrorist attacks, lots of different ideological conflicts, and that these all happened for lots of different reasons. People had different motives, and the nature of warfare was constantly changing and developing.

The only thing that remained constant was the pizza.

It had existed before I was born and would probably still be doing a brisk trade when I died, whenever that would be. In a world where Domino's was my only constant, it was hard to grasp the full mutability of all the variables of the world.

This, I suppose, was Washington's new White Man's Burden—to be born in America, land of the unchanging pizza chain and shopping mall, and to send people like me out into the big bad outside world to go and kill Mr. Johnny Foreigner for this-and-that reason. Whatever. I wouldn't like to be in the position of making those sorts of decisions. Give me the Empire of the Rising Pizza Dough any day of the week.

Give me my life.

And why not? Just like Williams, I had relinquished the unwelcome responsibility of having to decide things for myself. No buck stops with me. It gets passed up the chain to . . . who knows?

Huh? What was I trying to say with all this philosophical musing? I guess I was trying to articulate just how utterly impossible it was for me to try and articulate what I thought or felt about the fucked-up political situation down on the ground where I was now. I knew that there was some sort of Muslim-Christian divide involved, but that in truth this probably only accounted for about five percent of the real reasons behind the hostilities. What I did know was my orders—to track down the target, the man calling himself defense minister of the rabble that was calling itself the interim government. I knew that the NSC had identified him as Public Enemy Number One for this region. I knew that he was a bigwig. And I knew that back when this region had been called a proper country, he'd been a brigadier general in the army, and so he was now armed to the teeth.

I knew that his paramilitary outfit's MO was to go around to the far-flung villages of the country, drafting all able-bodied youths into their ranks. We were heading toward one such village right now. I knew that the paramilitary group, headed by the ex-brigadier-general-who-now-called-himself-defense-minister-of-the-interim-government, was engaged in the modern equivalent of witch-hunting: terrorist-hunting. That's what they called it, anyway—shooting dead any signs of opposition, only leaving alive youths who might be useful if impressed into service.

I could see a town in the distance through the front windshield, and I supposed that it would have been subjected to the same "with-us-or-against-us" massacre/draft. An orange light emanating from the town lit up the undersides of the clouds in the sky.

Huge chunks of the town were blazing, no doubt. Thick plumes of smoke rose into the sky, reminding me of a painting I once saw of Chinese dragons.

"Looks like we're getting close, boys. Let's keep it together," Williams called out from the cargo bay.

We pulled our scarves up over our mouths. A pathetic attempt at a disguise, maybe, but all of us knew full well that it would probably be enough to get us through any checkpoints.

We entered what once must have been a picturesque little town, now reduced to rubble. The old buildings that had been built and cared for over the years were now little more than a collection of bullet-ridden empty husks, such was the double whammy from the aerial bombardment at the start of the war and the mortar shelling that came later.

Soon there were people, and we arrived at a checkpoint. The guard beckoned for us to stop. Alex, who spoke the local lingo fluently, barked out gruffly that we were on patrol and were running short of food and fuel. The guard nodded and waved his handheld wand out toward each of us in term.

The blood-covered dog tags in their protective gel coatings that were in our stomachs did their jobs. We were identified as the soldiers we had recently killed, and the guard took down our details, cross-referenced them with the data on his laptop, and, satisfied, waved us on our way.

Candy from a baby, I thought, not for the first time.

The guard couldn't have cared less whether we were actually the people our IDs said we were. It was as if the only thing that mattered was the fact that the tags in our body said that we were *someone*.

Unthinkably lax security by American standards—but then, we were the most advanced capitalist nation in the world. Unlike this two-bit outfit, our data protection was enforced with sophisticated biometrics. In the States you couldn't just "identify" yourself. You had to prove beyond a shadow of a doubt that you were who you were claiming to be. They'd built a public database for exactly this purpose. Hell, Domino's wouldn't even hand over your pizza until you had your thumbprint checked by their finger reader.

In comparison, the soldier back there was satisfied by the simple ID that showed up in a simple database—who knows, maybe even something as basic as Microsoft Excel. The very fact that there *was* some sort of computerized data seemed to be enough. As was more or less the case in all countries suffering from this sort of civil war. When your country's falling apart at the seams, computer literacy just isn't a priority, I guess.

We pulled up alongside the ruins of an old church and dismounted from the truck.

"Gunfire, sir," said Alex. Sure enough, there was the intermittent sound of single shots being fired in the distance, somewhere to the east of the town. "I guess they haven't got this town totally under control yet."

"That's one possibility," said Leland as he inspected his dirty AK. A bit of mud wasn't going to stop it from working, but I guess he missed the SOPMODs that we'd had to ditch earlier. Still, he didn't forget to remove the first bullet from each full magazine: when the magazines were absolutely full they pressed down on the spring that released them, meaning that the bullets wouldn't always eject smoothly. "Although if I had to guess, I'd say it's more likely they're executing people."

With that, we walked quietly into enemy territory. Here and there were buildings still aflame, with civilian corpses scattered about the place. There was a woman with a shapely physique, who you could have called attractive were it not for the fact that half her face had been blown off, with the light from the flames illuminating the contents of her head for all to see. She held a hand attached to the arm of a child. Her son? Her daughter? Hard to tell, as it really was only the arm of a child that she held on to; the body had been blown away.

Over there—Alex tapped my shoulder, and I looked toward where he was indicating. The town square, full of youths in civilian clothing, lined up in rows, having ID tags implanted into their shoulders. Children being transformed into armed insurgents.

Children, still pliable and malleable, abducted and turned into soldiers. In fact, some of the children might not have been abducted—plenty came forth voluntarily. If you became a soldier you were given an ID tag, after all.

Ordinary ID tags at that—no different from ones used to sort inventory in a market stall. Only now they were being subcutaneously injected into the armed insurgents and drafted children. The ID tags being used in this war—including the ones that we all had in our stomachs—were no doubt mass produced cheaply in some factory somewhere, Oklahoma or Osaka or anywhere else in the world.

In countries like this one where the government had all but disintegrated due to civil war, it wasn't at all uncommon for family registers and birth records to be lost completely. Citizenship papers? Who was to tell whether you were even actually a citizen? Was someone going to take a census, dodging bullets as they did so? Sure, you might live here, work here, grow crops on the land, but you're not *from* here anymore—how could you be, when no one knew where *here* was? No, all you had left was your name, and you had to hope that was enough for you to get by in what now passed for the local community.

So, if you became a soldier, you'd be tagged, you'd have an identity that the armed insurgents' portable devices could read and process. You'd become somebody. A number on their free spreadsheet, with a record as to whether you lived or died. Even here, out in the boondocks, in a country where all semblance of rule of law had long since broken down, it still seemed the most natural thing in the world that people could—and should—be organized according to what was essentially an inventory management system.

That was how the children of the region became soldiers. So they could advance in the eyes of somebody—not even their fellow countrymen, as they didn't exist anymore. So that they could move up in rank, in status, as an item of infantry. They went to war so that they could stand shoulder-to-shoulder with Snickers and M&Ms and cans of Pringles.

As for the four of us who were now marching through the nightscape of this foreign land, we were a bit more sophisticated than supermarket merchandise. Our built-in internal sensors that monitored our physical status were able to transmit detailed information back home. Not something your typical merchandise tag can do.

It wasn't really much of a choice for the kids, of course. Basically they either joined the ranks of the men who had just killed their parents and raped their sisters and girlfriends, or they died along with the rest.

Leland had been right. The source of the intermittent gunfire was a firing squad.

There was a large circular pit that had apparently been dug in the ground by a piece of heavy machinery that probably would have been used on a construction site during peacetime. Men and women were lined up on the edge. The executioners gave the signal, the AK rifles were fired, and the men and women, shot in the head and torso, toppled into the pit.

I've seen corpses burnt to a crisp before. The skin blackens like charbroiled chicken. Muscle shrinks when it's cooked, causing the brittle bones to bend or snap, and when you look at the resultant mess you can't help but realize that humans are really just physical objects. By which I mean just a mass of raw ingredients. When it comes down to it a dead body really is just a thing, like any other thing.

The soldiers pushed the crumpled bodies further into the hole. A dead body isn't exactly light, and with the corpses that didn't conveniently fall backward into the pit, it took the soldiers much more than the couple of light kicks you'd imagine it would to push the lifeless bodies over the edge. In many cases, the soldiers had to kneel down and really put their backs into it.

Now, it's not as if I was unaffected by the scene in front of us, even if I had seen it all before. This was a blatant mass murder of innocent townsfolk, plain and simple—nothing can ever desensitize you to that completely. But the fact was that I'd seen so much casual, meaningless death in my life that I no longer felt the impulse to stop it at all costs. After all, it wasn't as if we were much better equipped than the soldiers here. We might have been able to take them, or we might not. Anyway, we weren't here as stakeholders. We were here as outsiders, neutral observers who had but one single-minded purpose: to kill our target.

Not only that, I was carrying the responsibility for both the mission and my three subordinates on the team. We might have been able to rescue some of the people dying in front of our eyes, but it would mean the mission would end in failure for sure, and the crazed ex-brigadier general would escape to kill and kill and kill again—creating more innocent victims that would otherwise be saved if we took our target out now.

Sure, some people might have called it a moral crossroads. All I knew was that now wasn't the time to meditate on the finer points of ethical semantics.

To be thick-skinned is to be enlightened. So, develop a thicker skin than the next man.

So, as usual, we hardened our hearts, thickened our skins, and proceeded with the mission. This was made easier by the fact that our target was approaching, or rather our two targets were about to have their rendezvous. We finished the necessary emotional adjustments so that we could cope with the tragic scene in front of us, and in an instant we were ready for action.

The ex-brigadier general who now styled himself defense minister led a peripatetic existence. He was always on the move, precisely to reduce the threat of assassination. Similar to what Saddam Hussein had done for many years to avoid capture. They say that Hitler too used to change his plans and his movements at the last minute, also to reduce the risk to his person. Once the sheer scale of the humanitarian disaster in the region became known to the world, the US decided to consider assassination as a tactic to help curb the chaos, but by that time the defense minister knew what to expect and what precautions to take to minimize the risk. After all, in his former incarnation he had been the beneficiary of training from the very same US intelligence apparatus that was now trying to assassinate him . . .

Which was why it was only dumb luck that allowed our people to happen upon the intelligence that our targets would be meeting in this former mosque at this time. If we let this opportunity slip, who knew when the next opportunity would come about to stop the murderous yet prudent ex-brigadier general? We simply couldn't afford to fail. And that was why we were able to abandon the dying people in front of us to their fates.

"I guess we're all going to hell," said Alex. Young, devout Alex, with his master's degree in Catholic theology. How he managed to cope with seeing hell on a daily basis in his work I never could work out. I guess he must have had some sympathetic—and very discreet—padre to whom he could make a copious confession after every mission.

"As an atheist, I don't really have a reply to that, I'm afraid," I said.

"You don't have to believe in God to know that hell's real," said Alex, a mournful smile passing his lips.

"Sure it exists. It's right here! Just take a look around you!" Williams said with a laugh. Well, if this was hell, our job was to go to hell and back. Mr. Dante, eat your heart out.

But Alex disagreed, pointing at his own head. "Respectfully, sir, no. Hell is *here*. Inside your head. Inside your mind. Seared into your cerebral cortex. This scene around us, it might be hellish, but it's not hell. After all, you can escape from all this. Just close your eyes and it's gone. And when you get back to America and return to normal life, the scene in front of us now will be gone forever. But you can't escape from hell. Because hell's right here, inside your mind, and you carry it around with you."

"Is that where heaven is too?" asked Leland, who was also laughing now. Leland was, I knew, a regular Sunday churchgoer, but in his case it was more of a social thing, to fit in with the neighbors. More habit than anything else. I doubted that most of your typical flock of Sunday sheep had the same level of fervent religiosity as young Alex.

"Who knows," Alex told Leland. "I know that hell is inside us because I've seen it. But I've never seen heaven. Heaven is the realm of God, after all. Man's feeble mind isn't enough to contain it in all its glory. I suppose you need to actually die before you can experience heaven."

"Ladies, ladies," said Williams, butting in, "let's leave the theological debates to one side for the time being, shall we? We've got a mosque to infiltrate, and I doubt that these shitty little disguises we're now wearing are going to be much use when it comes to getting us into the inner sanctum."

"Okay." Time for me to take charge. "They may have wall-mounted ID readers installed, so let's remove our tags. The guys they belonged to were just foot soldiers—there's no reason to believe they'd have clearance for a secure area like the one we're penetrating."

On my orders, we all pulled the strings attached to our soft palates and the dog tags out of our stomachs. They were all wrapped in string, encased in the pale blue protective gel, and still glistening with the blood of their original owners.

We slipped into a nearby ruin of a house and buried them in the ground. Then we went over our plans one last time. We sprayed ourselves in nanocoating and activated the Environmental Camouflage software. The disguise algorithms generated by the camouflage patterns fired through our systems, transmitting through the natural salts in our bodies to the nanocoating layer that covered our clothes and equipment.

The change was instantaneous. We disappeared into the background of the bullet-riddled ruins.

"As planned, then. Leland and Williams to wait here on standby, ready to secure our path of retreat in the event of unexpected developments. Alex and I to infiltrate the mosque and strike when the two targets meet. All clear?"

"Sure thing, boss," said Williams. "Just try and keep it down, huh? I could do without having to take on the whole town in a shootout afterwards. There's only four of us, right?"

Williams was fucking with us; that was his way of diffusing the tension. Of course there were "only" four of us. Four was exactly the right number for this sort of mission. That's the way it was—the way it had been ever since the Second World War. Fewer than four and you ran the risk of coming up short; you only needed to lose one guy and the whole mission was in jeopardy. More than four and you lost the clean, clear line of command, and it also became exponentially more difficult to move covertly.

The four-man formation was first perfected by the British SAS on their anticommunist ops in the tropical jungles of Malaya.

The real advantage was that it was possible to subdivide into two smaller battle units of two-man cells. The two-man cell, or buddy system, was effectively the smallest unit in Special Forces ops. Solo operation was virtually unheard of.

Two units of two. That was where we were at as we moved into the final stage of the plan. I was actually more used to buddying with Williams, but as we were the two ranking soldiers on this mission it didn't make sense to have us both in the same cell.

Alex and I moved smoothly and silently out of the ruined house toward the mosque walls. There were plenty of guards on the lookout, but the combination of our Environmental Camouflage, the route we took, and the cover of darkness combined to form the perfect storm of disguise. We were indistinguishable from the ruins that surrounded us.

When we arrived at the mosque I gave the hand signal for us to split. Given the darkness and the thoroughness of our disguises it should have been virtually impossible for us to have even seen each other's hand signals, but the software in our eyes was able to make out the contours of the other person and transmit their outline straight to each other's retinas. Alex nodded to show he understood and started moving toward the rear entrance of the mosque.

As long as we kept close to the ground and the walls, the combination of nightfall and our nanocoating disguise meant that we were for all practical intents and purposes undetectable without infrared scanning technology. I crept alongside the mosque wall until I found a hole that went underground.

In the distance I could still hear the sound of gunfire as the civilians were murdered. I put the sounds behind me as I started crawling under the floorboards and into the mosque. This once-holy place, built to praise Allah, now reeked of stale gunpowder and rotting human flesh. I was sure that the mosque would be full of decomposing corpses. Moreover, amid the carnage would be the source of all the trouble—the so-called defense minister who was running the whole show.

As I continued crawling under the floorboards, I heard classical music emanating from a point in the distance. I would love to say that it was Wagner's *Ride of the Valkyries* or something similarly cartoonish for the situation. But it wasn't. It was Beethoven's *Moonlight Sonata*. A beautiful melody, singularly inappropriate for this moonless night where the only light in the sky was from the burning fat of the corpses as they lit the clouds above with an eerie crimson hue. I scurried toward the source of the sound and before long found a hole in the floor above me.

Slowly, I raised my head from the hole in the ground. If I'd had my SOPMOD with me I would have been able to attach the probe unit and use that to have a look around, but as it was, armed with only a battered AK, I had to use the old-fashioned method of checking the space out with my own eyes. After confirming that there was, indeed, nobody out there, I climbed silently out of my hole.

The *Moonlight Sonata* was coming up to its melancholy refrain. I moved carefully and deliberately from room to room, getting a good mental picture of the mosque's layout as I did so.

The beautiful, swirling geometric patterns of the tiles, so typical of Islamic art, made the relatively simple layout of the mosque seem at first glance more like a maze than it really was. No doubt the 'effect of a cultural code I didn't understand, making the "other" seem different—cool, even. I moved deeper and deeper into the darkness of the maze, following the scent of the music.

The music grew louder. I realized that I had now neared its source. The one room in the mosque with a light on. I closed in, glued to the wall, and poked my head through the archway long enough to take quick stock of the contents of the room.

The former brigadier general was alone. The *Moonlight Sonata* was coming from a small portable radio set on top of a table— volume cranked up as high as it could go. The defense minister was evidently deep in contemplation, his sunken pupils glued to the radio, one hand outstretched toward the speakers, as if he were somehow trying to physically absorb the sound. He was dressed to the nines in his former military uniform, spick and span, as if he were about to attend a formal ceremony.

By the look of things the room was completely unguarded. Target A was alone. It would have been a piece of cake to dispatch him on the spot. The problem was that Target A wasn't currently deep in conversation with Target B as we expected he would be at this time. If the defense minister's corpse was discovered before Target B, the American, arrived, he might slip through our fingers.

Is Target B even here in the first place? I wondered. Perhaps that sense of unease that we had before the drop was justified after all. Now would be just the right time for Murphy's Law to kick in. Assassination was a complex job with many variables at the best of times. When you had two simultaneous targets, the difficulty level didn't increase arithmetically so much as geometrically.

What to do? The one thing I knew was that I had no time to waste. We were right in the middle of enemy heartland, and all it would take was one false move for us to be overrun; Alex and I, at the very least, would be sitting ducks.

Time for a decision. The ability to act quickly and under pressure was one of the hallmarks of special ops after all. I killed my breath and silently replaced my AK with my knife. The moment the former brigadier general turned his back, I leapt across the room and pounced. Using one of my arms to pin his arms behind his back, I held the tip of my knife to his throat.

"You're not my target," I said. "But if you make a noise or move, I'll kill you. Understand?" I was lying, of course, and I can't say I was particularly proud of the fact that I was lying to a man who was about to die. That I was about to kill, even. But this wasn't the time to be worrying about the finer points of battlefield ethics. "It's the American we're looking for. The man you were supposed to meet today."

"I didn't know he was American," the defense minister said, his breath remarkably steady considering the position he was in, with the deadly blade pricking his throat. "He's our press secretary. Was. Not is."

"So you killed him?" I asked, pressing the point of the blade further against his throat.

"No. He just suddenly up and left for no apparent reason. A few days ago, this was. I wanted to know the details. That's why we planned to rendezvous here today. I was expecting to meet him in person, but he just left a message for me."

Shit. That meant that Target B wouldn't be appearing tonight.

Well, we'd still be able to accomplish our first priority and eliminate the former brigadier general, so the mission wouldn't be a
complete washout, not by any means. Still, it was a loose end,
and that always left a bad taste in my mouth.

"What did the message say?" I asked.

"It was a short note on official government stationery. 'My
work here is done.' That's all it said," the ex-brigadier general said.

"Official government stationery my ass. What 'official government'? What 'government' at all? You're just a bunch of armed
thugs fighting over scraps of land and wreaking genocide on your
own people. Scum of the earth, that's what you are."

"Genocide, you say?" he said. "Is that what you call our peace-
keeping efforts? Our government needs to subdue the terrorist
threat for the good of our own people."

"As I said, it's not a government," I argued back. "Call yourself
defense minister or whatever you like, but it doesn't change
the fact that you're not recognized by the United Nations, and
more to the point you're the ones going around killing your
own people."

"What has the UN got to do with anything? You imperialists
are the ones who came here, trampling our indigenous culture to
the ground, laughing at our efforts at self-determination, stirring
up racial discord where our people have lived peacefully side
by side for years..." At this point the former brigadier general
seemed to run out of steam, and he abruptly stopped talking.
His eyes were glinting with a peculiar emotion, not quite fear,
not quite sorrow. Silence pressed down, punctuated only by the
distant *rat-tat-tat* of the ongoing executions.

"That's right. How did our country ever come to this?" He
started speaking again. "Weren't multiculturalism and tolerance
the cornerstones of our culture? Terrorists! That's right, it must
have been terrorists! Terrorists born of intolerance and hatred,
it's all their fault... no? No, it must have been something else.
The military didn't need to declare martial law in the capital
to deal with a routine terrorist threat, surely? The police had it
under control? So why? Why has it come to this? How has it
come to this?"

Rat-tat-tat. Rat-tat-tat.

There were no cries, no screams. The only testament to the anonymous dead whose corpses were piling up in the hole was the sound of the very gunfire that caused their deaths.

I was getting fed up with this bullshit. Nothing good ever came of having an old man staring his own death in the face. What was this, some sort of deathbed confession to atone for the stream of dead he left in his wake? Did he think he would earn absolution for his eternal soul or something? Seek forgiveness with a humble heart and you will be saved? That Christian shtick isn't going to work with me, buddy—I'm a confirmed atheist.

I told him as much. Called him out on his bullshit. I wasn't a priest or a pastor, I explained. I couldn't give him the absolution he asked for even if I wanted to. Which I didn't. Your repentance is bullshit—too little, too late. No religion can save you now, and if there is a hell you are going straight there.

"I'm sure I am. I'll go straight to hell, no doubt. But you misunderstand me, son. I'm not asking for forgiveness. I'm just trying to work out what went wrong. How this country has gone so wrong. It used to be such a wonderful place. So beautiful. Up until only a couple of years ago..."

And that was when it finally clicked. This man in front of me, the former brigadier general of this country, was genuinely puzzled. More than that, he was filled with dread, but not thanks to the knife I was holding to his throat. He was terrified because he didn't even comprehend his own motives for fighting in this civil war.

I shuddered. How illogical, how fucked-up it was to forget your reasons for fighting, now of all times. And how convenient.

"Why did you kill so many people?" I asked.

"Why did I kill so many people?"

That's against the rules, answering a question with another question, I thought.

The old man in front of me was now raving, his teeth chattering in fear. He was on the brink. His answers were too far gone for me to have any more faith in his words, but I continued regardless, pressing my knife even further up against his jugular.

"Why, old man? Answer me!"

"Why? I don't know why!"

"Answer me!"

In the short time our bodies had been pressed together my disguise had started adapting to the outfit the former brigadier general was wearing: full military regalia, replete with medals and decorations. A cold shudder ran down my spine—it was as if the old man's madness was infecting and about to possess me. Not that there was anything I could do about it while I had his arms pinned behind him and my blade to his throat.

"Won't you please tell *me*?" he was asking me now. His eyes were the eyes of a corpse, pupils hollow and void of any life. The phrase "looks as though he's seen a ghost" is bandied around a lot, but it occurred to me that he was what a person would actually look like if they had just been confronted with incontrovertible proof of a real, supernatural terror. I gritted my teeth, trying to force myself to blot out the absurdity of the situation in front of me.

"Shut up!" This was definitely not part of the plan—it absolutely had not occurred to us that this could have been one of the reactions. A groveling show of regret and remorse for the cameras, sure, and that would have been easy enough to deal with. As it was, the words that were now spilling forth from this man's mouth had an almost hypnotic effect, and as the words increased in intensity, I worried that the torrent of madness spewing forth was starting to encroach upon my own sanity.

"Please, sir, I'm begging you! Tell me why! Why have I killed so many people?"

He was completely oblivious to me now. Babbling. How the mighty had fallen.

"Look, old man, I can't help you. Won't you please just be quiet?" I'm ashamed to say that by now my own voice sounded as pitiful as his.

"Why did I kill everyone?"

"Shut up."

"But why?"

And that was that. I just couldn't take it anymore.

I drew my blade across his throat. Fresh blood splattered and turned the mosque wall into a Jackson Pollock painting. Before he had time to choke on his own blood I quickly hamstrung him so that I could force his once-imposing body to the ground and thrust my blade into his heart. As I did so, blood bubbled from his mouth and his eyes flared open.

The former brigadier general, the man who had called himself defense minister for the interim government, was dead.

The great commander of the estimated thirty-five thousand armed insurgents who terrorized the countryside was dead.

I felt as if reality had snapped back and hit me in the face. I realized for the first time that the piano melody that had been filling the room had long since faded without a trace.

Moonlight Sonata had finished without my noticing. I shook my head to clear my thoughts before looking around. It was as if I'd been in some sort of magical alternate dimension and forgotten to breathe while I was there. I gulped again for air.

Rat-a-tat-tat. Rat-tat.

The night that had briefly been caressed by the *Moonlight Sonata* had returned to echoing the sound of people killing each other.

"What on earth happened here, sir?"

I turned around to see Alex's troubled expression. All I could do by way of response was sigh. I didn't even want to start thinking about how to explain the old man's extraordinary behavior.

"Are you all right, sir?" Alex asked again. Ever the professional, even as he spoke to me he was checking the corpse of the ex-brigadier general that lay on the floor. He was using the recording capabilities of the nanolayer implants in his eyes to confirm and record the old man's death from as many angles as possible.

"Yeah. It looks like Target B isn't coming here tonight, though."

"Oh. Unlike Intelligence to get that wrong," Alex said calmly, going about his work.

I could hear more gunfire in the distance.

The atrocities in this area aren't quite over yet, I thought to myself.

late-night cable. I remember how it made me shudder: a scene with a woman in full mourning regalia wiping red bloodstains from the wall. I supposed she was the widow of the man who had just killed himself. The movie never did go into detail on that point, and in my mind that scene seemed curiously detached from the rest of the movie.

Come to think of it, I guess it could have been my mother who wiped up my father.

It's the nature of your work that is causing you so much stress.

I wondered if this was the sort of thing Alex's counselor would have said to him during their sessions—if he'd been going for any.

Kill, kill, and then kill some more. Plan missions down to the last detail so that you can kill even more people even more efficiently. Conjure up in your mind, vividly, an image of the target you are about to kill. Predict your target's next movements. Know whether he has a wife, whether he has children, whether he read *Harry Potter* to his daughter at bedtime.

Would *stressful* even be the right word to describe this line of work? Alex was a staunch Catholic, so I guess it's more likely he would have confessed to a priest than gone to counseling. When he was in that little confessional, would he have begged for absolution for all the men he had killed in the line of duty? If so, I wondered if the priest who heard his confession now felt guilty for not being able to grant that absolution, for not being able to provide Alex with the words that could have convinced him that he was indeed forgiven.

It's the nature of your work that is leading you into sin.

I could just imagine a priest saying something like that, a grotesque parody of my hypothetical counselor. *It seems that your work is inextricably linked with sin, and as long as you perform it you'll carry the weight of hell on your shoulders. Perhaps you should consider speaking to your superiors to see if you can be reassigned. Or maybe consider taking a holiday somewhere nice and warm this year? That'll take your mind off all the sin and hell around you.*

It was true that we had been worked to the hilt these past

couple of years. The orders from Washington had been coming down thick and fast, and perhaps it was the case that there was simply not enough time in between assassination assignments for us to be able to deal with our personal hells and sins.

Not that you could blame Washington entirely, of course. The past two years had been crazy, or rather it seemed like the world had decided to turn crazy round about the time we dispatched a certain former brigadier general. Africa, Asia, Europe: it was the whole world going mad, with civil wars and ethnic conflicts in quick succession. With most of these a UN resolution was quickly enacted. The principle of the day seemed to be "It is a crime against humanity to stand idly by while people kill each other."

It was as if one day somebody had changed the rules stating that you could no longer have a civil war without genocide.

The last two years alone had witnessed a ridiculous number of worldwide civilian casualties in internal conflicts—something like sixty percent of the number of all casualties of terrorism and civil war since the beginning of the twenty-first century. There were so many new reports of massacres popping up all over the place that journalists were finding it hard to keep track.

As a result, even the most atrocious genocide was getting buried, relegated to some corner of the web. Apart from a few particularly brutal ones that had managed somehow to grab the spotlight, most were simply reported like so much material for the archives, which is of course what all the webpages were when nobody much read them. It had become easier than ever to publish new information and harder than ever to get anyone to actually pay attention to it. The world only wanted the information that it was interested in. Information had become just another capitalist commodity.

The last two years had been a whirlwind for us headhunters. We were literally living a jetset lifestyle as we zipped around the world in high-speed aircraft, so much so that Williams would joke that the theory of relativity ought really to have kicked in by now and that time should pass differently for us than for average Americans. How we laughed.

We worked too hard.

The world made too many demands of us. People placed an

unbearable burden of responsibility on our shoulders. If even the quintessential genocidal leader, Adolf Hitler, had been voted in by the people—who must therefore on some level share the responsibility for the massacres committed in Hitler's name—then how right was it ever going to be to try and pin the blame for the killings in one region on a single individual? And yet this was what we were being asked to do, day in, day out.

If you kill this person, the armed insurgents will lose the unifying figure around which the people rally.

If you kill this person, it'll be easier for both sides to bury the hatchet.

Washington would choose the target—if you kill him, the genocide is most likely to stop—and our job was to take care of things. This first layer of victims could in a sense be seen as martyrs for peace.

Martyrs. In the two years since that incident I'd been directly involved in five more assassination ops, and on two of those I did the killing myself. In a couple of missions we entered the country covertly using the Intruder Pods; on others we entered the country in full view, as tourists or journalists on ordinary aircraft. Each mission was different, with different targets, and the tactics varied accordingly. However, there was one constant factor.

On four out of the five missions the same name cropped up as one of our targets.

The man who, two years ago, in a certain country in Eastern Europe, worked as the press secretary for a group of armed insurgents who were committing genocide. We realized that his name would inevitably be on our target list. It was unusual to say the least. It was almost as if this person was some sort of tourist traveling from war zone to war zone.

Given that Washington seemed to really have it in for this guy, it was inconceivable that he was just an ordinary civilian. The target data files that came with each mission became successively more detailed. It was as if Washington wanted us to get him but at the same time would reveal as little as possible about him. "Fucking bureaucrats, just give us the information we need from the start and stop dicking us around," Williams grumbled, and indeed it did seem an extraordinarily petty way of going about our task. Not only that, if Washington's aim was to keep attention away from the man, then their plan was backfiring spectacularly, as the veil of secrecy only added to the diabolical—or legendary—aura that was starting to build around this figure.

John Paul.

The strikingly nondescript name of the man who had been slipping through our fingers these past two years.

"So who is this elusive John Paul?" Williams spoke in an exaggerated parody of a Shakespearean actor. "The American who the American government loves to hate. The fugitive who is wanted dead, not alive. The tourist whose only interest is in viewing scenes of brutal crimes against humanity. Who can say who this John Paul really is?"

"Just a man, like you or me," I said.

Williams seemed unhappy at my answer, shaking his head sadly as if to say that I just didn't get it. "Jeez, not you too. Why's everyone so boring? I know he's a *man*, I'm talking about what *else!*"

"You do that, buddy," I said, "but he's still a *man*, and that's all we need to know. Men make mistakes. He'll make one sooner or later, and then we'll find him."

"Find him and kill him, you mean."

I wasn't really sure why the happily married Williams was here at all at my bachelor pad on a rare day off, let alone why he ordered in some Domino's without bothering to ask me and was now speculating out loud to himself. I guess Alex's funeral yesterday must have hit him harder than he cared to admit.

One of the living room walls was shaded from the sun so that we could watch TV and movies better. I was sitting on the couch with a can of Bud almost spilling from my hand, watching the Allies getting slaughtered over and over again at Omaha beach. I had the first fifteen minutes of *Saving Private Ryan* on loop. There was a reason behind this: not only were the first fifteen minutes the best part of the movie by far, it was also free to preview on the pay-per-view channel I was now watching.

Were we really thirty years old? There didn't seem anything particularly grown up about this college lifestyle. I guess that was all part of the American Dream—work and consume, work and consume, get sucked into the cycle, and then you never really had to worry about that sort of thing.

"I guess he had some shit on his mind, huh," Williams said out of nowhere.

"Yeah, I guess he did," I said.

"Motherfucker . . . why didn't he say anything to us?"

"Ask Alex."

Williams sighed as if to say that was exactly what he would have done, if he could. "Do you think he really was in that hell that he talked about all the time? Out in the field, in training, back at base when we sat around talking shit . . ."

"Ha ha, *we* sat around talking shit? *You* talked shit and we put up with it, don't you mean?"

I was only joking, but Williams looked at me, surprised. "You mean you never heard any of Alex's jokes?"

I couldn't help glancing away from the screen and at Williams for a second; after all, he was right. I had never heard any of Alex's jokes.

"They were pretty good, some of them, you know," continued Williams. "What's the word. Risqué."

"What, like when you asked him for a great novel and he gave you a Bible?"

"Nah, that was lame compared to his good stuff about Catholic priests, the Pope, choirboys, that sort of thing. He laid into the God of the Old Testament something good too, how retarded and inconsistent many of the commandments were. Had Leland and me rolling in the aisles, so to speak."

Huh. Not what I'd expected. I'd always thought Alex had been such a strict Catholic. "I . . . never had the chance to see that side of him," I said.

Williams looked at me for a while. The sound of Nazi machine-gun fire filled the room. Then Williams took his empty can of Budweiser and aimed for the trash can on the other side of the room. He was a good ten feet away, but it went straight in nonetheless.

"Damn, I'm one down on you and the pizza hasn't even arrived yet," I said out loud. But in reality I was still thinking about Alex. What did we use to talk about? God, mainly, I seemed to remember. I was an atheist but never felt the need to be too militant about it, and had neither the desire nor the ego to try and press my views on any believers in my vicinity. Alex was more or less the same but on the opposite side of the coin, and never felt the need to drag me into the light. It meant that we could discuss God, hell, and the nature of sin in an atmosphere of mutual respect. We had done so regularly.

Hell is here. That night two years ago on the mission wasn't the first time we had heard Alex use that phrase. I'd heard it from him before, lounging around at base. Then too, Alex had pointed at his forehead and said, "*Hell is here, Captain Shepherd. We're all hard-wired to march straight to hell. It's in our architecture.*"

I'd no idea what sort of personal hell Alex had been cultivating in his own mind, and now I never would. The one thing I did know was that Alex ended his own life in order to escape whatever hell he had been building. A preemptive strike against death, to ensure that he never fell into that hell he was so afraid of. What a fucked-up thing to do, and yet I could see the twisted logic in it, and I could imagine Alex taking himself seriously enough to go through with it.

The doorbell rang.

"Nice, the pizza," Williams said, jumping up to collect it. He identified himself by pressing his thumb down on the delivery boy's ID device. Confirmation came back from the military database that held all Williams's (and my) personal data, and the courier thanked us for our business and left.

"One of the perks of being Forces, huh?" said Williams, picking at the jalapeños even before he had thrown himself back down on the couch. "No need to worry about our data; it's all taken care of. Not much fun on civvy street where you have to pay for data storage."

"Sure, but Medicare covers most of it, and in any case, strictly speaking it's not the army that 'takes care of' our data.

It's outsourced to InfoSec, a private firm, about as civilian as you can get. The army just picks up the tab."

"Is that so? Well, whaddaya know. By the time I had any of my own money to play with, I was already career Forces. I couldn't tell you what life's like on the other side."

"Well, think about it," I said. "It's a pretty massive operation, taking down your full medical history, fingerprints, retinal scans, brainwave patterns, facial contours, and other details, not forgetting things like your full credit rating. They have to be kept absolutely secure but also easily accessible, so that any part can be checked at any time. It's not cheap."

"That's it!" said Williams, pointing at me. "John Paul. How is he getting around all this? All those layers of security? We needed our thumbprints just to get hold of these jalapeños here. When I was ten years old you could sometimes just about get away with a signature, but these days you need your fingerprints, your retina, your face scanned, to get anywhere. So how the hell is this John Paul getting from Europe to Africa to Asia and back again?"

I hadn't thought about that before. You needed ID before you could buy a plane ticket. Or rather, your ID was *how* you bought a plane ticket, no matter what type of bank account you used, or in what country.

So how on earth was John Paul managing to travel from civil war to civil war?

Then Williams's cell phone started ringing. I could barely believe my eyes as he shoved his greasy fingers, still dripping with pizza and jalapeño juices, straight into his pocket to retrieve his cell. He pressed the button without qualm. Well, it was his cell, he could do what he liked, but my body couldn't help but shudder, purely as a physiological reflex. That was Williams for you.

"Roger that, sir," he said into his phone, sucking the fingers of his other hand as he did so. "Yes, sir. Right away, sir, within the hour."

Williams cut the call. He used his still-greasy index finger on the wall to call up the command pad. I grimaced. The thin nanolayer membrane on the wall picked up his request and soon the command pad materialized out of nowhere on the wall, ready to accept his oily orders.

Williams tapped the stop button, and *Saving Private Ryan* stopped streaming. I asked him what happened, but he just sighed...

...and at that very moment my own cell started ringing. I fished it out of my back pocket. Headquarters.

"All units summoned to headquarters," said Williams.

2

"Take full precautions to avoid being identified along the way."

Williams and I followed our orders from the Pentagon and proceeded to Washington in our civvy suits. It would have been ridiculous to try to make it there in our uniforms, as our nameplates and decorations would have made us easily identifiable by definition. Basically, the orders were to come as you are, although Williams wasn't happy about this—he never felt comfortable meeting the top brass unless he was in uniform, he said. As long as you were squeezed into a tight uniform with plenty of medals and ribbons on your chest you didn't have any tiresome considerations such as fashion or style to worry about. Uniform is just uniform. With your own clothes you always had to worry about other people judging you based on their own values. I don't like people I don't know seeing me as an individual, said Williams.

We took an ordinary commercial flight rather than a military plane. It looked like they were trying to keep the general summons as low-key as possible, not just to the general public but within Forces as well. If John Paul was indeed part of a wider organization then it was quite likely they would have a surveillance network in place to monitor any unusual activity among the Secret Service and Special Forces. There was also probably something about the general summons that the Pentagon didn't want to be broadcasting to the forces at large.

So we did our best to blend in with the crowds as we made it to Washington on our own steam. We were under strict orders not to take a cab from Reagan National, so we took the metro to Pentagon Station and disembarked along with the throngs of the staffers and the other visitors.

It wasn't my first time in the Pentagon, but nonetheless I couldn't help but feel like something of a rube.

Watching the crowd disembarking at Pentagon Station it was nigh impossible to distinguish the staffers from the visitors. Due to developments in biometric IDs, clothes had become somewhat less important as a distinguishing feature than they had been years ago.

My ID, for example, was nowhere to be found in my clothes or shoes, of course—InfoSec's secure servers had done away with the need for all that.

The upshot of all this was that the people here, whether staffers or visitors, had a tendency to rough it somewhat. Take the visitors, civilians mostly. The fashion of the day was "Pentagon style," which was somewhere between an homage to and a parody of the typical desk-jockey uniforms of way back when—the era when the two worlds stared into each other's faces in a game of nuclear brinksmanship. So the civilians wore bland, nondescript (or so they seemed at first glance) outfits, and the military staffers either wore similar Pentagon-style clothes or something even more casual. Basically, the likes of me had no chance of telling who was who.

We pushed through the crowds of uniforms, suits, and Birdlegs and walked toward our destination. The Birdlegs, or Birdlegged Porters, always creeped me out, as they looked just like people with no upper bodies.

Walking robot legs made out of synthetic flesh—they'd been part of the furniture these past few years. The Pentagon was a much larger physical space than people gave it credit for—roughly three times the floor space of the Empire State Building, for example, although no one trumpets this fact. Having said that, it was easier to get around by the fact of its pentagonal shape—it was never too far from one point to another. What did slow things down was the constant security checks—we needed to have our palms and fingerprints read, our retinas scanned, and our ears and noses and eyes matched against their database before we reached our appointed conference room.

We arrived at the part of the building where the conference rooms were concentrated. Virtually all of them seemed to be in use, with a variety of signs hanging from each door, indicating the nature of the conference within.

THE COMMITTEE FOR THE LIBERATION OF LIBYA
EAST EUROPEAN STABILIZATION COMMISSION
PREPARATORY COMMISSION FOR HUMANITARIAN
INTERVENTION IN THE SUDANESE QUESTION
THE CONVENTION FOR DISSEMINATION OF BEST
PRACTICE IN COUNTERTERRORISM

All the world's problems could be found in this little corner of the Pentagon, and presumably some of the solutions too.

Words like *liberation* were used without compunction; I can't imagine that the governments of the countries concerned would have been too happy to be discussed in such explicit terms. But unlike the rest of Washington, this wasn't the place for diplomatic niceties. Indeed, the whole *raison d'être* of this place was to freely discuss how America was best going to intervene in the internal affairs of other countries.

One of the conference rooms was different, though. The plaque on the door simply read NO ENTRY.

"Here we are," said Williams, who then spun around to survey the other conference rooms. "Something a bit surreal about a room with a big 'No Entry' sign mixed in with all these others, huh?"

"I guess that's the White Man's Burden for you yet again," I said. "If the hegemon wants to rule the world, we just have to man up and shoulder our responsibilities alone, behind closed doors and away from the rest of the world."

Williams nodded in agreement. "There's something so Kafkaesque about this whole thing, isn't there?"

"When have you read any Kafka?" I asked.

Williams shrugged. "Never. I just wanted to see what it'd be like to use the word 'Kafkaesque' in a sentence."

Williams knocked on the door and a man's voice answered from within: "Identify yourselves using the device attached to the door."

I pressed my thumb onto the pale green glass pane about the size of a domino; the lock was released and the door opened an inch.

Inside the darkened room a group of men and women were watching a porn flick.

At least, that was what it looked like when we first entered the room. The projector was showing a black man tied up in restraints, and the audience was distinctly middle-aged. They all turned to glance at us as we entered. Amid the dim sea of faces peering at us I spotted our immediate superior officer and boss, Colonel Rockwell, the leader of Special Operations I Detachment.

"My men from Unit G," said Boss, beckoning to us to fill the empty seats. The men and women sitting at the table were all around Boss's age or older, so it looked like we were the babies of the group. A man rose from the table to introduce himself.

Undersecretary of defense for Intelligence, he told us. USD (I). In other words, the Defense Intelligence Agency reported to him—we had some civilian bigwigs in our midst, all right. Presumably he was here to speak for the DIA.

Sure enough, intelligence agencies from the CIA to the NSA were also represented to deputy director level, as were numerous members of the Senate Select Committee on Intelligence, including the senate majority leader. To see such a distinguished group of people huddled together in a room to watch a video of a black man being trussed up in what seemed like bondage gear was somewhat disconcerting, to say the least.

"This is a recording taken a week ago," the USD began explaining. "The fruits of the fourth UNOSOM IV deployment. We identified this man some time ago as being the chief culprit behind the Black Sea Massacre of last October."

"We arrested him, sir?" The words were out of my mouth before I could stop myself. To capture, rather than simply assassinate, the number one target was contrary to all protocol and operating procedure that had been established by the intelligence community these past years.

"Just so. There were special circumstances," explained Boss.

The USD continued. "Ms. Erica Sales here captured the man in the recording."

The woman sitting next to the undersecretary of defense nodded curtly.

Williams leaned forward. "Excuse me, ma'am. The undersecretary referred to you as 'Ms.' Does that mean you're not Forces?"

"If by 'forces' you mean those institutions that, at certain rare points in history, have been granted an official monopoly on organized violence by the state, then no, I'm not 'forces,'" replied the woman. She stood to take center stage, and the USD took a seat. As per the civilian fashion of the day, the woman was dressed in Pentagon style. "I'm the director of the third planning department at Eugene and Krupps."

I sighed inwardly with relief—I had chosen my words well—or at least luckily—when, earlier, I had asked, *We arrested him?* as opposed to what I really meant: *Why didn't we assassinate him?* That would have been too blatant for a civilian—after all, the US did not condone the assassination of foreign leaders, or so the official line still went.

"The latest UNOSOM IV deployment was essentially an outsourced project from its conception," the USD added in support of Erica Sales. "The forces deployed on the ground at the moment consist almost entirely of civilian contractors. Not just the usual suspects providing security arrangements for the Red Cross and NGOs—the actual execution of the business objectives of suppressing the armed insurgency in the area has also been assigned to independent civilian contractors."

The execution of the business objectives.

Such an interesting way of putting it. So telling. I was sure there were plenty of people who would be repulsed by such a phrase: peace activists, bleeding-heart liberals, and the like. But the phrase gave me a glimpse into a future I had never previously imagined, and it gave me an illicit thrill. As ever, words could have that effect on me.

I listened to the official DIA line: The business of war was no different, from a certain perspective at least, from that of a pizzeria making pizzas or of a pest control company killing bugs. People didn't have to fight for ethnic identity or to be a martyr for their religion—fighting could be just an occupation like any other. I thought about this. It was precisely because war was a

business that it became logistically possible to budget for it, to plan, to project manage, to place orders with manufacturers and contractors. Was modern warfare really nothing more than a purchase order to underwrite a country's desire to throw its weight around?

Of course, the idea that war was nothing more than a business laughed in the face of the blood-steeped casualties of war, just as it laughed at me and my job. The execution of war. The idea that war was just so much business to be taken care of. That it could be forecast, controlled, and managed like any other industry.

This line of thought had been developed in Cold War–era think tanks. It was determined that the only way to truly face the horrors of a full-blown nuclear war was to take a step back and consider all the factors as cold, objective facts. The futurist Herman Kahn, founder of the Hudson Institute think tank, advocated what he called "scenario planning" for a possible "hot" nuclear war and in doing so coined the phrase "to think the unthinkable." Wittgenstein would have approved.

Megadeath.

In order to deal with the apocalyptic reality of modern warfare, for people to be able to cope with dealing with scenes from the Book of Revelation on a daily basis, a certain finesse had become necessary when it came to terminology. Bland, bureaucratic phrases had become the norm, so that people didn't have to be constantly reminded of the families who had lost their children or bullet-riddled corpses.

"There are a multitude of tasks required in a massive operation like this: preparing and transporting provisions, canteen setup for local distribution, laundry services, constructing new government buildings, building and staffing rehabilitation camps for the former militia, and constructing and staffing prisons for war criminals. In the past we've always had to move in on the ground, establish a GHQ, and call in the military engineers. Now everything can be outsourced in advance to private military companies and UN-approved NGOs, and with UNOSOM IV they've gone one step further. No longer is it simply about delegating the logistics to civilian contractors, it's about having them on board at the strategic and tactical planning stages," explained the undersecretary of defense, who then turned to Erica Sales.

The woman from Eugene & Krupps, evidently some sort of private military company, picked up where he had left off without missing a beat. "There are only three people on the US government payroll in the entire UNOSOM IV operation. Their role is essentially that of resident auditors, there to monitor our performance and judgment. Eugene and Krupps has received similar instructions from the US, British, French, German, Turkish, and Japanese governments, and we're currently collaborating with a variety of organizations on the ground, from NGOs to the Red Cross to volunteer organizations to colleagues in the same line of work as us—such as Halliburton, who are responsible for supply train maintenance in this case—in order to lay the foundations for a lasting peace in Somalia."

At this point Erica Sales turned to us directly to give what seemed like a business pitch. "Our company employs a large number of former Special Forces personnel, and they played an integral role in our special projects last year."

"In other words they're Snake Eaters, just like us," Boss explained, his face expressionless. PMCs cherry-picking his top people by luring them away with "offers they couldn't refuse" was a perennial headache for Colonel Rockwell, but this wasn't the time or place for him to publicly tug on that particular thorn in his side. I glanced at Erica Sales's face to try and see if she had picked up on Boss's irony-laden use of the term "Snake Eater," but she was giving nothing away.

"Eugene and Krupps had the privilege of using the results of our R and D department's research to present a plan to the US government last September. A plan to capture alive Public Enemy Number One for the region, a certain Ahmed Hassan Salaad. Using numerous cross-corroborated sources from within the insurgency, we were able to convince the Senate Budget Committee that our plan was viable and stood a good chance of success."

I was hearing the businesslike spiel from this woman in front of me, and indeed she was painting a picture of an efficient bureaucratic procedure. But I had seen the other side—the reality that lay behind the anodyne, whitewashed words.

The walls painted red with the blood spurting out of the former brigadier general's throat.

The burning bodies of the bullet-riddled men and women.

The corpse of the little girl who had her pink brains spilling out from the back of her head.

The images piled vividly on top of each other. Erica Sales talked of being able to "present a plan" and had managed to weave all these words and phrases into her speech that seemed singularly inappropriate when describing war. Her words carefully chosen for their blandness had the effect of erasing all the colors of the battlefield, and it was as if in the version of war that she was weaving, nobody ever died and nobody ever killed, as if war was just like any other ordinary civilian enterprise. A whole layer of meaning was being stripped away . . .

. . . the layer that allowed you to describe in words the surprise, the astonishment, the sheer freshness of what it was like to be in the middle of battle where anyone and everyone could kill and be killed.

"After that, the Senate Budget Committee presented the précis to the Senate Appropriations Subcommittee on Defense, and once they'd greenlighted it, SOCOM was consulted," continued the USD.

Colonel Rockwell nodded. "Yes, and our answer—much as it pains me to say it—was that the plan was well conceptualized and completely viable."

"As such, we had an Extraordinary Grant approved by the budget committee and then assembled a unit to put the plan into effect. Our company suffered no casualties in the execution of the plan, and there were no unanticipated factors that interfered with the smooth running of the operation. Everything proceeded to plan, you could say," Erica Sales continued.

I looked at the man in the picture again. The top left corner of the screen showed the date and time, currently paused, and the coordinates where the recording was taken. The jerry-rigged interrogation room was a bleak white box, and we had our Ahmed sitting on a chair in the center. By the looks of it, this was right after he had been captured.

The man was trembling.

"Is this man really a key figure in the armed insurgency?" Williams asked bluntly, pointing a finger at the man. "Wouldn't one of these two-bit dictators be more likely to denounce us for illegally detaining him and for our Western imperialist ways, rather than just sit there trussed up like a trembling chicken?"

"Well, Ahmed Salaad is Oxford educated. He's familiar enough with the developed world to know that we're not about to torture a prisoner of war to death."

"So why does our boy Ahmed look like he's about to shit his pants, assuming he hasn't already?"

"Just sit tight and all will be revealed, sonny." The under-secretary of defense gave the signal, and I could tell that the footage was rolling again only by the fact that the timer in the top left corner had started counting. When all you were looking at was a single, motionless prisoner in restraints, it was hard to tell the difference. Then an off-screen interrogator started speaking to him in English.

Interrogator: We are an organization acting as a legal proxy of the United States of America, and you are being held as our captive. One of the explicit conditions of our contract with the United States government is that we voluntarily adhere to all the tenets of the Geneva Convention. We will be handing you over to the US government in due course, and provided you do not act in a violent manner yourself, no illegal force will be used on your person.

Ahmed: Aren't you using illegal force now?

Interrogator: Our client, the government of the United States of America, has gone through all the correct channels to ensure the international legitimacy

	of our actions in apprehending you. United Nations Resolution number 560097 gives us full authority to take whatever steps necessary to bring about the cessation of hostilities in Somalia.
Ahmed:	So this is a legitimate military operation. I wonder who gets to decide what exactly it is that makes an act of aggression legitimate.
Interrogator:	Perhaps it is the fact that an overwhelming majority of the international community sanctions our actions?
Ahmed:	You know, our actions were also sanctioned by our community. We were supported by the vast majority of our people. Everyone wanted it to happen.

"Seems he's not shy after all, shaking or no shaking," said Williams, who almost seemed relieved. "Looks like this is just another run-of-the-mill mass murderer, then. A fanatical worshipper of what's 'right.'"

"Of course he is," the USD shrugged. "But keep watching—this is where he starts to get all philosophical on us."

Interrogator:	The people can be wrong, of course. Look at how the German electorate voted in Hitler.
Ahmed:	Then who's to say that the people of the world aren't wrong about interfering in Somalia's internal affairs?

Interrogator: You have murdered huge numbers of
your own countrymen.

Ahmed: We had no choice.

Interrogator: Are you honestly expecting me to
accept that in the space of the last
six months you have come to believe
that there were all these people in
your midst that you now just had to
kill? I don't accept that people
can just flip a switch and go from
living harmoniously with their
neighbors to wanting to kill them
just like that.

Ahmed: And yet that's exactly what happened.

Interrogator: But why?

Ahmed: Who knows? All I know is that we had
good reason to kill them.

Interrogator: And yet one year ago such a notion
would have been inconceivable to you.

Ahmed: That's right . . . you're probably right
about that.

Interrogator: But how could such a mindset develop
in such a short time? I can just
about understand it happening in
one person. But for such a large,
disparate group of people to
suddenly develop such intense
hatred that they felt the need
to go about systematically
murdering their fellow countrymen?
Impossible!

Ahmed: I think you'll find that we're living
proof that it's very possible.

The clip came to an end.

"It's estimated that there were a total of forty-six thousand victims of the Black Sea Massacre," Erica Sales said, her voice dispassionate. "What we have to remember is that Ahmed here was an agent for peace in Somalia up until a year ago. There were bouts of civil unrest in the late twentieth century, but by the middle of the 2000s, that appeared to have been resolved once and for all. Somalia was about as stable a country as you could have found in the region."

I asked if some foreign military power had intervened to put an end to their previous civil strife. I was embarrassed to say that Somalia barely registered on my radar, and I couldn't have told you much about it. I'd been too occupied with work and eating pizza and watching *Saving Private Ryan* previews that my worldview was shaped almost exclusively by a combination of the dossiers handed to me in the line of duty, CNN, and the occasional TV movie.

"No, that was the impressive thing—it was the will of the Somalian people that brought about an end to their civil war," Sales answered. "Their troubles started in the 1970s and intensified in the 1990s to the extent that the international community tried to intervene once, just after the first Gulf War. The problem was that the operatives—your predecessors in US Special Forces, if you will—failed, and spectacularly at that. After seeing the battered corpses of his key operatives being dragged ignominiously and very publicly through the streets of Mogadishu, President Clinton decided that Africa was beyond hope and abandoned the whole area to its own devices. After 9/11, Somalia was initially suspected of being a hotbed of Al-Qaeda activity, but that soon died down once the full-scale invasions of Afghanistan and Iraq were underway. In fact, you could go as far as to say that the world at large had thoroughly forgotten about Somalia and its woes."

The land the world forgot. You could try and publicize its plight online, but you might as well try and push back the ocean for all the good it would do you. There was too much noise, too many layers, and the plaintive cries for help were all but buried. *Help us. Help us.* The silent death throes of many a country, sinking under the weight of its own plight. No one gave them a second glance.

"But then, in the 2010s, Somalia started to pull itself up by its own bootstraps," Colonel Rockwell suddenly interjected, and my eyes flicked over toward him to see him grinning. "You're looking at someone who was actually there on the ground in Mogadishu back in '93. I was part of Delta Force back then. I remember it like it was yesterday. I was in Bakaara Market when I heard the news of the Black Hawk going down. I'm one of the spectacularly failed predecessors that Ms. Sales refers to."

"Forgive me, Colonel, I had no idea. Of course. I meant no offense." Erica Sales put on a show of having the decency to look contrite.

"None taken. In fact, you're absolutely right. The operation *was* a spectacular failure. Not so much militarily, as it happens, but certainly a political failure. In any case, I've had a keen personal interest in keeping tabs on developments in Somalia ever since. Not that there's been much I've been able to actually do, other than send the odd donation. Anyway, my understanding of the situation—admittedly gleaned from what I've observed from afar—is that during the mid-2010s Somalia did indeed, as Ms. Sales suggests, start to drag itself out of the quagmire of civil war, entirely on its own initiative. The AKs and RPGs that had been the weapons of choice were gradually collected up in a general amnesty; civil order and education systems were restored, and the government, police force, and judiciary were rebuilt. The country found a semblance of order where there had been chaos. It's as if they were determined to prove Hobbes's theory wrong: that *bellum omnium contra omnes*, the war of all against all, was not always the inevitable and final result of civil breakdown. And by 'they,' I'm talking about one person in particular who was the driving force behind this recovery: a quiet but passionately determined man."

"And that man's name was Ahmed Hassan Salaad," said Erica Sales.

To be honest, I wasn't surprised when I heard this news. Just saddened a little, though mostly numb. The men who fought oppression on behalf of the weak, children, women, the destitute, and dying—had a habit of transforming into the next generation of oppressor once they had seized power. Power corrupts. It was a common story, and I couldn't afford to be surprised or affected too much by a common story.

"It wasn't an easy path, but Ahmed's group managed to forge a semblance of peace in Somalia for a while. They established a consensus that however poor, however needy, however destitute the country was, there were still fundamental principles that could not be abandoned. Children went to school and learned to read and write. Jerry-rigged armored trucks no longer patrolled the streets at night, and people could sleep peacefully again. Once that basic level of law and order had been established as a fundamental principle, the country could start focusing on its desperate poverty."

"What sort of natural resources does Somalia have?" asked Williams.

Erica Sales shook her head. "Virtually none to speak of. It is possible that there are some marginal sources of income that remain undiscovered or untapped, but as of the end of the twentieth century there were no significant resources along the lines of oil, ores, or even agricultural products. Investigations were made and surveys were taken, and no potential prospects for an income stream from exports were discovered."

"They were screwed, in other words," Williams continued tactfully.

"Not true—not so long as they had their people." Erica Sales shrugged. "Humans mean human resources, which means potential labor for hire. The UN's Millennium Development Goals have fostered a reasonably successful track record of seeing under-developed, resource-poor countries achieve a level of economic stability. And the African scenery always has significant potential for tourism, given appropriate development of infrastructure. The problem is—"

"—the country was stuck in a messy war for so long that no one wanted to invest, and all the tourists have long since been scared away, huh?" Williams interrupted.

"Just so," Erica Sales said with an air of finality and looked over at the undersecretary of defense.

The USD nodded and took the stage again. "Thank you, Ms. Sales, for your thorough briefing. We will now proceed to discuss internal matters."

"Thank you, ladies and gentlemen, for your time and attention." With that, Erica Sales turned sharply and left the room without further ado. The audience watched the Pentagon style–attired PMC director as she exited.

"Very well, ladies and gentlemen. I will be taking it from here," the USD said, clearing his throat in such an exaggerated and pompous manner that I had to bite down on my tongue to keep from laughing.

"So, Somalia had experienced some success in its disarmament drive and was making some progress. But the poverty and hardship continued. Some sort of drastic measure was needed to change the world's attitude toward the country in order to attract some foreign capital. To convince the world that Somalia was once again a civilized country with an educated and willing workforce and a safe place for tourists to visit. After all, all this was true, up until a year ago at least. But it wasn't enough that it was true—it had to *be seen to be true*."

"Public relations, in other words?" I asked.

The USD nodded. "Exactly. Ahmed had studied International Relations at the University of Oxford, and he recognized just how powerful a factor PR was in the creation of Bosnia and Herzegovina out of the ruins of the Yugoslav Wars."

Hope is a powerful weapon, but exceedingly difficult to wield effectively. Wasn't that written in some book somewhere? Well, the American people were going to have to believe in Somalia, believe that there was something to be hopeful about, if Somalia were to succeed as a nation. The American politicians in Washington were going to have to believe, as were the news networks. Lobbyists would have to be mobilized. How to achieve all this? Step onto the scene a certain PR specialist who was prepared to take Somalia on as a client.

A press conference was held in Washington. Somalia's cabinet ministers were trotted out. They were granted an audience with key US political figures. The dire straits of the Somalian economy were impressed upon them. Articles were written for the media. The word got out. And so the wheel started turning, and the powerful weapon called hope started creaking into action—at least, that was how the world was supposed to work...

"They needed to get the word out one way or another. The world needed to know that the fighting in Somalia was over, and that Somalia was now a progressive, forward-looking country with massive potential that just happened to be desperately poor at the moment. And that's when Ahmed made the decision to hire a former PR man as press advisor to the Somalian government," explained the USD.

He didn't need to say any more—I could see what was coming next. "John Paul, of course," I said out loud.

The whole room seemed to swivel toward me. I hadn't particularly intended—or expected—to draw focus, but apparently everyone was surprised at my prescience.

"Exactly. And I'm sure, Captain Shepherd, that you know exactly what happened next after John Paul entered Somalia."

Think of a murder case. Except the murderer is a country.

A reporter interviews the next-door neighbor for a sound bite. "He was a quiet type," Mrs. Smith (56) says. "His lawn was neat and trimmed, and he always took the trash out on time. Never in a million years would we have imagined him doing a thing like this. It's such a shock to the entire neighborhood..."

That was the best analogy they could give us. I nodded, listening to the USD's words. "Yes, in other words, that's where we are now. The country was plunged back into chaos in a heartbeat. A Hobbesian war of all against all. Chaos. Lines were drawn: the killers and the killed. And then—"

"—the famous scenes on the beaches of the Black Sea with the thousands of corpses like so many beached whales." Williams finished the story. The room was heavy with silence.

John Paul.

It was pretty clear now that he wasn't just some tourist with a bizarre penchant for seeing civil war zones. Well, it had been clear from the start to those at HQ who had given us the command to assassinate him; this was just the first time anyone had properly explained the situation to us.

This man who we'd tried and failed to kill on numerous occasions had somehow been a catalyst for genocide in locations throughout the world.

For some reason, when this man went into a country, it plunged into chaos.

For some reason, when this man went into a country, the blood of innocents would pour forth.

"The time span for all of this was a mere six months," the USD continued. "Now, the silver lining was that these countries that attracted nothing but the world's indifference when they were peaceful did at least manage to capture the world's attention when the massacres were as graphic and vivid as they were. With public opinion being what it was and with a presidential election looming, the US's response was all but inevitable. The problem was, the US Army was already massively overcommitted, thanks to all the existing civil wars and terrorist cells and ethnic conflicts around the world, and was in danger of spreading itself too thin to be effective. That's how, for the first time in modern warfare, outsourcing on a massive scale became the norm."

"The US forces are being worked to the bone," interjected one of the Congressmen. "This sudden escalation in overseas conflicts is simply unnatural, that's what it is. All these countries that have pulled themselves away from their violent pasts and were looking forward to bright futures suddenly seemed to collapse. It's one step forward, ten steps back! Even countries with absolutely no history of racial tension suddenly find their citizens at one another's throats. We've commissioned all the major think tanks to analyze the situation to come up with *some* sort of explanation, but so far they've been firing blanks."

"And yet you've all known the answer from the start, haven't you?" I asked. "From before I received orders to assassinate John Paul?"

Nobody said a word.

I didn't move. My eyes were fixed on the men and women around the table.

The sea of faces also remained motionless, except for almost imperceptible twitches. Who could be used as the scapegoat?

None of them wanted to be the first to speak in response to my question, lest a wrong answer cost them their job. Such were the dynamics of Washington.

Eventually a woman in a navy blue suit broke the abstruse Washingtonian silence. "That's right. We attempted to capture John Paul a number of times prior to issuing the assassination order."

"Who's 'we'?" Williams asked bluntly, pointing a finger at the woman's face. The woman was visibly taken aback by his bluntness and lack of respect but said nothing to object—neither did Boss or the undersecretary of defense.

"CIA. Overseas is our territory after all," the woman in the blue suit replied.

"No it's not. It's not your 'territory.' The world is what it is, a giant mess of a place full of confusion and chaos. Thinking that it's somehow 'your territory' is what's caused this whole clusterfuck in the first place."

Despite the extraordinary words that were coming from his mouth, Williams was absolutely calm. He wasn't riled up or trying to pick a fight, particularly. He just had no time for amateurs.

Colonel Rockwell had to rein him in. "Watch your tongue, Captain."

"Apologies, sir. I take my words back fully, although not the sentiment behind them. If there's anyone who's being rude here, it's the lady over there. Calling the world her territory is disrespectful to the rest of the world and disrespectful to us." Williams seemed to accept his reprimand but showed no remorse for his outspokenness. We were the ones who had been fighting for the US abroad after all, unlike the CIA, who basically played teddy bears' picnic with their "paramilitary" activities. What right did they have to call the world their territory? I could figure what Williams was thinking.

The USD urged the CIA woman to continue, and she did so without changing her blank expression.

"As you say, we did indeed fail on a number of occasions to capture John Paul. In our defense, it hadn't yet been established at that stage that he was instrumental in fanning the flames of conflict around the world. There was a correlation, but there were numerous factors involved at that stage, and all we could say for sure was that he seemed to be cropping up in the shadows quite a lot whenever there was some sort of atrocity. It was only when the level of the atrocities started intensifying exponentially that we started receiving reliable intel confirming that John Paul was at the heart of all this."

I wondered how many innocent people had been murdered in John Paul's wars and atrocities in the time it had taken the CIA lady to explain this to us with her arms folded in front of her.

Just one single man, traveling around the world, leaving a bloodbath in his wake. He seemed to find his way to the heart of power—government or insurgency forces, it didn't seem to matter to him, so long as he could whisper his seductive spell into the ears of those who had the power; and then, as if by magic, piles of dead bodies would start appearing.

Was that a credible explanation of events?

I thought back. Two years ago, when I had killed the ex-brigadier general. *Why? Why? Why has my country ended up like this?* The former brigadier general hadn't been asking a hypothetical question born of regret, he'd been genuinely trying to work out what had happened. I remembered his expression when I confronted him; even though he knew *what* his motives were, *what* he was trying to achieve by causing those atrocious scenes of mass murder, he didn't know *why*.

I remembered that expression and I saw it now, on a different face, right in front of me: the trembling face of Ahmed Salaad projected onto the wall.

"So, Boss, why have we been summoned here today?" I asked. Colonel Rockwell adjusted his beret as he looked around at the other people in the room to secure their tacit consent to continue. Having received it, he said in a calm voice:

"It's been decided that we'll be putting into effect a plan to assassinate John Paul."

Williams frowned. *Uh, wasn't that already decided a couple of years ago when you first sent us in to try and kill him?* he obviously wanted to say.

I, on the other hand, immediately grasped what Boss meant. "A search and kill op, sir? Will we be trailing him?"

"Exactly."

A trailing op. Find him and hunt him down like a dog. A team of us were going to be dispatched into the thick of a war zone, armed to the teeth with the latest gadgets, primed with all the prep work the intelligence community could throw at us, and then left to it.

"It's thought that John Paul is currently entrenched somewhere in Europe. Now, Intelligence Corps assassination work has, of late, been producing spectacular results. In particular, Unit G's stock has never been higher. There's only one fly in the ointment, and that's John Paul."

"So you want us to go undercover? Like spies?" I asked.

"Exactly," the navy-blue-suited CIA lady spoke up. "As much as we hate to admit it, the CIA simply doesn't have the experience or the track record that you do at assassination, and even our best operatives simply don't match up to your level of toughness and training. We did consider the option of having one of our moles on the ground do the work, one of the local radicals, but this is an extremely delicate and precisely planned operation, and we need to do everything we can to maximize our chance of success. Once upon a time this was the sort of plan we would have put in the hands of the Green Berets or Delta Force. As it is, Special Operations I Detachment is undoubtedly the most suited to this line of work."

"Most of all, the important thing to remember is that this is a preemptive strike," Colonel Rockwell continued, turning to look directly at us. "So far, it's always been a case of a massacre occurring followed by Intelligence determining that John Paul has somehow been involved, before finally sending us in to try and tidy up the mess. Considered from this perspective, our missions in the past have essentially been nothing more than glorified police work after the event.

"This time, though, it's different. This may be a tracking mission, but it's not a simple case of finding a target of opportunity and taking him out. When the chance presents itself, you're not just to kill him—you'll need to discover the seeds of the next genocide he's planting."

Colonel Rockwell finished speaking, and the undersecretary

of defense took over. "You will be appointed staff officers and temporarily attached to the Intelligence Department of the Joint Chiefs of Staff."

No surprises, given how closely integrated the two intelligence departments of the DIA and the Joint Chiefs of Staff were. "In other words, under your command," I said.

"You're being assigned to J2," said Boss, "but as this is a joint operation between Intelligence and DIA, we'll be able to provide you with comprehensive support from our end too. This is a crucial mission after all. There are a lot of people relying on our success.

"In short, gentlemen, to coin a phrase, you could well be our only hope. Our last line of defense before another massacre takes place. Shit, even as we speak, what's to say that John Paul isn't trying to turn a country somewhere in the world into a new living hell?"

3

Corpses.

The crater in the ground was like a giant's stockpot, packed full of the remnants of charred people.

Humans have a higher proportion of subcutaneous fat than most mammals, which means that when they're heated up good and proper, their skin crisps up like pork crackling, and were it not for all the other things that inevitably end up getting burnt to a crisp with them, they would give off a similar savory aroma. Burning corpses get their characteristic foul odor from things like clothes and hair in particular. Were it not for those, burning humans wouldn't smell much different from any other meaty barbecue.

All these thoughts ran through my head as I sat on the edge of the still-warm crater and surveyed the mass of human flesh that spread out before me. A thought flickered through my mind: the carnage in front of me was really no different from a meal that someone, somewhere was about to eat. As I brooded, one of the corpses opened its eyes, its eyelids cracking as it did so. Its skin and bone and flesh were all burnt to a crisp, and the eyes that stared out through the eye sockets made the corpse look like something from a Hammer horror movie.

"I'm all burnt to a crisp," my mom muttered, looking at her charred hands.

"Yep, like a crispy Peking duck," I said.

"I wonder if I taste as good as Peking duck," my mother said with a laugh. As she did so, a crack appeared in her hardened cheeks. She was like a painting that had been in the sun for too long.

This was really funny. "Looking at you like this, Mom, I can't help think that you're nothing more than a pile of flesh and bones."

"Manners, manners! After all, you're not exactly much more yourself, are you?" Mom seemed offended. "If a corpse is just a pile of flesh and bones, then how can you pretend that a person who just happens to be alive is any more than that either? We're all just objects."

"Just objects, huh? Try telling that to Williams. Better still, try using him as an object . . . what, like an ashtray, maybe?"

"I'm sure he wouldn't be too happy at first. But he'd come around sooner or later."

Warplanes were circling the sky at a dangerously low altitude; they reminded me of the underbellies of great whales. There was an occasional smattering of gunfire, and the smell of gunpowder permeated the area.

"He'd come around to what?" I asked. "The idea that he's just an object?"

"Yes, that he's just a piece of meat, O-son-of-mine-who-calls-himself-an-atheist-but-can't-quite-bring-himself-to-accept-one-of-the-central-tenets-of-his-so-called-belief-system."

I laughed. *O son of mine.* That's what Mom always used to call me when we played our high-falutin' language games. Putting me in my place for being the innocent that I was.

" 'I am naught but flesh, and the flesh profiteth nothing,' " I countered.

"Naught but flesh, maybe, but don't take that as a bad thing. Your body is not a prison, you know."

I nodded. Because Mom was always right. If she said something was so, it must be so.

"Look, your friends are here to pick you up," she said.

There was a roar. A transport craft was descending from the skies, and the blast was whipping up the air around us, causing the trees around the crater to blow this way and that. I lifted a hand to my face to shield myself from the debris that swirled in the air. The plane's hatch opened, and there was Williams, beckoning me toward him.

"See you later then, Mom."

"See you later, O son of mine."

I waved goodbye to my charred mother.

My mother waved her blackened matchstick arm back at me.

The personnel carrier started its ascent. I lay back in my recliner seat and before I knew it I was asleep and the crater full of corpses was no more than a speck in the distance, a memory.

I fell asleep on a passenger craft in the world of the dead; when I awoke it was on a passenger craft in the world of the living.

My visits to the land of the dead had become more frequent since Alex's death. So much so that I'd even considered seeing one of the counselors that the forces supplied for us. I hadn't quite gotten around to it, though, and I probably wouldn't. After all, it wasn't like it was affecting my work in any way. Basically, I'd resigned myself to the nightly call of the deadlands.

The scenes in which Mom had something to tell me were really just an echo of my childhood. Mom never remarried and brought me up by herself. She used to talk to me about anything and everything. My abnormal interest in literature and words, my teenage obsession with movies, all were due to Mom's influence on me. In other words, the scenes in the land of the dead were really just like the sort of everyday interactions we had when I was growing up, at dinnertime or just lounging about in the living room. Apart from the obvious fact that Mom was now dead, of course.

Mom watched over me constantly. Her greatest fear was for me to be out of her sight. I guess she thought I might disappear. Just like my father did. People could disappear in the most inexplicable of ways. My mom was terrified that would happen with me.

I was fairly young when I cottoned on to this fact about my mom, and I guess I did my best to try and assuage her fears. I became a careful child. I took pains never to get into fights and always paid close attention to how other children spoke and acted to make sure I kept under the radar. I never stood out, never rubbed anyone the wrong way. On those rare occasions that something did happen, I made absolutely sure that Mom would never find out. I made sure she had nothing to fear. To constantly prove that she didn't need to worry, that I wasn't about to suddenly disappear. Reassuring Mom had always been my number one priority, dawn through dusk, kindergarten through college.

I guess I joined the forces, and put in for Special Forces to boot, because I'd grown bored with myself. I applied to the brand-spanking-new Intelligence Department, put myself forward for the fifty-to-one selection procedure for their new, experimental Special Forces, and passed. Strangely enough, my mom didn't have too much to say about that. She smiled and said, *You have to follow your own path.*

Despite the perilous line of work I was now in, ultimately it wasn't me who was to suddenly disappear one day like my father did. It was my mother, she who had spent her days worrying about *me* disappearing. And now her body was in a cemetery in Washington and her soul visited me every night to talk to me in the land of the dead.

For now though, when I opened my eyes the land of the dead disappeared, and I found that the aircraft was about to land. I looked out the window and saw the surface of the plane pulsing and rippling grotesquely, just as the surfaces of Intruder Pods did. As with the Intruder Pods, the wings of these Meatplanes could twist and contort in the air to absorb and adapt to the worst of the air currents, making for a supremely stable flight.

I wondered how much flesh there was on one of these giant wings. These aircraft weren't called Meatplanes for nothing. I felt like stripping the wing down to its bones with a knife to see what the flesh was like underneath, to see the blood dripping from its carcass.

I swallowed a Regionsync pill to reset my body clock. These pills always reminded me of the pill women take to regulate their fertility. Still, I had no desire to meet up with Williams while I was suffering from jet lag, so I gulped it down.

The Meatplane touched down gently on the runway at Ruzyne Airport. Its wings contorted—pretty alarming, if you're watching it for the first time—and the forward momentum of the plane was absorbed. It was like being inside a bird who uses its wings to elegantly guide its landing onto a tree branch. As a result, these Meatplanes could land on the narrowest strip of runway, decelerate massively, and yet the people inside would barely feel a thing—g-force was kept almost constant. This was also helped by the polymer seats going into shock absorption mode, of course. An electric current subtly modified the seats on a macromolecular level to turn them into something like giant mushrooms, and by the time the seats returned to normal, we passengers were greeted by the smiling faces of the cabin crew guiding us toward the exits. I always enjoyed my flights on these sorts of civilian planes—they beat the hell out of those surreal military stealth craft on the comfort stakes.

Prague. City of culture. City of a hundred spires.

I left Ruzyne Airport and took the metro to emerge on an overcast morning.

"Which genius's bright idea was it to use Charles Bridge as the dead drop?" Williams asked.

We were standing on the bridge watching the amber clouds cast their shadow over Vltava River.

Williams had been late for our rendezvous, of course, and as usual was just trying to bluster his way out of it. I nodded and said nothing. He did sort of have a point: Charles Bridge was indeed overloaded with tourists. It was as if some mob had decided to get together to try and sink the bridge using its own body mass.

Having said that, Williams was still a paid-up veteran of the elite Special Forces, and his job over the last few years had, to a greater or lesser extent, consisted of playing "Where's Waldo?"—tracking down and identifying his target from the surrounding rabble. Finding a person for a prearranged rendezvous was surely easier than when you were trying to neutralize them. On a scale of one to ten, the likelihood that Williams had simply been a bit lazy and arrived late was probably an eleven. As always. I knew from experience that it wasn't worth calling him out on it, though—not unless I wanted to get into a heated debate that would soon descend into a farce.

I asked Williams how things were. Williams scowled—he seemed almost disappointed that I wasn't challenging him. He had obviously rehearsed his story in his mind and had been ready to stand his ground.

"Not bad. Same old, same old," he said.

" 'Same old, same old'? Williams—you just got here forty-eight hours before I did!"

"And there it is. Dude, I knew you were annoyed about having to wait. I told you, it's not my fault, there are too many people on this stupid—"

That's our Williams for you...

"Williams, have we really come to Prague to act out a Monty Python sketch?"

"Well, it's not like we've got anything better to do. John Paul ain't here."

Huh. Well, it looked like we were in the middle of some sort of comedy after all. Or at least a shit-show. Not that I was too surprised; this was hardly the first time we'd been sent halfway around the world to a place where John Paul wasn't.

"Isn't here? Does that mean he *was* here up until—"

Williams cut me off. "Yeah, the morning I arrived I had a coffee with the latest CIA genius in a Starbucks. 'Unfortunately, sir, we appear to have temporarily let him out of our sights.' Fucking Langley brat. Straight out of Harvard, wet as piss behind the ears, not even enough Czech to read the sports pages, and still he's landed himself a nice little posting at the embassy here."

"Huh. Says all you need to know about Langley, putting a greenhorn like that on such an important target." I sighed, but truth be told I was hardly surprised. These days the CIA was little more than a throwback to a bygone era, a vestigial bastard child of the Cold War. As had just been proven, again. And, yet again, it was up to us in Intelligence to pick up the slack and clean up after their latest operational clusterfuck.

"Yeah. You know those spy novels where the agents can always rely on the desk jockeys? M to cover your back, Q to give you just the right gadget at the right time? I say we burn those books. Every time Langley fucks up, we burn them all."

Williams was only half joking—I could tell he was seriously pissed. With good cause, to be fair. *The CIA just can't get the staff anymore.* I surveyed the statues of the saints that lined the bridge. One of them in particular caught my eye: the saint had a number of samurai-like figures kneeling at his feet, waiting to be baptized. It was like a scene from a Kurosawa movie. I knew that quite a lot of these statues were of famous Jesuits, so I guessed that this one was probably one of the missionaries who first proselytized Christianity in Japan.

I wondered how this saint could have gotten his message across when he was a stranger in a strange land. How did he communicate with the Japanese? What did they understand by his reverential treatment of God? What did they even understand by the word "God"? How was it translated?

"Dude, are you even listening to me?" Williams interrupted my reverie.

"Sure, sure. I was just thinking about that wet-behind-the-ears CIA brat. How he feels in a country where he barely has enough of the local language to get by."

"What? Fuck him and the fucking horse he rode in on. And fuck Langley for not sending some fucker who speaks the fucking lingo."

"Indeed. Anyhow. What now?" I asked.

Williams shrugged. "Look up John Paul's woman, I guess."

"He has a woman?" The first I'd heard of this.

"A woman John Paul visited, at least. That's how the Secret Service knew he was in the area."

"Shit, sounds like we'd have captured him already if they'd been doing their job properly."

"Well, the CIA say that they've been keeping a close watch

on her. Not that I believe anything those idiots say anymore. But that's what they say. And according to them, John Paul's recent appearance by her side was the first incident since they've been tracking her."

"What's the probability John Paul has already left the Czech Republic?"

"Dunno. Hard to say. His ID doesn't seem to register at airports after all. Maybe he left, maybe he's still hanging around. I guess our best bet is to hope he's still here and keep a close watch on the woman," Williams said half-heartedly. He was right, of course; there wasn't exactly anything else we could do, according to procedure. That didn't make it any better, though.

"Hey, Clavis. This is just like that Kafka play, no? Except in our case it's *Waiting for John Paul.*"

Williams was being uncharacteristically literary again, or at least was trying to be, so I felt I needed to point out two things. Number one, *Waiting for Godot* was by Beckett and not Kafka. And number two, Godot never actually appears in the play, leaving the two protagonists to speculate about his whereabouts with an ever-increasing sense of futility. Don't jinx us, in other words.

"Meh. It's all Kafka to me," said Williams.

4

Gregor Samsa woke up one morning to discover that he had turned into some sort of disgusting insect.

Kafka had written these words in German.

The Hapsburg dynasty that once ruled the Czech lands had wanted German to be the *lingua franca* of their empire. German was decreed the second official language in all Czech lands in 1627 and was gradually adopted in all governmental offices, while Czech became the language of the peasantry. German remained an official language until the fall of the Austro-Hungarian Empire. Fast-forward thirty-something years after the collapse and the Czech lands were, for the second time in living memory, one with their Slovak neighbors. This time they were the Czechoslovak Socialistic Republic, although still commonly referred to by their pre-WWII name of Czechoslovakia.

Anyhow, that's why you could buy maps in German in this country, and that's why there were plenty of Slovak-speaking natives. Not that there was much by the way of difference between Czech and Slovak—it was perfectly possible for two people to have a conversation where one was speaking Czech and the other Slovak. And the older generation, in particular, were in the habit of peppering their Czech-Slovak conversations with a liberal sprinkling of German nouns.

So there were still three languages in this country, really. There was only one official language now, Czech, but there were plenty of landmarks that had a number of names, which could be pretty confusing for tourists when they wanted the Opera House and were given directions to the Státní Opera by one local, the Smetana Theater by another, and the Opernhaus by yet another without realizing that they were all one and the same building.

The many place names, and the many languages spoken by the old folk...

Czech was a hard enough language as it was without having to worry about "interference" from Slovak on one side and German on the other.

"So I suppose that Czech could be considered something of a 'hard language' compared to your run-of-the-mill romance languages." Lucia Sukrova was explaining all this to me as she served tea. "Czech is a Slavic language, just like Russian and Croatian, and like all Slavic languages there are a huge number of possible noun declensions. Some nouns have over two hundred possible different forms, depending on which way you count them."

"That's very interesting, ma'am. So you could spend a whole month on a single word and not master it," I observed, placing a slice of lemon in my tea.

"Yes, although admittedly that's an extreme case." Lucia smiled. "But the really tricky thing about Czech isn't so much the nouns *per se,* as the difficulty of getting them out in the correct order to say exactly what you mean, and in an accent that comes even close to a native speaker's. Did you know, for example, that some Czech words don't have any vowels in them? How's this for a sentence: *Strč prst skrz krk.* And we even have our own unique phoneme, the Ř. Linguists call it the raised alveolar non-sonorant trill, and it's a rare bored housewife who can master *that* with any degree of panache, I can tell you."

"I see," I said.

"That's why it's hard to teach this sort of direct interpersonal communication over the Internet. There's just too much you miss, too many subtleties."

She was absolutely right, of course. Web-based learning could only ever get you so far, even with the advanced e-learning technologies we had at our disposal these days. Virtual reality learning environments were the order of the day for most of our classroom training sessions, but language learning was still firmly a face-to-face, offline experience, precisely for the reasons she named.

Lucia Sukrova's livelihood was teaching Czech to foreigners. We were in her studio, a spacious room in her traditional apartment in the center of Prague's old town, where all her students came to study.

"I have to confess, ma'am, that I'm relieved that your English is so good. You speak like a native, unlike some language teachers I've worked with in the past."

"Well, English does seem to be the hegemonic language these days, after all . . ." Lucia smiled. If this was a subtle dig, for once it didn't seem to bother me, even though I was usually pretty weary of having my country's foreign policy rubbed in my face by disgruntled locals.

"I'm sure it must seem that way to you, ma'am, although you might be interested to know that according to the latest web traffic analysis that might not strictly be true. More content is created by Japanese bloggers than in English, for example. Perhaps because the Japanese like to have a virtual outlet for their opinions and feelings that they suppress in everyday life."

My cover is that I'm in advertising, recently transferred over here to manage a big new account. Here to be a pioneer in the burgeoning interstitial market. To infest and infect beautiful Czech websites with opportunistic pop-ups of airbrushed models proclaiming their undying loyalty to a diet pill du jour. And these sorts of ads did, as it happened, have a tendency to appear on both English and Japanese blogs.

"Is that so? I have to admit I can't really relate to that on a personal level, as I've never felt the compulsion to document my life for the whole world to read. But if what you say is true, I imagine that the web is drowning in a sea of words."

"Did you ever keep a diary?" I asked, trying to find a way to relate the conversation to her.

"Hmmm...yes, I believe I did. Some time ago, though."

"And if you don't mind my asking, ma'am, where did you learn your English?"

"In the States. I studied linguistics," she said.

"So you could say you're a master of words?" I asked.

"Hardly. If I were so good with words I'd have ensnared a man or two to look after me by now, no? I studied the academic framework of language, not its sensual power."

"Sure, you could describe Noam Chomsky as many things, but sexy is probably not one of them," I joked.

"I don't know about that. Not for most people, you're right, but there are some oddballs in this world who feel the sensuous beauty in his work. Take me, for instance."

Lucia smiled again. She sure liked to smile, I thought. And not just any old smile. Hers wasn't the superficial smile of someone trying to make polite conversation. It was the smile of someone who loved words and loved communicating exactly what she meant in her heart. When she smiled she looked so much younger than the thirty-three-year-old she was. When she smiled, she could have probably passed for a teenage girl.

"Where were you based in the States?" I continued.

"I was at grad school in Massachusetts."

"MIT?" I asked, and she nodded. "Wow! Impressive! I had no idea."

Not true. I had every idea. It was my job to seem impressed by this piece of information, as if it were new to me, as if Intelligence hadn't profiled this woman down to the last minute detail. It was my job as a spy to be able to pull off this sort of lie convincingly. Normally I could. Right now, though, I had no idea whether or not she was convinced.

"It's not that impressive really. It happened to be the only school where I could continue my research in my field, and so that's where I went."

"Oh, really? What sort of research was that exactly?"

The conversation that had been flowing so naturally up until this point now hit a wall. This was one question too many for a casual conversation, evidently, although Lucia did her best not to show it.

Who's asking? she must have wanted to say.

Instead, she chose her words carefully, blandly. "I suppose you could say it was mainly to do with how language can exert influence on people's behavior."

"You mean linguistic relativity? Like how Eskimos have over twenty different words for snow, and how the very existence of these words affects their worldview?"

"You mean the old Sapir-Whorf hypothesis? No, not quite." Lucia smiled again. And truth be told I was relieved. Not so much because I was worried about her being suspicious, but because I didn't like looking at her face when she frowned. She was a beautiful woman when she smiled.

"Actually, the story about the Inuit is something of an urban legend. The number of words that they apparently have for 'snow' seems to increase every time the story's told. When Boas first reported his findings it was four, Whorf spoke of seven in his hypothesis, and the seven became 'almost ten,' 'over ten,' and so on and so forth, until you get 'the Eskimos have a hundred different words for snow!' being reported as fact in *National Geographic*. Scratch a little deeper, though, and you'll see that they really just have a handful. Not that different from English, when you think about it: 'snow,' 'sleet,' 'slush,' 'hail,' and so on."

This I didn't know. I'd put up with plenty of dinner party snobs in my time, idly jibber-jabbering about how the Inuits have *such different realities from us, don't you know*, and how their lives must be so much more *real, y'know, being centered around snow and all that*. And so I guess it was these idle gossips who were the carriers of the Eskimo meme from one middle-class dinner party to another.

I wondered how many words the Inuits would allegedly have for snow by the time the meme finally ran its course. A hundred? Two hundred? More?

"Sadly, real life tends to be a little less exciting than all that,"

Lucia continued. "And contrary to popular belief, there seems to be very little correlation between language and people's perception of reality. No matter where you're born or where you grow up, reality is just that little bit too resilient to be buffeted about by language. The thought always comes before the language used to express the thought."

"And yet I'm thinking in English right now."

"Well, it might seem like that, because your reality is one that incorporates the English language into itself. But actually your thought process consists of a number of different factors, and language is just one of the tools at its disposal. Language is a subset of thought, if you will, not the other way around. Trying to argue that people think with language just because we have a keenly developed linguistic sensibility is a bit like saying that beavers have evolved to think with their teeth."

"That's an...interesting analogy." I wasn't being sarcastic. I had to acknowledge that there was a certain attractiveness to the idea that reality was determined by words and that it was the meanings that people attached to words that acted as a filter to construct their own versions of reality. But at the same time, something had always struck a false chord with me about this theory. I remembered back in high school our English teacher proudly relating the story of Eskimos having many different words for snow (twenty, was it, in that telling?) and feeling profoundly uncomfortable about this. After all, words were real, they were bundles of reality that existed in the outside world, independent from me. I remembered wondering how they could possibly influence my thought in that way when they weren't really part of me.

"What sort of units do you imagine a mathematician or a theoretical physicist thinks in? When they first conceptualize their ideas?" Lucia asked me.

I answered that I supposed they would use more numbers and numerical formulae.

Lucia shook her head. "You would have thought so—but Einstein's actually on record saying that it was always a visual image that came to his mind in the first instance. Other so-called geniuses have said similar things. That it's actually a sort of diagram that comes to mind first, and it's only by manipulating that diagram in their minds that they're able to come up with formulae as the output."

"That's hard to believe. To understand, I mean. How do you visualize an imaginary number, or infinity for that matter?" I asked.

"Hard to believe for you or me. That's because our realities are different from those genius scientists. So, you see, it's probably more accurate to speak of different realities as being determined by thought processes, not language as such."

"May I ask you a question?" I decided to press the point. "What are words to *you*? If they're not objects that determine our realities, then what are they there for?"

"Tools for communication, of course. Or... organs, maybe, I guess?"

It was at this moment that I realized that Lucia's language had shifted in register—slightly, subtly, but definitely. At the start of our conversation, she had been talking to me as a prospective student and customer—and that was supposed to have set the boundaries of the conversation.

But here she was now, *enjoying* her conversation with me.

"Organs?" I said. "You mean, as in body parts? Kidneys and bowels and arms and eyes?"

"Exactly."

"But isn't language a human abstraction?"

"So are you saying that abstractions can never be real? Do you believe that there's no way the human soul could be contained in a pitiful little organ such as the brain, maybe?" Then Lucia appeared to stop herself. "Oh, forgive me if I've overstepped the mark. You are, perhaps, a religious man?"

I thought of Alex.

Hell is here.

Alex pointing at his own forehead.

"No, I'm an atheist," I said.

Alex had been a religious man. He had believed in God.

And that same Alex had said that hell was inside our minds. Hidden among the folds and creases of our brains.

"That's a relief. I know this sort of conversation can be offensive to some people."

I laughed. "Lucky escape for you, I guess. Besides," I pointed out, "if I were the Bible-thumping type, you would have already offended me earlier with your talk of souls and whatnot."

"You're right. I guess I'm the sort of person that has to rely on having lucky escapes." Lucia laughed. "Anyway, what I was saying was that language is one of the fruits of evolution, of humanity's natural tendency to adapt to the environment. Humans had to acquire the ability to somehow compare themselves with other things; that way they could run crude mental simulations to try and forecast the outcome of a particular action or inter-action. Human thought processes—or maybe you could call it raw emotion—came up with a way of differentiating our selves from the other: the ego, they call it in psychology. After all, without having an idea of the self, you have no way of comparing yourself with the outside world, no way of making any sort of comparisons or judgment calls. But with a sense of self, man was able to avoid all sorts of danger through his 'forecasts.' You could say that language developed as a way of trading these 'forecasts' with other similar beings. This allowed us to build up a mental database of information without necessarily having to experience it firsthand, and this in turn further reduced our exposure to danger and allowed us to adapt even more perfectly to a wide variety of environments."

"So you're saying that language is basically just a product of evolutionary adaptation?"

"Yes. Just like our other organs."

So the very fact that I was here now, talking to Lucia, was nothing more than an incidental byproduct of evolutionary adaptation of the brain? Was language really no more than an organ, like an elephant's trunk or a giraffe's neck?

Language was indeed a precise and delicate instrument, I supposed. It occurred to me that even though we now had technology such as giant artificial flesh Meatplanes and the like, we still didn't have a way of fully replicating the complex filtration systems of human kidneys and livers on a miniature scale. Those organs were, in their own way, just as precise and delicate, as exquisite, as language. For medical science, the perfect artificial organ was still some way over the horizon.

When even our internal organs still contained countless mysteries hidden to us, what right did we have to think of language as being this unique, divine gift?

I needed to know who I was. I needed to use words to communicate with other people. Surely then, language was just another inevitable evolutionary process. Language was part of my flesh. An organ called the self. An organ called language.

"If that's the case, isn't it a particularly human conceit, this idea that living things will necessarily develop language once they've evolved past a certain point?"

"You're thinking that another species might have other 'organs' develop instead, you mean?" Lucia said. "So in a super-advanced civilization of crows, they'd all have incredibly sharp beaks rather than language?"

Language, and my own sense of self—both mere adaptive mechanisms. That much I got and was prepared to accept. Having said that, if language really was nothing more than an adaptive organ—well, there were examples, weren't there, of species that became extinct through over-adaptation?

Wasn't the saber-toothed tiger eventually driven to extinction by the weight of its own canines?

5

"Well, whaddaya know—I guess that English major came in handy after all."

These were Williams's first words to me to welcome me back when I returned from Lucia Sukrova's apartment via a pre-arranged back route in an apartment on the opposite side of the building.

"Just the way the conversation flowed," I said as I pulled myself out of my suit.

Williams's eyes stayed glued to his monitor. "If you say so, dude. Sounded to me like you were quite happy to let the conversation flow that way, though, huh?"

"Not getting much at home these days, Williams?"

"Hey, buddy, I've still got it when I want it, you know? Ten minutes with that little lady and she'd be putty in my hands."

"Uh-huh. What would you do, sit there and grunt at her until she submitted?"

"Nah, I'd spin some line about Eskimos and snow. Or maybe talk about Kafka."

"I thought it was all Kafka to you?" I said.

"You don't get it, do you? You're allowed to leave some gaps in a conversation with a woman—hell, you're *supposed* to. Gives her a chance to stick her pretty little oar in."

"Gaps in the conversation are one thing, but in your case you'd be leaving hulking great craters. Anyway, women can't stand self-assured pricks like you, in case you haven't noticed."

If I sounded like I was crossing the line from banter into something more irritable, it was because I was sometimes genuinely tired of Williams's incessant braggadocio. Besides, he had it all wrong. You don't try and engage a Czech language teacher by talking at them about Kafka, any more than you become buddies with a fishmonger by lecturing him about fish. If there's one thing worse than shop talk, it's shop talk with an amateur who thinks he knows it all. I shuddered at the memory of those godawful presentations on special ops we used to have to sit through given by slack-jawed CIA goons.

"Nice. Anyhow—any sniff of John Paul along the way?" Williams asked.

I thought back to the room. I'd kept an eye out for all the usual indicators—a ring, photographs, magazines, general cleanliness, and decor—but I had detected no obvious signs that a man had been there recently.

It turned out that the electronic sensors had had better luck than my own limited human sensory organs. A man *had* been in the room recently. We knew this thanks to the tiny sensor patch that I placed inside my nostril beforehand to record the airborne particles in the room. Or rather, the patch sent the data to a device stuck to my torso, the nostril-patch being merely the sensor that transmitted the data to the processor under my shirt, via the natural salts on my skin.

The smoking gun: Penhaligon Eau de Cologne.

"I guess even John Paul likes to make an effort for his lady.". Williams sneered.

The CIA had reported that no men had entered Lucia's apartment since John Paul had left a few days ago. Only a few women, mainly bored housewives who had recently moved to Prague with their businessman husbands.

So the cologne must have been the lingering scent of John Paul. My own nose might not have picked it up, but it *was* picked up by something in my nose.

"Damn. No semen," continued Williams. He was referring, of course, to the results of the analysis that were now displayed on the screen in front of him. "I guess he didn't miss his girlfriend all that much, then."

I sat down, tasted the bowl of Czech sauerkraut soup in front of me—not bad—and started reading Lucia Sukrova's file. Poring over the details of her life like some sort of stalker. Sure, I could justify it by telling myself it was just work, but was what I was doing any less sordid than Williams's search for cum stains? I couldn't really concentrate and closed the file.

I decided to access USA, partly to forget that I was in this den of professional peeping toms.

The network acknowledged my account, and the USA home page opened up.

Recently updated Intellipedia pages and the latest news items popped up in the topics area. The "hot topic" illustrated RSS feed was about the pictures of the massacres in India captured on keyhole satellite, complete with furious commentary from other members of the intelligence community who were logged in. The developments in post-nuclear-war India were a source of heated discussion for members of intelligence agencies across the world, and the discussion boards were buzzing.

A subpage in a window also showed a number of topics particular to my level of security clearance, along with dictionaries and wikis. USA's official name was something like the National Defense Information Sharing Network, but for some reason everyone referred to it as the United Spooks Association, or USA for short.

Could you ever imagine a situation in which a company could easily store its information on a network for all its departments to access as necessary, saving time and money, and yet its various departments bypassed the network completely and kept on using their own local systems for the pettiest of reasons, such as not trusting the developers of the network, or due to simple precedent and inertia? To keep their entire infrastructure offline, despite the obvious cost and inefficiency? Well, this was exactly what had happened on a national scale—with the old United States information systems.

Departments insisted on sending executives to rendezvous with other departments in person despite the costs involved. Offices insisted on sending and receiving faxes, laboriously reentering data by hand every time. Administrations persisted in using outdated systems when far more efficient ones existed, and they did not even know where and how to look for them. Everyone looking out for their own little patch, battening down the hatches, reinventing the wheel that had been invented—and would continue to be invented—countless times by countless other organizations, all ostensibly on the same side. Such was the daily reality of the information agencies in the US.

Or so it went until the World Trade Center disappeared from New York. After that, everything had to change, and quick.

America got serious. Heavyweights were drafted in to build a massive information network from scratch. Administrators who showed the slightest bit of resistance to the new system found that their previously cozy little jobs weren't so secure after all and were rapidly replaced by people who could get with the program. A truly integrated information service for the various branches of the intelligence infrastructure. And while they might have fallen short of their grandiose claim to have all the information in the world under one roof, they did at least succeed in dragging the US's information systems kicking and screaming into the twenty-first century.

Right now though, there weren't that many people who knew about John Paul. A handful of bigwigs and a few of my comrades in I Detachment. The fewer people who knew about a topic, the less likely that someone would update USA with useful leads.

Even so, I was in luck. I had posted on John Paul before I set out for Prague, and there were a couple of replies to my thread from some of my comrades who had also been assigned to this case.

"Donald's left us a message about Prague," I told Williams. "Check out USA. A topic I started. Search for 'Prague' and it should be your first hit."

Williams logged in and opened the browser on the index page.

"He posted it only three minutes ago. Damn, the indexing on this thing is fast," Williams said.

Prague is notorious as a place where people can disappear, Donald had written. According to European agencies, someone who disappeared in Prague was considered untraceable, allegedly.

This was news. These days it was virtually impossible to disappear from a developed country, whether you were in the US, Western Europe, Singapore or Japan. You needed to constantly prove who you were to buy food or to travel anywhere. This was true even if you were homeless, so if you were serious about wanting to disappear in any of these countries, you didn't have many options other than to die in secret or to be locked up in isolation like a modern-day Kasper Hauser.

This was interesting information from Donald, though it was an "allegedly" because his information came from a friend of his in the State Department who had just attended the NATO Antiterrorism Best Practice Cooperation Conference in Frankfurt. The friend had heard it from a Dutchman who was in the same working group as him at the conference, and that Dutchman knew because he had heard so from a French acquaintance who worked in the MAEE, and the Frenchman had in turn surmised this from his own informants and spies and *agents provocateur*... Something like that, anyway, Donald had explained.

Conjecture and hearsay, in other words. Par for the course in the intelligence field. Gossip became rumor became urban legend and was reported at a later date as gospel truth and even old news. There are alligators living in the sewers of New York, that sort of thing. The UN has a secret fleet of black helicopters ready to invade the US at a moment's notice, and the US government is in cahoots with aliens, with whom they've signed a covert treaty. Mostly idle gossip, in other words. The problem was that there were occasionally some useful gems of information among the sea of half-truths and falsehood. Look at Iran-Contra: a broken clock is right twice a day, and sometimes the conspiracy theorists are right. Rumors couldn't just be dismissed out of hand, as much as that would have made my life easier in this instance.

Prague is notorious for people disappearing. Sure, I could have ignored this piece of information as two-bit gossip.

But the fact was that John Paul *did* disappear here, correct? And not just the once. A few years ago, when he first disappeared from the world. And now, again, only a few days ago.

Checkpoint, Checkpoint. Another checkpoint.

I passed through how many checkpoints as I tailed Lucia Sukrova?

When I entered the metro. When I rode a streetcar. When I entered a shopping mall.

After 9/11 the world was dragged into a war against terror. The president granted the NSA authority to spy on American citizens, and military presence in cities became commonplace. Other countries followed suit to a greater or lesser extent. But however hard the world seemed to tighten the screws, terrorist acts seemed to keep slipping through. And so it went, until finally an Islamic fundamentalist group set off an atomic bomb in Sarajevo, wiping it from the map.

Hiroshima and Nagasaki were no longer the only ones in their select club. Sarajevo had become a giant crater, a land contaminated with death in the air and in the soil.

Hence these checkpoints today. We paid for our daily freedom and existence by having our movements recorded in minute detail. Big Brother is watching you. An invasion of privacy. That's what some people said, anyway. Most of us—including me—felt that every time we passed through a checkpoint, we were on our way to somewhere safer.

This was somewhere between fantasy and delusion, of course. Each checkpoint was just that, a checkpoint. It showed that you were somewhere. If you traveled from one to another, the checkpoint showed that you'd traveled from one to another. That was all.

Nonetheless, most people were happy to go about their daily business passing through a forest of checkpoints.

As if there were somehow the holy grail of safe places at the end of it all.

I arrived at a square where some sort of demonstration was going on—an NGO demanding more civil liberties. Most people passed by indifferently without giving them a second glance. Lucia Sukrova did briefly look at the changing nanodisplays on the demonstrators' placards, but she carried on regardless, never slowing her pace. It was impossible to read what her reaction to the demonstration was.

I'd been in many countries in the line of duty.

I'd seen men use old-style gallows to hang opposition forces that they'd captured. Civilized nations were supposed to recognize prisoners of war as such, and according to the strictures of the Geneva Convention POWs were not supposed to be executed. But in countries where there was no rule of law, POWs were dead men walking.

I thought of the country where the boys were injected with ID tags and became soldiers. There was no law in that land. From a philosophical perspective, anything was permitted there. Government had collapsed, and there was no authority to bring order to Hobbesian chaos.

Anything was permitted in that land. In theory, at least. In practice, a boy had two choices—to become a soldier or to die. They were in the land of the free, and yet they were not free to choose life.

You sacrificed one type of freedom in order to gain another. We handed over a portion of our freedoms in order that we might gain freedom from being blown up by an atomic bomb, the freedom not to have airplanes smashed into the buildings where we work, the freedom not to be attacked by chemical weapons while we ride the subway.

Freedom was a matter of balance. It didn't exist in an absolute sense, in and of itself. It was either a freedom *to do* something or a freedom *from* something. In that sense, freedom was a bit like love, in that there was no such thing in an absolute sense, only a love for someone or a love between people.

Take today. Lucia Sukrova had made the decision to sacrifice the freedom of her privacy in order to gain the freedom to go shopping. She seemed mainly to be shopping for groceries and clothing. Williams, the CIA, and I were tailing her in shifts, and I was now looking at her face from afar.

She wasn't what you would have called conventionally beautiful, but I found her face curiously attractive. Her cheeks had some freckles on them, as if she hadn't quite finished being a teenager. She had quite a prominent nose, slightly crooked at the tip.

The feature that stood out the most, though, was definitely her eyes. Not because they were big—although they were—but because her eyelids drooped down over them so that her eyes always appeared at least half shut. Personally, I liked this European look, although it would have been considered too melancholy by American standards. I think it was Brian Eno who said after seeing *Pulp Fiction* that a California girl is just too lively to be a true femme fatale.

Lucia Sukrova was no California girl, that was for sure. She was a long way away from anyone's definition of *lively*. If I had to settle on a word to describe her, it would probably have been *worldly*.

"So, we'll start off with one month's lessons and see how we go from there," Lucia said.

"Yes, please," I replied shamelessly. After all, this was probably the most straightforward way of gaining regular access to both Lucia and her apartment.

"That'll be fine. Could I just ask you to confirm the details here?" She passed me her mobile device, and I pressed down on the light green plate. A contract was formed between my businessman alter ego and Lucia's Czech language school.

"I do hope that one day I'll be able to read Kafka in Czech," I said out loud, just enough for Lucia to hear. It was a more subtle version of the Kafka gambit Williams had suggested a while back—not that he would have even known why.

"Oh, I'm afraid you'll be disappointed then," Lucia chimed in, taking my bait. "Kafka wrote all his fiction in German. Kafka's father raised him to speak German, you see. It was much more useful to speak German if you wanted to find a good job back then. You did know this country used to be part of the Austro-Hungarian Empire?"

"Yes, I think I heard that."

"On top of that Kafka was also Jewish. Czech Jews at the time could never really integrate into society, so they spoke German—it made things much easier if they spoke in this 'borrowed' language."

I said that this made sense, given the themes of his works such as *The Castle* and *Amerika*, and asked whether she thought that he was trying to convey his ambiguity toward the place where he lived but could never really call home. I took a sip of the tea that Lucia placed before me.

She answered, "I'm sure that Kafka would have seen himself as a man living in a borrowed country using borrowed words, yes. Like the surveyor in *The Castle*."

"Another point in favor of your hypothesis that language doesn't frame your thought process, I think, Ms. Sukrova. And, come to think of it, Nabokov didn't write *Lolita* in his mother tongue either."

"You certainly are well read, Mr. Bishop," Lucia said. Bishop was my alias.

"Well, you know, quite a few English majors end up as advertising agents like me."

"Maybe so, but I can tell that you didn't just study literature for school. You really do love reading," Lucia said, lifting her hand from the armrest and stroking her chin. There was something about this gesture that struck me. I wondered if she had ever sat there discussing literature with John Paul sitting where I was sitting.

Discussing literature—or genocide.

"I'm hardly what you'd call a bibliophile, though. My job is to talk to people, you know? You've got to be a bit of a dilettante in all sorts of subjects. Tricks of the trade, nothing more. And if it gets the conversation flowing with a charming lady such as yourself, then so much the better."

"Well, you certainly do know how to spin a line, Mr. Bishop!"

Except it wasn't a line, not completely. Part of me was absolutely serious. But rather than say this, I decided to carry on playing the part.

"And what about you, Ms. Sukrova? There must be someone in your life who can read you a good bedtime story?"

"No," Lucia replied, shaking her head. "Not anymore."

"Not anymore?"

"If you don't mind my saying so, Mr. Bishop, you're in danger of straying into some rather personal territory. Do I have to remind you that you have a wife and a child?"

I opened my arms. "Forgive me. But it's precisely because I'm happily married that I sometimes overstep the mark. After all, it's not as if I'm going to try and seduce anyone."

"Well, forgive me, Mr. Bishop, but being married is no guarantee these days."

"Maybe not, these days. But I'm an old-fashioned guy with old-fashioned morals. I assure you, your virtue is quite safe with me."

"I'll just have to take your word on that," Lucia said. Then, hesitantly, "It was a while ago, now. A fellow linguistics researcher."

"At MIT?"

"Yes. Although when I say fellow researcher, he really was on another level. He was involved in a language project for the National Military Establishment."

"I didn't realize that the National Military Establishment funded linguistics research."

"Well, he told me that an agency called DARPA provided the research grant. I never knew the exact details."

This was news to me. There was nothing in John Paul's profile that said anything about his working on a project for national defense—it had just said he was involved in a federally funded language project. It had never occurred to us that his linguistics research could have been directly involved in what came next; Williams and I had both been content to gloss over his early life as being more or less irrelevant.

"He sounds like quite a guy."

"Yes, I met him at MIT and was going out with him for a while. But then one day he went away. Just disappeared completely.

After that, I returned home to the Czech Republic and started this line of work here."

"Couldn't you find any work over there?"

"Oh, there was some, but it wasn't easy. I'm a researcher at heart, so I probably should have remained with the university. I just couldn't quite bring myself to stay..." Lucia shrugged.

I nodded sympathetically. "And did he like books too?"

"Well...he read a lot of Ballard. Have you heard of *Empire of the Sun*? It was made into a movie last century."

"The Spielberg film, right? Sure, I love old movies."

"Well, the movie was based on a book by an author called J. G. Ballard. The book's even better—full of dry humor, but at the same time so wonderfully evocative of the end of the era."

"Doesn't sound much like the film."

"Well, the adaptation was faithful enough to the story. But the original was much bleaker, more harsh. Ballard's work often has themes of decay and of things coming to an end. He was a science fiction author, mainly."

"Sorry...I'm not so up on my sci-fi."

"That's fine. John was always reading Ballard, though. Novels set in nuclear wastelands or on a desolate space station."

"This John...he sounds like he sure did like a good apocalypse," I said, trying to visualize the sort of scene that attracted John Paul. The eschatological stories favored by the man who now traveled from land to land leaving piles of corpses in his wake.

I wondered if John Paul dreamed of a world in ruins. Spaceship Mother Earth, a giant, unmanned satellite that silently orbited the sun. A world where aliens would land one day and find only the traces of civilization long destroyed, the empty husks of building after building whose inhabitants had long since disappeared.

As I imagined the scene, I realized that I was feeling a strange tranquility wash over me.

After all, how different was John Paul's dream from my dream of the land of the dead?

6

I noticed them as soon as I left Lucia's apartment.

There were at least two of them. Tailing me? Or staking out the building?

Given that we'd been keeping a lookout on the front of the apartment ourselves, I figured that it must have been me they were tailing.

I suppressed a grin and stepped out into the street.

I could tell that adrenaline was starting to pump through my veins, so I adjusted my internal tension to counterbalance its effects.

One step. Two steps. I could feel the ground beneath my feet clearly, so clearly. My senses were heightened so much that the mere act of walking almost tickled my feet.

I couldn't very well just cross the road to our apartment where Williams was currently holed up. That would have been just too funny. So I wondered which way I should go now. After all, I had only used this exit to double back so that Lucia wouldn't be able to detect our movements while we were watching her . . .

I wondered if my tails knew about our stakeout of Lucia's place. Possibly. They probably knew it existed at least, even if not exactly where it was. I didn't know if they were John Paul's men or not, but we'd already factored in the possibility that we would come up against some sort of organized resistance, hence our precautionary measures such as entering the country at different times and avoiding all real-time wireless transmission of data from Lucia's apartment as proof against interception.

I scratched the back of my head. My signal to Williams that I was being followed. I decided to take a stroll through the streets of Prague and discover the identity of my tails.

I arrived at a busy street, and my field of vision went into overdrive. My AR contact lenses were flooded with virtual banners.

Prague was a tourist hotspot, so its Alternative Reality databank was pretty well developed. Shop after shop, street after street, all had labels, links, a cornucopia of secrets to be revealed. On the film of my contacts, the noble city of a hundred spires was plastered with virtual neon writing and lighting, turning the elegant historic vista into a cross between a neon-soaked Hong Kong night and Ridley Scott's Los Angeles. The type of store, hours of operation, the number of Michelin Stars a restaurant had—all kinds of landmarks were liberally annotated with virtual neon, creating an alternative reality for the benefit of travelers.

But what I needed was a plan.

I looked around for a Touchboard terminal. Prague's roads were AR-optimized, so there were plenty of terminals scattered about the place. Groups of tourists were huddled in front of giant plastic boards, and each board was illustrated with a picture of a smaller keyboard. I went to stand in front of one of them, staring at the keyboard for three seconds until my contact lenses paired with the Touchboard. I started "typing" on the picture of the keyboard, which functioned every bit as well as a normal keyboard as long as you didn't need the luxury of spring-loaded keys.

A while back they actually introduced technology that allowed you to type just by looking at a key—the machine scanned your eye movements—but these visual keyboards died a quick death once it became clear that they were never going to work at any real speed; it turned out that good old-fashioned touch typing was faster than anything the human eye could do.

I activated a filter that blocked out all tourist information and logged into USA.

I flicked through the data on Prague's transportation and infrastructure. Nothing helpful. Damn, I should have done my research beforehand. On the off-chance that someone had something useful, I started a thread requesting a map of Prague with footfall data. I set it up so that I'd be messaged the instant the topic had a reply and sent the link over to Williams for good measure.

Having done all I could do at that moment, I severed my connection with the Touchboard and set off to find a lonely alleyway somewhere—a dark corner where I could turn the tables on my pursuers without fear of being disturbed.

I jumped onto a passing streetcar, reflexively stealing a glance behind me as I did. Two men and a woman had also jumped on with me at the last minute. They sat apart from each other. One of the men in particular—a rough-looking youth—was keeping his distance. Were they too far away from me to tail me effectively, or was it a double bluff? Too soon to tell. The streetcar made a few stops, and just as we were approaching central Prague I jumped off. The two men and the woman stayed on the trolley.

Just in case something was about to happen to me that meant I would never see the light of day again, I picked at a pheromone capsule embedded in one of my fingernails and let a couple of drops fall to the ground. If I vanished, Williams or someone else would be able to follow my scent using tracer dogs. Worst-case scenario, these pheromones would be my epitaph, marking my last stand.

I started winding my way through the old stone buildings of the city of a hundred spires. This was an old city, even by European standards—it had remained mostly untouched in the great wars of the twentieth century. Neither the Nazis nor the Russians had penetrated the core of the old town. This city was a survivor. And I was determined to use it to help me to survive.

The ancient, winding alleyways and the looming shadow of Kafka conspired together to transform this town into my own personal labyrinth. Not like the Latin American labyrinths of which Borges wrote, but something distinctly European—a pale, chilling entity against the backdrop of the harsh midnight-blue sky.

They were still following me.

I walked among Prague's spires and churches, past Saint Vitus Cathedral, over her cold stone slabs. After a couple of careful feints and misdirections I managed to get a clearer picture of the people following me. The two men and the woman from the streetcar were here. There was also a youth in standard-issue, minimalist, trendy Pentagon-style gear, and a woman wearing a vintage jersey.

All of them were young. None of them could have been my age.

Some sort of youth cult that worshipped John Paul, maybe? My mind spun through the possibilities as I walked around, staking out my pursuers. I could easily have taken any one of them out, but the others were sure to converge on me as I made my move. Was discretion the better part of valor right now? I could always shake them off here, but they'd be back on my tail the next time I showed my face at Lucia's, no doubt.

Was I going to have to take an hour-long detour to get home every time I went for my Czech conversation class?

Fuck that.

My thoughts were interrupted by a new transmission to my AR contact lenses. Someone had replied to my thread on USA. I headed for the nearest Contact Board and logged in to find that someone had uploaded a detailed, color-coded map with all traffic data for Prague during the last four months. Bingo. They'd only gone and found me an open-source map straight from the Czech Ministry of Transport, complete with mean footfall figures, recorded from an aerial blimp that observed the action from sixty thousand feet.

I scanned the map and spotted a nearby side alley that was virtually never used.

Now that John Paul had disappeared, my tails were our biggest lead. A gift, really. I started cricking my shoulders and stretching my arms—a public warm-up for the violent exercise that I was about to engage in. It was the scruffy youth from the streetcar who was following me at that moment, and he stopped for a second, bewildered by my sudden burst of energy. I guess it just didn't occur to him that he had just gone from predator to prey.

And so it came to pass that I was able to launch a total surprise attack on this unlucky youth.

I slipped into the deserted alleyway. He scurried after me, oblivious to the fact that I was waiting and ready to deliver a sucker punch straight to the solar plexus. He went down with a pitiful gurgle. Exactly as I planned. I was almost disappointed at how easy this was.

"Surprise," I whispered in his ear and then delivered another powerful blow. For now, my aim was to beat all resistance out of him, no more.

It was a delicate balance, hurting someone enough that they have absolutely no fight left in them without actually knocking them out cold. Easy to misjudge. This time, though, I seemed to get it right—helped by a few more well-placed punches and kicks to the face.

"Now then," I said. "You're going to tell me who you are."

"I'll never speak," said the youth, through swollen lips. I dug the tip of my foot sharply into the prostrate youth's kidney.

"Now then," I said again. "You're going to tell me who you are."

"I'm nobody," the youth said.

I brought my weight down on his kidney again. Oops, my foot must have missed, and I must have pressed down on his stomach instead. Warm vomit erupted from his mouth.

"Who are you? Tell me," I said for the third time. Except this time I spoke in Czech, using the vocabulary and grammar from the lesson I just had with Lucia. An interrogative sentence or a normal one, the rules are the same in Czech: the phrase you want to emphasize comes first.

"I'm nobody. Please. Please believe me, sir. I really am nobody."

Hmm. It seemed that my Czech lessons weren't destined to bear fruit so quickly. Well, enough talking. Time to find out what I needed directly from his body. I pried open his swollen eyelids and photographed his bloodshot retinas, and then pressed his fingertips onto my portable reader to get his prints. If we'd been in a better location I could have really tightened the thumbscrews and had him singing in no time, but we were still in the middle of the city, after all, so I decided to call it a day.

Probably hard to believe after what I've just described, but I'm no sadist. I was just fulfilling my professional duties. My job is violence. My job is deciding whether people live or die. Die, mostly.

My job *is* this pain, these whimpers, this vomit.

The guy's buddies were probably starting to miss him. I figured they'd come looking for him shortly. I slipped away and left the scene behind me.

After a couple of minutes of browsing through the data I had obtained from the kid, I was overcome by the desire to apologize to him for what I'd done. If I ever came across him again, I'd man up and ask his forgiveness, straight to his face.

The youth's fingerprints and retina scans apparently belonged to different people.

"Man, that was some nasty shit you pulled on that kid, though." Williams laughed as he chomped down on a jalapeño pepper that he had just picked off the Domino's Pizza that was apparently available in the Czech Republic too.

I'm nobody. According to the database, the youth's words were literally true. It was hard to imagine that either of the so-called identities that his biometric data matched with were actually his.

"Yeah, well, I guess I *am* just a nasty shit," I said, digging into the pizza Williams had secured for us. Lucia Sukrova was having her dinner now too. We glanced occasionally at the monitor that showed the comings and goings of her apartment as we discussed this bizarre ID case.

Had the youth suffered a finger-losing accident and had a new set transplanted? Unlikely—we might have been living in a world where nanomachines and synthetic flesh were the order of the day, but medical science hadn't yet nailed the thorny issue of immunologic organ rejection. It would have been one thing to regrow fingers from a person's own tissue, but transplanting from another person? Technically possible, maybe, but a huge operation. It would, at the very least, have left some sort of paper trail. Yet we could find no record of any such operation.

Could it have been a simple case of a mistake in the database? Conceivable way back when human error could have caused an entry to be inputted incorrectly. But now the databases containing personal information were managed by giant insurance companies and their subcontracted InfoSec firms. There was basically no margin for error. They had redundancy systems in place to double and triple check every single process. After all, these days it was impossible to do anything or travel anywhere without relying on personal data systems, which meant they had to be failsafe: as accurate as, say, aviation equipment or medical life-support systems.

In other words, neither scenario was particularly likely.

I'm nobody.

The young man had said these words repeatedly through his tears. He hadn't exactly been crying because he was being forced to talk, of course—it was my well-placed shot to his kidneys that brought forth those tears. But that didn't necessarily make the words that he managed to force out over his sobs any less true.

How, though? Shadowy figures able to manipulate the contents of the database at will? After all, "Mr. Bishop," my assumed identity for this mission, was obviously a fiction. But this was only possible because I was a government agent and because the army had farmed out its own ID systems to an independent contractor rather than one of the standard civilian insurance companies. Even then, there were still lots of hoops for us to jump through, as with any country with a properly developed ID management system; every time the CIA or Special Forces needed a fake identity for one of their agents, they needed to secure explicit permission in advance. The chairman of the Senate Committee on Information Security and at least one other member of the committee needed to sign off on every request.

In other words, it was highly likely that the youth was some sort of government agent.

Which country could be acting on behalf of John Paul? Maybe that was the reason why the Pentagon was so keen on expediting John Paul's elimination—because some other country was now getting involved?

"Yeah, that's a possibility. He's quite the little internationalist, isn't he, this John Paul?" Williams nodded. So maybe we were being tailed not by John Paul, but by some foreign government agency that thought that *we* were somehow involved with him? That would fit: we had suddenly appeared out of nowhere and started spending a lot of time with Lucia Sukrova after all.

Damn. Secret agents from another country sure would put a monkey wrench in the works. The mood in the room darkened.

Anyhow, all of this was just guesswork and speculation. No point in fretting over the hypotheticals. What we had to do now was narrow down the possibilities. This was exactly what we had touched on in my conversation with Lucia: it was the act of narrowing down the possibilities, making logical predictions based on this information, and then *surviving*, that acted as the catalyst for the development of language and the ego. But spend too much time obsessing over the endless possible variations and you ended up missing your chance to actually *do* something.

And that's why I decided to stop thinking too hard and focus on the facts that were in front of us.

Our character profile of John Paul was at best like a partially completed crossword puzzle, filling in the blanks one at a time but with the final few entries remaining tantalizingly out of reach. When he was our secondary target on our mission two years ago we had very few blanks filled in. Each mission since then had helped us to fill in some more of the blanks. Now we were almost there.

Conventional wisdom was that this was a terrible way to gather intelligence. As a basic military strategy, starting off with an insufficient force to achieve your objectives and then gradually increasing your resource allocation trickle by trickle as the war goes on was more or less the textbook way of how *not* to fight a war. As a tactic, it showed that you severely underestimated your opposition in the planning stages and wasted a significant amount of resources, time, and opportunity at the early stages of your campaign.

For Intelligence, information was power. It was our only real military resource. For regular forces, information was there to support the battle on the front lines, but to us in Intelligence information was our lifeblood, as powerful as live ammunition, as vital as a supply train. That was why we couldn't understand, couldn't stand, the indecisive, secretive attitude of the top brass over this mission. Trickling the information down piece by piece was just as stupid a strategy as slowly increasing your resource allocation bit by bit until you had enough of an edge to win. If only they'd just let us know all the facts up front, we wouldn't be in this mess right now. On this point, at least, Williams and I were in agreement.

John Paul lost his wife and only child at Sarajevo.

John Paul's wife and daughter, soon to turn six years old, were seeing the sights when they both vanished in a flash of fire as the city around them was turned into a giant crater. The beautiful city, its inhabitants, and a large number of visitors and tourists were all vaporized and scattered into the atmosphere along with copious quantities of radioactive debris. A mushroom cloud rose above Europe, marking the end of the post-Hiroshima era.

According to an ID trace, John Paul was in the apartment of a certain college student, one Lucia Sukrova, when the bomb detonated. Of course, I wouldn't have known any of this or been allowed to learn of his private life unless it was strictly related to military and Intelligence business. I had no particular feelings about John Paul's actual affair and made no judgment about his adultery. But I was trained to feel his pain, vividly. *He betrayed them*—the guilt, the pain, the self-recrimination and self-flagellation. All these feelings I could empathize with in abundance. It was my job.

A month after the explosion, John Paul had traveled to the camp near the perimeter of what was now called the Sarajevo Crater. Surrounded by NATO troops and an international task force there to guard the perimeter, John Paul waited in silence, patiently, for his turn to be loaned a protective suit to guard him from the nuclear radiation permeating the air of the ruins of Sarajevo. There were so many victims who had "disappeared" that it was impossible to tell with any degree of certainty who had gone missing and who was dead. At the time, genetic markers weren't in widespread use as personal identification measures, so even when remains were discovered, it was rare that they could be identified as belonging to an individual. Most ended up in a mass grave.

Three weeks later, John Paul stood on the edge of the Sarajevo Crater, looking down into the abyss. There was no way to tell what this man who had lost his wife and daughter was thinking at that moment, but it was my job to try and imagine it.

And yet, I thought, what could a man possibly be thinking when confronted with the desolate landscape so typical of his favorite SF novels? When looking at the place that only a short while ago was a city but now had been scorched into a smooth, glassy wasteland surrounding a giant crater? What would the white-radiation-suit-clad figure think as he stood on the edge, looking down at the giant mortar bowl, imagining his family being crushed into paste?

Shortly after he returned home, John Paul dropped out of MIT and shut himself away for six months. He ordered his groceries online. For half a year there was not a single record of him ever having used the subway, a bus, a tollbooth, a shopping mall, or a store. His web receipts showed that the only purchases he ever made online were for food. John Paul isolated himself from the world as much as was physically possible.

What depths of despair had John Paul been cultivating during these six months? Did he make attempts on his own life? Was every night a sleepless one? And then, emerging from his self-imposed silence, John Paul suddenly decided to take a job at a prestigious PR firm. A firm that regularly worked for governments and big business, coordinating "hearts and minds" propaganda campaigns. At the time John Paul joined the company his new employers were being retained by a certain developing country in an effort to persuade the international community that said country was an excellent prospect for direct foreign investment.

Whether he was hired for his White House and National Military Establishment connections from his MIT days or just for his phenomenal linguistic ability—he was apparently able to speak thirteen languages fluently—John Paul's role was to take care of business for the firm's nation-state clients.

His role was to attend the important functions in Washington, meet the right bureaucrats and Congresspeople so that he could plant seeds of sympathy in receptive minds. On the client side, John Paul had to select and prep the government ministers who would go down the most easily with the Western media, and then, when they were ready, fly them over to the US to place them on the right news programs. He set up a press center to receive foreign correspondents in style, building up a picture of his client country as a place where business could be done and foreign visitors were welcome.

After his first success, it was a simple case of rinse and repeat, and before long John Paul had become the go-to man in the field. He had become an official aide to various ministers for public information, press, media, culture, and propaganda for numerous developing countries.

And then the atrocities began.

The countries John Paul had worked for found themselves

plunged into civil war in quick succession. The only variable was who started the troubles—in one country it seemed to be armed insurgents, in another the regular army, and in yet another the ordinary townsfolk—but one way or another they all seemed to lead to genocide on a massive scale. Even so, John Paul was seen as a success by some segments of society, for he always appeared to be at least partially successful, particularly in initially winning the hearts and minds and sympathy of the American people to the plight of his latest client. America would then be the country's savior and guiding light, right up until the moment that the rug was pulled from under them when the people of their nice new client state inconsiderately decided to start killing each other. America had assumed the role of the shepherd toward a new democratic and civilized era for its adopted states, so Americans were understandably a little shocked when they found out that they seemed to be driving their little flocks into vicious civil wars.

It was as if the US had become an assassin of emergent developing countries. Initially though, no one would have dreamed of pinning the blame on John Paul. Why would they? How was anyone to suspect that this single, mild-mannered company man was capable of fooling all his bosses and colleagues and, unbeknownst to any of them, was coordinating a deliberate campaign to incite civil war and mass murder?

It was only when the evidence became too strong—when every single one of his clients ended up in some sort of horrific internal conflict—that people started looking at the possibility of a causal and not just a correlative relationship between John Paul and the atrocities emerging worldwide. Even then, John Paul was able to stick around at the company for a little while longer, as he paid no attention to his detractors. He was never worried about his company's approval, after all. He didn't need to play the game because he had no true interest in working there. He had only joined the company in the first place as a means of getting the genocidal ball rolling.

Eventually though, enough was enough, and John Paul was forced to leave the PR company. And then he seemed to disappear off the face of the earth. No trace of him in any country's transport systems, no sign of him even buying food, anywhere, ever. Indeed, the last confirmed sighting was in a Prague shopping mall.

And here we were now, trying to track down the man who disappeared off the radar only a few days ago.

Since John Paul's departure from the PR company he had only been visible through his works. His signatures on military orders. Whenever we heard John Paul was at the heart of another bloody civil war, we'd fly there to find he was already gone. Whenever we heard that he was orchestrating another massacre, we'd fly straight out there to find, yet again, that he had long since left. The greenhorn from the CIA must have seen his face at least one time, or else how else would he have kept tabs on him? And yet, according to his ID, John Paul had never been anywhere near the city...

It was then I realized that we were chasing a ghost. A specter born of the death and destruction of the Sarajevo Crater.

Waiting for Godot, huh? Maybe Williams's analogy wasn't such a stupid one after all.

CHAPTER

THREE

1

The storm had passed, and Prague was calm.

There were gaps in the stone paving where the insurgents had salvaged rocks and hurled them at the police. Underneath the old paving there was synthetic flesh: exposed, red-raw, veins throbbing in a lattice.

I wandered through the deserted streets in a daze. The nano-layer ads that had once coated the historical buildings had been ripped off by the mob and burnt. Plumes of black smoke still emanated from all corners of the city, even though the insurgents that had caused the fires had long since melted away. Just like that pied piper who had disappeared from Hamelin without a trace.

The blood-red flesh of the streets gave the cityscape some blotches of color. I stepped onto it—it was hard, but elastic enough that it felt like I really was on top of a living organism.

I headed for the outskirts of the town, careful not to trip on the stone paving that now stood a couple of inches above the flesh. I felt like the only person left in the entire city after the riots. I was the last bastion of civilization. Maybe even the last person still alive in Europe.

I reached the outskirts of Prague and was confronted with fields of scarlet meadows, as far as the eye could see.

"What's the matter, O son of mine?"

A sound from above. I looked up to find a giant object looming over the fields. The wing of a jumbo jet. Its white coating had peeled off and fallen to the earth, where it had formed a giant tower. I looked back at the wing: where there had been the white protective coating, there was now more exposed red flesh.

"Here! Over here!"

I turned to face the voice. It was my mother, although I couldn't make her out at first, as her skin had been flayed just like the jumbo jet's, and she too was a mass of exposed crimson.

It was then that I realized that the red fields that stretched out to the horizon were dotted with Intruder Pods. I hadn't noticed earlier because these, too, were stripped bare, their black Stealth Coating removed to reveal the red muscle and blood beneath. Sinewy threads were dangling off them, fluttering in the breeze: blood-red seaweed floating in a blood-red ocean.

"Mom, you know you're kind of ... exposed?"

"Uh-huh. Atomic bomb, you know?"

"But Mom, you died back in Washington! I was the one who killed you!"

"Now who's getting all melodramatic, O son of mine? It was the car that killed me, really, and the doctors who ended it all. You're not to blame."

"But I could have chosen to keep you on that machine. You'd still be alive ..."

"Huh! Call that living, being plugged into that machine like a vegetable? You must be joking."

"But your heart ... your heart was still beating," I said, on the verge of tears. "Call me old-fashioned, but as long as your heart and other vital organs are still working, you're alive."

"Okay. Mr. Old-Fashioned. You're so twentieth century." Mom gave a wan smile. Looking at her now was a glimpse into the inner workings of the human musculature—I could see clearly which muscles were at play in constructing her facial expressions. "But come clean, O son of mine—it's not really the boundary between life and death that's troubling you right now, is it?"

I shook my head. "I just want to know. If I was the one who killed you. Did you die when I gave the order? Won't you tell me, Mom?"

"Ah, so we're talking about guilt and sin." Mom nodded. "You did the right thing. You made a difficult decision, and you did it for me. You pulled the plug on your own mother's life-support machine. You called off the life-sustaining nanomachines. You placed your mother in her coffin. It must have been hard for you, so hard, but you did the right thing because you were only doing the right thing."

"Really, Mom? Is that the truth?"

"Of course not." My mother's voice was suddenly cold. "I'm just telling you what you want to hear, right? How can anyone say for sure what the truth is? How can you know what I feel? I'm dead, remember?"

I was afraid now. Mom's voice had taken on a harsh edge. "I know how you think, how you rationalize your life," she continued. "You're just following orders, right? When you kill people in your line of duty, you're just doing so in order to prevent a greater tragedy? You're just the messenger, the tool, the loaded gun, and it's someone else who pulls the trigger. As if that somehow absolves you from responsibility for your own actions."

"Mom, stop it!" I begged, tears streaming down my face.

"Well, guess what? When you killed your own mother *that was* your own choice. You told yourself that she was in pain, and that she would suffer more alive than dead? Fine. But I was lying there on that bed, and *I* didn't tell you that, did I? You were projecting your own thoughts onto me. So when the doctors pressed you for an answer, you had to make the judgment call on your own. You shouldered the responsibility. No Pentagon or SOCOM to make your decisions for you. You made your own bed—man up and lie in it."

My mother's words pounded at my mind. I tried to block her out, to shut my ears, but the cruel torrent continued unabated.

"And that's made you think, hasn't it? You've started to realize that it isn't just me. All those generals and colonels and self-styled presidents that you've killed in the name of your 'duty.' You've *always* had choices. And you've made your choices. You've just stopped thinking about them. When was the last time you actually sat down to think about why you're doing all this?"

I'm sorry, Mom. I'm sorry. I turned away and started running back into the empty streets of Prague.

"That's right. If it was your own choice to kill me, then it was also your own choice to kill every single person you've ever assassinated. How is there any real difference? Do you think this is a plea bargain? Are you somehow imagining that by accepting responsibility for your decision to kill me you're somehow excused from all the rest of your murders?"

I ran farther and farther away, but my mother's voice still followed me, distinct and clear, like an evil spell.

I covered my head, desperate to block out the whole world.

"You can run, sir, but you can't hide." A new voice, young, clear. I looked up to see Alex's smiling face. My dead colleague tapped his head. "After all, hell is here, inside your mind."

"Leave me alone!"

"What is a human being?" Alex continued. "A collection of brain cells, water, carbon compounds. A magnificent creation and yet no more than a small clump of DNA. From the moment a person is born, he's no more than physical matter. Just like that synthetic flesh down there. You can project lofty ideals and morals onto human beings all you want, but in the end you're just deluding yourself. Sin, hell, whatever you want to call it, only exists insofar as it's inside us. There is nothing more."

Then the stone pavement exploded beneath my feet.

The crimson flesh was expanding, penetrating and enveloping the layers of historical Prague. The torrent of flesh spread out toward the heavens, and before long it had enshrouded the entire city.

The tsunami of flesh surged on relentlessly, pushing me farther and farther up into the sky. Forever.

Toward a place where there was no sin, no hell.

"Jesus, buddy. That's quite a nightmare you were having. Are you okay?"

Williams was doing his best to calm me down. He handed me a cold towel. I must have sweat buckets while I was sleeping.

I felt my cheek. I had been crying.

"The land of the dead again, huh?" Williams asked.

I hesitated, but then decided to answer truthfully. "I've been seeing it constantly since Alex died."

"Me too."

That was a reply I had not expected.

"Oh, I haven't given it a fancy name like your land of the dead," Williams continued. "With me, it's just a dream. About Alex. I can never remember what happens. All I know is I feel shit when I wake up. Which, I guess, makes it a nightmare, huh?"

"Maybe I should see a counselor." I sighed. "Like we have to see before we go on a mission to kill children. Alex had his padre to talk to, but I don't believe in any of that stuff, so I don't have anyone..."

"I went to counseling once," Williams said as he fetched me a glass of cold water. "Couples counseling. We were in a rut, the old woman and me. So one day we got a babysitter for our daughter and headed on over to a Forces counselor."

"And? Any good?"

"Yeah. It helped. Some. I'd recommend it for minor marital problems. Whether the old dude would be much help dealing with something as serious as Alex's death, I'm not so sure."

"I don't think it's just Alex's death that's bothering me."

"Oh? What else is on your mind?"

I tried to find the words to explain, but they just weren't there. Williams saw that I was drawing blanks and continued. "Anyhow, even more so, if there's other stuff you're worried about. There's only so much a desk jockey like that can do for people like us. Basically, you've got to work it out for yourself, I figure. At least you don't believe in God, so you're not about to start blaming yourself by calling it karma or divine retribution or whatever."

Work it out for myself. Yeah. I know. I've known that from the start.

The problem was that I just couldn't stand being ordered about by my own unconscious, even when it took the shape of Mom or Alex.

"Anyway, thanks, Williams, I'll take over watch duty for a while. I'm wide awake now and not likely to get back to sleep anytime soon."

I passed him my sheets. Williams started muttering something about how outrageous it was that we had to share the same sweat-drenched bedclothes, but I knew that he wasn't really complaining. He was just trying to take my mind off my nightmares.

There were three cemeteries near the station: Olšany, Vinohrady, and Židov.

Kafka's grave was in Židov, and it was easy enough to find. The office at the entrance to the cemetery gave me a small cap. It was covered in Hebrew script, which I couldn't read. The Hebrew alphabet sure did look bizarre, I thought. Almost like it was designed by an alien computer. It had an artificial, constructed feel about it. The cap itself was on the small side—not really something to wear so much as something to pop on your head when necessary.

"You should cover your head before we go inside. This is the Jewish Cemetery after all," Lucia explained.

I couldn't be bothered with the hassle of having to shake off a tail or deal with my pursuers with violence, as I undoubtedly would have had to do if I visited Lucia's apartment again. But Williams came up with a good idea: why didn't I arrange to meet Lucia in town? Depending on whether she was tailed, we might be able to determine if the enemy was interested in Lucia too, or whether they only had eyes for me, or indeed whether they were only interested in Lucia and therefore me by extension. Then there was also the possibility that Lucia and the youths were all working together. Whichever it was, meeting Lucia outside would surely help us narrow down the possibilities.

So I told Lucia I was interested in seeing Kafka's grave and asked if she would act as my guide to Prague. Given how widespread alternative reality contacts were these days, it was a bit of a risky move—why would anyone need a human guide when you had all the tourist information you could ever want at the blink of an eye, literally? But after some hesitation, Lucia assented, and so I ended up taking the metro with Lucia to the outskirts of the city where the New Jewish Cemetery was located.

The cemetery was covered in a canopy of lush foliage that

seemed to block off what little of the pale sunlight managed to creep through the amber clouds in the sky.

There were a few other visitors to Kafka's grave. They were leaving pebble stones as an offering, as was the Czech custom.

"Kafka's sisters?" I asked, pointing at the gilded lettering that had been added at the bottom of the gravestone, where three feminine-sounding names had been inscribed.

"I believe so."

"They all died around the same time too. 1942, 1943—ah..."

"Yes, Auschwitz." Lucia nodded. "They all died in the Holocaust. Even his youngest sister, Ottla. She had married a German, but she divorced him to voluntarily move to the Ghetto. Ottla's husband tried to stop her from divorcing him. As the wife of an Aryan, she was eligible to have her Jewish status overlooked. Still, she chose to go. She left their daughter with him."

I never knew that, I told her, although she explained that it was quite widely known—common knowledge in Prague, at least. Franz, the eldest of the Kafkas, was most fond of the youngest, Ottla.

"Well, I take my hat off to you, Ms. Lucia—you sure do know your Kafka."

"Well, my Holocaust more than my Kafka. John used to talk about it all the time."

"John? Oh, you mean the gentleman that you used to see?" I maintained my facade of barely remembering his details.

Lucia nodded. "John was always discussing the Holocaust. It must have been the subject of his research. It's not as if he were actually Jewish himself..."

"You said he was involved in a DARPA research project, right? Studying history? That's unusual."

"Well, I never knew the details. Say, Mr. Bishop, you seem awfully interested all of a sudden."

"Not particularly," I assured her, covering my tracks as deftly as I could. "It just struck me as somewhat incongruous, that's all, the US Army spending their time and money researching a well-worn subject such as the Holocaust. I would have thought they'd want to spend their time on more practical things, like,

I don't know, robots, or artificial intelligence, or high-tech polymers or something."

"When you put it like that, I suppose you're right," said Lucia. "But it wasn't just the Holocaust he was interested in. He also talked about Stalin a lot. And Cambodia. Sudan, Rwanda, places like that too. His research always seemed to be focused around all the cruelest episodes in recent history."

"Okay, so the Holocaust was just a part of that."

"Yes, I think so."

Lucia and I left a pebble each as an offering to the Kafkas. For Franz and his three sisters. Unlike Franz, his sisters had only the years of their deaths inscribed, not the actual dates. These were unknown, as with so many Jews who met their fate during the Holocaust. The Holocaust was such an all-encompassing word that the details were soon swallowed up in the dark depths of history.

"But we do know exactly when they were transported to the concentration camps. Those records survive," Lucia told me in a voice so soft it was almost a whisper. "It's like with us—whenever we move, take the metro, buy some food, or ride a tram, there's always a record."

"I guess so. And I guess, like with Sarajevo and New York, it's not just to act as a deterrent to terrorists but to quickly and accurately identify any victims if the terrorists succeed. Killing two birds with one stone, you might say: preventative measures and help with the mop-up if the worst ever does happen."

Lucia smiled. "Mr. Bishop, you almost sound like you're lecturing me. But you don't need to convince me. Don't worry, you're preaching to the converted. I don't particularly feel that Big Brother is watching us in a totalitarian Orwellian nightmare." She laughed. "But while we're on the subject of historical lectures, what I will say, though, is that the government at the time didn't have anywhere near as clear a picture of their own citizens as they made out. No database or central records. They were basically relying on a ten-year-old national census. So how did they record, analyze, sort, and compile effective records of who actually was and wasn't Jewish? Punch cards. The operation to transport Jews to the concentration camps was the largest coordinated transport effort in human history at the time. The

Nazis could only do this by generating and tabulating data on punch cards, based on the results of the old census. They used IBM machines to organize all of this. IBM hadn't invented the modern PC yet, of course, but they did have tabulators that they called 'computing machines' that were already being used for industrial purposes, and it was relatively straightforward for the Nazis to set these up for their own purposes."

"So you're saying that without IBM's . . . tabulators, the Nazis would never have been able to organize the mass transit of Jews to the concentration camps?" I asked, as if I were reviewing information for a quiz. "Well, they say that the modern computer was born out of cryptanalysis and grew up on ballistics. It looks like the computer's ancestors can't escape the shadow of war either."

"John showed me one once. A transportation schedule for the Jews, tabulated by IBM. John's actual research was top secret, but the schedules themselves were open source, so I guess he didn't see any harm in it."

"Hmm. I'm getting a mental image of a couple snuggling down on a couch to spend the evening poring over Holocaust memorabilia. Not exactly your usual dinner and a movie, eh?"

"I guess not. We were an odd couple, that's for sure." Lucia laughed. "He often used to say that genocide had a unique odor about it."

"Odor?"

"According to him, the Holocaust, Katyn Forest, and the killing fields of the Khmer Rouge all had a lingering scent about them. Whenever there was some sort of genocide—a deliberate, large-scale massacre—that country always had this distinct odor about it."

The smell of genocide.

John Paul must have come across this theory in the course of his historical research.

"Presumably he wasn't talking literally about the smell of dead bodies?"

"No, I don't think so. I guess he was using poetic license. Maybe he was trying to discuss a discovery he made during the course of his research without actually having to compromise any of the secret details."

"And so you never really found out what exactly his research was about..."

"Yes. I don't think he told anybody. He had a small team around him doing some of the legwork, but I think he did most of the heavy lifting himself. I don't think he even discussed his work with his wife."

"His wife. Oh. Uh...so you were...uh..." It was never an easy job, trying to seem surprised by information that you already knew full well. I gave it my best shot.

"Yes," Lucia said, "he had a wife. And a daughter. I knew about them both. You must think I'm the worst sort of woman..." Lucia trailed off and then turned away from me and started walking toward the metro station alone.

I hurried after her. "Um...look...Ms. Sukrova. I'm really sorry, I was prying. None of this is any of my business, and I had no right..."

"No, it's my own fault. I shouldn't be so careless with my tongue." Her eyes were filled with sadness. "I'm so sorry for ruining a perfectly good day."

"Please. The fault really is all mine...I was being far too familiar with all my questions. If there's any way I could make it up to you, I would."

Inside, I was sneering at myself. Laughing at how low I was stooping at this moment.

Ms. Lucia Sukrova. I already know full well that you used to date a married man.

I know which restaurants you ate in. I know what magazines you bought. I know which branches of Starbucks you took your coffee in. I know how many condoms John Paul used to buy.

I know all this, and yet here I am talking to you, putting on a bare-faced facade, painfully dragging all this information out from your own lips just so that I can pretend to you that I've acquired this information from you "naturally."

"Mr. Bishop? If you do really mean that about making it up to me, I wonder if you'd be kind enough to accompany me to just one more place?" Lucia asked. She was still smiling sadly.

I was overwhelmed by remorse at my own shamelessness. I had no right to look on her face. I was no man.

2

The club was pounding with youthful vitality. The dance music pumping through the club was like an alien being to me. I'd long since stopped following the latest trends in music, so I wouldn't have known whether to describe the setup as a Prague thing or just a young person thing.

"You know, this isn't really my scene..." I said, though my face undoubtedly already showed that fact.

"I thought you said you'd do anything to make it up to me." Lucia pulled me in by my arm. "Just to keep me company?"

Truth be told I found it hard to believe this was Lucia's sort of scene either. She seemed out of place in such a lively atmosphere. She was most beautiful when talking about books, and there was nothing in her classroom to suggest she was interested in this sort of hedonism.

As I was cajoled into the club by Lucia and crossed the threshold, I was assailed by an uneasy feeling. Something wasn't quite right, though I couldn't put my finger on exactly what. I was alert, anxious. Something was missing.

We arrived at the bar.

I looked over to the dance floor to see a mass of writhing young men and women—hardly more than boys and girls—grinding, making out, sharing hormone hits. The tiles of the dance floor were covered by a strikingly realistic video projection of the abyss. I could imagine myself tripping over the edge and plunging downward for all eternity—except that the young people were dancing right above it, floating on the void.

One of the young people stood out: a skinhead who'd coated himself with a holographic nanolayer. A thin film on the back of his head created a display field that made it look as though his skull was transparent and his brain was visible for all to see. Just CGI, of course, but I couldn't help but wonder if hell was in there too...

Lucia had already found us a couple of empty bar stools and fired off a drinks order.

"Have you had a proper beer since you arrived in this country?" she asked. "A proper Czech beer, I mean."

"Uh . . . just a Budweiser or two."

"The real Budweiser Budvar? Or just what you Americans call Budweiser?"

"Um, the second one, I think. It's what I drink back home, anyway."

"Well, we'll have to change that, won't we? Oh, I'm sure your stuff's fine as far as it goes, but this here's the real deal."

Two glasses arrived on cue.

"What you Americans call 'Budweiser' is really just a brand name, no more. And, in fact, if you look closely at the label of the stuff you usually drink, you'll see that it's made by an American company called Anheuser-Busch, unlike our stuff, which comes from the city of České Budějovice—Budweis in English—a bit to the south of here. That's why your Budweiser can't be marketed by that name in many European countries; Budweiser Budvar is the only one allowed to use the trademark. Anyway, more to the point, this is a great Czech beer—the best in the world, I think."

I listened to her speech and I was surprised. Not because of anything she said, but because she casually flipped out a change purse from her jeans. I hadn't seen such a thing for years. I was even more surprised to see Lucia take a bill out and hand it to the bartender as a tip. This was a blast from the past—a flashback to the pre-automatic-transaction era.

Then it hit me. The reason why I felt something was not quite right when I entered this joint.

We hadn't been ID'd on our way in.

If Lucia clocked my surprise, she didn't show it. She just took a swig of her beer. A hearty one at that. Maybe there was more to this lady than first met the eye.

I was evidently reeling from the shock, as Lucia eventually did catch on to my dazed expression.

"Aren't you going to drink anything?" she asked.

"Uh, sure. I was just a little surprised, is all . . ."

"By what?"

"Well, it's not exactly every day you see paper money."

"I suppose you're right—since Mobs became widespread, you mean?" she said, referring to the ubiquitous mobile terminals.

"So... is this place black market or something?"

Lucia laughed. "Hardly. It's all above board, just about. The Czech government, or I guess I should say the Euro government, still acknowledges bills as legal tender. Not too many places are happy taking them, of course, but—"

"Here is one of them?"

"Exactly. It's a regional thing. Actually, come to think of it, I'm not sure that paper money is technically legal tender as such, although it's certainly not illegal. It's more like what would you call in America... scrip?"

"Scrip, huh? I've heard of it, but I thought it had been abandoned last century, given up as a failed experiment."

"Last century's grassroots attempts at establishing parallel currencies, you mean? Yes, they were abandoned, even if some of them were successful enough while they lasted. Based on cooperative ideals, issued by local organizations with lofty socialist goals such as 'back to basics' localism. They were usually well meaning enough but, like most things based on idealism rather than harsh day-to-day pragmatism, never really took off. Whereas the money in my pocket now comes from a very different sort of impetus. A punk spirit, if you will."

"Punk scrip? I'm not sure I follow you," I said.

"Money that's untraceable. The government isn't too happy about it. It's something of a thorn in their side, and there are plenty among the powers that be who'd like to see it eradicated. But they've never succeeded in passing a law to ban it. Even within government, not everyone's in favor of tightening the surveillance state further, and I suppose that paper money is something that helps even the odds in the little person's favor."

I looked around the club again. This time I noticed, dotted among the youths, a number of older people, older than us. People who would have remembered a time when they didn't have their identity and movements checked and tracked and cross-corroborated twenty-four seven, 365 days a year. And then I realized that one of the older customers was waving at us and making his way over here. He wore a well-cut sports jacket, casually carried off over a cashmere turtleneck.

"Lucia ahoy!"

"Ciao, Lucius!"

An acquaintance of Lucia's evidently. She beckoned him over to the bar and bade him sit down next to me.

"Lucius is the owner of this club," Lucia said by way of introduction. "A shrewd operator, but don't let that fool you—he also has an introspective streak and is a gentleman to boot."

"Haha. The only 'introspection' you'll see from me on a day like this is when I consider what to do with my delivery boy if he doesn't get my Budweiser kegs here on time." His was a deep, steady voice.

"This gentleman here's Mr. Charles Bishop," Lucia said, completing the introductions. "Recently arrived in Prague, sent here by his advertising company."

"Bishop," I said, savoring the ring of my alias. "Swell place you got here."

"Oh, you're too kind. It's nothing."

We were sticking to small talk for now—there was nothing bigger to talk about yet.

"So, Lucia, what's been keeping you from us this past while?" Lucius asked.

"I'm sorry—work's just been crazy," said Lucia. A lie. Certainly for the last few days, while Williams and I kept a watch on her, traffic to and from her apartment had been pretty light.

"Well, it's good to be busy," Lucius said. "But we've missed you here. Tyrone in particular. He's madly in love with you, you know."

"If you say so," Lucia replied, but she was laughing.

Lucius pointed toward the other end of the bar. "Don't believe me? Just go and ask him yourself. He's standing over there on his own like a lost soul."

"So he is. Well, we can't have that, can we?" Lucia stood up and started walking over toward the man Lucius had just identified as Tyrone. It was just Lucius and me at the bar now. I took a sip of the Budvar.

It really was good.

"So, how do you know Lucia?" Lucius asked. I glanced up, checking for any signs of wariness or jealousy on his part—was I encroaching on his territory? But no, judging from his tone of voice and demeanor, he was just making light chitchat, asking as a friend.

"I'm her student. She's teaching me Czech."

Lucius made a show of mock surprise. "Well what do you know! There's a first time for everything. Normally Lucia never brings her students here."

"Well, I wanted to see Kafka's grave today, so she was kind enough to act as my guide, to help me find it. We were out and about anyway, so here we are, I guess."

"Kafka's grave, huh? Right opposite the metro station? Pretty tough to find, I imagine?"

Was he testing me? My guard went up. Still, better to try and deflect any suspicion or hostility rather than tackle it head on.

"Yeah, boy did I feel a fool. Still, better safe than sorry." I grinned broadly. The quintessential clownish American tourist. Lucius smiled too—my story seemed to be washing.

"So, how do you like our humble little joint? Paying your way with real money and no tedious ID checks."

"It's great! Is this pretty normal for the Czech Republic?"

Lucius laughed and shook his head. "Hardly. The government isn't too keen on this sort of place. We're black sheep, too far under the radar for their liking. Not that they can do anything to us legally. I expect they've got a few plainclothes public safety officers mixed in with the rest of my clientele to try and keep the peace. As if we're going to have any trouble when the beer's so good!"

"Well, this is certainly new to me—there are no places like this left in the States."

"Yep, Europe does have its advantages. The US might be the home of the free, but these days there's probably more you can get away with on this side of the Atlantic," Lucius said. He caught the bartender's eye and ordered a dry Cinzano on the rocks.

"Necessary sacrifices in the war against terror, I suppose. You have to admire the European sangfroid, though, losing Sarajevo like that and still being as liberal as this when it comes to freedom."

"Freedom always involves choices, though, doesn't it?" Lucius replied, lifting his glass of vermouth to his lips the moment it arrived. "Like the worker who voluntarily submits himself to losing his individual liberty while he labors but in exchange gains the freedoms that his salary affords him. He can now buy things. No longer is he tied down to having to till his own fields and reap his own harvest and hunt for his own meat. He can pay farmers to do all that for him and enjoy the benefits of fresh vegetables delivered to his doorstep, meat that's already been painstakingly butchered and deboned, even have his entire meals prepared for him. Is he a wage slave or a freedom fighter?"

"Like in the States, how the citizen has voluntarily given up a portion of his privacy in order to be free from the threat of terrorism?" I added.

Lucius thought about that for a moment. "Yes, I think you're right. It's a continuum, and Europe is just a couple of steps further down the spectrum toward individual freedoms. That said, there's not exactly a whole lot in it. This sort of joint here is about as far as we go."

"So do you see yourself as running this place to protect your freedoms?"

Lucius's eyes flickered, as if he were searching for an answer. "I don't think I'd go quite that far. I guess I'm just trying to articulate a feeling that, say, the kids on the dance floor over there don't understand. The fact that you only become aware of the trade-offs you make for freedom when you're already having it eroded from all sides." He turned to face the young people gyrating over the abyss. "Many of the young people over there believe in freedom as something that's pure and absolute. It's a phase they have to go through, this idealized notion of liberty. That way, when they finally grow up and are put in the position of actually having to make real decisions, they appreciate 'real' freedom—the fruits of their own choices—all the more."

"You sound like you see yourself as a guidance counselor," I said.

"I guess I do. Well, I like to think of myself as enlightened, at least, and I'm always happy to spread the love." With that, Lucius lapsed into silence as he surveyed the room in a deliberate, calm manner. I could see what Lucia had meant when she described him as introspective. He was contemplative, a philosopher. Even his conversation had been carefully chosen; we had touched on some deep topics, but he had given very little away. This was definitely a man who liked to think before he spoke.

I decided to push the conversation a little further. "Well, the Enlightenment was a European movement after all. Not so easy for us simple Americans to relate to."

"I'd hardly say that. Isn't the US always instrumental in exporting its freedom and democracy around the world? Your own unique brand of Enlightenment?"

"Hey, there's no need to go all sarcastic on me."

"No sarcasm intended," Lucius said with a straight face. "Think about how much the cost of modern warfare has skyrocketed, even compared to just a few decades ago. The huge costs associated with the latest high-tech weaponry, the increased personnel costs, the opportunity cost. War just isn't profitable anymore, no matter how much oil might be at stake. And yet America still soldiers on, policing the world. Why? Even going to the trouble and massive expense of hiring private contractors around the world to put out fires that have nothing to do with the US. Sure, there are those who criticize your actions as Team America trying to impose their righteousness on the whole world, but I see it differently. Given that it's the US who's picking up the tab, I see America's wars as a new form of Enlightenment, where war is no longer an extension of diplomacy—diplomacy is now an extension of war."

"War...as Enlightenment?"

"Whether or not Americans see it that way, yes. I'd argue that their military actions are exactly that. The so-called war against terror is an extremely principled war, devoted, even, to certain ideologies: humanity, altruism, the Golden Rule. The US is not the only country who acts this way—most modern democracies support this way of thinking, to a greater or lesser extent—but America's the leader of the pack."

"Uh, thank you, I think..." I managed to say.

"No," Lucius said bluntly. "Don't get me wrong. I'm neither praising nor condemning US foreign policy. I'm just calling it like I see it. After all, who says Enlightenment is always a good thing? What might seem like progress to one person might be a self-righteous imposition of values to another."

I didn't really know what to say to this man. Was he really just a club owner? I decided to ask him straight up.

Lucius laughed. "Am I 'just' a club owner? I guess so, in the sense that Eric Hoffer was 'just' a longshoreman, or your dear friend Kafka was 'just' a petty bureaucrat. The Japanese have a saying that all honest trades are equally honorable. And I think it was Joseph Conrad who said that thought is no respecter of persons."

"Lucius, what are you two talking about?" I turned around—Lucia was back.

"Not much. Just how freedom is a currency we spend, and how war is Enlightenment..."

"Just the usual idle chitchat then?" Lucia laughed.

Lucius smiled. "Actually, there aren't too many people who I can talk to like Mr. Bishop here. Sadly, though, I'm going to have to call it a day and retire to the office. My stevedoring duties call, as it were. But it was interesting talking to you, Mr. Bishop, and I do hope you'll come by again sometime so we can pick up where we left off."

"I'd like that," I said.

Lucia and I watched Lucius as he disappeared into the back office.

What was it about the disappearing figure that made me feel nervous?

3

"Well, you weren't wrong when you described him as being the introspective sort," I said to Lucia after Lucius had left. "He struck me as being more the Gallic philosopher than the stereotypical Czech businessman." I took another sip of my Budvar.

"I told you so. He keeps you entertained, though, doesn't he?"

"It can't be easy to make a success of a club like this, though?"

"Maybe not. But as long as there are people who remember what life was like before the surveillance crackdown, and as long as there are youths who don't remember, but who still feel clamped down on and claustrophobic without being quite able to explain why, there will always be a need for places like this. It's just a case of supply and demand."

"So the people who are here now are the people who demand their freedom—is that what you're saying?" I asked.

"A taste of it, at least. Take me—I'm scared of terrorists, why wouldn't I be? I'm glad of the war on terror, as they call it, and the fact that our society is now organized enough to nip potential threats in the bud. In that sense, I suppose I might be different from those boys and girls on the dance floor. But that doesn't mean I don't sometimes want a breather, a time-out. Just once in a while, it's nice to be able to relax and spend time in a place where nobody knows what you're eating, what you're drinking, who you're dancing with, for how long..."

Me time. In the truest sense of the phrase. That was what Lucia got from this place.

A place where nothing is observed, nothing recorded, and anything goes.

And Lucia wanted to share it with me.

"It was very kind of you to bring me with you to this place," I said. "Thank you."

"It's nothing. It just felt like the right thing to do. I'm not sure why," Lucia mumbled, staring at her beer glass.

"To talk about John?" I asked, as I placed my own glass down on the counter.

"Maybe. I'm not religious. I have no priest to talk to. And I don't believe in counseling."

"I know what you mean. I'm the same."

Lucia's eyes glinted with the faintest hint of a smile. "Poor little me, huh? No sympathetic priest to pour my heart out to, and I'm not in the habit of keeping a journal to sort out my thoughts."

"Maybe you should write a book? They're all the rage, aren't they, confessional memoirs. A coming-of-age story or something."

"I just don't seem to have the talent or the inclination for it. Pretty pathetic, I know, considering I studied language."

"Well, I guess that leaves just one option. You'll have to tell me all about it."

Lucia's eyes flicked away from mine and toward the abyss that threatened to pull in the dancers. It was as if she longed to be sucked down into that bottomless pit herself.

"I was in bed with him when Sarajevo disappeared." So began Lucia's story.

Her voice was completely different from that point on. A thin whisper. Really, I shouldn't have been able to hear her without bringing my ear right up to her lips. The music should have drowned her out. And yet, somehow, I could hear every one of her words with absolute clarity.

"John's wife had gone to visit her sister in Sarajevo, taking their daughter with her. John and I were making the most of that precious time together without them. Cambridge was our oyster. It was a time when we didn't have to worry, when John wasn't constantly looking over his shoulder. It was such a lovely time. I was happy. So happy that I couldn't even bring myself to feel the slightest bit guilty at what we were doing. Every spare moment I had, I spent with him."

Then Lucia paused and bit down hard on her lip. An act of self-flagellation to punish herself?

"I remember it clearly. We had just made love, and I had gone for a shower. I emerged clean and fresh to find John frozen stiff, glued to the nanolayer projection. The front page was showing an update flashing across the top. Sarajevo had been hit by a nuclear bomb. He was watching the linked video clip.

"I was terrified. I just stood there, still wrapped in my towel. He, too, was paralyzed, just watching the same clip over and over again. The anchorwoman in the clip was just reading out information as it was transmitted to her, and the subpage below the clip was saturated with constant updates, links to new clips. John made no effort to look at any of them. He wasn't interested in finding out any new information. He was stunned enough by what he had already seen, and all he could do was keep his eyes glued to that."

Lucia stopped to take a sip of her beer. Her voice was calm

and disinterested; it was as if she were talking about events that had happened to somebody else. I almost expected her to start the next part of her story with something along the lines of "once upon a time, in a faraway land, there lived a woman called Lucia Sukrova." But when she continued, it was about how John Paul flew to Sarajevo.

"I wanted to go with him, but even I had some sense of shame—it would hardly do for a mistress to accompany her lover as he traveled to discover the fate of his wife and daughter. Had John and I been in bed laughing when the bomb exploded? Was he inside me when his wife and only child were obliterated from this earth? I didn't know what to do, what I could do. I had no idea how I was going to act, how I was meant to act, when he returned from Sarajevo. The worst part of it was that I still loved John, with all my heart. I ached for him as soon as he got on that flight. I needed to feel his body wrapped around mine again. And I wanted to mortify the part of myself that had these unbearably selfish feelings.

"In the end, I didn't need to worry about what to say to him when he came back. He just silently returned, dropped out of school, and went away somewhere. I didn't try and look for him. I was afraid of seeing him again. After all, he had become the living embodiment of my own terrible sin. And I didn't have the confidence or the strength to face the consequences of my own actions."

Lucia's story was over.

I had been listening in silence. There was nothing I could have said. After she finished, she stared in silence at the bottom of her glass. I had no idea what I was supposed to say next. What to say to help ease the massive burden she was carrying on her shoulders.

I particularly couldn't say anything because her story hit so close to home.

That vague sense of emptiness that I remember feeling when I read her profile back at briefing. It was crystallizing, coming together. The gaps were being filled in, the skeleton fleshed out with Lucia's story. The written word only encompasses so much; Lucia's voice was so much more revealing.

I remember someone once saying that we have eyelids but no earlids for a reason. You can shut your eyes and be oblivious to the words written down in front of you, but you can never quite block out a story that someone else shares with you from their own mouth, with their own lips. Not unless you can completely shut off your ego from your body.

It was only now that Lucia had shared her story with me that this fact really hit home.

The human voice adds color to a story.

The color of penitence. Thick, heavy slabs, dark and red like dried blood, saturated like a Mark Rothko abstract.

John Paul's wife and daughter disappeared that day in Sarajevo. And Lucia had no way of atoning for her sins against them. No way of begging for forgiveness. Because they were dead. Not even their corpses remained.

To lose the subject of your feelings of guilt is to lose your hope that you can ever truly be forgiven. That's why murder was such a taboo in all cultures—there was no way of atoning to your victim. No possibility of pardon.

The dead cannot forgive.

That was why Lucia was suffering so. She had already started her irreversible descent down that slippery slope and had learned too late that her actions were painfully, hauntingly irrevocable. In her mind, there was no one and nothing left in this world who could possibly forgive her for what she had done to John Paul's wife and daughter.

God is dead. Which meant that sin was now solely in the realm of humanity. Humans were always the ones to commit sin, but now, instead of praying for divine forgiveness, humans had to find some way to work it all out for themselves. When the spirit was no longer living, the flesh could no longer afford to be weak. But when the target of the sin was gone...

This must have been why I was so drawn to Lucia. She was a kindred spirit—*a fellow unforgivable*. Like me, she was beholden to the dead.

Which was why I decided to tell her about my own sins.

It was the least I could do. And looking back on it now, I see that it was my own way of acknowledging that I liked her.

4

I asked if my mother was in pain.

The doctor explained that it was not so much a case of *if* she was in pain, but whether she was still able to *feel* pain.

I thought of the corpse of the girl who'd had her cranium split open by the rifle round, the body of the boy who'd had his guts blown out from behind, the villagers roasted like so many chickens, and the dead body of the ex-brigadier general who had fashioned all these atrocities.

The accident happened three days before my return to Washington from the death and destruction of central Asia. I didn't panic when Colonel Rockwell told me the news; I felt a strange calm as I headed toward the hospital.

It had been an old-school Cadillac that had run over my mother—a real piece of junk that had never been retrofitted with modern safety devices. A throwback to the twentieth century. It was pink. It almost seemed hilarious. Except that at some stage, I would have to face the fact that it wasn't a joke. Mom really was run over by a Hollywood cliché pink Cadillac. To round out the joke, the driver had been a textbook drunk who'd had no interest in installing the sort of automated soundness-of-mind checker that now came standard on modern vehicles. How else would the pink Caddy have had the freedom to lunge onto the sidewalk where my mother was walking, taking her out along with the booze-addled driver and a couple of other pedestrians for good measure?

Putting aside the absurdity of the fact that such a car was somehow still considered roadworthy in this day and age, the end result was that the pink Cadillac finally came to a stop only when its momentum was killed by its smashing into the flank of another car across the way that had been minding its own business at a traffic light. The pink Caddy's momentum wasn't the only thing killed at that point: the driver's drink-sodden life was snuffed out instantly.

My mother died too. Her lungs had stopped moving by the time the ambulances arrived, and although she had been put on a respirator, she was pronounced DOA at the hospital.

But then she was brought back to life. The hospital had the right equipment and performed the correct medical procedures. Mom was given the same treatment as we were after being wounded in battle: the processes of her internal organs were suspended, nanomachines stopped her internal hemorrhaging, and finally her heart started beating again.

She came back to life for a reason: so that she could force me to decide her fate. To punish me for joining the army.

It was none other than my own mother now treading that fine line between life and death. And yet I couldn't bring myself to rush to the hospital—I felt no sense of urgency, no compulsion to hurry. Thanks to my occupation, everyday life was so saturated with the color of death that I was now inured to it. My inoculation had started even before I joined the Forces, of course, what with my father disappearing one day when I was young, and thanks to my friend who died of cancer as a kid. So was I now supposed to wallow in the luxury of fretting about whether another person close to me was going to die?

I walked. During the whole length of the journey from my lodgings to the plane to Washington, then to the cab ride to the hospital, there wasn't a single moment when I started running. My heart was full of sadness, but it was of a chronic sort rather than acute—not so much a response to this latest tragedy, but a world-weariness at my preconceptions about the painful nature of life being reconfirmed. Nothing surprised me anymore. Such was the way of the world.

It was summer. I stepped out of the August sun into the crisp air of the hospital reception area and signed in. It was only when the receptionist asked me if I wanted to upload a hospital guide for my alternative reality contacts that I realized I had left my ARs at home. At no point at the airport or in the taxi had I even noticed I was missing them. I told the receptionist I didn't have my ARs in, so she activated the hospital beacon so that I would be led automatically to my destination. A black beacon appeared on the floor, swimming across the pressurized floor pads like a goldfish in a bowl, leading me toward the ICU. The hospital floor looked almost like a work of art.

I walked along the hospital corridor, guided by the slow-moving black beacon as it crept through the wards and public spaces. Each of these were clearly marked to distinguish them. A faint dreamlike aroma was pervading my senses.

Without the beacon I would never have been able to find my destination, but with its help it wasn't too long before I arrived at the ICU. I was given antiseptic whites to change into before crossing the threshold into the unit via a set of sliding double doors. Inside the ward, beds were cordoned off via transparent curtains, and beyond them were the patients, many of whom looked as though they were not much longer for this world.

Most of them would probably make a full recovery, of course. But I didn't know about my mother yet.

The black homing beacon crept on and slid underneath one of the sets of curtains, so I parted them and went through.

I saw a morass of tubes and monitors. The tubes that plugged into my mother's body were there to pump in life-giving nano-machines to make up for whichever of her internal organs had given out. Her normally luxuriant hair had been completely shaved off, and the gash in her head was sewn up, stapled, and covered in hemostatic pads dripping with blood. There were also a number of places on her shaved skull where somebody—a doctor, probably—had written notes in shorthand, presumably to indicate where to aim the electromagnetic waves that would guide the nanomachines to their destinations inside her skull. I was reminded of Post-Its on a refrigerator door or of the clutter at Williams's house that was punctuated with week-old memos to self: *Don't forget to pick up the groceries.* A whole corner of his kitchen was dedicated to such notes. And then there were those police procedurals on TV, with the detective's desk in organized chaos...

Yes, I was reminded of all of these by the jottings on my

mother's shiny head, which now looked liked a bizarre modern version of those old phrenological models.

I wasn't sure how long I stood there in front of my mother. At some point I heard a gentle voice—*Captain Clavis Shepherd?*—and I turned around to see who had spoken.

The man introduced himself as my mother's attending physician.

I asked about my mother.

She had multiple fractures and extensive subcutaneous bleeding. Many of her internal organs had been damaged to the point of impaired function. Nothing, though, that the technology couldn't keep stable. Her life was not in immediate danger.

I didn't press him on his precise definition of "life." What "life" currently meant for my mother as she lay there, on her side, oblivious to the world.

"Is she conscious?" I asked, and I noticed the doctor's lips tightening. At the time, I read the doctor's expression as a sign that I should give up all hope for that, but looking back on it now I realize that I was subtly wrong on that count. His troubled expression was probably more that of a specialist trying to search for the right words with which to explain the nuances of a difficult and complicated situation to a layman. A situation I was somewhat familiar with as a specialist in my own field. What to do when friends or family—or even desk jockeys within your own organization—asked you for a yes or no answer when there were only shades of gray. For every subtle and complicated question, there was an answer that was perfectly simple, straightforward, and wrong.

"Unfortunately, that's not an easy question to answer," the doctor eventually said. "Your mother suffered from severe blunt-force trauma directly to her head, resulting in what is known medically as a cerebral contusion. She has a comparatively small area damaged on the side that was hit, but the damage on the other side is much more extensive, with multiple microhemorrhages deep inside her brain."

"I don't understand—on the other side?"

"If you can forgive a somewhat insensitive analogy, it's a bit like hitting a billiard ball with a cue. The area you hit is quite small, but when the ball then hits the cushion on the other side there's a lot of force absorbed. When the brain is hit in this manner, it has nowhere to go except into the hard skull wall on the other side..."

A billiard match inside my mother's skull but with a cue ball as soft as marshmallows.

The doctor went on to explain that, as a result of the trauma, the part of my mother's brain around her neocortex was severely damaged. She had lost her respiratory function entirely, although that could be artificially maintained with the machines.

"Mr. Shepherd. We're able to isolate the different functions of the cerebral cortex into separate compartments. Modules, if you will. And we can confirm that many of your mother's cerebral cortex modules are still alive. We can even positively identify which ones. But..." The doctor hesitated.

"But?"

"Well, medical science just doesn't have any frame of reference to help us determine which and how many modules need to be alive before we can describe the person as being meaningfully 'conscious.' In the same way that medical science can't describe what it's like to be dead."

My mother's house. The house that had once been my home.

The house was in a quiet corner of Georgetown, not too far from the Exorcist Steps, named after the old movie. The steps had always been covered in graffiti, sometimes of a pretty creative variety. Once, around the time I was in high school, someone covered the whole surface of the steps with display paint and projected an image of Father Karras tumbling to his doom, looped over and over. The incident was briefly on the network news, I remember.

I opened the door. The place smelled of my mother. Her life. Her air.

"Anybody home?" I found myself muttering under my breath, out of habit. The house had always been a place of words. Now silence prevailed.

I started walking around the place that should have been my own home. I felt like a detective looking for evidence, or even a thief. My own room was still there, kept in place. I ran a finger across the surface of my old desk. There was hardly any dust. The room had been cleaned regularly.

Eyes, I thought to myself.

This house was a pair of eyes. My mother's eyes, watching over me to make sure I didn't suddenly disappear like my father. I grew up under the gaze of those eyes. Even when Mom was out of the house and I was in the living room on my own, on the network, I still always felt something over my shoulder.

My mother had been an expert at tracing my movements. Nothing escaped her—it was uncanny. What candy bar I'd been eating, which of my friends I'd been secretly hanging out with—there was always something in the house that would give me away and land me in trouble.

I sat down on my bed, the bed that had once been mine. She would have made an excellent tracker, I thought to myself, and almost burst into laughter at the thought.

This had been my mother's world.

The world of a hundred eyes focused on a single objective: to make sure a person would never disappear.

At some point that world became stifling, suffocating. That was why I joined the army and signed up for Special Forces. Well, you got what you wanted, didn't you, Clavis Shepherd? Plenty of danger, more dead bodies than you could shake a stick at. And you're not dead yet! You've even lost a comrade— admittedly due to suicide rather than in the field, but hey, it still counts. You're the real deal. What more could you want from life?

I forced myself to stop thinking. I was afraid of where it would lead me.

I went into the kitchen. It, too, was clean and orderly. Not a single magnet or memo on the refrigerator door, a fact I found eerie.

My mother didn't like photographs. There were no framed pictures in the living room. It occurred to me that I had never seen a single photo of my father. There probably wasn't a photo anywhere in the entire house—not of my father, not of my mother, not of me.

I wondered if there would be anything on Mom's server space. If I were to log in, would I have found us all there, safely preserved and easily accessible?

The wallpaper was still the same as when I was a kid. It had yellowed a little with age, but remained neat and clean. I tapped a wall with my fingertips to bring up an access port. I tried to see if I could log into my mother's account, but—obviously—I was asked for authentication, which I couldn't provide.

Was Mom's life recorded here in minute detail? If I were to summon up her Life Graph and order the computer to edit it into a biography, would there be a clue at the end as to what she would have wanted me to do with her now?

And then I realized how much I was focusing on physical records.

Logs. Life Graphs. Rather than worry about these external documents of Mom's life, shouldn't I have been thinking about the internal ones? My mother as she was inside myself, as I remembered her? And then I realized that my motive in coming to this house—to try and somehow figure out the right thing to do—was no more than procrastination. More than that—I was evading the truth.

The truth that I had no idea what my mother would have wanted.

My job was to read the psychological profiles of my targets. The NSA or the National Counterterrorism Center handed over their logs, and I read them so as to make accurate predictions regarding the likely movements and behavior of the target I was assigned to kill. And yet here I was, utterly unable to guess what my own mother would have wanted.

Even if I had been able to access my mother's logs at that point, there wasn't a lot I would have been able to do with the unedited raw data, and even if some program had been able to collate it into a narrative, I doubt it would have been of much use to me at this juncture. And yet I wanted those records desperately. Not because I needed a basis for my decision, but because I couldn't bear to acknowledge that I couldn't even *make* that decision on my own.

I was starting to panic. I needed to sit down. I collapsed onto the sofa.

I did love my mother. I was sure of that much.

But I was terrified. What if I also hated her? I was mortified by the possibility that there was a part of me that was repulsed by this woman who had struggled so hard to raise me, this single mother who had given me so much.

I thought of the constant gaze that had followed me around in this house. From the other side of the room. From the kitchen. The eyes that were always there, trailing me, glued to my back long after the meal was over and I had retired to my room.

I was constantly being watched. Incessantly.

I felt a flashback—of what it was like when I was a kid. In the hall, in the kitchen, in the bathroom, in the shower. Mom's gaze was always there, penetrating. Through this gap, that crevice, from this angle. I could still visualize all the sight lines in the house. My mother wasn't overprotective—she never coddled me. If anything, her parenting style could have been described as almost laissez-faire. I got up to the usual share of kid's tricks, and in most ways my childhood could have been described as normal, unexceptional. The only thing that marked me as being in any way different from the other kids was the vague feeling I had that my mother's gaze was always on the back of my head.

The house. The house where my father disappeared from this world.

The house of my mother's gaze.

It was comforting to be watched over, and then it was suffocatingly oppressive. Two sides of the same coin.

I knew at that moment I couldn't stay the night there. I had to leave.

Later that day I found a small motel and checked in. I told the doctor that my mother wasn't the sort of person to have prepared a will.

The doctor laid it out for me. "If your mother gave no instructions for her terminal care, and given that she was not religious, the choice falls to you. You are going to have to decide whether or not to continue her life-support treatment."

I spent a day on the ward with my mother, staring at her face, quietly, agonizingly trying to work out the answer. What would Mom do? What would Mom want me to do?

That was when I asked if my mother was in pain, and the doctor explained that it was not so much a case of *if* she was in pain but whether she was still able to *feel* pain. Furthermore, the doctor explained, it wasn't clear to him where the precise line was where we couldn't continue referring to my mother as "her" or "she."

How many of the cerebral cortex modules that determined a person's personality and consciousness needed to remain intact for you to refer to them as the same person? What "she" would have wanted? We had no way of vicariously experiencing my mother's current mental state. So the question "Is she in pain?" was inadequate on so many levels. Did "she" still remain "she" in a meaningful sense? Could the nerve receptors that remained alive in her brain receive pain stimulus? Did "she" experience that stimulus in the form of pain as we know it?

The doctor was up front with me: he didn't have the answers to any of these questions.

"Isn't there someone who can decide for me?" I asked. I'm sure I was sobbing.

I was afraid. I had no idea what this doctor was trying to do. How could I make such an important decision when it was such a gray area?

It wasn't the doctor's fault, of course. We were now in the realm of philosophy, not medicine. And yet, frustratingly, modern technological developments were all useless when it came to the realm of philosophy. Technology could analyze and dissect human beings so well, but philosophy just didn't want to know.

And I didn't want to know. I didn't want to decide. I realized this might have seemed selfish—hypocritical, even—given the number of people I'd sent to their deaths. But when it comes to someone close, someone you love, you lose your mind. No one tells you of the huge, ambiguous gulf between the lands of the living and the dead. I longed for the days when we had that simple, black-and-white phrase: "brain dead."

I returned to the motel, where I cried some more. I cried for the world that had gone past the point of no return in creating this awful ambiguity between life and death. I cried in terror. I cried at the prospect of having to decide, on the sheer harshness and cruelty of my position. I cried so much I felt nauseated. I fell prostrate on the bed, crying until I needed to run to the bathroom to dry-heave my guts out, and all that emerged was saliva and more tears.

At the end of the night I had decided what to do.

However difficult the question, when it came down to it there were only two alternatives, and I had to pick one of them.

I barely even skimmed over the letter of consent to terminate treatment.

I gave my consent where consent was needed, and my mother's life support was switched off. The doctor asked me how I felt and offered the services of a recommended counselor. Yep, sure enough, it was the counselors again. Marriage on the rocks? About to head into battle? Relative just died? Counseling was the panacea, it seemed.

"No thanks. But I appreciate the offer."

Basically, I was worn out.

I realized this at the funeral service. I'd worn myself out thinking about all the details, and that was why I'd been able to make my decision. If I hadn't been so exhausted, I might have still been at the hospital, sitting with Mom and her life-support systems, still turning over the options in my head.

At the time I had convinced myself that I was thinking of Mom's best interests when I pulled the plug. When I pressed my fingerprint down on the device to give my consent, I believed that Mom wouldn't have wanted a grim half-existence, that she would have wanted to be either alive or dead, one way or another, and that if she had been alive she would have been in terrible pain.

But, as the doctor had said, there was no way for me to know whether she was in pain. After all, she was no more than a thin remnant of her former self, and it wasn't even clear whether the new "she" could feel pain.

Then there was that atmosphere. The oppressive feeling of my mother's gaze that was reignited inside me when I visited the house.

Had I really arrived at my decision by considering my mother's best interests? I searched deep inside myself, and by the time the funeral service was over I could no longer convince myself that I had.

From that moment onward I'd been plagued by the subconscious belief that I killed my own mother.

5

During the entire time it took for me to tell my story—minus the direct references to the army and my work, of course—I think I must have taken four sips of my beer. I don't think Lucia's glass touched her lips the entire time.

"Well, for what it's worth I think you did the right thing. You shouldn't be so hard on yourself. You're not a sinner, unlike me," she finally said.

I was ready to explode. It was a mistake to have sought partial release by confiding a watered-down version of my story to a civilian. There was a huge part of me that wanted to spit it all out—the deaths I had caused in the line of duty, my own "sins" as Lucia would have said—but I had to remain professional to the end. And it was killing me.

Because I had killed Mom.

Because I had killed the brigadier general.

Because I had killed the troops on patrol.

Because I had left the people in the village to their certain deaths.

Don't forgive me, Lucia. The burden of guilt I carry with me is larger than you can even imagine. I've killed so many people, and

soon I'm going to kill your former lover. So don't grant me your
pardon. If you were to pardon me...I don't know what I'd do.

"That's good of you to say. It makes me feel a little better," I
replied, subduing my bursting heart, turning it to stone. See? I
could still give any answer I needed to give, any answer I wanted.
After all, that's how I dealt with the hundreds of innocents I
left to their fate; that's how I could kill children when they had
their guns pointed at me; that's how I could cope with seeing
the girl with the glistening brains sprouting from the back of
her head and the youth with the slippery guts spilling from his
lifeless body.

"I'm not just saying that to comfort you, Mr. Bishop. You knew
how much it was going to hurt you when you made your decision.
You knew, even as you gave your order to terminate treatment,
that you were never going to be able to forgive yourself. You
knew, and still you went ahead with it, because you knew it was
best for your mother that way. That's not a sin. You were doing
it for your mother's sake."

"Was I really?" I asked.

"Humans aren't so bad, really. We're not designed to go to hell.
People like us—we're predisposed to be basically good, not evil."

"Lucia, I thought you were an atheist." The conversation had
suddenly taken a turn for the pious, and I blurted this out almost
without thinking.

"I'm not talking about religion, though. I'm talking about
the evolution of species."

"Evolution?"

"Yes. The evolutionary default setting for humans isn't to go
to hell. And that's not just true of humans. There are all sorts
of animals who are naturally programmed to perform all sorts
of acts of altruism."

"Oh, so you're not actually talking about Darwin's theory of
evolution as such, then, about adaptation and natural selection.
The survival of the fittest. Because he'd disagree with you and
argue that the highest aim of all life is to survive and protect
itself," I said.

"No, I am talking about Darwin. Think about a swarm of
insects, for example. It's only when they give themselves over

to the host that they're able to achieve their full potential as a species. Or take honeybees. They'll sting an intruder to protect their hive even if doing so rips out their own guts in the process. They act altruistically in order to benefit their species as a whole."

"But that's just genetic programming at an instinctual level," I countered. After all, how are bees acting any differently from robots? Whereas *I* wasn't a robot. *I* didn't robotically decide to kill my mother. That was something I decided with my own will.

"Well, what's to say that man's conscience isn't also a product of programming at a genetic level?" Lucia fired back.

"If that's the case, how do you explain criminals and villains who just don't care about other people? And morality and conscience are completely subjective notions at the best of times—see how much they vary between rich and poor countries. No, conscience is a social construct."

"The details of what makes up an individual's conscience, maybe. But conscience per se—including its offshoot, religion—is a product of evolutionary processes."

"Don't tell me you're seriously trying to suggest that altruism can coexist with social Darwinism?"

"You've heard of game theory, right? Well, there's this simulation that takes the model several iterations down the line. It's true that at first people tend to act purely in their own short-term self-interest and have no qualms about trampling over other people to get what they want. The prisoner in the prisoner's dilemma is usually happy to rat out his companion if it means shaving a few years off his own sentence. But when you allow the simulation to develop, and you introduce new factors—you make the model closer to being like real life, in other words—then you start to see an interesting change. The long-term equilibrium position is almost always one of cooperation rather than competition. People become prepared to give up a short-term benefit, even when it's dangling there right in front of their eyes, in order to act in a way that benefits the group as a whole."

"I find that hard to believe," I said.

"It might seem counterintuitive at first, but it makes perfect logical sense when you start to think about it. Individuals may gain some benefit in betraying others in the early stages, but sooner or later some of them realize that cooperation within a community results in a better outcome all around. If an individual still persists in being a betrayer, the cooperators refuse to deal with him, so his only option left is to try and form a community with other betrayers, and these communities are never stable, as the betrayers are, by definition, always stabbing each other in the back."

"So you're saying that conscience stems from when living things first started grouping together into communities?" I asked.

"Think about it. Most animals are weak, at least as individuals. In order to adapt to their harsh surroundings they needed to adapt to working together as a community. These communities of cooperators become more successful evolutionarily, so they effectively outbreed the betrayers and pass on their genes to their offspring. As a species, then, the genes that are most likely to get passed down to the next generation are those of the cooperators, rather than the betrayers. Is it that far-fetched to imagine that in time cooperation becomes embedded into the species' genetic structure and that altruism effectively becomes an instinct?"

"So you're saying that my decision to kill my own mother had nothing to do with my soul and everything to do with my genetics? That it was the default decision for my brain, as you put it?"

"Not exactly." Lucia shook her head. "Although I do understand why some people like the idea of being able to reduce all human decisions to genetics or biological determinism. Anyway, I thought you said you didn't subscribe to any religious beliefs."

"That's true, yes—"

"Riddle me this, then. Why do you have to fall back on metaphysical ideas such as the soul in order to explain your actions?"

That stopped me short. What did it mean, exactly, to say that you had a soul? What were the implications of saying that humanity had some sort of fundamental essence existing in lofty seclusion, untouched by the harsh and dirty realities of this world? Could it be that the idea of the spirit was just some fiction I bought into so that I could lighten the burden I carried, of all the dictators and villains that I had killed and all the innocent victims that I had abandoned to their fates? So that their deaths would somehow be tempered by the thought that at least a part of them would continue existing in an alternative universe—one that we called heaven, or hell, or whatever?

Fuck. I was no atheist. When it came down to it, I believed in exactly the same sort of shit that all religious people believed in.

I did so because I wanted to run away from the full implications of my actions. Alex hadn't run away. Or perhaps he couldn't run away. Unlike me, Alex had chosen to face religion head-on. Alex had never used religion as an excuse.

That was why Alex had killed himself. It all made sense now.

"Evolution gave birth to conscience. And culture. Humanity, warmth between parent and child, between fellow humans. You've heard of memes?" Lucia said.

"Memes as in the cultural equivalent of genes? Sure. Although I thought you said that conscience was a product of biological evolution, not culture."

"The existence of conscience, yes. It's the *details* that are the social construct. Memes are what's passed on from generation to generation. Some details survive, others are weeded out. That's what culture is."

"So, are you saying that we're all slaves to memes? That my actions are somehow controlled by them?"

"Not exactly. There are some people who might like to think of genes and memes as things that control our actions, but that's putting the cart before the horse. Memes don't control us. Rather, they're parasites, riding the coattails of human thought. Humans think, make decisions, and memes piggyback on these decisions to spread from person to person. Genes and memes are not get-out-of-jail-free cards. We might inherit hereditary characteristics or be influenced by memes, but we can never entirely give them credit for our consciences or pin the blame on them for our sins."

"Okay, so let's say I had a gene in me that, I don't know, made me inclined to rape women," I said. "If I then decided to rape you senseless, that's not the fault of my genes? Or what about if I'd been horrifically abused as a child and as a result never developed a moral compass that told me that love and kindness are good things, and I turned out to be a serial killer. Would that not be down to my environment and upbringing?"

"I don't believe that," Lucia said. "People always have a choice. Regardless of what's come before. People are free, which means that people can choose to throw away that freedom. People are free precisely because they have the choice to decide for themselves what they're free *not* to do, for their own sake or for the sake of someone else."

I looked once more at Lucia's face. Suddenly, I felt free. Pardoned. Not because I'd received affirmation that what I had done was right. Not because my sins had been forgiven.

All that had happened was that Lucia had shown me how my sin was my own. It was my cross to bear, not something that had been thrust on me by anyone else.

"Thank you," I said.

Lucia accepted my gratitude in silence.

Although there were checkpoints all over town and a person's progress through them could easily be monitored, crime had not completely disappeared. The surveillance society we now lived in was a great deterrent against systematic or premeditated crimes because the perpetrators knew they were almost certainly going to be tracked down, caught, and punished. But the flip side of this was that the surveillance state was almost useless at stopping impulsive, desperate, or suicidal crimes where the perpetrator was fully prepared for capture—or too far gone to care if they got caught. As such, the tradition of seeing a lady safely home to her front door at the end of an evening had not gone entirely out of fashion.

We took the metro and then a streetcar. I'd only had a couple of beers, so I wasn't really under the influence, so to speak. I was certainly alert enough to sense that we were being watched from the moment we alighted at the streetcar stop closest to Lucia's apartment.

What to do? If this was just an ordinary tail, I'd have no problem seeing Lucia safely home and then dealing with it afterward. But if it consisted of associates of the kid I'd beaten up last time, well, they wouldn't fall into the same trap so easily.

I couldn't discount the possibility of an attack. In fact, given how bold they were being—barely keeping any distance at all—it was more than a possibility. It was a good fifteen minutes' walk along quiet side streets to Lucia's place. Our base was directly opposite her apartment, of course, so that was hardly a better option to aim for at this juncture. I sent a distress call to Williams. If he managed to reach us in time we'd be able to find a way out of this.

I grabbed hold of Lucia's hand and started picking up the pace.

My gut feeling had been correct. Our tail sped up, barely even bothering to keep hidden anymore. Not even the most amateurish pursuers would come out in the open like this unless they meant business. I resigned myself to the fact that we would be attacked somewhere between here and Lucia's place.

I wasn't sure exactly how many of them there were yet, but I could be pretty sure that, given what I did last time, there'd be more than one of them.

I was in a bind. If the chips were down I'd be forced to draw my gun, and at that instant my cover with Lucia would be blown, and all my effort so far would be in vain. Well, unless Lucia had any other advertising executive friends who enjoyed publicly brandishing handguns on their days off.

The problem was, then, one of timing. I didn't want to draw too soon, or indeed at all, if possible—my gun was my ace in my sleeve. If the other side had no such qualms, though, I'd be at a distinct disadvantage when it came to showtime.

"What's the matter, Mr. Bishop? Why have we sped up all of a sudden?" Lucia asked, her voice clearly troubled. I ignored her and pulled her along. Hoping, praying for some passersby that would make it harder for us to be assaulted openly.

A man appeared ahead of us. One of the young men from the other day. I charged straight on toward him without letting up in pace. At the same time the figure tailing us from behind broke into a dash—

—but had mistimed his run—

—and I reached the man in front of me faster than he had expected and gripped his gun slide tightly as he tried to pull his gun from his jacket pocket. The gun was immobilized, and the man couldn't pull the trigger. I wrenched it from his grasp in a fluid circular movement, snapping his finger that I'd trapped in the trigger.

The man screamed in pain and fell to the stone paving. I spun around, pointed the gun I had just snatched, and fired at our assailant coming at us from behind.

Then a surprise—the gun was ID-registered.

The grip rejected my fingerprints and the gun went into safety lockdown. So maybe these bozos were foreign intelligence agents after all?

I gritted my teeth and chucked the gun away.

All this happened in a flash—Lucia was still standing where I had left her.

I scanned the area quickly but could see only the man approaching from behind. But I couldn't believe there were only two of them. I had to be on the lookout for an ambush.

So far I had avoided drawing my gun. At this rate, I might still be able to explain away my actions and my skill without blowing my cover. A stint in the army during my youth or something. I was still in control. At least, that's what I thought until the man behind us caught up to us.

Then I was no longer in control.

Fire.

Indexfingermiddlefingerringfingerlittlefingerthumb.

Electric shock.

My senses were blown away in a blast of thunder.

My fingertips, my toes, my eyes, all throughout my body—an unbelievable, searing hot pain. All the extremities of my body were on fire, as if they'd all decided to go insane at the same moment. I almost blacked out from sheer agony.

"Mr. Bishop? What's the matter? Charles? Charles?"

This was what it must have felt like to burn up from the inside out.

Lucia had a look of panic on her face. She placed a hand on my shoulder. I realized the man approaching us from behind was no longer running. He had his mobile device pointed at me and was strolling gently in my direction.

"Run away." The pain in my extremities was so severe it took me a few seconds to squeeze the words out. "Lucia, run." The man kept on walking toward us. I realized it was the scruffy young man I had beaten up in the alleyway.

Perhaps the pain I was feeling numbed my sense of time, but it seemed to me to take an eternity before Lucia finally took heed of my words and turned to run away. The pain in my legs grew too much to bear, and I collapsed prostrate onto the historic cobblestones of old Prague.

I screamed wordlessly, acknowledging my total and utter defeat.

"There's no need for you to run away, Lucia."

I could just about make out the voice. Through the pain that was forcing my body apart, through my seeping consciousness, I turned toward the speaker to see his face.

A face I had seen numerous times in various pre-mission briefings.

The face of the man who had eluded us all these years.

Lucia was rooted to the spot, staring at John Paul.

6

I felt cold stone against my face long before I could open my eyes.

I checked for the searing agony, but it was gone. I managed to look at the fingers that had been causing me so much pain only a minute ago. Neither red nor white. No different from usual.

My wrists had been taped together. Gingerly I stretched out my fingertips and pressed them against the ground, ever so gently at first. No pain. I pushed myself up and looked around. I was in a dark room, surrounded by what looked like a giant chessboard.

"I have no idea who you are, although I assume you're here to try and kill me."

I turned around to see who the voice had come from. It was a shadowy figure, his face backlit by moonlight that crept in through a window covered by a metal grill.

John Paul.

The Lord of Genocide.

"It seems that the American government has been sending hit squads into the countries where I've been. I've been hearing reports that the generals and politicians I helped out were being killed off," he said.

"That can't be a nice feeling, knowing that any day you could be next," I said.

John Paul shrugged. "When I tried to return to Lucia's apartment I realized immediately that some clumsy Secret Service agent was trying to tail me. So I put the place under surveillance for a while, and sure enough you showed up. You were obviously Forces, which did trouble me somewhat, I'll admit."

"Why do you think I'm in the Forces?" I stared at John Paul. A trained linguist turned PR flak. It bothered me that this civilian could tell the difference between the CIA and Special Forces so easily. It also bothered me that he was talking to me as if we were fellow professionals.

"As I'm sure you know, I've spent the last few years of my life in war zones," John Paul said. "A long time. Places where no UN troops, let alone US soldiers, ever intervened. But there were occasionally PMCs, there to provide tactical and strategic consultancy. They would train up local troops, molding the rabble into a semblance of a proper army. Most PMC soldiers are, as I'm sure you know, ex-Special Forces who crossed over to private work in order to double their paycheck. Well, I started watching these people, and in watching them I started to notice the special type of walk that only trained soldiers have. It wasn't that hard for me to do. After all, my work as a linguistics researcher was basically frequency analysis—identifying the hidden patterns that lurk behind apparently mundane agglomerations of data."

I pushed myself up with my bound wrists so that I was sitting on the floor and facing John Paul directly. Like one of Jesus's disciples sitting at the feet of his master.

"Speaking of patterns," I said, "the NME was funding your language research, and you were looking for some sort of patterns there. What I don't understand was why DARPA was involved in the first place. What benefit was there to them in funding an academic thesis? Why was that a matter of national security?"

"Ha. So you're telling me that neither your superior officers nor the fine staffers of Washington ever bothered to explain that to you? How typical."

The moonlight was now shining brightly on my face. From where John Paul was standing I would have looked deathly white.

The former scholar put his hand to his mouth before launching into a calm, deliberate lecture by way of explanation.

"The defense establishment wasn't involved with my research at first. It was academic work, pure and simple. All the materials I was using were in the public domain. Archives from Nazi Germany, radio broadcasts, magazines, literature, military communications. I acquired all sorts of data from the Nazi era—prewar as well as wartime. Much of it was already digitized; I had my assistants convert the materials that only existed in hard copy. Then I parsed it all. Grammatical analysis, in layman's terms."

Research into Nazi rhetoric. I tried to imagine how it would relate to university work. Class 101: Fascist Communications—Discourse for Dummies. Don't embarrass yourself in front of your fellow National Socialists by making a linguistic faux pas! All this was interesting enough, as an interdisciplinary elective that fell between the domains of linguistics and history. But I still didn't see how that could be of such interest to the military.

"I published a thesis based on my work," John Paul continued. "The MIT budget committee called me in not long after. The chairman coolly informed me that my research had been selected for funding by the National Military Establishment, so I needed to run along and present them with my research. I wasn't wild about the idea at first—it would mean that any further research on the topic would be classified and impossible to publish—but when I realized how many perks there would be other than just the actual funding, I reluctantly accepted. After all, it meant full access to confidential CIA documents and to international traffic intercepted by the NSA. Everything from Pol Pot's wireless transmissions to the Khmer Rouge to Rwandan radio broadcasts. The NME even arranged for me to have full access to the Russian archives on the Katyn Forest Massacre. Most valuable of all to my research, though, was the raw data from the traffic that the NSA and the CIA had intercepted."

"And you discovered something from all this?"

"Yes. That there is a grammar to genocide."

I didn't understand.

John Paul saw my incomprehension and explained. "Whatever the country, the political climate, or the syntactical framework of the language used, the data always showed that there was one thing in common: a deep structure of the grammar of genocide. There were always certain patterns in the media of a society that was about to start committing genocide, present in its newspaper articles, radio and television broadcasts, even the novels and short stories published. We're talking about at a deep structural level, not something noticeable in the surface structures that non-linguists are used to accepting at face value. In other words, only a trained linguist who was specifically looking for these patterns would ever have been able to find them."

The grammar of genocide.

A predictor of atrocities to come.

I couldn't believe it. "Language is something humans learn. It's the result of acquired learning. *A posteriori* knowledge. It's just language. It can't affect people's souls in such a fundamental way," I said.

"Ah, the old *tabula rasa* canard. Touching to think that there are still people who believe it. The human mind is a blank slate? I suppose next you'll be telling me that autism is caused by people not receiving enough love and affection when they were children."

"Isn't it?" I asked.

"Genetics predetermine most things about the way a person turns out, from their personality to any physical or mental handicaps, even down to their political leanings. Environmental factors play a marginal role at best. There are those who have tried to argue that human beings are purely a product of their environment, and that all people are essentially born equal. Well, I'm an egalitarian myself, and I believe that it's a uniquely human trait to be able to transcend our genetics by creating this concept called 'culture.' But I can't allow my belief in the potential of humanity to muddy the objective results of my scientific inquiry. All I'm saying is that every human action has a source, with perfectly good biological and neurological explanations. We need to start by acknowledging to ourselves that we are no more than bundles of flesh assembled according to a genetic code. Our livers and bowels and kidneys were made according to a predetermined genetic formula, so why should there be a special exemption for our minds or hearts, or anywhere else we choose to believe our mysterious spirit might reside?"

I thought of Lucia's words that the human heart was a product of evolution.

Had she just been regurgitating John Paul's philosophy?

The thought made me sick to the core.

"But the language that a child learns while growing up is the language spoken by the people around him," I said. "It's not as if babies are born with Esperanto carved into their brains or anything. Isn't that what scholars mean when they call linguistics an *a posteriori* discipline?"

"No. Let me give you an example. Back when slavery was still legal, the old plantation owners could have cared less what sort of language their slaves spoke. The slaves had been abducted from all four corners of Africa and were just thrown together to work, regardless of whether they had any language or culture in common. Now, this state of affairs wasn't going to last for long. Soon, the slaves started picking up fragments of their masters' language—English. But their version of the language was much more simplistic than the original and grammatically all over the place, but at the same time much more rigid and restrictive than English. You couldn't change word order in a sentence or collocate words easily, for example. In its first generation, this was called Pidgin English."

John Paul took a deep breath, readying himself to continue his lecture.

"The children of those slaves grew up with Pidgin English as their mother tongue. When they interacted with other 'native' pidgin speakers, interesting things started happening: the language started shifting from the rigid original toward a much livelier and more fluid language. A more naturalistic grammar emerged. Grammatical rules that the parents had never used started coming into play, effectively invented by the children. This new language was based on English but was definitely not a language developed by people who had grown up listening to the original. Linguistically and grammatically speaking it was an entirely new language that developed out of a pale imitation of the original. Today it's called Creole. The children, in other words, acquired a sophisticated grammar that eluded their parents. The only convincing explanation for this is that the human brain has an inherent ability to generate its own grammar out of the linguistic components it has on hand."

"And that's what you mean by deep structure—our innate grammatical potential?" I asked.

"Yes, an ability seared into our brains by our genetic code. An organ that gives birth to language."

A built-in organ inside our brain that gives birth to language. The organ that contains the portents of massacres.

I was starting to understand. "So DARPA was interested in your research because they figured that if there was a hidden grammatical code inside the human mind that led to chaos and disorder, then they might be able to preempt outbreaks of genocide by monitoring and analyzing communications in countries that were already known to be politically and ethnically unstable."

John Paul nodded. "As my research progressed, I soon became able to identify omens of escalating violence in patterns of language that people used to communicate with each other. It wasn't something that you could identify from individual conversations, but rather something that happened at the structural level of a society. You could even see it in the language used by the society's victims. You can see it in the discourse of the Jews who lived in the Third Reich, for example. And to get a true picture you need to perform frequency analysis on an entire region. What you end up seeing is an outbreak of a particular type of change inside the minds of people who've been subjected to this discourse over an extended period of time. Specifically, the part of the brain that makes certain value judgments becomes inhibited. That thing that we have come to call 'conscience' becomes twisted. Biased, if you will, in a certain direction."

John Paul had said enough. The horrific logical conclusion to his story was now looming before me.

I wondered when he had experienced his "eureka" moment. When he lost his wife and child? Or when he was with Lucia replaying that initial report of the news from Sarajevo over and over?

After a pause, I timidly ventured my conclusion. John Paul's conclusion.

"So you wondered which came first, the chicken or the egg..."

John Paul smiled. "Just so."

Genocide could be predicted by the frequency of certain types of deep grammatical structures used within a country's discourse.

So what would happen if you took a stable country where no such discourse was happening and somehow deliberately increased the frequency of this type of deep grammatical structure?

What would happen to a region when its people started speaking with the grammar of genocide?

You'd have to be a lunatic even to consider it, I thought. It was an idea that might crop up during the course of research—a whimsical hypothesis, a joke almost. But you wouldn't actually try it out. How could you, for starters? As John Paul had said, this wasn't a hypothesis that manifested itself on an individual level, only at the level of a whole society. You'd need to be able to influence public discourse on a massive scale—the logistics were mind-boggling.

And yet...

"So you experimented? With a Third World country?"

"Why do you think I joined a public relations firm?" John Paul said. "The perfect opportunity to embed myself in the core of a country's propaganda machine. All I had to do was influence the national media broadcasters, sign off on the head of state's speeches, tell the cabinet ministers what to say, and make sure that no government announcement went out without being checked by me first. It was easy. I had left MIT by then and my government funding had dried up, but I already knew everything I needed to know. And sure enough, the experiment proved successful."

"But what about the other countries?" I said. "They didn't give you the same level of access to influence the core of their government communications."

"And they didn't have to," John Paul said. "A little judicious application of SNDGA and it was easy enough to work out which branches of communication I needed to focus on to yield maximal returns. Not so different from you guys, right?"

"SNDGA?"

"Not your field, perhaps? SNDGA stands for Social Network Directed Graph Analysis. It's what your bosses use to work out which target you need to kill next in order to have the biggest chance of suppressing the violence in a region."

He's Public Enemy Number One. The leader who is causing the massacres, fanning the flames of chaos, bringing about death and destruction to his society. That's why he's your target. You need to kill him for the greater good. The sort of thing I had always been told on a pre-mission briefing. Same with Williams, Alex, Leland.

Well, I suppose someone in Washington or Fort Mead must have had a way of identifying our targets.

John Paul seemed to have seen something in my momentarily blank expression because he squatted down next to me and looked straight into my eyes as if he were talking to a crawling toddler.

"Have you ever heard of Six Degrees of Kevin Bacon?" he asked me. "A party game named after an old movie star."

Footloose was one of my guilty pleasures.

"You take two actors who've never been in a movie together and try and connect them in as few steps as possible," John Paul continued. "If there's an actor they've both been in a movie with, that's one degree of separation. If the first actor has been in a movie with an actor who in turn has been in a movie with an actor who has been in a movie with the second, then that's two degrees of separation, and so on. Virtually every actor ever known can reach Kevin Bacon within three degrees of separation. In other words, the game is about personal networks."

"Thanks for the explanation, but I doubt there's an American alive who hasn't heard of the Kevin Bacon game."

"Do excuse me. I wasn't trying to patronize you. It's just a useful analogy for explaining graph theory. The study of analyzing networks made up of these sorts of links. The NSA, the Center for Counterterrorism, and DARPA all poured money into the field of graph theory once it became clear that the new type of terrorist threat was decentralized and not tied down to a specific geographical location. Graph theory became a subject of interdisciplinary military research, just like my field. Graph theorists would study data intercepted at Echelon and observe the interactions between different people in different regions— how data were exchanged. It wasn't the contents of the data as such that was important, but the flow: how information dispersed and which channels would cause it to disseminate most effectively. All this can be ascertained through network analysis."

That made sense. I supposed that was indeed how the powers that be chose our targets.

"But how do you know all of this?" I asked.

"They let me use their research to help my own research into the grammar of genocide. The lines that connected one point to another. The nodes and edges. Digraphs that incorporated directional markers showing the trends of information flow. Add a little bit of SNDGA, and it's easy to work out where the most important sources of communication are. You don't always need access to a president or a general. In fact, in one country I chose to play the role of a priest, and in another I was part of an influential NGO. More chance to propagate the genocidal grammar that way—a more extensive network, you see? Of course, the specifics vary from country to country."

This man was calmly describing the results of a series of experiments to me as if they were entirely theoretical. It was as if he had conveniently forgotten that his research into genocide was built on top of a mountain of human misery.

"I don't believe it," I said. "I don't believe that language has the ability to influence our subconscious in such a way. The Sapir-Whorf hypothesis has already been comprehensively discredited. Human thought isn't regulated by language. Are you seriously trying to say that this weird function has been left in our brains as a result of evolution? Impossible!"

For some reason this made John Paul laugh out loud. It wasn't a villain's laugh, but a healthy, hearty, normal laugh. And that made it all the more freakish.

"What's so funny?" I asked.

"Nothing, nothing. I just never expected to come across a spy who was so up to date on linguistic theory, that's all."

I sneered at him. "Spending time with the lovely Ms. Lucia has been very educational."

"Yes, it seems the two of you have been spending a fair bit of time together," John Paul said. His voice was that of supreme indifference. Damn. I'd hoped that would have affected him at least a little bit. But it seemed there was nothing I could do or say that would have any effect on this man.

John Paul started speaking again. "Do you ever think to yourself that perhaps words have no meaning?"

I said nothing. I had no idea where he was trying to go with this.

"I wonder who it was who first said that they liked something," John Paul continued. "Or that they didn't like something. Such simple expressions. Compare those with the conversation that the two of us are having now. Aren't we basically saying the same thing, just in a much more long-winded and circumlocutory way? We're basically just expressing primitive emotions, no different from saying that something tastes good or that we feel bad."

I squirmed in embarrassment as I thought of the long conversation I had had with Lucia about my mother's death, when I poured my heart out to her. Maybe John Paul was right. Was that not just a roundabout way of telling her that I liked her?

"Whenever I've studied a country undergoing a period of militarization, I entertained this charming little theory. It's occurred to me that the slogans that inevitably end up being scrawled on the street corners aren't really about the words at all. They're more primitive than that. The slogans are just manifestations of a deep, primeval resonance. 'Hate enemy.' 'Protect self.' I like to think of them as little fragments of music in an underlying symphony of primeval urges."

"People aren't animals," I said. "Human language is different from the howling of wild beasts."

"Do you really believe that? I'm not sure that I do," John Paul said. "Goethe himself admitted that something as simple as a military march could cause him to feel his spine tingling to attention. And it's not just airports and cafés that have background music playing. Auschwitz had a soundtrack too. The sound of the wake-up bell in the morning, the drums to make the prisoners march. However exhausted and utterly despondent the Jewish inmates were, as soon as the drums broke out in rhythm they found their bodies moving along with the beat whether they wanted them to or not. Unlike what we see, what we hear has the capacity to touch our souls directly. Music rapes our senses. Meaning? What meaning? Pure sound can and will bypass all that noble-sounding guff."

The thing that lurks under the words we use.

Meaning is just skin deep.

That's what John Paul was trying to say. When we speak, it's not just the contents of our words that matter. The "meaning" of the words is only ever a small part of the equation. That's what John Paul meant: there was also music, rhythm, hidden esoteric layers that I couldn't hope to grasp or notice or understand.

"People can close their eyes, but they can never completely block off their ears. No one is immune to my words," John Paul explained.

I forced myself to look into the moonlight and at John Paul's eyes. I was expecting, hoping that I would see madness there, that I would find a lunatic bathed in a lunar glow. But I was granted no such satisfaction. All I could see was a perfectly rational and calm pair of eyes, staring down at me. If anything, they were twinged with melancholy, not madness.

"You're insane."

I didn't believe it, but I had to say it anyway.

7

John Paul left the room, and about fifteen minutes later I found myself being prodded along a dirty corridor by one of my other assailants. The corridor was covered in graffiti that, by the looks of it, had been done fairly recently. This wasn't a scene I expected to see in this day and age when all petty crimes could be traced quickly back to the perpetrator.

I was nudged through a doorway, my assailant's gun still in my back. I emerged on the other side to find myself in a fairly

large room that contained a bar lined with glass bottles and an
open space with its floor covered with a nanolayer portraying
the image of an unending abyss.

Lucius's club.

"Nice to see you again so soon," I said to the emerging figures
of Lucius, Lucia, and a number of men who could only be
described as underlings. The men were all armed and looking
at me warily. "You surprise me, Lucius. To think you're on the
same side as John Paul."

Lucius shook his head. "John is our client, nothing more.
We just did what we had to do in order to protect ourselves."

"And who is 'we' exactly?" I asked, looking at both Lucius and
Lucia, who was standing next to him with a bewildered expression
on her face. So was she not on Lucius's—or John Paul's—side?
Had she been unwittingly duped into becoming an accomplice?

Lucius paused for a while, as if trying to remember something.
Then he spoke.

"'And it came to pass in those days, that there went out a
decree from Caesar Augustus that all the world should be taxed.
And this taxing was first made when Cyrenius was governor of
Syria. And all went to be taxed, every one into his own city.'
Are you familiar with this passage?"

It was Lucia who answered, before I had a chance to focus
on what was going on. "No, although it sounds like something
from the Bible."

Lucius turned to me. "And what about you, sir?"

"I'm an atheist. I don't go to church," I said.

"It's Luke, chapter 1. Even back then, citizens were turned
into numbers and counted," Lucius said.

"So what?" I asked. Lucia was looking at my bound wrists.
She was obviously concerned.

"Well, we here are the uncounted," said Lucius, looking at
the armed men around him. "We are nothing more than an
unidentifiable mass in the eyes of the surveillance society. We are
vagabonds who slip through the cracks of security behemoths."

"You live under false identities?" I asked. I was incredulous.
Only Forces and governments should have been able to fake
IDs. It was virtually impossible to hack the InfoSec company

databases, and its employees were basically incorruptible. The slightest leak, whether internally or from outside hackers, was treated with the utmost seriousness, with long jail sentences for anyone who even tried. No, security breaches were all but unheard of.

"It's practically impossible to assume a false identity as such, more's the pity," Lucius said, shaking his head. "But that doesn't mean that there aren't certain workarounds. We can start with low-tech methods. Mapping the locations of sensors, for example. We're inundated with a multitude of sensors, but individually they tend to be monofunctional. They scan just your retina, or just your veins, or just your fingerprints. Then here's a brainwave scan, and here's a camera. Well, by painstakingly entering all the details of these sensors we've managed to come up with maps of all major American and European cities. A Rough Guide for the Surveillance Evader. Using computer analysis it's been possible to find loopholes, shortcuts—paths of least resistance. There are ways to trick some of the sensors, and then all you need is a fake set of nanolayer fingerprints and somebody else's eyes, and suddenly it becomes very difficult for them to track you."

Come to think of it, that youth I roughed up had had different retina and fingerprint IDs.

"But surely you still need fake IDs, even if just for the fake fingers and the fake eyes," I said.

Lucius shrugged. "We cultivated our ID database carefully and over a long period of time. Babies who died shortly after birth, before they were fully registered. Travelers who went missing abroad. Civilian contractors and PMCs who went MIA in war zones. And, most of all, Sarajevo."

The corpses that never even had the chance to become corpses. The missing.

Names in purgatory.

"We carefully select IDs from among the missing and make them live again. We archive them so that they are out of the sights of governments and can be drawn on at a moments' notice if needed. You can imagine how valuable this archive is to us. Short of terrorism and genocide we'll do whatever we need to protect it," Lucius said.

"And yet I remember a time only a few short hours ago when you were telling me how there was no such thing as pure freedom, how everything was a matter of checks and balances," I said. I never would have guessed from his demeanor at the time that Lucius was such a radical ideologue.

"I stand by that. The issue we have is that the trade-off society forces us to make is massively one-sided. The privacy we've been asked to give up just isn't rewarded with a corresponding increase in security." Lucius advanced so that he was now standing right in front of me. "The current security regime is pointless. After 9/11, the world steadily increased its surveillance levels on individuals. 'Traceability' became the order of the day. And yet, the more the screws were tightened, the more terrorist incidents there were across the world's major cities."

"That's a lie," I said.

"It's not a lie," Lucius snapped. "Even you have to acknowledge the truth about Sarajevo. Am I wrong? Even the official published statistics show a correlation between the surveillance clampdown and increased terrorist activity—just take any government data and plot it on a graph. It's all there, in black and white, for anyone to see. And yet for some reason most people choose not to."

"In that case, why does everybody believe that personal traceability is the best protection against terrorists?" I asked.

Lucius's lips twisted into an ironic smile. "Is that what people believe? Or just what people *want* to believe?" He laughed, a sad, hollow sound. "It's not as if the government is lying to us. Or rather, it's not as if it's *only* the government that's lying to us. The media lie too, and, worst of all, so do the people, the citizens. We all lie to each other. We've all been taken in by this collective myth of traceability, and that's how our modern surveillance state was born. It might be true that terrorist activity has died down recently, but that's only because most terrorists have been diverted by the recent explosion of civil wars and ethnic conflicts around the world. It's nothing to do with the security crackdown."

We see what we want to see.

We believe what we want to believe.

What good was hard statistical evidence in the face of belief?

The government, industry, the people—none were interested in looking at graphs, not when mere facts contradicted their core beliefs.

"Reality is such a pathetic and weak thing," Lucius continued, shaking his head sadly. "There are so many horrific things in the world that go unreported. Do you know, for example, how artificial flesh is created? Genetically modified dolphins. Aquatic mammals engineered to be able to live in freshwater. They're raised—or maybe 'cultured' is a better word, given the circumstances—in Lake Victoria, before being dissected alive so that their muscle can be put to industrial use. The rest of them becomes animal feed. Children on starvation wages work round the clock in giant sweatshop factories off the shores of Lake Victoria, forcing the red blubbery flesh into giant cans using biostaplers."

"Live dolphin muscle..." I trailed off.

The Intruder Pods that we used to penetrate enemy lines. The short-range jets that hopped us from continent to continent. All covered in raw flesh. How many people knew that sex lotion was made out of seaweed?

"No one. No one knows. Just as no one will try and stop you from selling dyed lumpfish roe as caviar," Lucius said.

"But how can that—"

"Anyone remotely interested in doing so can work all this out for themselves. Just use your AR contact lenses to track the provenance of whatever is in front of you. Where and when an object is made. The space and the time is there for all to see. We live in what the science fiction author Bruce Sterling might have called a spime society. People want to know whether their Budweiser is brewed under sanitary conditions and which ranch a burger can be traced back to. You can even find out which forest provided the trees for your house. The metahistory of everything in the universe is bare, raw, there for the taking. And yet no one is interested in anything other than their own little personal narratives. No one wants to know about the tragedy of the origins of artificial flesh, they just want to know that it will continue to provide the airplanes and machines that will prop up their comfortable lifestyle."

At this point, Lucius's warped smile surfaced again. "And you, Mr. Bishop. You know all too well about the massacres that happen all over the globe. How many of those is the world interested in? As you know all too well, only a fraction are ever reported. People are designed to see only what they want to see."

He had a point. Outside my work, all I knew of the world came from clips on CNN. I lived in a Domino's Pizza world. I lived in a world of fifteen-minute chunks of free movie previews.

"Basically, the issue we have is that the idea that submitting ourselves to permanent surveillance somehow makes us safer is one great lie. An unfair trade. The reason we choose to live anonymously is because we don't want to live in a society that forces this trade upon us."

Lucius stepped away from the abyss surrounding us. He sighed, then continued. "John noticed that the CIA were staking out Lucia's apartment. He warned us of this fact—he's a good customer. We figured that you might be using Lucia to get to us. You'd already roughed up one of us, after all."

One of the men took out a mobile terminal and tapped the keypad.

The tips of my body were flooded with that searing pain again, and I yelled and collapsed.

"Stop it, please! You're killing him! Please!" Lucia screamed.

Lucius glanced at the man who was frying me. The man was, of course, the youth that I had worked over in the alleyway. His face was still covered with bruises. He slowly put away the Mob in his back pocket.

"A Paingiver," Lucius explained. "Nanomachines designed to deliver an unbearable shock to your nerve endings. I slipped some into your Budweiser earlier. I hope you don't mind. A useful little present we received from John—military issue, apparently. The machines lodge inside your capillary vessels, which means that when they're activated they cause incredible pain in your extremities—fingers, toes, the like."

The pain had miraculously disappeared, although my body was still reeling from shock. Gasping for breath, I looked over at Lucia's face. Her tears made her black eyeliner run all the way down her cheeks.

The face of a woman crying for a man who had betrayed her. Crushed by conflicting, overwhelming emotions.

"Unfortunately, Lucia brought you right into our club. That raised the stakes. Now, if it had just been a matter of my own personal liberty, well, that might have been one thing. I could have coped with being arrested. But there was the danger of having our entire library seized. If that happened, all our friends, colleagues, and customers, all our compatriots fighting for personal liberties in Europe and America—they'd all be outed. We had to preempt that at all costs. That was why I needed to stake out Lucia's place."

"So you've been watching me all this time?" Lucia asked.

"Forgive me. As I explained, it was for the greater good."

"I thought you were the anonymous heroes who went underground to avoid the constant surveillance of government and industry. And yet you're happy to put other people under surveillance yourselves?" Lucia asked.

"It's a truly troubling dilemma," Lucius replied.

I thought of Orwell's *Animal Farm.* Where all animals are equal, but some animals are more equal than others. And those who were already free watched over others so that all could be "equally" free.

"I seem to remember Stalin and Pol Pot also being 'troubled' by similar dilemmas," I said, sneeering, and immediately received another payload of pain for my efforts.

"Tuvi, could you hold off for a moment, please?" Lucius calmly asked the youth. Luckily for me, the kid complied.

"You'll have to forgive Tuvi—it seems you roughed him up good and proper, so you'll have to think of this as your just deserts," Lucius said.

"Ha, so this is *Crime and Punishment* now, is it? Well, I wonder when you're going to get your punishment for what you've done in the name of freedom."

"Don't worry about us. And besides, people in glass houses... you were observing Lucia just as much as we were, no?"

"What?" Lucia looked at me, stunned.

I knew it. I had always known it. Sooner or later we would end up here. It had been inevitable from the start. Really, why had I ever expected anything else?

Yes, I know all about you, Ms. Lucia Sukrova.

I know that you were mistress to a married man.

I know the restaurants where you and John Paul dined together.

I know at which branches of Starbucks you drank your morning cappuccinos.

I know how many condoms John Paul bought.

I wanted to scream out loud. For the youth to press the button on his Mob and never let go. For my fingers and toes and all my body to explode and blast my consciousness into tiny fragments. I wanted and deserved any and all pain that the world could throw at me.

"You see, Lucia," Lucius said, "this man has been watching you in order to try and capture John Paul. He's an American secret agent. A somewhat cultured American agent, perhaps, but a secret agent nonetheless. Cultured enough to capture your heart, at least."

I looked at the young man, Tuvi. *Press the button,* I willed. Make me squirm in agony. Show me in my wretched agony to Lucia. But Tuvi saw through me. He looked down on me. I was a deer in the headlights, not worthy of another thought.

Hell is here. Inside your mind. Job done. No need for any more pain.

"John's waiting for you outside, Lucia." Lucius pointed Lucia toward the exit. Gently but firmly. Time to go.

Lucia glanced toward the exit before turning her gaze back on me. Was she hesitating? Or condemning me? I was so overwhelmed by guilt that I could no longer tell.

An eternity of agony. It was agony to be looked at by Lucia. Her piercing gaze was unbearable. And yet I didn't want her to go. I wanted her to stay here.

Your ex is a mass murderer. He's responsible for more deaths than Stalin. I could have told her that. Shouted it out. Except... except—what right did I have to tell her?

"Lucius...don't let this man die," Lucia said.

"Lucia, please. I abhor killing."

Upon hearing what she needed to hear, Lucia turned around and left the club. I listened to her fading footfalls, my insides churning in a cocktail of regret.

The door closed, and the footsteps faded away completely. Lucius and his henchmen stared down at the abyss, at me, the wretched insect.

No one was speaking anymore. They were weighed down by the burden of what was about to happen, what had to happen. They were gritting their teeth. Doing what they had to do for the sake of freedom. To resist the evil will of those who insisted on watching them.

That was why I now had to die.

"I thought you abhorred killing," I said.

"Indeed, I do." Lucius actually did look genuinely sorry for what he was about to do. Just as, I'm sure, Hitler once did, and Stalin. Or, indeed, the ex-brigadier general that I had dispatched once upon a time, or our captive Ahmed from Somalia. Lucius might have felt guilty, but his guilt was of no value. Just as my guilt toward Lucia was of no value.

"That's why it pains me so much to have to do this," he said.

It was at that moment that a mosquito buzzed in front of me. It was as if I were in a dream—a final mirage I was seeing in the face of death. The mosquito hovered and settled on my middle finger.

The middle finger I had dabbed with pheromones earlier.

Lucius noticed the mosquito.

"You . . . a Tracer Dog—"

I lifted my bound hands to cover my right ear, using my shoulder to cover the left. I opened my mouth wide and braced myself.

The world roared, and the south wall exploded. A huge shock wave slammed through the room. Fragments of the wall and dust and debris filled the room, blinding us all. Lucius and his group were instantaneously immobilized. Many of them would have ruptured eardrums. I had managed to block my ears and open my mouth in time, just about, and even so my head was ringing.

All Special Operations I Detachment personnel had indoor assault training drilled into us during basic training at Killing House. During the training we had to take turns in shifts: who would be the assailants, who would be the targets, and who would be the hostages. The one thing I took away from my turn as a hostage was that when Special Forces attack, you had better eat dirt if you want to survive. Hit the ground and wait until it's all over. Stay standing and you had no right to complain if your putative rescuers shot you dead. Your average Special Forces man was a crack headshot.

Because of this, I had no idea who on my team did what and who killed who. If ever there was a situation where curiosity would have killed the cat, it was this.

The entire assault operation took less than three minutes. It was a fairly small club after all. The dust never even had a chance to settle.

"How's it hanging, Clavis?"

I recognized that voice. I stumbled up and beckoned for Williams to untie me.

"You look like a ghost under all that dust," Williams said, brushing some of the powdered concrete from my body. "Anyway, where's the girl? Lucia."

I stared out through the giant hole in the wall that now looked out onto the cityscape of a Prague evening. The labyrinth of stone. The city of a hundred spires.

"I don't know. She's gone."

I was shattered. Everything was numb, and I longed for pain. If only I had pain, I could escape from my weariness. I knew it. I needed pain, punishment, urgently.

And yet all Williams could do was kill me with kindness. Gentle, thoughtful, funny Williams. The last thing in the world that I needed right now.

CHAPTER

FOUR

1

A war zone.

The National Geospatial-Intelligence Agency had taken high-resolution satellite images of the territory formerly known as India and Pakistan.

A mass of craters. Their circumferences in direct proportion to the size of the warheads used to create them. The effects of the nuclear war had been as far reaching as they had been unsubtle. It was as though the earth had bubbled up and boiled over. Over the years, purling mountain rivers had poured into craters where warheads had dented the ground, gradually filling them up to form giant concentric reservoirs. The craters themselves were desolate places, reddish-brown pits devoid of all life; the radiation had seen to that. But venturing away from the circumference, the ground gradually started to turn greener until finally the stench of death had all but disappeared and you were back into the territory of India's verdant forests.

The picture zoomed in. The numerous NGA lenses in orbit shifted in their trajectory, enlarging the image of the land far below. The heat radiation present in over ten kilometers of atmosphere, combined with minuscule imperfections in the lenses themselves, caused the new image to momentarily blur until the adaptive optic software embedded in each of the lenses kicked in to correct the final image so that it was crystal clear again.

The cameras employed twenty-four bits per RGB channel, which meant that it was possible to identify green pixels on the mountain roads and distinguish them from the deep greens of the forest all around them. This paler green color was the green of war, the green of the army. Antiaircraft guns, armored vehicles, personnel carriers, tanks. When the generals who had pressed the nuclear button had fled from justice, the courtroom, and their inevitable death sentences, they were welcomed with open arms by the paramilitary organizations—provided they brought along with them a handful of toys.

The cameras zoomed farther in, five centimeters to a pixel, the maximum resolution. We could now distinctly see faces of the dead villagers scattered across the center of the paramilitary's latest stronghold. There must have been at least fifty corpses, burnt and twisted into various fetal positions. The satellite video was still focusing, showing an ever-clearer image of the agglomeration of dead bodies.

People had been killed there. An entire village. At the hands of other people.

There was an acronym that we in the Special Forces had come to hate. CEEP: Child Enemy Encounter Probability.

It meant exactly what it sounded like. The possibility that we'd end up in a shootout with prepubescent girls.

The possibility that we'd end up having to blast their little skulls open and riddle their developing bodies with bullets.

Probability. Traceability. Countability. Searchability. Viability. Everything was "-bility" this and "-bility" that. It was enough to drive the world mad.

In reality, when the word *probability* was used, we were looking at a hundred percent chance. The suffix *-bility* lost all meaning. It was a weasel phrase, a phrase used only by fraudsters and fools.

Words don't have any smell.

Neither do images or satellite recordings.

For some reason, this fact annoyed me.

The smell of fat frying and muscle shrinking. The stink of proteins in human hairs turning into ash. The distinctive odor of people burning. I knew it all too well. I wouldn't quite say that I had become used to it, but I had encountered it enough times over the years in the line of duty that I was at least familiar with it.

The smell of gunpowder. The smell of old rubber tires aflame, lit as beacons by the soldiers.

The smell of the battlefield.

There was something inherently vile about watching these satellite images, and it was making me feel uneasy. Not because of the horrific nature of the images—though they were horrific enough, all right—but because they were so sanitized. Sitting here, it made no difference to us whether we were looking at people burned whole, with guts spilling out, or with blood seeping out onto the ground. It was all so clean and deodorized. That was the most disgusting thing of all. The lenses that coldly looked down at the corpses from on high in the freezing void of space were like an omniscient yet supremely indifferent god.

The only smell associated with these images right now was the smell of the conference room at HQ in Fort Bragg. A brand-new smell, the smell of concrete and plastic and resins and monomers and adhesives and chemical wizardry.

"These images were taken by the air force's space recon satellites four days ago," the man from the National Counterterrorism Center explained. "At the New India government's behest, the prosecutor at the International Criminal Court at The Hague has issued arrest warrants for eight leaders of a Hindu fundamentalist faction currently active in rural areas. The charges include crimes against humanity, use of child soldiers, and genocide."

He sounded like every other civilian state official. There was a complete, bizarre mismatch between the bland tone of voice he affected and the gravity of the actual words. It was as though he was taking half-digested pieces of jargon and spinning them ever further away from their true meaning, taking them to the point where they became almost completely nonsensical, before presenting them in a nice and orderly fashion. I would have called it superficial, except that the word didn't really do justice to that weird sense of detachment he was projecting. When he talked of crimes against humanity and crimes of genocide, you had no sense that he actually understood or felt what these words meant. At that moment I felt a lot of sympathy for the soldiers who listened to Robert McNamara's account of the Vietnam War and simply couldn't relate to it in a meaningful way.

Still, this man from the NCTC was here, now, in this meeting room in Fort Bragg, giving a skillful, efficient, and entirely superficial briefing to the assembled soldiers.

"Eugene and Krupps are on the ground as the Japanese government's proxy, carrying out the UNOIND remit for postwar reconstruction and stabilization. As the US Armed Forces maintain only a token presence in this area, it's fair to say that Eugene and Krupps are effectively the dominant military power on the ground."

The next image was brought up on the screens of the notepads of the assembled meeting. A picture of children mingled with skinny adults, smiling at the camera without a care in the world as they brandished AK rifles that seemed comically oversized in their tiny hands.

"This group that now calls itself the Hindu India Provisionals was founded by the same faction that started the nuclear war. The official postwar Indian government that had formed following international intervention established a secular state. Hindu India smoldered away in the rural hinterlands for a number of years without causing any real damage, but recently their activities have escalated. They have started attacking remote Muslim villages, massacring their inhabitants, raping their women, and abducting and indoctrinating their children and assimilating them into their own ranks."

I watched as the screen in front of me started graphically enumerating a list of the atrocities. Rows of corpses lined up and bleached white with caustic lime. The lime looked like flour and the bodies almost like pieces of chicken ready to be breaded and fried. Then there were the charred black houses and the alleyways between them littered with the naked bodies of women. Just images. No smell, no sound. Just pixels trapped inside our notebooks on our desks.

"The postwar New India government has, for the most part, exceeded international expectations. The Hindu India Provisionals were until recently a mere fringe cult group with limited influence. The population of India is still poor, but the government managed to hold a successful round of democratic elections. Infant mortality was dropping rapidly. And then, as of last year, things started going downhill."

"Who are these Hindu India when they're at home?" blurted out a voice from behind me. Williams.

"They are a fundamentalist paramilitary group who draw their strength mainly from the rural poor. For the last year or so they've been inexplicably growing and expanding the scope of their activities. They mostly kept their heads down in the immediate postwar reconstruction period, confining their activities to the countryside, far away from any center of power. They offer a simplistic solution to the national identity crisis brought about by years of foreign intervention. Up until recently, though, there weren't many subscribers to their particular brand of antigovernment fundamentalist religious rhetoric, as most of the populace quite rightly associated it with the sort of rhetoric that caused the nuclear war in the first place."

"So why the sudden escalation?" Williams asked again. "I thought everyone in the region had their fill of war?"

"Indeed, that is what we all believed. Our political scientists and economists have tried to come up with a hypothesis to explain the sudden surge in Hindu nationalism, but no one has yet been able to posit a model that's in any way convincing."

"Ah, they're just missing the battlefield," Williams said, grinning. "Just like us—we get blue balls when we've been away from the action for too long. Am I right or am I right, Clavis?"

And with that, all eyes were on me. I sighed.

"Whatever floats your boat, Williams. To each his own, I guess. All I know is it's best to keep your dirty thoughts to yourself rather than air them in public—it scares off the pretty ladies."

The NCTC man coughed theatrically in a plea not to let the atmosphere descend any further toward that of a high school locker room. We all settled down for the next part of the briefing, albeit with smirks on our faces.

"The ICC prosecutor investigated and found that the New India government's accusations were well founded. The prosecutor found evidence of crimes against humanity, mobilization of child combatants, and genocide. Accordingly, The Hague has issued arrest warrants for the leaders of this brutal paramilitary group, but as yet the New India government has lacked the firepower to do anything about it."

"Aaand that's where we come in, the poor bloody infantry!" Williams interjected.

The speaker nodded. "Exactly. Your mission is to capture the head of the Hindu India Provisionals along with three of the eight leaders. We are acting as a military proxy for the Japanese government and will capture these villains and bring them to account at the International Criminal Court. There they will answer for their crimes against humanity. However, I should warn you that there is a, uh, delicate matter regarding your combat status. As you will technically be tasked by the Japanese military as their proxy, you will officially be classified as mercenaries under the Geneva Convention. As such, should you be apprehended by the enemy, the standard terms of the Geneva Convention for enemy combatants will not be available—"

"Get captured and you're on your own, we don't know you—that's what you're saying, right, Phelpsie?" Williams was thoroughly enjoying himself now. If ever there was a man who enjoyed living on the edge, it was Williams. The greater the odds, the more enjoyable the challenge. In that sense he was one of nature's supreme masochists.

A more serious interjection came from Leland. "What I don't understand is why we have to somehow be representing the Japs in the first place. What's that all about?"

The speaker, Phelps, smiled indulgently. "The US is not a signatory to the Hague Conventions. The Hague has given the Japanese government the mandate to act; the US is able to intervene legitimately only as an external contractor."

Williams groaned. "Shit, so we're no better than Eugene and *Krapps* now?"

"Lame. This is so totally lame," Leland agreed.

"We're not some amateur mercs, you know," Williams said.

At this point Colonel Rockwell rose from the corner of the room where he had been sitting quietly up until a moment ago. "Thank you very much, Evan. We'll take it from here."

And with that, Evan Phelps of the NCTC was summarily dismissed. He looked somewhat doubtfully at the colonel—he still had plenty he wanted to say, no doubt—but in the end he scurried off, overwhelmed by the colonel's military aura.

Now it was time for the briefing to start in earnest. The room went silent. Just like a secret society, I thought. A world without outsiders, just us band of brothers. Phelps had been ejected from the room, of course, because what happened now was need to know, for our eyes only. But the instant he left the atmosphere also changed—the members of the conference collectively straightened their spines and sat alert. No more cocky teenagers putting on a show of defiance toward the world. This was now a sacred ritual of a secret society. If the scene now looked like some sort of macho fascist gathering, it was also somewhere between black magic and shamanism. We were a secret gathering here to participate in an esoteric ceremony.

"We were the ones who requested the mission from the Japanese government. We asked that it take this form," the colonel said without preamble. "There is a strong possibility that John Paul is currently with the official targets."

Suddenly my world exploded into life.

John Paul was in India.

Which meant that Lucia could be with him too.

"When the arrest warrants were issued by The Hague, Eugene and Krupps's operations department presented the Japanese government with a plan. Naturally, as Eugene and Krupps are the effective military power in the region. But we can't have E and K be the ones who capture John Paul. They'd pass him on to the ICC, and then he'd be out of our hands for good. The other targets are secondary and can be handed over if necessary, but we need to be the ones to bring in John Paul."

At this point I thought I saw the colonel glance over at me. Of the people in the room, the colonel and I were the only ones who knew about John Paul's grammar of genocide. We were the only ones who knew just how he was spreading his death and chaos around the world and the reason why he had to die.

Phelps had said that Hindu India had been inexplicably expanding the scope of their activities. Inexplicable to Phelps, perhaps, but there were two people in this room who knew exactly why. Because of the evil spell woven by that man. The pied piper who led his children to genocide.

The monitor behind the colonel froze, and I could make out glimpses of burning bodies on the frozen image.

Leland spoke up. "We accepted this mission so that Johnny wouldn't end up in the hands of the ICC, sir?"

The colonel shook his head. " 'Accepted' is not quite the right word. No, we actively went out of our way to pull some strings with the Japanese government. We made sure they turned down Eugene and Krupps's initial proposal so that they could give it to us instead."

"Yes, sir."

"If the US had been a signatory to the Rome Statute it would have been much easier. But signatories cannot make use of anti-terrorist evidence obtained by torture by third party countries. It's deemed inadmissible. We'd have to close down Guantanamo Bay for starters."

"So our main objective is to take out John Paul?"

"Not take out. Capture and bring in alive. Just don't let him fall into the hands of the ICC or the New India government."

We all understood our duty. It was obvious now why the civilian staffer Phelps had been kept in the dark.

"It's the basic drill: aerial drop. Pickup will be via UAV," the colonel said.

Someone asked what sort of unmanned aerial vehicle.

"Helicopter. In addition, we'll be laying on some Flying Seaweed to provide you with close air support. You'll be able to call on them for tactical bombing."

"What's the CEEP, sir?" Williams asked the question that was always asked. I could feel the room bracing itself.

As usual, the colonel answered without hesitation, compunction, or emotion. "One hundred percent."

"I almost feel bad for asking," Williams said, his smile sardonic now. He knew all too well from ten years of bitter experience that there was rarely such a thing as a mission with zero Child Enemy Encounter Probability. But he still needed to ask. To know. It wasn't just Williams either. All of us in the room felt the same.

Man, it wasn't a nice feeling to know you were about to go out into the field and start killing kids. Even if modern technology made it easier, it never quite became easy.

"Intelligence tells us that the hostile ground forces are comprised of roughly sixty percent minors under eighteen. All units to report for battle counseling starting tomorrow morning. The plan will commence one week from today. Gentlemen, you are dismissed."

2

The air smelled of the desire to kill.

No, not the air.

I did.

There was a figure on the crosshair. I pulled the trigger, and it went down. Like a twig snapping. Another figure emerged. It was carrying an AK. It wanted to kill me. I pulled the trigger again. The figure went down.

The act of killing wasn't that important in and of itself. It was the mission that was important. We had to do our duty, and if we had to remove obstacles as we did so, then so be it. Sometimes the enemy would try to stop us and attack. Often, the enemy's attacks were virtually suicide charges. In the arena of war, life was cheap. Cheaper even than the secondhand laptops used by the leaders to keep track of their troops like the cannon fodder they were.

It was as if the figures in my scope had never even heard of the word "cover." They just kept on charging into my crosshair. Bullets leapt out of my rifle and into the skulls of the children, exploding all the potential out of their brains and splattering it onto the terrain behind them. Or, occasionally, through their bellies, sending a mixture of their intestines and liver and kidneys to spray out. Or into a pelvis or thigh, cutting clean through an artery, causing the flesh to well up with an unstoppable flow of lifeblood.

Cheap lives. I started doubting myself even as I was snuffing them out one by one. Why was I shooting the enemy? Was it really just survival instinct? Or was that something imprinted onto me by counseling?

These killing fields. Were they really because of me?

"Of course. It's your own free will. Without a shadow of a

doubt." The counselor had smiled as he answered my question. Skillfully, without missing a beat. The interviewer must have been used to all sorts of curveball questions. Why should an existentialist one faze him? Psychology and philosophy have always been bedfellows. When most non-specialists—myself included—thought of psychology, what they usually imagined was an interdisciplinary subject that contained elements of academic psychology. Sociology, epistemology: related, but not psychology per se. Whenever a psychologist appeared on the news, what we really wanted to hear from him was a cocktail of philosophy, sociology, and other disciplines that wouldn't challenge our preconceptions.

I asked my question of the counselor during the battle prepara-tions that Colonel Rockwell had ordered on the last day of our BEAR neurotreatment—Battle Emotion Adaptive Regulation. The core members of the battle plan were lined up in the offices of a Viennese School clinical psychologist having our mental states adjusted. We had all received sensitivity maskers, local anesthe-sia to our frontal lobes, and extensive counseling, and now the psychological barriers to optimum performance on the battlefield were reduced to the minimum. We were getting ready to fight.

Special Forces were all subjected to these treatments every time they went into battle. Well, of course we were: we were the elite, the best of the best, so why shouldn't we use every means at our disposal to maximize our battlefield performance? It was just a series of standard medical procedures after all. And yet, even though I'd undergone the procedure countless times without incident, there was always a lingering doubt, and that was now starting to press on me.

"Without a shadow of a doubt?" I repeated.

The counselor nodded. "Absolutely. It's a wonderful thing for an emerging young mind to spend time carefully analyzing itself, but out in the real world you soon realize that you simply don't have time to spare second-guessing yourself."

He stopped and paused for words, then took a breath and continued. "Think about when you last caught a bad cold. Did you perhaps see a doctor, who prescribed some medicine and gave you advice? You then got some bed rest, took it easy for a couple of days. Now. A question for you, Mr. Shepherd. Who was it who actually cured your cold?"

"I don't know." I didn't want to give a stupid answer and have this young counselor laugh at me.

He pointed theatrically at my chest. "It was you, Captain. You, not the doctor. Your body fought off the infection, but more importantly, it was you who decided to find a cure. You were the one who went to see the doctor, to ask for a prescription. It was your intention, your will, your purpose. The doctor, and the medicine he gave you, were just there to help. People are allowed to use tools in order to help achieve their objectives, are they not? Well, that's what your frontal lobe masking and counseling sessions are: tools. After all, you were the one who decided that you would fight, long before you first came to us for treatment."

The counselor was right. What would be the point of deciding to fight in a traumatic theater of war and then choosing voluntarily to experience that trauma, with all its attendant side effects, when there was perfectly good preventive treatment available?

"What we counselors do is regulate your emotions so that they are at their most appropriate for war. You wouldn't want any ethical noise to creep into your consciousness during the heat of battle—it could result in a split-second delay with lethal consequences for you or your comrades. That's why we have these mechanisms to filter the world so that your brain receives it in a way that allows it to process information efficiently. That's all that happens when the frontal lobe module of your brain is masked and you receive your counseling."

Ethical noise. It was true that the battlefield was neither the time nor the place to be meditating on ethical dilemmas. Emotions were shortcuts to value judgments, whereas working through dilemmas using reason took time and effort. If a person had no values and relied solely on cold hard reason, he would never be able to decide anything. Pushed through to its logical conclusion, a supremely rational being would necessarily take every single little factor into consideration and end up being paralyzed by inertia.

Humans weren't the same as wild beasts, though. We had to decide who needed to be killed and who needed only to be wounded. A bear could kill, all right, but only humans had the capacity to truly fight. To choose to neutralize the enemy not from base instinct but out of free will.

"Your actions and thoughts derive from a network of extensive modules in your brain. You subconsciously refer to an internal library of judgments and actions. This is true of your conscience. Your nervous system is hardwired to favor cooperation with other people that will mutually enhance your lives and therefore your chances of survival. Well, this conscience manifests itself physically inside your brain. It has a specific set of coordinates."

"A module?" I asked, and the counselor smiled.

But I already knew all this. How the brain worked. And how unreliable our own sense of self was.

I kept it all pent up inside me, though, and listened to the counselor's continued explanation.

"Exactly. It's the same principle as the sensory masking that we use for Special Forces. I'm sure it must be quite unusual at first to have the feeling of pain masked so that only the knowledge of it remains."

Sensory masking. That grotesque form of preemptive battle-field anesthesia invented by DARPA. It took away any feelings of pain from wounds received on the battlefield so that the soldier could fight on unhindered while at the same time being fully aware of the fact that he had been hurt, so that he could tend to his injuries as appropriate. This bizarre disconnect was only possible because the acts of acknowledging pain and feeling pain occurred in different modules of the brain.

"In other words, if we mask the correct combination of the brains modules, we can do more than just suppress pain. We can also give the person certain behavioral characteristics that will help him succeed in his mission. Despite all the advances in neuroscience, our detailed knowledge of the inner workings of modules is still really only in its infancy, so we're not able to make precise adjustments, but we can at least do enough to ensure that our heroes in Special Forces aren't weighed down by an unnecessary emotional burden during battle."

His explanation of the brain's inner workings was just the same as the explanation that I had received that summer, in that hospital, back when I chose to kill my mother.

There were forty or fifty cross-sections of my mother's brain on display in the examining room. The slides were all in square frames, neatly covering the wall, so that from a distance they almost looked like they were a single giant slab of marble.

"So she's not conscious?" I asked, or rather confirmed, for the umpteenth time. Looking back now, I can't remember the exact number of times I posed a variation of this question. But it must have been a considerable number. It took me a lot of time and effort to accept that the question itself was flawed, and even after I came round to that fact, I was still never confident in my newfound understanding.

The doctor looked at the slides again and closed his mouth while he was thinking. Eventually, he opened it again.

"Mr. Shepherd. Are you a religious man?"

"No."

"Well, no matter—even if you were religious, this would still require some explanation," the doctor said. "It's true that we used to believe that consciousness was a two-way state: at any given time, a person was either conscious or not. Sleep was, after all, the dominant paradigm and our main frame of reference."

"Well, yes, people fall unconscious and sleep," I said, without adding the unspoken third option that they die. "Are you saying that there are other states?"

There were, the doctor told me, and then began explaining some of the developments in neuroscience over the past ten years. He explained how advances in mapping techniques had allowed medical science to identify which mental processes happened in which parts of the brain, and that so far a total of 572 discrete modules had been identified.

It was easy enough, with modern techniques, to perform sensory masking that blocked out feelings, but there were more interesting developments. For example, there was a documented case of a blind subject being able to consistently dodge a tennis ball thrown at him. The subject himself insisted that he was blind, and as far as he was concerned he did indeed live in a world of darkness. And yet the fact was that he was able to register an object coming toward him. In other words, his mind was unable to process the fact that he was seeing the ball in a different channel.

In this instance, there was nothing wrong with the subject's optic nerves. The reason for the disconnect was that the act of "seeing" something actually consists of two different components. In other words, the ability to see colors and shapes is processed separately from the ability to notice that something is there in front of you.

Yes, to "see" and to "perceive" are different things, processed in different corners of the brain. We might intuitively think of our sense of sight as being primarily related to the senses: "the apple is green," "the pillar is rectangular," and so on, but there is actually another part of sight that isn't so much a sense as a focus, and the eyes constantly send optic information to this part of the brain too.

So even the simple act of looking at something translates into a complicated series of parallel functions for the brain. It was mind-boggling to think how many different combinations of functions could be identified. Five hundred seventy-two and counting, the doctor had said.

"There are something like twenty different substates between the states that we popularly call *asleep* and *awake*. So it's not as if a person has a fixed sense of self. Some modules can be functioning while others are sleeping. And there are times when a person tries to call upon a module only to find it asleep. That's how we forget or misremember things. Intoxication by alcohol or drugs also falls into this category. Even as we're speaking now, your and my consciousnesses are—how to say it—fluctuating? There's no quality control on consciousness. It's constantly ebbing and flowing from strong to . . . dilute."

"A person is ebbing and flowing?" I said.

The doctor explained that we were now heading into the territory of semantics. A person—Descartes's "I"—could only be understood as a purely linguistic concept these days.

Take a crowd. If ten thousand people gather together in one place, that's unmistakably a crowd. Same with a thousand, obviously. So what about a hundred? Fifty? Ten people? How many need to be in a group before it can unequivocally be called a crowd?

This was what the doctor had been driving at. "Consciousness," "I," "self"—all became a matter of semantics. How many modules needed to be alive before you could describe someone as being the person you knew and loved? How many modules needed to be functioning before you could decide whether they were "conscious"? Society had yet to come up with satisfactory answers.

Take my mother. Was enough of her "alive" in a meaningful sense that I could still call her my mother?

That was the judgment call that I was being asked to make. How on earth was I supposed to give an answer?

So we had our emotions masked along with our senses.

BEAR was about anesthetizing part of yourself. Deliberately diluting your own essence. The domain of conscience was essentially an emotional function of the brain, not a logical one.

"Emotional judgments play a large role in the act of eliminating your battlefield targets," the counselor said. The screen in front of me was displaying an array of the world's horrors: natural catastrophes, towns turned into battlefields, hordes of starving children.

"For example, the act of rescuing bloodied victims with your own hands has an overwhelmingly larger impact on your conscience and emotion modules than a more abstract act, such as sending a donation to hurricane victims. It's stating the obvious to say that people respond more emotionally to what is happening right in front of their eyes. In contrast, the act of donation is essentially a rational one. But even then, emotion is ultimately responsible for many so-called rational decisions, because emotions form the basis of human value judgments. Most logic is really no more than *a posteriori* rationalization."

"So you're saying that when I kill children on the battlefield it's not the hammer of cold logic but rather my own emotions that are blasting their brains out?" I decided to try and push the counselor's arguments through to their violent conclusion.

The counselor just nodded as if this were the most natural question in the world. "Emotion has the ability to shortcut logic and deliver a swift, accurate response to stimuli. Even though people are reluctant to admit it, conscience can be just as powerful a driving force as the intent to kill. It might be fashionable to take the view that humans are fundamentally weak and prone to violence. But the fact is that even soldiers such as yourself are in thrall to the driving—and potentially limiting—force of conscience. It doesn't sit easily alongside your watchwords of ruthlessness and thoroughness. That's why it becomes imperative to use the technology at our disposal to temporarily subdue this powerful force, particularly with people such as us who were raised in America with its strong moral values. It goes against the grain, but our lives depend on it."

"So we're being brainwashed, basically," I said.

Again the counselor had an answer—well, this was a question he was used to answering, I was sure. His answer began with a nod. "I can see why you think that, but there's an important difference. With medicines, they say the poison is in the dose, don't they? You don't even need to overdose as such in order to abuse medications. Think of people who use tranquilizers as recreational drugs."

"So it's not brainwashing because we're voluntarily submitting to it?"

"Exactly."

When you entered a battlefield, you needed to be able to kill people with a light heart. If counseling helped in that then surely it was okay? If that was your intention then it should be fine? Were there no ethical problems about subjugating yourself to a process that suppressed your ethical compunctions, even temporarily? I just didn't know anymore.

There were actually plenty of my teammates who saw the whole counseling process as a farce from the get-go. What right did scientists have to appropriate tactical decision-making from officers who had earned their stripes the hard way? Soldiers signed up for Special Forces with eyes wide open. Why would they need all this girly counseling to firm up their resolve? If they weren't prepared for what was ahead, they shouldn't have signed up in the first place. If you can't stand the heat, get out of the kitchen.

The flip side of the coin was, of course, that Forces provided these counselors for us at great expense because they valued us as soldiers. Or rather they *had* to value us—public opinion in an advanced capitalist society such as ours had, in the space of a single generation, grown astonishingly intolerant of the idea of any of "our troops" being left to die in foreign climes. It was as if the general public had forgotten the simple fact that, in war, people tend to die. The result of this was that in our military system a soldier became a valuable—and expensive—commodity. Salary, training, the latest technology. Which in turn meant that no standing army could afford to support too many soldiers. So an industry sprang up trying to supply artificial substitutes for human fighters. Most such robotic entities ended up on an ever-growing scrap heap, but a small handful of inventions were granted the honor of a place on the battlefield alongside us human soldiers so that they could help us kill other human soldiers.

Ironically though, the further the field of human neuroscience was explored, the fewer resources there were available for research into artificial intelligence, which as a discipline had become pauperized. Once scientists had established that strong AI—computers that could replicate the more complex functions of the brain—and relative redundancy in particular were not on the horizon, interest in the field of AI for military purposes had waned. There were still simply too many roles on the battlefield that could only be carried out by humans.

Given the ever-escalating cost of training and maintaining soldiers to full combat effectiveness, governments were understandably loath to lose their prime military workforce to the civilian companies that sought to hire us away, so they began taking measures to prevent a general hemorrhage. One by one, countries enacted "gardening leave" legislation preventing discharged soldiers from joining PMCs before a fixed period of time had passed since their retirement. This, in turn, made it harder for the PMCs to cherry-pick candidates speculatively, so the stock of well-qualified mercenaries had soared.

As a result, no matter where you were in the developed world, a trained soldier was not something that you could afford to have break down on you. Maintenance became a top priority.

America had already had some experience of mental health care for its troops, stretching back to the previous century. Veterans of the Vietnam War and the Gulf Wars would return home and be troubled by recurring nightmares. Post-traumatic stress disorder began to eat away at the heart of America's military, and something needed to be done about it. A cure was needed.

What I was receiving now, though, wasn't the cure. It was the vaccine.

The goal of my counseling was to make it easier for me to kill.

"Essentially this is no different from an inoculation, Mr. Shepherd. We want you to be able to use your skills on the battlefield to your heart's content, so to speak. At the same time, it's important that we reduce your risk of psychological damage to the absolute minimum. When we send you to a country where you are at risk of the effects of infectious diseases, we're always sure to give you a battery of shots, right? Well, think of the counseling we give you as a vaccine against the effects of war. Now, I understand completely that you might feel you've already built up a natural immunity, but just think of this as a sort of booster, a purely precautionary measure."

I realized just then that this counselor had misunderstood, or rather misread, me. He was thinking that I was like my obstinate teammates who liked to make fun of the whole counseling process.

No. I wasn't a macho poseur like them. I was fully aware how fragile I was as a person, given the situation I was going into. I had to shoot and people had to die. If I hesitated, I would die. But could I truly take responsibility for the enemy I killed so that I might live? Was my essence of self strong enough for me to accept that burden and carry it on my shoulders?

I realized that I wasn't trying to evade responsibility for my sins. Rather, I was terrified that I wasn't worthy to bear those sins. That the sins themselves were nothing more than fictions, figments of my imagination.

In the heat of battle, when the specter of death loomed large, I was paradoxically most aware of being alive. I felt my own life force vigorously pulsing against the backdrop of the death all around me. Sure, look down on me and call me a thrill seeker or an adrenaline junkie if you like. But the fact was that I killed other people so that my own life span could be extended. If I needed to step over others in order to prioritize my own existence, then so be it. It was this sensation that made me go back to the battlefield again and again for more.

But what if this killing force inside me was not truly mine? Not my own free will, but rather something engineered by a combination of these Viennese School counselors and chemical substances? I was still alive, here and now, but should I be celebrating that fact in the same way? Was that life-affirming sensation a manufactured lie?

I realized that this counseling was a real threat to my *raison d'être*. Not because of the techniques or substances used, but by virtue of its very existence.

My stomach welled up with a bizarre, mysterious, nauseating feeling.

Could I ever trust my own motives on the battlefield again? I didn't fight for a greater good, to protect my family, or even for money, but rather for the overwhelming sensation of life-affirming reality. Most soldiers rationalized this motive, lying even to themselves, dressing it up as patriotism or comradeship. It was a base motive perhaps, but one that no wild beast would ever have on an instinctual level. It raised me above them.

But what if my will to kill was a fabrication, based on a foundation of lies? I would be absolved of all my sins, sure, but the sins were supposed to be *mine,* my burden to carry, my proof to myself that I was still alive. Without them, the thrill of raw, live reality was nothing but an illusion.

Why wouldn't someone just tell me that I was a murderer? That I was a killer?

I wanted someone other than this counselor to tell me that I had shed real blood, killed real people, of my own real free will. I wanted to feel what I felt during battle, staring over the edge of the precipice into the abyss. The rifle-shot cry that screamed *I am still alive!* existing, right here, right now. Tell me, someone, that this isn't just one big fake.

I wondered if the counselor could guess the source of my unease. My brain was being monitored right this moment by the electrodes that had been stuck on at the start of the session.

Neuroscience had come so far and had identified 572 discrete modules of the brain, but it was not yet at a point where it could read thoughts. Nonetheless, my brain would have been giving off all sorts of signals, and it would have been possible to deduce something from these.

The psycho-auxiliary software that was monitoring my brain had a real-time feed of this data into my interviewer's psychological model of my psyche, which was being constantly updated and adjusted. This information would in turn have been fed to the counselor via his earpiece, giving him suggestions as to the most appropriate next step for him to take. I noticed he was indeed periodically tapping and readjusting his earpiece.

The counselor asked me a question. I had no idea what part of BEAR it was supposed to relate to, nor how it was supposed to help prepare me to adapt emotionally for battle. I didn't know what the counselor was going to do with my answer. I didn't know how his questions so far were supposed to have affected my emotions or my reason. I was sure his words were affecting me on a subconscious level that I could never hope to know. As long as my will was still my own and it was truly still "me" in charge of myself, I would never know and never be able to know.

"So. Are you ready to go and kill some children?" the counselor asked.

I told him, honestly, that I thought I was.

The psychotech officer had adjusted my emotions. The senses I didn't need for this mission had been masked. My teamwork instincts had been medically boosted. I had used my AR contacts to practice, drill, and plan for what was about to come.

Everything was ready. It was the day before my departure to India. I stood before a mirror and pricked my finger with a pin until blood welled up.

It hurt. I knew that it hurt.

But I felt no pain.

3

The world changed the day the bomb exploded in Sarajevo.

The era of Hiroshima was brought to a close once and for all. All around the world the military suddenly started waking up to the fact that their theoretical weapons of mutually assured destruction were maybe not so theoretical after all. Nuclear weapons were back on the table as an option.

During the Cold War, nuclear weapons were the ultimate symbol of the eschaton. If the USSR and the USA went nuclear on each other, then a giant radiation cloud was sure to form a canopy in the skies that would herald an eternal nuclear winter. Humanity would perish. Nuclear war was to be avoided at all costs, and indeed, it had been avoided. Because people believed in the myth of nuclear apocalypse.

But that myth was exposed at Sarajevo.

A huge number of people died. Even so, military establishments around the world saw it as a "controlled" explosion. The casualties were confined to the target area. When politicians and generals around the world looked at the crater in the ground created by an improvised nuclear bomb, they realized that nuclear weapons might have their uses after all.

That was why, when India and Pakistan finally pulled the nuclear trigger on each other, the rest of the world wasn't overly concerned. It was, of course, a dreadful event, and one that shouldn't have happened.

But it was neither the end of everything nor the beginning of anything.

The world had already experienced Sarajevo after all.

We had become accustomed to people dying in large numbers.

Here, there *was* a smell.

A smell to stick in your craw. A smell that made you think that humans really were no more than beasts. Yes, India smelled all right. It smelled of poverty and sacred cows and feral dogs and shit and piss. It smelled of the pungent spices used in the preparation of every meal. It smelled of men, and it smelled of women.

And, of course, where it smelled of life, it also smelled of death in equal measure.

It was pervasive. The air even penetrated into our base.

We arrived at our Mumbai base ahead of our equipment and waited for the cargo shipment containing it to follow us. It was still on the outskirts of Mumbai, in the form of giant crates full of support equipment and Eugene & Krupps–branded weaponry, stewing in the hot air, waiting to be processed so that we could take delivery.

We had started to become accustomed to the oppressive heat and humidity. We spent our time at base camp reviewing the battle plan while we waited patiently for intel from our agents in the field. As soon as we had the tip-off, we would be bundled into our Intruder Pods and launched toward our target destination, and as soon as we captured our targets we would hightail it out of there in unmanned helicopters back to the nearest local base. Then, once everything was secure, we would escort our prisoners back to Mumbai by train.

It was a flawless plan. Of course, for a plan to work, things had to go according to it.

We headed out into the city once known as Bombay to acclimatize ourselves to our surroundings. New Delhi and Kolkata had been incinerated in nuclear infernos and were now somewhere at the bottom of giant craters. Mumbai had miraculously survived the nuclear exchanges of the war and so had naturally become a magnet for refugees from the rest of the country. Eugene & Krupps, the UN, and various NGOs all stationed their headquarters here for the postwar reconstruction effort, in this city that had once been the heartland of India's awesome computer industry.

As we walked through the city we came across a Eugene & Krupps armored vehicle that had come to a standstill amid an ocean of people. It was a Stryker, probably US Army surplus, and its path was currently blocked by a herd of holy cows that was ambling across the road at a snail's pace. On top of the vehicle stood a number of E&K PMC soldiers clad in Blackhawk

Commando Chest Harnesses. They had guns dangling by their sides in holsters, and one of them drew a pack of smokes from one of the many pouches velcroed to his harness. He lit up a cigarette, blowing the smoke irritably into the crowd. Some jokers had evidently decided to take advantage of the standstill to cover the olive drab Stryker in bright pink stickers of Ganesha, which made the normally imposing armored vehicle look somewhat kitsch.

You could buy sacred icons on every street corner of this city, from the old-fashioned portraits and dolls to garish stickers and Mob straps. Shiva, Ganesha, Hanuman, and pretty much any other deity who took your fancy. All shapes and sizes, every possible permutation of god and consumer good you could possibly want, and then some.

Amid all this, Eugene & Krupps made its presence felt.

There were enough sentries to man virtually every intersection. There were probably more soldiers than police in this city by the looks of it, and each one wore his own interpretation of the uniform. Some had full protective gear, others just caps, and others wore nothing at all on their heads. There didn't even seem to be any regulation-issue firearms—I even saw one middle-aged dude with an old-style Colt revolver. Talk about a cobbled-together single-action army. The silver-haired dandy glared back at us. I guess he could tell from the way we walked that we were in the same profession as him.

In contrast to the sentries who patrolled on foot, the men sitting on the Stryker were in coordinated uniform. They were disciplined enough to have passed for a national army. I figured these were probably the ex-Special Forces that Erica Sales woman had been talking about back in the conference room at the Pentagon.

Eugene & Krupps weren't the only private contractors involved in India's postwar reconstruction efforts, of course. The prisons for war criminals were run by the Dutch private security company Panopticon, and our very own good old Halliburton were tasked with public works.

Eugene & Krupps might have sounded vaguely middle-European in origin, but it was more or less an American company these days—over seventy percent of its stock was owned by US corporations, and most of its management ranks were staffed by Americans. I'd heard that there were even a couple of US senators on its board of directors.

In other words, the US was not a signatory to the Rome Statutes—and so couldn't officially be directly involved in the postwar reconstruction—but could still exert its influence in more subtle ways through companies such as Eugene & Krupps. The US didn't have to send in its ground troops in order to have a military presence. UNOIND might have tasked Japan with the postwar reconstruction and security of India, and Japan in turn tasked Eugene & Krupps as her proxy, but the US had ways of pulling strings behind the scenes.

The interesting thing, though, was that this powerful Eugene & Krupps had the direct backing of the Japanese government and the indirect support of the US and yet were still wary of the Hindu India forces. That gave us an idea of the odds we were up against.

Hindu fundamentalism. Caste discrimination had officially been made illegal long before the war. On paper at least. But centuries of entrenched social order can't simply be legislated away overnight. The history of India *was* the caste system. All countries have their own forms of discrimination surreptitiously built into their national psyche, and India was no exception. That was why Hindu India had been able to survive. And it was why they were now able to thrive.

We arrived at a riverbank and found ourselves in the middle of a giant shantytown of a slum. Rows of corrugated iron roofs ran along either bank, making the river itself seem like a blood vessel flanked by vascular walls of makeshift housing.

The people who lived and worked here were the so-called laundry caste. A subsection of the untouchable caste, which was really no more than an umbrella term for various so-called untouchable professions. People born here spent their entire lives doing other people's laundry. Social mobility was more or less unheard of.

This was another one of the reasons why the US didn't intervene more proactively in the postwar India reconstruction. They would have had to deal with these messy human rights issues head-on. As it was, the governments that did intervene—Europe, Singapore, Japan—soon arrived at an unofficial policy of turning a blind eye to whatever entrenched abuses there were.

Leland and I decided to go and have a look at the railway that the New India government would be using to transport us during the final stages of the plan we were about to embark upon. We climbed to the top of a knoll on the outskirts of Mumbai, and from there we could look down over the sprawling slums that engulfed the train line. There was a train speeding through at that moment, showing no sign of slowing down as it powered its way through the shantytown. Leland was visibly shocked by how little concern people seemed to pay the tons of speeding steel flying past them. It was almost as if they had a death wish, but in fact they were just supremely unconcerned; the old men, children, young mothers, all shades of humanity slept, ate, and did their business right next to the tracks.

"Doesn't the way the train runs through the slums make you think of Moses parting the Red Sea, sir?" Leland asked as he surveyed the scene from the top of the hill.

The slums used anything and everything as material—all kinds of trash were appropriated and incorporated. Galvanized iron, cardboard, hay, MDF, newspapers. The cornucopia of life that surrounded the tracks was like a flattened low-tech version of Kowloon.

Paupers and war orphans seemed to be drawn to the few working railroads that had survived the war. These refugees were the cholesterol clogging up the arteries of the train tracks. If trains were the lifeblood, then the people did actually cause accidents that stopped the flow of blood. The residents of the slums had no qualms about crossing the tracks or performing their bodily functions over them. It wasn't uncommon for a person to be hit by a train as he squatted down to take his morning shit. The Mumbai municipal authorities did what little they could for the refugees of society to try and keep them out of harm's way, but there were simply too many of them, and they kept on returning to the railroads no matter what the authorities did.

As bad as things were now, they had been worse. Before the

UN intervened, postwar India had been teetering on anarchy. Its decimated industry showed no signs of life, and most of India's famed engineers and scientists had died in the war. Before the UN accords took place, this country had been a Mad Max world, only greener.

A message arrived for me, flashing up in my AR contacts. The subject line read NATIONAL STOCK NUMBER X HAS ARRIVED. IMADS was a fully trackable courier service, just like Fedex. If you wanted to know which porter was carrying your gun over which ocean, it could tell you down to the nth degree.

"Time to head back, Leland. Our shit's arrived."

The delivery depot was next to Mumbai Airport's runways. It was overrun by people trying to slot things together. It was like Black Friday at a new Ikea. We were issued IDs at the entrance and given a printout of a map pointing to the rough location of our crates. We piled back into our truck and proceeded to start looking for our stuff.

It seemed like the collection depot was full of invisible elves trilling out to their masters. When you approached a tagged container your IDs started chirping in high-pitched beeps. The collection depot was vast, and much of the cargo there had apparently been abandoned unidentified and unclaimed. That was why they had introduced an audio-guided tracking system half a year ago.

Williams was driving, one hand on the wheel and one wrapped around a First Strike bar that he proceeded to chomp down on as if it were a Snickers. "We better get out into the field soon or these things'll give me a coronary," he said.

First Strike bars were developed as rations for Marines for when they had to land on enemy beaches and form the vanguard of an invasion. Gram for gram they were the most efficient way known to man of delivering protein and calories to the human body. They were definitely not something you wanted to get into the habit of eating outside of mission time—it'd be a question of which gave out first, your heart or your liver.

We were cruising along in the truck when Williams turned to me. "Yo, Clavis. You spoke to John Paul, didn't you?"

I had no idea why he would ask me that now, all of a sudden. "What makes you say that?"

"Just a feeling I had," Williams said. "You haven't been the same since that night in Prague."

So I told him. Then and there. All about the siren songs that John Paul had discovered with the help of DARPA—the grammatical tune that lured countries to their deaths amid a sea of hatred and mistrust.

"Pretty hard to swallow though, isn't it?" Williams said when I'd finished. He rolled down the truck window and chucked his empty candy-ration wrapper out without looking. "It's a bit like that killer joke."

"What's that?"

"You know, the British Army's secret weapon during World War II. The funniest joke in the world. British troops used to run through open fields, dodging artillery fire, shouting a German translation of the joke at the enemy, who dropped dead from laughter as soon as they heard it."

I sighed. It was a real talent that Williams had, taking the most serious of conversations and pulling the rug out from under them.

"Another one of your fucking Python sketches, I'm guessing."

"Bingo. How did you guess?" Williams said.

"Only you, Williams, could think of something as dumb as that to say at a time like this."

Williams shrugged and carried on talking. Clearly nothing I said would have any effect on his mood. But when he spoke, he was serious again. "So, basically, this thing makes people act like lemmings."

"I suppose that's one way of putting it," I said, looking at the forest of containers spread out before us. "The way I understand it, grammatical patterns in words transmit and reproduce themselves like a virus, and once a critical mass is reached, there's something about the hidden deep structure of the grammar that induces a mass state of chaos, and this leads to people massacring each other."

Williams lifted his finger toward me. "Here's one for you,

though. You know how lemmings are supposed to mass-migrate to their deaths when there are too many of them in a certain area? Well, apparently that's just a story, no different from what you were saying back in Prague about Eskimos and their words for snow. An urban legend."

"Huh?"

"Yeah, apparently the lemming myth originates from a Disney documentary of all places. Crazy shit, huh? There's this film that shows all these lemmings leaping off a cliff into a river, where they all drown. But apparently it was all staged. The lemmings had to be flown in from Canada and launched off the cliff using a turntable. The producers of the film even had to pay for the lemmings—they bought them from some Inuits, apparently."

I had to admit this wasn't quite what I was expecting by way of a response to my confession about John Paul. But when I thought about it, it was the sort of response I should have expected from Williams.

"So all that stuff about lemmings committing mass suicide as an evolutionary mechanism to regulate their numbers to keep their overall population at a sustainable level—"

"Yeah, bullshit, all of it," Williams said. "Apparently, that's not how evolution really works. It ain't all about survival of the species at all costs. It's the *individual* that likes to live on, and so it adapts to its environment, and the characteristics that help it adapt become the dominant traits that are passed down to the next generation of the species. Evolution is about what the species can do for the individual, not the other way around. A self-sacrificing instinct isn't much good from an evolutionary point of view. You hardly ever actually see it in real life."

I thought about this and what it meant. So the grammar of genocide couldn't possibly be an evolutionary mechanism. John Paul was either delusional or had simply made up a wild cover story to rationalize his evil actions.

I vocalized my thoughts in an effort to drive away my doubts. "But it wasn't a very convincing lie that John Paul told me then, was it? If he really had wanted to fool me, he could have come up with something better, surely?"

"Do you think he was trying to cover something up? There was some deeper secret he was trying to hide from you or something?" Williams asked.

No. That wasn't it, surely. That was the sort of thing that an over-possessive husband would do—kill his wife in a fit of jealous rage when he found her talking to another man and then invent a stupid lie when questioned: *aliens came down in a spaceship and forced me to do it.* This wasn't like that at all. John Paul wasn't trying to plead insanity to claim diminished responsibility.

"Anyhow, that's all academic now," Williams said. "What we *do* know for sure is that the sonofabitch is behind all these murders worldwide, and what we need to do now is take him out once and for all."

I glanced away from Williams. I realized that I wasn't particularly interested in capturing or killing John Paul. I was interested in him because wherever he was, Lucia Sukrova would probably be there too.

My target now was Lucia Sukrova.

I wanted to see Lucia again.

I wanted Lucia to tell me that she forgave me.

God was dead. God is dead. So what?

As long as Lucia could grant me absolution.

Of course, I wasn't about to share my selfish thoughts with Williams, so I kept my head down and carried on pretending to look for our cargo. Fortunately our ID tags started singing, and Williams drove on.

4

Seaweed to passengers. Calling Flying Seaweed to all passengers. Brace yourselves for high-altitude drop. Over.

We were ready when we heard the pilot's voice come over the loudspeakers in the cargo bay.

The Flying Seaweed of which the captain spoke was hurtling through the sky, a miracle of engineering and stability. Black and thin, it did indeed from a distance look like its namesake. If there was such a thing as a type of seaweed that was a hundred meters long and fitted with jet engines, that is.

If a satellite was looking down on us now it would have

seen a monolith cutting through a forest of clouds. The Flying
Seaweed did technically have parts that functioned like wings,
but they were so long and streamlined that you'd be hard-pressed
to describe them as such.

It would have been impossible to tell just by looking where
the belly of this bizarre-looking aerial assault craft was. It would
also have been impossible to discern that, instead of its more
usual payload of incendiary bombs, it was currently carrying a
cargo of Intruder Pods as it flew into the heartland of crater-
pockmarked India, using its assortment of precision micro-flaps
to help guide its flight.

In the cargo bay, we busied ourselves with preparations for
our impending descent. As always, there were a million and one
last-minute checks to be performed. The final Pod check was
particularly important because if the Pod didn't activate, then
it would effectively end up being hurled from a great height
toward the ground and its doom.

Once the Pod checks were complete the medical staff came
to insert tubes into our nostrils.

"Hot damn, that's the stuff! Give it to papa!" Williams shouted,
ripping the tubes from his nose as soon as the technicians had
given him his dose. "That bromance juice sure does get you going.
Clavis, buddy, I sure wish you could be here with me in my
Pod right now so that I could show you how much I love you!"

Williams was kidding around even more than usual, and I
knew exactly why. He had sensed my unease and was doing
what he could to distract me. His buffoonery was supposed
to help loosen me up. But it only had the effect of driving my
doubts to a meta level. What if Williams was only acting that
way because the cooperation hormone injection—what Williams
called "bromance juice"— was kicking in? What if this was all
a product of artificially engineered mirror neurons designed
to make us feel that we all had each others' backs? I shook my
head. Our descent was about to start. I didn't have time for
these childish doubts.

The Combat Medical technicians pulled the apparatus from
my nose. Snot poured from my nostril, a reaction to the hormones
that had just been pumped into me.

Most of the medical treatment for Special Forces was outsourced to Combat Medical. Our BEAR counselors were also Combat Medical. Like most mature markets in a capitalist society, the military auxiliary service market was outsourced to the nth degree. There were companies that maintained and leased us our weapons, companies that operated our recon satellites, and companies that specialized in intelligence. Even the supply train was broken down into the smallest possible constituent parts: there were separate companies to provide food and water.

The business of war had become entrenched and was now a vital consideration in any analysis of modern warfare. Each individual component was only a small part in the grand scheme of the modern military-industrial complex but at the same time was indispensable. You couldn't fight a war without weapons. You couldn't continue a war without food. You wouldn't know where to start without intelligence. Private military companies became an integral part of the system, providing reciprocal services for regular armies and eventually becoming fully integrated into the system themselves. Dystopian visions of PMC behemoths with enough military power to threaten G9 countries became obsolete as PMCs were fully coopted into the system as interdependent suppliers of military services. At the same time, official armies were now dependent on civilian contractors to mobilize.

"Here, your ARs." Williams passed the nanolayer liquid to me. AR contacts had the potential to fall out during strenuous maneuvers, so during battle it was better to use nanodisplay film. I dabbed my eyelids with cream so that the nanolayer wouldn't form anywhere other than directly on my eyeballs and then dribbled the liquid into my eyes. The liquid quickly sensed the electric potential in my eyes and formed a thin membrane that would act as my AR display for the duration of the battle. The cream around my eyes insulated the rest of my face, preventing the liquid from setting anywhere it didn't need to.

"All units check AR efficacy," I called out, although by now this was no more than a formality—the other soldiers were already turning on their combat datalinks and checking the test patterns showing in their ARs.

"All correct here," Williams called out. His eyelids were covered in huge globs of the white cream. "And as per usual I'm tripping out on the test pattern." His eyes were wide open, staring into nowhere in particular, and he was grinning like a spaced-out junkie.

"Dude, you know you don't need to pop your eyeballs out of their sockets in order to see the test pattern," I said.

The test pattern had started coming up on my retinal film too. Complex rows of alphanumeric displays were swirling round, finding their benchmark for an alternative reality to be superimposed over the reality before me: a room full of Special Forces soldiers waiting in silent anticipation.

"Yo, panda face," I said to Williams, "wipe that crap off your eyes." I chucked him the towel I'd used to wipe off my own insulator cream. Williams tried to think of a comeback but ended up mumbling something lame about how pandas actually had black patches around their eyes and not white.

I ran a final equipment check. The BHI Combat Harness that I was wearing had a multitude of pouches attached, so checking everything bit by bit actually took a fair while.

"Hurry up, boss! We're all in our coffins already!" Williams heckled, but I wasn't about to be rushed. I double-checked at my own pace until I was absolutely satisfied that I had missed nothing, and then I joined the others in the coffins—the black Intruder Pods.

The Seaweed's loadmaster entered and shut the lids on the apertures.

All light disappeared.

The Pods were lifted up. There was a slight tremor and the sound of something slotting into place. I closed my eyes and listened to the sound of the servo moving the Pod along. I realized that the low-frequency waves being generated by the movement were making me feel tense, so I clenched my fists, opened them, and clenched them again. Then there was a stronger vibration, and the Pod stopped moving. I knew I was now fixed into position in the airdrop bay.

There was another mechanical sound, and then I heard the sound of the outside air beating against the walls of the Pod.

It sounded like cloth ripping and became louder and louder as the Flying Seaweed opened its belly.

"You've got the lead, Jaeger One. Godspeed to you."

And then I was falling from a great height.

Free-fall, as per usual.

Final guidance mode.

Unlike the time in Eastern Europe, our drogue chutes weren't due to be activated until the very last minute. Back in Europe we had landed some distance away from our final destination, but this time we were going to land right in the enemy's lap, and there was no time for foreplay. If we were to open our chutes at the same altitude we did in Europe, we'd be shot to shit by AKs and RPGs before we reached the ground.

Legs sprouted from the bottom of the Pod in order to help absorb the inevitable shock that was going to hit us as a result of leaving the chute opening to the very last minute. Four legs, very muscular—well, they were made out of artificial flesh—emerged to brace me against the Pod's upcoming near crash landing. From below, it would have looked like a bowlegged giant hurtling down. I'd seen this sort of landing in training before, and I was shocked at how real, how fleshy the whole thing looked.

Just before I was about to hit the ground, the machine guns attached to the thighs (if you could call them that) of the artificial legs started firing to secure the landing area. The recoil from the machine guns set the Pod vibrating. I linked in to the Pod using my AR, and I could sense the ammo being used up at an extraordinary rate. I connected to the external visuals, and I could see three or four freshly bullet-riddled corpses of enemy soldiers near the landing area.

I felt an intense shock run through my body, but the antigravity mechanisms absorbed the worst of it. The next moment the Pod peeled away from me like a banana skin, and part of the Pod detached itself from the main body in order to take the shape of a Pathbreaker Unmanned Aerial Vehicle that would provide me with aerial support.

"Jaeger One touchdown," I called and ran to take cover in the shadow of the nearest building. The other seven soldiers in my team landed in quick succession after me, and within fifteen seconds of my touchdown, all the Pods had entered self-destruct mode, their electrical parts destroyed by acid and the artificial flesh killed by having its supply of life-giving enzymes cut off.

I stuck my head out of the shadows to quickly confirm that the Pods were all dying properly and that the soldiers that had been shot by the auto-fire on our way down were indeed all dead.

The Pathbreakers that had emerged from the Pods were now in autonomous scouting mode; they were gathering information about the terrain and relaying messages among the team.

We converged on the building that we had identified as our target and slipped inside before the enemy had the chance to raise the alarm. Children with AKs charged us, and our guns cut through their little bodies like hot knives through butter. Outside was the sound of the covering fire and the chainsaw-like buzzing of the giant upside-down salad bowls we called Pathbreakers, and inside was the sound of screaming children.

We quickly killed all the children encamped in the lobby. Aiming for the leg or shoulder was simply not an option on a mission like this—it was shoot to kill from the get-go. Had we been facing adults, who had somewhat more predictable attack patterns, it might have been a different story. But children, children were fearless, and they never knew when to give up, and that made them unpredictable and dangerous.

The building was overflowing with children. The Praetorian Guard. Boys and girls of all shapes and sizes and ages kept coming at us, and we kept taking them down, one tiny shadow and one headshot at a time. Williams and I pushed our way down what once would have been a hotel corridor and started ascending a flight of stairs.

If this had been a battle between equals, of one modern army against another, the best strategy would have been to shoot to maim rather than shoot to kill. A severely wounded soldier didn't just mean one enemy taken out of action, it could mean up to three, as two of his comrades would be tied up getting him to a place of safety. But on this battlefield, life was cheap, too cheap, and there was no culture of stopping to rescue an injured comrade. It just wasn't done. As such, the optimal strategy changed: the safest course of action was to make sure that every single enemy combatant that you faced was instantly and one hundred percent dead. The leaders of these sorts of paramilitary groups would often supply their child troops with copious quantities of mind-numbing drugs to keep them revved up, obedient, and focused on battle. It became the children's only way of temporary relief from their harsh lives. And when a drug-addled kid was charging at you with an AK rifle, shooting off a limb or two was simply not going to cut it. Even a fatal shot to the chest or guts might give them time to fire off a final salvo or two in your direction.

That was why we always had to take them down first time. As I was calmly advancing and killing every child in my way, it occurred to me that Williams and I were effectively drugged up in the same way by our own superiors. We had subjected ourselves to nanomachine sensory-masking treatment. If Williams or I were to take a shot right now, we wouldn't *feel* any pain, we would only *know* about it.

So if the enemy wanted to stop us, they'd have to fire a lethal shot too.

I shuddered. If, for argument's sake, Williams and I had to turn on each other, the only possible outcome would be that one or the other of us would have to die. We would keep firing at each other until a deathblow had been dealt. We were no different from the children in front of us.

My ARs flared up: armored vehicles and trucks from all around the town were converging on the building we were in. Having said that, their leaders were in here too, so it was not as if the vehicles outside could start blasting at us. They could have the biggest cannons in the world, but they'd still have to leave them behind and come in here on foot if they wanted to get us without harming their bosses.

The enemy redoubled its useless efforts to try and stop us from advancing, screaming like angry angels as they charged. Most of the boys' voices had not yet broken, so it was impossible to tell just from the screams whether a particular voice belonged to a boy or a girl. A young girl, naked, breasts not yet formed, emerged through one of the doors. She had probably been servicing one of her commanders. She held an AK rifle to her skinny flank and started firing randomly in our direction. I calmly took aim at her naked torso and fired. Her flat chest split open and she collapsed. I stuck my head around the door frame to the room she had jumped out of. A man who looked like he could have been a commander was struggling to do up his pants. I shot him dead too.

At that moment I was in a perfect state. What I mean by perfect is that I could kill children without the slightest bit of hesitation. Anyone who thinks I'm stating the obvious—they were shooting at me, for God's sake!—is seriously underestimating the power of both human morality and emotion. You never knew when either of those things was likely to spark up at the most inopportune moment and influence your judgment. Even highly trained soldiers. Of course, even in a normal state of mind I'd be able to kill children without compunction if my life depended on it. Most of the time. But you could never quite say one hundred percent. Not if you'd been brought up as a normal citizen in America.

Humans can, on occasion, end up prioritizing love or morality over their own lives. We're warped. We're a perverse species, capable of sacrificing ourselves in the name of altruism. Never underestimate morality. As Lucia said, altruism is to a certain extent an evolutionary instinct and as such has taken root deep inside the brain. Plenty of soldiers were, quite rightly, afraid of this instinct taking hold in them, blindsiding them, controlling their actions when they least expected or needed it.

That's what BEAR was for. To protect against that worst-case scenario. Because the worst-case scenario would inevitably result in death. There was no recovery from it. That was why the ability to protect yourself absolutely against the unexpected encroachment of emotion and morality, even if only for that specific window of time, that little festival called war, where you were detached from society and a different set of rules applied, was so powerful.

I had been made perfect by counseling and chemical substances.

My ARs showed me where my targets were. On this floor. The team had the whole hotel under control. Our targets were trapped.

And then a bullet brushed my cheek. I ducked for cover as soon as I perceived the pain, and Williams fired off a salvo at the window where the shot had come from. Had my sense of pain not been totally subdued, I would undoubtedly have been unable to react so quickly and efficiently. I acknowledged the pain in my body without feeling it in any sense at all. A sniper had fired the shot from the fourth floor of a building some distance away. About five meters in front of me there was a girl whose head had just been opened up like a rafflesia plant. The sniper must have thought she was one of us.

"What do we do now, boss?" Williams asked, scowling. "It's not safe to advance. Should we crawl under the windowsill?"

I used my battle link to contact Leland. "Calling Blue Boy. This is Jaeger One. Your current location is the corridor on the opposite side of the target room from us, correct? Over."

"Roger that, Jaeger One. But there are also windows on this side en route to the target room. I'd say odds on that there's a sniper or two pointed this way too. Over."

"Let's smoke the corridors, boss," said Williams.

I considered this idea for a couple of seconds but discarded it. "No." It'd stop the sniper fire, but it'd also make it too difficult to fight off another enemy charge.

"Then I guess we just have to pray to God," Williams said.

He wasn't being facetious. I nodded and linked up to the Flying Seaweed.

"Come in, Seaweed. This is Jaeger One. What is your current location? Over."

I heard a crackle and over that the voice of the pilot who had wished me Godspeed.

"Just overhead, circling the fireworks. Over."

"Good. I need you to take a building out for us. We'll identify the target with laser. Over."

"Roger that, Jaeger One. Over and out."

I nodded, and Williams stuck the tip of his rifle out of the window. He used the SOPMOD laser pointer and activated his

ARs so that he could send a visual confirmation of the building where the sniper was hiding.

"Gotcha!" Williams smiled viciously. Data regarding our location and that of the target was beamed up to the Seaweed, and the pilot confirmed that the data had been received.

A few seconds later there was an almighty roar. Our hotel shook, and pieces of plaster fell from the ceiling. I stuck my head quickly over the windowsill to see what was left of the sniper's hideout collapse to the ground in the distance. The Seaweed had used one of its emergency Smart Bombs.

"Thanks, Seaweed!" Williams shouted, and he was already off, charging through the dusty corridor toward our final target. I shrugged inwardly and followed. Williams arrived at the door to the room, unstrapped a sawed-off shotgun from his back, and made sure it was loaded before blasting the door open. Meanwhile, I had a stun grenade timed perfectly, two seconds exactly, and I tossed it in. I plugged my ears and opened my mouth just before light and noise erupted on the other side of the doorway.

Williams and I charged in, followed by Leland's unit, who had joined us. I pumped a bullet into the forehead of a boy who was still floundering in shock from the blast of the stun grenade, and while I was at it I took out a half-naked young girl who held a PPSh semiautomatic in her hands. No doubt she had been one of the boss's bodyguard-slash-sex-slaves. In no time flat the leadership of Hindu India had surrendered unconditionally, either cowering in the back room or kneeling before us, hands in the air.

Williams brandished his sawed-off shotgun theatrically. "*Nobody* expects the Spanish Inquisition!" he cried.

"Who are you people?" one of our prisoners asked. No trace of an accent—his English sounded pretty fluent. Well, it wasn't too unusual for an intellectual elite or two to be mixed in with monkeys such as these. No doubt educated at Eton and Oxford.

"We're agents of the ICC. You know there are arrest warrants out on you sons of bitches—who the hell were you expecting?" Williams laughed. A little too diabolically for my liking.

"Mercenary scum. Vultures of war," the prisoner spat.

I was perplexed by this. We were US Army regulars, of course, but he was technically right in that we were classified as mercenaries for the purposes of this mission. If we were doing things by the book, I guess Williams should have said we were military proxies of the Japanese government here to arrest you on their behalf. But that didn't quite have the same ring to it. Anyhow, Williams didn't seem too troubled by such niceties.

"Yup, and it takes one to know one, buster," he said, his maniacal smile now twisted into something closer to a scowl. He and the Blue Boy team were now calmly binding and tagging the Hindu India leadership, who had all lost the will to fight.

All except one. "We are most certainly *not* the same. We are warriors protecting our holy motherland against encroachment from Muslim scum. We are on a crusade. The only God you worship is Mammon," the educated prisoner said.

But to be honest, his words no longer had any effect on me. All fanatics were the same. Regardless of which sect, which religion, which cult, which battlefield, which tragedy they were involved in. It was always the same type of person.

Williams, too, saw this and laughed. It was like watching a bad sitcom in reruns, he said.

In addition to the Indian leaders that we had captured, there was a white man standing in the corner of the back room, watching silently as we bound the others. I remembered that figure and that face.

John Paul.

"Good to see you again, sir," John Paul said with a smile. "I have to say, I am impressed—not just a spy, but Special Forces too." Now that I was looking at his face in the sunlight I could believe that he was indeed a former scholar, something I never quite saw when I met him in the dark basement in Prague. But there was one thing in common with the time I met him in Prague: his eyes were not the eyes of a madman but rather of someone who could not be more lucid.

"This is the day job," I said, taking off my protective goggles so that I could look him straight in the eye. "Where's Lucia?"

John Paul seemed overjoyed to hear me ask the question. "She's not here. And it looks like your target is not exactly congruent with the mission you've been tasked to perform by your country."

"I'm arresting you," I said, keeping my emotions in check. I taped his arms together. John Paul didn't resist.

I linked up with the Seaweed again. "The goods are in the shopping basket. Check her out. Over."

"*Roger, Jaeger One. Over and out.*"

Leland switched his guidance marker on. It would act as a beacon for the Seaweed's retrieval craft, which would now be here shortly. Our comrades who had been holding the line for us on the other floors were starting to arrive too.

"Get to the roof, everyone," I called out.

Leland's team had planted SWDs on the backs of the heads of the Hindu India bigwigs, and these now kicked in, forcing the men to start marching in the direction we ordered, even if they resisted and their bodies flailed behind them. No one could remember what the official name was of these contraptions that forced prisoners to march, but within I Detachment we called them Silly Walk Devices, or SWDs for short, after the comical way in which the body and arms sprawled behind the legs when the prisoner tried to resist. No prizes for guessing who came up with the name and where he got his inspiration from.

As the last of our detachment arrived on the top floor, a deep rumble shook the whole building. The enemy forces who were trying to climb the building must have triggered a sensor and activated a booby trap of water gel explosives. They'd probably destroyed all the internal stairs by now. The children would have a job getting up here.

We climbed the stairs toward the roof, and as we did so a bird's-eye view of the town flashed up in the corner of my eye. Images from the nose camera of the UAV helicopter sent down from the Seaweed.

We arrived on the roof and the right corner of my ARs started flashing. I kept a steady lookout for the aircraft, as indicated, and by and by a flying pig-like contraption entered my field of vision, closing in on us from the south. I could see various RPGs being fired uselessly at it—the only effect they had was to create a number of pretty little arcs in its wake—and as it approached, I could see it with my real eyes and at the same time could see myself and the hotel grow closer via the helicopter's eyes projected back at me through my ARs.

What a motley crew and what a bizarre situation, I thought. The miniguns attached to the helicopter were strafing the ground as it approached us, sweeping away all the ill-mannered resistance that was daring to try and fire antitank weapons in its direction. The underside of the fast-approaching aircraft was twinkling with muzzle flash as it unleashed a torrent of tracer bullets on soldiers below. This was one machine that was determined to live up to its privileged status as a people killer.

In no time flat the helicopter had reached us and landed on the roof. My comrades provided cover fire, suppressing the paramilitary soldiers who were trying to shoot RPGs at us from the road below. Williams noisily rounded up our prisoners and herded them into the helicopter, where he promptly fixed them with knockout patches so that fell unconscious. They wouldn't be allowed the opportunity to get up to any mischief.

The north section of the roof exploded and shards of rock flew everywhere. An enemy RPG had slipped through our barrage and hit us.

"Damage report from all units!" I shouted over the roar of our suppressing fire. The two soldiers protecting our north flank stuck their thumbs up. No one was hurt, but the enemy sensed weakness and started focusing their firepower to our north. There was a hail of bullets and more RPGs. The north wall was crumbling. Time to go.

"All prisoners secured!" I heard Williams shout. I gave the signal to withdraw. The team all pulled out their hand grenades.

"Jaeger One, sir, how many floors does this hotel have again?" one of the others asked.

"Four floors, each roughly eight feet high," I called out so that all could hear. Everyone did the math, pulled the pins, waited till the precise moment, and then dropped their grenades over the edge of the roof.

We heard the explosions as the grenades hit the ground in the distance. The gunfire coming from below subsided, and this was our cue to climb aboard the helicopter. With a sure hand

Williams deactivated the autopilot mode and took the helm. It took less than fifteen seconds for us all to pile in, and during that time Williams brought the helicopter fully under his control.

"Here we go, ladies!" Williams whooped for joy, and suddenly the g-force was pulling me down. The paramilitary stronghold started shrinking into the distance. The soldiers near the gun booth rained down a goodbye salvo on the soldiers below, but we were quickly at a height where neither the adults nor the children on the ground could have any effect on us or vice versa.

I activated my ARs and linked to the fuselage cameras. Through one reality I could see the faces of men satisfied with a successful mission and a job well done; through the alternative reality of the abdominal cameras I could see paramilitary troops firing wildly and uselessly up into the air and the makeshift beacons of burning tires.

As the scene drifted farther and farther away I could also feel the adrenaline in my body ebbing like waves retreating from the seashore. The battle was over. Now I could return to the dream, the dream of normality and everyday life. I could return until duty called again.

The long wait until the next battle.

And the long wait until I could next meet Lucia Sukrova.

I felt myself overcome with weariness. I forced myself to remember my duty and pull myself back to reality, and contacted the local base camp.

"Jaeger One calling. The battle is over and our duties discharged. The packages have all been secured. The jewel has also been secured. No casualties. We are now returning to base. Over and out."

5

The train was a relic from last century. It had survived the nuclear war and still chugged on today, a link between India's regions. Its antique simplicity was its strength. We had escaped the Hindu India organization's sphere of influence by helicopter and regrouped at a Eugene & Krupps frontline base, and now all that was left to do was escort the prisoners back to Mumbai by train as per the plan. There we would hand them over—excepting John Paul, of course—to the prosecutor from The Hague, who in turn would pass them on to Panopticon for safekeeping. Our duty would then be done.

The base camp was close to the Pakistan border. The atmosphere there was heavily charged. The handpicked Eugene & Krupps sentinels there would stand guard all night, scowling at the Hindu India–controlled hinterlands on the other side of the forest. The catering company that normally supplied E&K rations refused to come this far, it seemed—during the four days we spent at the base we never saw any of the garrison rations that we had grown accustomed to back in Mumbai. Not that I'm particularly complaining about the rations they provided us with or anything.

The Eugene & Krupps soldiers—technically "employees" I suppose, but if it carries a gun and looks like a soldier and smells like a soldier, then it's a soldier so far as I'm concerned—spent their days gazing into the surrounding forests. Leland asked one of them what he was looking for and received the answer that he wasn't looking but rather listening. The sound of a large number of people dying at once created a huge pillar of sound, a choir of tens or even hundreds of voices that rent the heavens of the Indian sky. The soldiers here called this sound a Ligeti. Some E&K soldier must have been a classical music buff and had decided to name the discordant wailing after the modernist composer who, among other things, provided the eerie soundtrack to *2001: A Space Odyssey*.

The E&K troops told us that they never ventured into the forest. A while back they had tried a massive offensive push in collaboration with UN peacekeepers, but it proved a massive failure. After that, E&K came to an informal understanding with Hindu India that the forest was the boundary line.

The E&K troops, then, were all interested in our story, as we had returned from the mythical land beyond the forest. What was it like? Were there corpses everywhere? It was as if we were all Captain Willard, returning from Colonel Kurtz's unholy kingdom beyond the border.

They eat their Muslim captives, right? No, they worship an idol

*made out of an unused nuclear warhead and decorate it with the
ears of their victims as offerings.* These tall tales might have seemed
ridiculous, but it was amazing how quickly people reverted from
being rational purveyors of information to Chinese whisperers
when lines of communication were cut off. When soldiers were
garrisoned in the asshole of the world, in the boiling heat, surrounded by hostile forest and with the threat of an unknown
enemy constantly looming, it was almost inevitable that stories
would be born about the horrors of war.

Stories of the brutality and inhumanity of the unknown enemy
were par for the course during war. So were ghost stories. Ghost
ships, ghost submarines, ghosts of German soldiers haunting
Lithuanian forests. Which was why I was hardly surprised that
ghost stories had sprung up here too: tales of swarms of ghosts
of massacred Buddhist and Muslim villagers who roamed the
forest by night. These were passed on from sentry to sentry.

Why did soldiers fear the imaginary dead when real death
was always around them?

Why should a submarine traversing enemy waters be worried
about ghost submarines when they faced the very real threat of
an unknown enemy minefield that could blow them out of the
water at any minute? Why should a soldier stuck in the trenches
worry about ghostly comrades beckoning him to the land of
the dead when he was up against the real risk of a deadly hail
of mortar fire? And yet people could always find ways of being
afraid of the dead. Even on the battlefield, where life couldn't
get any more real, people found ways of believing in fictions—or
is "delusions" a better word?—that could shock them to their
existential core.

There had been a number of times when I wondered whether
John Paul was such a delusion—a figment of my imagination that
I had invented to scare myself. A ghostly figure who traversed
the world to spread a trail of death in his wake. A mythical
monster created out of human fears. After all, even though I
had captured the man who called himself John Paul, I couldn't
feel any sense of closure. Could this mild-mannered scholar's
a capella song really have been the catalyst for all that death?

Dawn broke, and we climbed into a doubly reinforced Stryker

to begin our six-hour journey to the nearest railway station. We used KO pads to keep our captives unconscious for the duration of the journey, so when the time came to wake them up and bundle them out, their muscles had gone to sleep. The prisoners did what they could to loosen up their stiff joints as we roughed them out of the vehicle and onto the platform. One of the prisoners moaned about how we were abusing prisoners of war. He was one of the Indian generals who had given the order to use nuclear warheads on unarmed civilian targets.

"Kneel!" Leland's battle cell lined the prisoners up along the railway platform. The prisoners were made to kneel, and we kept a close watch on them. If any of them wanted to escape they would have to stand up first, one leg after another. Not too easy when you had eagle eyes watching your every move.

The prisoners stayed in position until they found themselves looking up at an old diesel engine pulling into the station. We had the front three carriages to ourselves, sandwiched by police wagons, and the rear carriages of the train were crammed full of passengers on their way to Mumbai. There were even passengers on the roof. A scene that epitomized this desperately poor country.

I wondered why these people were heading to Mumbai. Were they trying to escape the clutches of Hindu India or just fleeing from grinding rural poverty? I thought of the shantytowns where the laundry workers lived and worked and the slums on either side of the railway line. Was that what awaited the passengers of the train? Or would they end up as beggars on the streets? Did they have relatives in Mumbai who had promised to lend their rural cousins a hand? In any case, one thing was for sure: this train was a container of humanity ready to be dumped into the teeming ocean of life that was Mumbai. But if the passengers were just going to be dropped into the slums, the internment camps of poverty and despair, then they were on a journey out of the frying pan and into the fire. It brought to my mind the Nazi trains that transported Jews from the ghetto to the concentration camp.

The wheels started moving, rattling over the rails. It was a jarring ride—solid, but rough. A Kalashnikov of a train. It was hardly surprising that people occasionally fell from the roof on this sort of journey. A couple of hours sitting on the hard wooden benches and my ass was completely numb.

"I'm going to take a look at the prisoners," I said. I stood up and walked toward the carriage behind me.

Two of our detachment were in with the prisoners, watching them closely, while the rest of us were split into two groups, guarding the carriages in front and behind respectively. We had made it safely out of the high danger zone about an hour ago and were now down to yellow alert. If Hindu India had been planning to attack us, they would have done so back there. Whatever they might have thought about losing their top leadership, it was unlikely that the remaining Hindu India paramilitary were about to go completely crazy and attempt a suicide charge into territory firmly under the control of the New India government, UN troops, and Eugene & Krupps.

When I arrived in the prisoners' carriage, the apes all had their mouths shut, although they seemed to be taking their captivity in different ways. Some of them were paralyzed by fear the moment they stepped into the passenger car that was taking them to justice; others were trembling, some were indignant, and yet others tried to maintain a dignified silence—as if the monkeys had any dignity to begin with. The only thing they had in common was that they had become so accustomed to being switched off by the KO pads that they had learned not to show any sign of resistance.

One of the men, who had evidently determined that I was the leader of our detachment, opened his mouth. "It'll be interesting to see what happens when we get to our destination. Do you really think the cowardly government troops will be able to contain us?"

"Oh, no need to worry about that," I replied. "Your faithful followers won't have much luck if they try and spring you from your cells. Panopticon's secure facilities are like a cleaner version of Alcatraz."

"Panopticon? We're being taken to a private detention center?" he asked.

"A prison, strictly speaking. A correctional facility. Panopticon has been tasked to provide security for the New India government and the UN. You won't find any of your 'cowardly government troops' in their facilities, I'm afraid. Only elite private military forces, handpicked for their experience and security know-how. They're the best in the world. I wouldn't count on being rescued, if I were you."

The man didn't seem to believe me—his eyebrows were raised in a silent smirk. He evidently had no idea that this sort of thing was standard practice these days. He was an old man. The ID spot check we performed when we arrested him told us that he had been a colonel in the old Indian army. He was a product of a different era, a time when the state still did everything.

I left the old man and moved toward the back of the carriage where John Paul was sitting on his own, next to a window covered with iron bars.

"Iron bars, eh? You did well to find a carriage like this," John Paul said, staring out the window. He lifted up his bound hands and pointed at the scenery that was drifting by. "Look, that billboard there."

I only managed to catch a glimpse before it flitted by: some writing in what I suppose would be called gothic script, with a heavy, angular font. It was superimposed over a realistic if somewhat old-fashioned painting of soldiers.

"I came up with that," John Paul said. "The grammar of genocide isn't always dependent on the content of the message. You can sneak it into the most innocuous of everyday conversations, if you want to. But it's best if you can incorporate it into slogans and propaganda, like on that billboard back there. There grammar is at its most concentrated form. You can embed the grammar into sentences in different ways, with different degrees of concentration, but stirring messages like the one on that billboard really give you the opportunity to lay it on nice and thick and dense."

"What the hell are you talking about?" I said.

"I have this little theory. Consider this. It's not political extremism that leads to genocide. Rather it's the need to prepare for genocide that makes people express their opinions in terms of political extremism."

"What the hell? You've got it all fucked up," I said.

"If by 'fucked up' you mean that I have my cause and effect the wrong way around, then yes, I agree with you. But then again, I'm sure you'll agree with me that the fact that all it takes is a few words for people to systematically start murdering each other is also 'fucked up,' as you put it."

The Lord of Genocide shrugged.

Amber clouds hovered over the paddy fields outside. A pillar of light appeared in the distant forests, a Jacob's Ladder. Were there more massacres going on over there, perhaps? Was God sucking up the souls of the innocent victims with a straw of light? The vista looked almost like a caricature—surely if there was a god up there waiting at the top of that, it would have been the one from Monty Python.

Time was nothing to me anymore. If you'd asked me what time of day it was I would only have been able to describe it as being "battle time." A no-man's land where your sense of time and emotion was masked by your BEAR. I found myself being drawn into the rhythm of the train, which made this already endless and timeless period stretch out even further and simultaneously pass in an instant. It was like wading through jelly, and yet completely normal and natural at the same time.

I was drawn back into the carriage by another piece of Hindu India agitprop out of the window. John Paul noticed that I was looking at it and spoke.

"You'll notice how the picture to go with the slogan is rooted in the socialist realism school? I've noticed that beyond a certain point, right-wing and left-wing extremists alike tend to share the same aesthetic sensibilities, or should I say lack of—"

"You really are something else, aren't you," I interrupted calmly. "You fucking piece of shit. I'm not just talking about your genocides either. Even your friends over there, the fundamentalist nuts, you've been laughing at them while you used them as tools for your own ends."

"And you can't abide my looking down on them?" John Paul asked.

"Not just looking down on them—looking down on them

and manipulating them into killing each other. At least they have the integrity to get their own hands dirty."

"Yes. The problem is that I've committed myself to more than I could possibly do with my own little pair of hands. Unfortunately I just don't have the time to busy myself with the manual labor. But I do accept responsibility for everything they do," John Paul said.

"They'll be standing trial soon," I said. "The ICC will see they take their share of the blame. But not you. You're different."

"Back to the National Military Establishment for me?"

"Exactly. And after that, even I don't know."

I stopped speaking to try and read John Paul's reaction. Nothing. He didn't show anything. No fear. No resignation.

After a little while, John Paul spoke again. "I'm thirsty. Could you get me a glass of water?"

"How about a glass of 'quit your bitching or I'll slap you with another KO pad,'" I said.

"How hospitable of you. I think I'll pass."

"Where's Lucia?"

"Not here."

"I know she's not here, you fuck. That's why I'm asking you where she is."

John Paul shrugged. "How is that question relevant to your duty?"

"Maybe it's not." I felt myself getting more agitated, and my voice grew deeper and colder. "Maybe I just want Lucia."

"And you're prepared to kill as many children as it takes to get to her," he said.

I looked at John Paul. It was ironic. This was the first time John Paul had ever revealed anything approaching a human emotion. Sure, that emotion might have been animosity toward me. And it did make me angrier still. But there was also a little part of me that was . . . relieved?

"Sure, it's tough. But I was just doing my job."

I tried to give as bland an answer as I could, but it made John Paul laugh out loud.

"Tough? You're lying, and you know it. I know all about the emotion regulation that you go through before battle. So that you can kill children without worrying, either before or after. You don't even feel any guilt as you pull the trigger. I'm right, aren't I?"

I didn't say anything.

"And 'I was just doing my job'? Please. Have you any idea how many ordinary people, people who wouldn't hurt a fly in their day-to-day lives, have used that as an excuse to commit the most cruel and brutal acts imaginable? The Nazis who sent the Jews to the gas chambers were 'just doing their job.' The East German border guards who shot their own countrymen dead for trying to cross the Berlin Wall were 'just doing their job.' Just doing your job, eh? Well, if everyone 'just did their job' then we wouldn't have any need for soldiers or bodyguards. Jobs exist to paralyze the human conscience. Where did capitalism come from? The Protestant work ethic: do your job, save money, and God will be pleased with you. A job is a form of religion. The only thing that varies from person to person is how pious they are. Most people actually understand this on some level. They just don't want to admit it to themselves."

"What about you?" I said. "You don't seem to have any problem with your job of traveling around the world and massacring everyone!"

"Absolutely. Absolutely. You see, we're not so different, are we, you and I?"

"Fuck off!"

"But we are! I admit that I only cast the spell, of course. I don't pull the trigger or light the fuse myself. I have no direct involvement on the front lines. And what about you? Are you directly involved when you're in battle? *Really directly involved?* When you shoot and kill the children that are charging you? Do you feel the mixture of relief and guilt and revulsion that any normal person would feel? Or do you feel flat? Does your *optimized* emotional state wipe everything out and keep you calm and distant? Let's be honest with each other. You might be physically taking part in battle, but you're not really there. Something's missing. I'm sure the same goes for all your comrades too. You kill enemies right in front of your own eyes and yet you never feel the accompanying emotions or reactions. You wonder whether the intent to kill was ever really yours. You start to doubt whether you can take ownership of the deaths that you cause."

Bull's-eye. This man in front of me had hit the nail on the head, and I hated him for it. It bothered me that he could be so calm. He was so untroubled by the scene around him that it was almost as if he had been Photoshopped into the picture.

"That's right, isn't it?" he continued. "You don't want your work to trouble you, so your emotions are adjusted away, nice and simple. Factory workers wear protective gloves, and you wear a protective shroud for your heart. Or allow someone else to shroud it for you, at least. You allow yourself to feel nothing for other people's lives, not even for the lives of young children. In my book that's a far more cruel thing to do than the actual act of killing."

"Who the *fuck* are you to lecture me about cruelty?"

"Fine, fine, so let's agree to disagree. But let me tell you an interesting fact. The way that the grammar of genocide works on your brain is not all that different from the emotional regulation process that you go through before battle."

"Yeah? Well, we're different from *them*," I hissed, pointing at the Hindu India mob in the center of the carriage. "*Our* BEAR treatment is defensive. It's designed to protect us. It heightens our self-preservation instincts, that's all. We don't start performing stupid rituals where we cut off the arms of children just for fun."

"No, you're not that different. Defense and offense are just two sides of the same coin. The grammar of genocide takes effect by regulating the function of the brain that relates to conscience. Not so different from your so-called BEAR treatment, right? The grammar of genocide modifies your conscience, guiding it in a particular direction. It's no different from what you do to yourselves to prevent any residual altruism from surfacing, so that you can kill children unimpeded. It's about suppressing the activity of certain modules in the brain. The only real difference is that you use technology to do it, where as I draw on the primordial power of language."

"Sure, our counselors told me all about how people are basically good. Sounded like holier-than-thou bullshit to me." I smiled ironically.

"The problem here is with this word 'conscience,'" John Paul said, ignoring my cynicism. "This thing that we've come to call 'conscience' is basically the sum total of our value judgments. It acts as a mediator for the desires of the brain's various modules, calculating the risks and rewards of a particular course of action, and what comes out the other end—the optimal course of action—is what we call conscience. But it only takes a gentle nudge to one of the modules before that delicate balance is destroyed. The grammar of genocide only affects a tiny little corner of the brain, suppressing its function. But that's all that it takes for a society to fall into chaos, and voilà, the groundwork for genocide is laid. There's no fundamental difference between this process and the way you suppress the functions of parts of your brain before battle using neurotransmitters and counseling."

Hindu India created its killing fields under John Paul's spell. In the same way, I created a trail of child corpses under the spell of Forces psychologists.

John Paul was just pointing out the obvious. What could I possibly say in response to this?

One thing was different from that night in Prague, though. John Paul now seemed to get a rise out of needling me with his words. Was this just because he had his back up against a wall, and fear was loosening his tongue? Either way, John Paul was now in full stride. He even seemed to be enjoying himself. He might have been a good actor—but this just didn't seem like an act. It wasn't fear that was making him babble. This was abnormal. He seemed positively *at ease*.

Something suddenly occurred to me.

"You have a mole, don't you? Someone inside the administration."

John Paul seemed taken aback by the abrupt change of subject. "I beg your pardon?"

"I've been wondering. How have you always been able to escape us at the last minute? There aren't that many people who can get hold of the details of our plans. Just those of us in Special Operations I Detachment and the higher-ups."

"So what does that prove?"

"You said back in Prague that you used an NSA program to

look for the optimal position from which you could influence a country's media. Well, you might have been able to do that back when you were a researcher, but now? How do you get access to the program? And more to the point, how do you get yourself into that position in the society? You have an associate high up in the US administration, no? Or a supporter, at least."

John Paul nodded. "I'm not saying that I do or I don't. But what I will say is that even if there is a leak, I'm sure your superiors know all about it."

"What's that supposed to mean?"

"Well, every time I evaded capture, the pool of candidates of possible moles must have shrunk somewhat, no?" John Paul said. "Have you thought that maybe they were prioritizing finding the leak over killing me? That it's been more important for them to tighten the noose around the high-up mole, whoever he is, than for you to actually succeed in any of your missions? If something were to happen now and I were somehow able to escape, helped by inside information, I would surely lose my 'supporter,' I think you called him, in the process."

"*Calling Jaeger One.*" Williams was suddenly in my ear. "*Please come to the rear carriage immediately. Over.*"

I glanced at John Paul again and headed for the rear carriage.

"Clavis and I are cutting loose," Williams said to the others. He led me into the next carriage behind me where the civilian passengers were. They looked at us in dumb astonishment—they couldn't have been used to seeing foreign soldiers armed to the teeth with guns and flak jackets.

"What's up, chief?" I asked Williams.

"Something's following us. One of the passengers came and told us. Looks like a helicopter."

"Do we have a visual?" I asked.

"Not from our carriages. We need to get to the train's ass for some proper recon."

We pushed our way through the rest of the carriages until we reached the end of the line. The passengers swarmed around us, jabbing their fingers frantically toward the back of the train. We used international sign language to assure them that we understood—that is to say, we nodded our heads over and over again. When we reached the final door we swung it open. There, amid the noise, was a young boy, sitting on the roof, his legs dangling over the edge. He was pointing at the sky.

I looked up from the track.

"See anything?" Williams asked.

"No."

I put on my combat glasses and adjusted my ARs.

Now I could see a black dot on the horizon. A helicopter. Low altitude—virtually on the train tracks. It was closing in, fast.

"Chinese," Williams said. Just what you would expect for a civil war in a poor country. It used to be Russians who supplied arms to the Third World; now China was the go-to country of choice. A basic Chinese battle helicopter was a fraction of the price of the high-tech American or European models. Most AKs going around these days were actually Chinese rip-offs too.

In other words, a Chinese-made helicopter closing in on us could have meant any number of things. It could be the Pakistan Army, Hindu India, the New India Army, or Eugene & Krupps.

Looking closer, I could see what looked like machine guns attached to its sides.

"Calling Blue Boy, this is Jaeger One. There is an armed helicopter closing in from the rear of—"

I had already turned and started heading back into the carriage, but suddenly I was cut off by the fact that the front end of the car was speeding toward me. For some reason the whole carriage was drifting behind me. It took me a split second to realize that it had come to a sudden stop and its contents were being tossed around like clothes in a washing machine.

And then I realized that I had been out cold. For how long? A minute? An hour?

There was a high-pitched ringing in my ear, and I felt curiously dissociated from my surroundings. It reminded me of how I felt in the hospital that summer when I killed Mom. I felt a squirming sensation all over my body. No doubt it was my SmartSuit, diagnosing my injuries and adjusting accordingly to stem any open wounds and compensate for any bruising.

The passenger seats were to my right and the ceiling was to my left. I paused to consider which way gravity was.

I felt like I was trapped in a one-dimensional world, except instead of there being only one dimension, there was only one sense: sight. I could see, but I couldn't work out my x and y axes. Most of the passengers were piled up on the side where the window was. Williams too. I could see a bloody arm protruding from the layer of people. I vaguely remembered seeing something like this in a movie once, but I couldn't remember which one.

Presently, I could hear something that sounded like fireworks in the distance.

Ah, gunfire, I thought to myself, and tried to move my body. I'd been bruised all over, but fortunately nothing more serious than that. I knew that I'd been hurt, and I knew where I'd been hurt, but as I didn't feel the pain I was able to move without trouble. I exited the carriage from the rear door.

The rail tracks seemed to have moved over to our right.

The carriages toward the front of the train didn't seem to have shifted quite so much. We must have been thrown around by a centrifugal force. The coupling had broken off, and we had been slingshotted into the air. I couldn't begin to imagine how far the people on the roof had been thrown. Our whole carriage was lying on its side. I ignored the buzzing in my ears to look over toward the train cars way in front: one was on fire. There was a black metallic vehicle skimming the ground, borne aloft by a rotary wing. And I could see figures in the distance, dancing the dance of Special Forces, moving in elegant formation.

A bullet flew in my direction and landed right in front of me.

That jerked me back to reality. I leapt for cover behind the overturned carriage. From this distance the figures up front were mere specters; I could barely even see them in their camouflage gear. I activated my ARs—any of the vanguard who had survived would be engaging with our ambushers now, so I called for a status update.

I didn't have time to be looking at their names individually. Cardiac arrest. No response. Arm torn off. Broken legs. Having said that, my own entry showed multiple fractures and internal hemorrhaging, and I was still combat effective, so our SmartSuit injury sensors weren't the be-all and end-all.

"Blue Boy! This is Jaeger One calling Blue Boy! Do you read me?"

No response.

Using the carriage for cover I moved toward the action as quickly as was prudent under the circumstances. The screams and groans of the passengers who were still conscious melded together to form an unearthly cacophony. This must have been what the Ligeti sounded like to the Eugene & Krupps sentinels. Some of the passengers were now crawling out through the door and stumbling away to freedom. The lucky ones were starting to recover.

And then one of the survivors who tried to run ahead of me had his face blown off. A bullet intended for me, no doubt.

I retreated back into the shadows and decided to try Leland's team again.

"Blue Boy. Are you there, Blue Boy? Blue Boy?"

This time I was met by what seemed like an excessively cheerful reply.

"Blue Boy here! Is this Jaeger One? Over."

Shit, I'd forgotten to state my name.

"Affirmative, this is Jaeger One. My position is currently four carriages back from yours. What's your status there? Over."

"The engine appears to have been blown up, sir." Leland still sounded as cheerful as ever. *"Immediately after the explosion we were attacked and surrounded by airborne assault troops. We're currently exchanging fire with them. We're all trapped inside the overturned carriage. They're using their machine guns to open holes in the walls, sir! Over!"*

Like a Clint Eastwood movie, I remembered. A movie where the side of a bus was opened up by machine-gun fire. Clint played a detective whose job it was to defend a woman who was a key witness in a case and was being targeted by crooked cops. And that made me think of the person we had been tasked to guard: John Paul.

"What about the prisoners? Over."

"We can't tell what's happening in the next carriage, sir. We're pinned down. I do know that the guys guarding the car aren't responding. SmartSuits are reporting them dead. When I tried to

leave this car to investigate my left arm was blown off my shoulder, sir! Over."

Leland's voice was as positive as ever as he rattled off the list of disasters. Damn him—it almost made me laugh. But I could tell he wasn't joking. That was just the state we were in now, we who could perceive pain without feeling it. The Special Forces with our sensory masking. An arm ripped out of its socket? The SmartSuit would soon see to the blood, no worries. You could imagine the stories the guys would be telling down at the bar later. *Hey guys, I was charging along without a care in the world and fuck me, I never noticed that my own head had been blown off! Whaddaya know!*

"Are you hurt?" I vocalized almost unconsciously.

I suppose Leland was a bit taken aback to be asked such an irrelevant question under the circumstances. *"Uh, yes, sir, I guess I am. I can tell I've been hurt, I mean. I can't feel anything of course. No problem, sir. Pain's not too much of a—motherfucker! Clavis, they got Nelson. Shit! Nelson's down, sir! Fuck! Goddamn! Over!"*

I gritted my teeth and started advancing again. The enemy had our train car surrounded in siege formation. I took a hand grenade out and threw it toward the car.

A rumble. I took advantage of the collapse in their formation caused by the explosion to move closer by another carriage. From my new cover I looked out to examine the situation.

I could just about make out some figures in camouflage gear. Many of them were streaked with scarlet. I realized that these were open wounds. Stumps, even. Two soldiers standing near the point where my grenade went off had lost arms and legs. They were now moving for cover, most of their bodies camouflaged except for their newly acquired stumps that were spurting crimson blood onto the terrain. Leland's crew took full advantage of the lull to launch a counteroffensive, throwing a grenade at the enemies on the other side and following it with a fusillade. I used the opportunity to move closer by yet another carriage. Almost there. Almost ready to link up.

I performed another quick recon. We'd managed to kill a few of them in the short time since I launched my grenade.

But the walking wounded seemed impervious to their pain.

There were men who had lost arms or legs or were bleeding out but still maintained battle formation and were firing away. Who were these assailants? How far did we have to grind them down before they would die? This was like a zombie film, I thought. And not the twentieth-century sort with the shambling walking dead—these were the lean, mean, fast zombies of the early twenty-first century.

Sensory masking.

Finally it hit me. The enemy had received pain masking too. They'd had their brains messed with so that they could have their pain temporarily filtered out; they could sense when they had been hurt without really feeling it. The nightmarish vision I'd had back in the hotel while I was mowing down the children had now proved to be strikingly prescient. We were finding out what would happen when two groups met up—two groups that had both received BEAR treatment.

That's right. None of the G9 countries had ever had cause to meet one another on the battlefield, obviously. There had never been a test case where two equally technologically advanced militaries had been pitted against each other. Modern warfare, as far as we were concerned, meant asymmetric warfare in its truest sense. It meant rich white guys invading enemy territory and blowing seven shades of shit out of poor brown guys. That was what all of our plans and missions essentially came down to.

That was why no one had predicted or planned for or trained us for a situation such as this one. *A zombie shootout.* Our ambushers had evidently been at the receiving end of some fairly high-tech military support treatment before coming here. Technology that made them impervious to pain and indifferent to the fact that they were losing blood and even limbs in the course of engaging the enemy.

"The enemy has received sensory masking!" I told Leland.

"Yes sir, we noticed that! We'll just have to flatten them into hamburgers, sir! Over!"

I was lost for words. This was...grotesque. This just wasn't *war* anymore.

I admit it. I lost my nerve.

The mental image of both sides standing there, firing away at each other until we were literally no more than piles of mince-meat. It shocked me to my core. The fear of death is always with you when you're on a mission. Our job is to take that fear and link it to our desire to live. So it wasn't the fear of death that was paralyzing me. It was the vision of a battle taken to its logical conclusion of an eternal shootout without pain or feeling.

I hadn't yet reached the train car where Leland and the others were under siege. I wasn't yet close enough to properly engage with the soldiers who had taken ten bullets to the belly and lost their fingers and arms and legs and ears and jaws and cheeks but were still fighting. I was out of range. And worst of all, I was glad that I was out of range.

The limits of this battle were no longer the effective firing range of the weapons, though. The limit was now how far you could imagine yourself being pushed into the realm of the gro-tesque, how happy you were to keep fighting even when injured to the point of permanent disfigurement. The limit was the map of the mind that showed what to do to suppress emotion and feeling.

I was spurred on by guilt now—guilt that I had yet to join my comrades on the battlefield. I leapt out of my hiding place and ran full speed toward the carriage where Leland was holed up. Not a professional judgment call or a pragmatic decision, just a blind dash.

The world was a cruel place. For some reason, not a single bullet hit me during my desperado charge. I later realized that it was probably because our assailants were already retreating at that point, but at the time it felt bizarre, like I was being cheated out of my chance to take part in the battle. Why? Why couldn't I be part of it? I was frustrated, vexed, even, that no one was shooting me.

I slipped into the carriage where Leland and what was left of the crew were making their stand.

"Jaeger One, sir, how are things outside?" was the first thing Leland said to me.

The men were collapsed across the floor. Various parts of their bodies were soaked in red. Most of them held guns in their hands and even now were ready to counterattack. I realized that a hand grenade had exploded inside the carriage, and evil-looking fragments were scattered about the place, embedded in the walls and furniture and ceiling, leaving the room glittering like a bizarre planetarium.

I looked at Leland. Jesus. It wasn't just his arm that he'd lost.

The lower half of his body had been blown away, and his guts were dribbling out. His SmartSuit was doing its futile best to keep him alive. The floor—or, to be precise, what used to be the left wall of the train car—was covered in a slippery, half-congealed black film of the men's blood.

I looked around to see if I could spot Leland's legs. Nelson had an extra pair of legs in his lap and by the looks of things wouldn't be needing them: his face had been ripped off from his jaw to his right ear. You could see right through his exposed cheek to his upper teeth, which shone pearly white, making him look like a grinning skeleton that hadn't yet been properly cleaned of its skin. I picked up the pair of legs, and then realized that they might not have even been Leland's.

I handed them over to Leland anyway—they would have to do for the time being. He gave a strained laugh. I realized that his consciousness was fading. Ready to disappear for good any minute now.

"What's...happening outside...sir? The bastards...did... we get all..." Leland's voice trailed off and was gone. He was gone. All traces of consciousness in his brain, gone.

"Who knows," I said to Leland's corpse.

Outside, the thrum of the helicopter engine was turning into a high-pitched whine in the distance.

There were no more gunshots or explosions. They were replaced by the wailing of the injured passengers.

A Ligeti.

CHAPTER

FIVE

One.
Two.
I was counting the coffins.
Three.
Four.

I stared up at the sky for a long time. A real long time. Long enough that I never wanted to have to look at the sky again. I stared so much that the motherly form of the Globemaster gradually approaching the runway was starting to look like a whale or a dolphin, or maybe some nameless prehistoric fish. A black fish swimming through the gray June skies. And I was standing at the bottom of the sea. The fish swam through the ocean of grayness and eventually touched down gently in our vicinity and opened its giant womb to the world to release the eggs it had been carrying in its belly.

The eggs emerged from the womb. The eggs of the deceased. The steel fish gave birth to eggs of death.
One, two. I counted them. The coffins emerging from the gaping womb. The eggs.
The corpses that had been scraped up, patched together,

reconstructed from nearly nothing restored, draped with the Stars and Stripes, and tagged.

Five, six. I counted the coffins.

I wasn't the only one counting. The US Armed Forces were also counting.

They counted the coffins and let the appropriate people know of their arrival. One, two, three, four. To be precise, it was IMADS doing the counting: the International Military Auxiliary Delivery Service. Using the metadata embedded in the tags in the coffins. Fedex let you know when your parcel arrived; IMADS let you know when your coffin arrived.

Soldiers carried the coffins. I carried the coffins. Williams carried the coffins. The survivors carried the coffins.

Inside them were fragments of flesh.

They had been carefully pieced together and reconstructed. I caught a glimpse of the operation back at base camp. Technicians skillfully piecing things together. They needed to have something resembling a body before they could send the remains back home to their families. The technicians used genetic markers and the tags on the fragments of clothes to match the correct pieces of flesh to the correct bodies. The correct intestines, the correct fingers, the correct skin, the correct eyeball.

The coffins were full of corpses that had been fabricated just like that.

As I carried the coffins I tried to figure out if I was angry. My comrades had died. Many of them. I was allowed to be angry. I was *supposed* to be angry. I should be hating someone. The soldiers who ambushed us. Or the mastermind behind the surprise attack.

But the harsh reality was that the anger and the hatred that should have been welling up inside me was nowhere to be found.

Without turning my head I looked over to Williams, who was carrying the same coffin on the other side. There, in his face, were anger, hatred, sadness, just as they should be. Tight lips and a shining desire to kill the as-yet-unidentified mastermind.

I tried copying him by stiffening my lips and squinting. After holding the face for a couple of minutes I started to think that maybe I was beginning to feel angry after all. I didn't know who I was supposed to be hating yet, but maybe I could hate them once I found out.

I wondered if Williams's righteous anger, his anger for his fallen comrades, could be called a manifestation of the conscience. To be angry on behalf of somebody else. To hate on behalf of people who were not yourself.

I didn't have that feeling. I did feel sorrow, but that sorrow steadfastly refused to blossom into anger. And who was I *supposed* to hate, anyway? Our assailants? The mastermind behind the attack? John Paul?

I was empty. I had no idea who I was supposed to hate.

Not that I could share this fact with anybody. Not my buddies, not Williams, not Colonel Rockwell, not the counselors.

We had orders from above to receive post-combat counseling. To avoid developing PTSD.

Williams was angry. Really pissed, just as a real soldier should be. "Who needs that shit! Just let us at the bastards who attacked us! I'll shove my PTSD so far up their asses—"

He didn't feel any emotional trauma. Just anger toward the ambushers. That was what he was trying to say.

I tried to adopt the same attitude. I put on a show of being angry. *Esprit de corps* and all that. But then it was announced that any soldier who failed to turn up for his prescribed counseling session would face court martial. *You Special Forces troops are highly valued human resources,* we were told. *It's our duty to make sure you're properly maintained.*

I didn't need any counseling.

What I needed was punishment.

I needed someone who could punish me.

I desperately wanted to be punished for all the crimes I had committed.

"This beats any counseling bullshit." That was what Williams said when he left his wife and daughter at home to come round to my house. What did he want? Why, the usual holy trinity, of course: Domino's Pizza, beer, and a movie. I wasn't really in the mood, but then I had no good reason to say no, so I let him stay.

This was what we'd done when Alex died too, I realized as I opened a Bud. And Williams wasn't necessarily wrong when he said that this was better than any counseling. Whenever Williams or I experienced anything traumatic at work, beer and junk food and lazing around really did seem to relieve the stress.

I took a sip of my Budweiser. Definitely a different taste from the Budvar. Williams was chomping down on the pizza and choosing a movie from his own archive.

Williams didn't have much to say for himself today. Well, not compared to his usual self. I could tell he was fed up with the counseling, tired of forcing out the emotions that were allegedly trapped inside him.

The film started. King Arthur appeared from the mist, closely followed by his squire, who was tapping a pair of coconut halves together to emulate the sound of horses trotting. It was Williams's favorite, *Monty Python and the Holy Grail*. He laughed loudly at all the jokes as usual, but every once in a while he cast a glance at me as if to seek confirmation. *It's okay to laugh at this stuff, isn't it?*

Williams had been out for the count during the whole ambush, safely out of harm's way in the rear car. So he hadn't been hit, and he did not take part in or even witness the battle of the soldiers who felt no pain even though they knew it was there, the soldiers who turned one another into mincemeat. I was sure Williams couldn't forgive himself for not being there. Not being part of the battle that saw his comrades slip away one by one. The shame and the frustration of not being part of it was hitting Williams just as hard as the reality of losing his comrades.

"*None shall pass! None shall pass!*"

In the movie, the Black Knight was speaking to Arthur and his squire. The battle began.

Williams spoke. "It's scary how much Terry Gilliam looks like a servant in this, don't you think?"

"Well, he's supposed to be the servant, no? He plays the squire, right?"

"Nah, I don't mean that. You know. He's too convincing. Makes it hard to believe he went on to be a famous director."

I turned back to the screen to continue watching the film. King Arthur had just sliced the Black Knight's left arm off. Orangey fake blood spurted from the stump where the arm had been.

" *'Tis but a scratch!"* The Black Knight continued fighting.

Just like the battle in the train, I thought, gulping back some beer. Except we had all been Black Knights, the enemy and us included.

In the movie another one of the Black Knight's arms went flying off. *"Just a flesh wound!"* The knight carried on, kicking Arthur, hurling insults at him, bleeding from both shoulders. By the end of the scene he had lost all his limbs and was a stump on the ground, but he was still threatening to bite Arthur to death right up until the very end.

I remember, back in the mortuary in India, just before the bodies were about to be stitched back together, staring at the mounds of flesh laid out unceremoniously on slabs and thinking some dark thoughts. That the wings of the Meatplanes and the flesh of the Intruder Pods under their cellulose husks and the Achilles tendons of the Chicken Leg Porters were all made of the same stuff. The only difference was that one was human flesh and the others came from dolphins. But flesh was flesh. Both worked in the same way, both needed blood and a pulse to function.

I remember thinking how convenient it'd be if our bodies had metahistories. If each cell had its individual tag full of metadata, then how easy it would be to slot these piles of flesh back together.

Metahistories. Alpha consumers could spend all day staring history in the face in the form of the provenance of whatever consumer good they were considering purchasing. You could trace each individual ingredient of a Domino's Pizza back to where it came from. A microhistory of each constituent part: cheese, jalapeños, ham, pineapple, the wheat and egg in the dough. All were fully traceable, not just back to where they were made, but how, when they were harvested, which distributor transported them, how they were prepared. The history of the flour. The history of the cheese. Once known as "smart consumers," these influential early adopters did at least have the collective modesty not to want to have to refer to themselves as "smart," so their name was changed to "alpha consumer" in order not to offend their own sensibilities. They were a highly influential bunch, not afraid of spending great time and effort discussing the products, founding consumer forums, gently or not-so-gently encouraging producers toward improved best practices.

Some of these alpha consumers became real opinion leaders when it came to particular consumer goods, and every brand had at least one champion. These champions would take an advisory role on the forums, helping to create public opinion and in some cases having substantial influence over the sales of a particular item. They would take a particular type of shoelace used in a particular type of shoe, investigate its metahistory, and debate and discuss the merits of other laces (cheaper?) and even the materials used in them (would this type of fiber be stronger?).

Thus each consumer product became an accumulation of discussions and memories.

Having said that, we didn't actually need to have each individual fragment of flesh be tagged, as our lives were already replete with metadata of their own. We would have to make do with that for now.

If you had a free hand over someone's records—power of attorney—then you could bring up almost anything about them. Records of their purchases and movements. Records of all sorts of communications. Their personal albums and diary, of course, and even a computer-generated biography if you wanted one. A person's complete metadata in one handy volume. The editorial skills of the software programs that autocollated biographies were something else, and could make even the most mundane existence sound like a lifelong roller-coaster ride. Most people of my generation would be lying if they told you they hadn't Biogged themselves at least once. A thirty-year-old, for example, would have to wait only about three hours or so for a machine to render their life so far into a four-hundred-page masterpiece.

I thought back to those few days one summer ago when my mother was awaiting my verdict as to whether she would live or die. I had looked through all the useful documents I could find on her family pages and the guest account for her personal pages, but there were no Life Graph documents available. I didn't even know if Mom had ever bothered to have her biography collated. According to a report published last year, at least seventy percent of Americans had had biographies done at one time or another. It wasn't as if it required any effort—you just pressed a button and the software did the rest—and it was hard to imagine that there were too many people around who weren't at all interested in what a machine had to say about their lives.

More to the point, even if I had been able to access my mother's biography, would there have been anything that would have affected my decision? If I'd been able to read a full account of her life, as pieced together by millions of pieces of metadata, would things be different now? Would I have chosen to keep my mother in that ambiguous space between life and death? Would I have quit the Forces and taken a desk job in an office nearby so that I could visit her once a week to see how she was doing?

As it was, I'd outlived my mother, and the survivor can only guess at what the departed would have wanted. You'd have to be quite a narcissist to believe that those guesses were ever anything more than a subjective shot in the dark aimed at reality.

The fact was that the deceased always held dominion over us. Because it was impossible for us to experience what they experienced.

Apart from Williams and myself, the only ones left in I Detachment were Sean, Bob, and Daniel. It had been the worst surprise attack that the US Armed Forces had experienced these past two decades and the first time the US had ever been up against an enemy that was on a level footing in terms of training and firepower. We were the first Special Forces unit in living memory to experience defeat on the battlefield.

The corpses of the enemy soldiers were also all over the place, literally. One reason why it took a full week to fully reassemble the bodies was that our dead assailants were dead people in more than one sense. They were all PMC soldiers who had somehow "died" in the past—MIA on the battlefield, or abducted and allegedly beheaded by enemy insurgents. It had taken a week for their data to catch up with their bodies.

There were no records of our attackers having entered India through official channels. Dead people can't travel, of course, so they must have acquired fake IDs from somewhere. Perhaps from the Uncounted of Prague. In any case, we still had no idea where this well-equipped, BEAR-treated unit of soldiers had come from. Judging from the trace quantities of radioactive material found on their equipment we could speculate that they could have come through Pakistan, over the craters and through the Hindu India heartlands, but Pakistan was still a failed state following the nuclear war, and there was no way to get in to follow the trail.

Despite this, it wasn't really a big problem for us that our assailants would remain ghosts. Because we had been able to identify the prime suspect almost immediately. A mole within Eugene & Krupps: one of the directors, namely the senate majority leader. It was the magic of technology that brought him down. The oracle of SNDGA. The NSA's very own Deep Throat. A global game of Six Degrees of Kevin Bacon. It seemed that SNDGA held the key to all the world's mysteries. I wondered how many degrees of separation between the fine senator and the now bloodied and limbless corpses of our assailants.

A top-secret internal investigative team within Intelligence had apparently been watching the majority leader for some time. Each assassination attempt on John Paul had led them closer to him, and by delicately adjusting the details of the information they leaked to the senator Intelligence had been able to tighten the noose. The corpses of our ambushers were, apparently, the final pieces of the jigsaw puzzle.

I could still remember the exact words that John Paul had said to me just before the train had been ambushed. *"If something were to happen now and I were somehow able to escape, helped by inside information, I would surely lose my 'supporter,' I think you called him, in the process."* John Paul had fully anticipated that the majority leader would intervene to rescue him, even if that meant the majority leader would implicate himself in the process.

No one in the government wanted a public hearing and the associated scandal. That was why the White House and the NME swept the whole thing under the carpet. Of course, when it did finally all come out down the line it was a scandal the size of Watergate or the Iran-Contra scandal. But that's another story.

Legal action against the majority leader would have meant all sorts of things coming out in the wash: John Paul's close involvement with DARPA's research and the secrets of the NSA's Deep Throat. No, that just wouldn't do. So the government and the politician came to a quiet deal—he would retire from politics citing ill health and disappear from their world. He went on to work full time for Eugene & Krupps.

Meanwhile, my comrades were sealed in caskets and brought back to the US. The ambushers' corpses were also reconstructed, and following autopsies their bodies were repatriated to their various countries of origin. Of course there were also other corpses. When the engine had exploded the train was speeding through a curved portion of the track. The pent-up centrifugal force acted as a slingshot, hurling the rear carriages away in an arc. Williams and I really had drawn long straws that day, but many of the Indian passengers hadn't—they'd been thrown around like the contents of an old-style tumble dryer. The passengers sitting on the roof were simply flung into the heavens. The record holder was a child who landed a full five hundred feet away, head first, ramming his face and neck all the way up into his torso.

As for the Hindu India leaders that we had captured, they never did have to stand trial at The Hague. They never even made it to the Panopticon facility. They just went straight to their graves. They had all been shot dead, cleanly, one bullet per person, right in the forehead. The ambushers evidently had no interest in Indian politics. The entire assault was staged for one reason and one reason only: to free John Paul. He was all that the ghost soldiers had ever wanted.

And now there was really only one thing left to deal with. John Paul.

2

This had to be our last Seaweed drop.

We were flying through the African skies, en route to what was supposed to be the final leg of the John Paul saga. It was still a full three months before the whole scandal was due to break—soon, the twelve-member investigative committee would look into the irregularities behind the sudden retirement from public life of the former senate majority leader and find that the trail of the official cover-up led them all the way to the Senate Select Committee for Intelligence, the head of DARPA's research arm, various generals in Intelligence, Colonel Rockwell, and finally to me.

I wondered what Williams and the others were up to. We had been sheathed in our Pods back at the aircraft hangar at base camp, so we could only communicate by wireless.

"This is Mouse Two. I'm going for gold, Seaweed!" Williams was chatting to the pilot.

"Looking forward to it, Mouse Two. Commencing countdown. Over."

The copilot started the count. I could barely contain my rising excitement. Not because I was feeling tense about the drop. Because I was ready to carry out the first step of the plan. I had been waiting for it.

Lucia was going to be at our next destination.

"Enemy sirens have activated!" The copilot sounded nervous. *"Ground radar has detected us. How the hell? Can they see us or something?"*

"This is Jaeger One. Cut us loose now, Captain. Immediately. Over."

"What are you talking about, Jaeger One? They've spotted us!"

The copilot was losing it. Stealth bomber crews weren't used to the idea of being targeted by enemy fire just before they were about to unleash their payload. Particularly if the enemy was supposed to be some third-rate African tin-pot dictatorship.

"All you have to do is press the release button. Quickly! Over."

"But that's against all protocol—enemy missile incoming!"

I gritted my teeth and activated the manual override, preparing to cut loose the external safety hook from the inside. I pressed the buttons and pulled the manual release lever just as we'd been taught in training. I heard a shrill beeping in my inner ear and then a woman's voice. *"Priority override ejection request activated. Five seconds to release. Three, two, one, release."*

I heard the faint sound of the flesh hook releasing my Pod.

I was weightless—the Pod had been released. A moment later I heard a roaring noise, and the Pod was buffeted from side to side. Maybe the missile had hit the Seaweed. But I had no way of knowing anything—I was sealed off from the world, no way of making wireless contact, no way of speaking to the pilot or even Williams.

It suddenly occurred to me that all of our missions involving John Paul had started with HALO drops of Intruder Pods. It was never a straightforward land or sea assault. The only exception had been the secret agent business in Prague. Why was it that we always had to *emerge* from something in order to deal with John Paul? It was as if we had to experience an arcane birthing ritual before we had the right to engage with him.

The Pod calculated the variation in course that my early release and the shock wave had caused and quickly adjusted the thrusters that covered its shell. I knew that I had been thrown off course, and there was no longer any guarantee that I'd safely land anywhere near the vast surface of Lake Victoria.

I was falling. But I felt no need to pray.

"Here's the situation." Colonel Rockwell was briefing us in a windowless SOCOM meeting room. "Lake Victoria used to support over four hundred distinct species. It was a prime example of biodiversity in action. Anyone know what other name the lake was known by?"

"Darwin's Dreampond," said Williams. "Boss, is this going to be a geography lecture? Should I go grab us some popcorn?"

As usual, Boss ignored Williams's backchat and plowed on. "Until the middle of the twentieth century, the primary industry in the area was, unsurprisingly, fishing. I say 'industry,' but it was mostly subsistence fishing. Small, self-sufficient communities living comfortably on the lake's shores. Then in 1954 the ecosystem of the lake was irreversibly altered by the experimental release of an exotic fish called the Nile perch."

Not just altered—violently assaulted. The Nile perch was a delicacy in foreign climes, but in the lake it was a highly aggressive invasive species. The Nile perch thrived and were fished commercially and exported as far away as Russia and Japan, where people were prepared to pay good money for it. Ironically, this pushed its price out of the reach of locals. Not only that, the perch thrived by eating the cichlids native to the lake that the locals had traditionally used as their food supply. The only difference between the locals and the perch was that the perch preyed on the small fish so aggressively that they were virtually driven to extinction. The people of Lake Victoria had lost their heritage and their livelihoods in one fell swoop. There was no other industry in the area. The locals were driven to despair. Local women were driven to prostitution, and AIDS spread like wildfire; local men were reduced to scavenging scrap heaps to look for—ironically—Nile perch bones to gnaw on.

"But then the era of the Nile perch came to an end. Because smaller fish were driven to extinction, the plants in the lake that they normally fed on started thriving in their absence and soon started growing out of control. Water hyacinth—itself an invasive species—proliferated, deoxygenating vast tracts of the lake, smothering aquatic life underneath it and depleting the nutrients in the sheltered bays where the young fish could mature in relative safety. As a result, the Nile perch died out."

"So things returned to normal, sir?" Williams asked.

"No. During the 2010s some businessmen realized that there was massive potential in the lake that had been brought to its knees by aquatic monoculture. They released nanomachines designed to eradicate the water hyacinth, and then started to bring the lake back to life. The goal of these businessmen was industrial mass-production of a recently discovered technology utilizing a breakthrough in neuroscience: artificial flesh. Even today, artificial flesh is insufficiently sophisticated to transmit visual data or thought or sensory information, but the technology to manipulate artificial flesh into contracting at will was already well into development."

"Is artificial flesh made in Lake Victoria, sir?" Williams asked.

It was. Though most people didn't know that. Or that lube was made from seaweed.

"Strictly speaking, there's nothing artificial about artificial flesh, so it's not 'made' anywhere. It's harvested from genetically modified aquatic mammals such as dolphins and whales."

"You gotta be bullshitting me, sir."

No bullshitting going on here, Williams.

And the thing called caviar that you eat? Lumpfish roe with black food dye.

I spent some of our substantial downtime between Prague and India looking into all this. Artificial flesh was basically used only for industrial purposes, and it didn't really come up as a consumer good that the general public could buy. The only place you could find it in what you could possibly call a consumer good were the Chicken Leg Porters that you occasionally saw in offices or in the houses of the rich—and even that was a stretch. They were contraptions consisting of a sturdy pair of legs topped by a pair of long arms, designed to carry heavy items between floors and across warehouses, hopping up and down stairways or in and out of elevators. I remember looking at the online catalogues of one of the leading brands of Porters so that I could investigate its metahistory.

I clicked through the various metadata links, cycling through the details of the Porter's component parts. The outer layers were made of organic resins and highly malleable smart alloys. The operating software had its own complicated history, as did the internal balancer module. The smart alloys in turn had their own alternative prehistories, as they consisted of recycled metals that had rich commercial pasts of their own. Finally I arrived at the artificial flesh components, but when I traced their histories they all led me to the same dead end: a factory on the shore of Lake Victoria. That was where the flesh was "produced." There were no further details.

There were no further details on the web forums either. There was no lobby group, no alpha consumers who had any opinion whatsoever on artificial flesh. There certainly wasn't any discussion about the fact that the flesh came from dolphins and whales. Not that I had really expected there to be any discussion. It was only largeish enterprises and government organizations who bought Porters in any sort of quantity. They weren't exactly top of the list of any consumer group discussion. Consumers were interested in household goods and commodities in the private sphere. Food and vacuum cleaners, now, they *were* important. There was plenty of discussion about those. Capital inputs such as artificial flesh? Not so much. People see only what they want to see.

Most people, of course, weren't even particularly interested in the metahistories of the goods around them. Myself included, at least until Lucius opened my eyes back at his club in Prague. What right did I have to call out Williams for not believing this briefing on the provenance of artificial flesh?

"Not bullshit, Williams. Exceedingly not bullshit." Colonel Rockwell turned to include me as he continued. "The whole lake has been turned into a giant breeding ground for whales and dolphins that have been genetically modified to live in freshwater. The animals are then dissected at local factories, and the product is exported worldwide. Lake Victoria basically came back to life by reinventing itself as a giant fish tank."

"Jeez, how can you call that 'coming back to life'?" Williams gave his head a vigorous shake, as if he were trying to rid himself of the disgusting mental image.

"The production of artificial flesh is currently the region's staple industry. Its only industry, in fact. And it was all going smoothly until the inhabitants of the lakeshores started agitating for independence. The lake borders three different countries: Kenya, Uganda, and Tanzania. But its inhabitants miraculously agreed to forget the usual tribal distinctions and cooperated to unilaterally declare independence."

"And they made enemies of all three surrounding countries?" Williams asked.

"Effectively, yes. The coastal dwellers declared themselves to be the Lake Victoria Shores Industrial Federation and are now recognized as an independent state by the UN. The name might sound more like a chamber of commerce than a fully formed nation, but as their war of independence was essentially fought over trading rights, it's actually pretty appropriate. After all, given their effective monopoly over the world's supply of artificial flesh, their relationship with the advanced world is essentially an economic one."

"And John Paul is there right now?" It was the first thing I'd said all meeting.

"Yes." The colonel touched one of the briefing room's walls, and a nanoscreen appeared. It showed pictures of child soldiers carrying AKs.

"Captain Shepherd successfully tagged Lucia Sukrova with pheromones back during the Prague mission. We were able to use Tracer Dogs to follow her as far as Prague Airport. Of course, she and John Paul were using multiple fake IDs, so we were unable to track them any farther. But then we hit upon the idea of reverse-engineering tracking, or tracking via process of elimination. We investigated all the IDs of the people who boarded the plane at the gate the Tracer Dog led us to. We then followed up on their movements from the moment they left their destination airport. Most people went straight to their homes, or to the shops, or basically acted in a consistent manner. We discounted all these people one by one until we were left with a number of IDs who behaved unusually, avoiding certain types of checkpoints. We identified the people whose trail ran dry. It was a huge undertaking. A painstakingly dull operation," the colonel said, rubbing his beret.

"Anyway, the end result of all this is that we now know that John Paul is staying at this guesthouse, where he's bringing together all the domestic media. The anticipated enemy military presence is the Lake Victoria Shores Industrial Federation Armed Forces. They have no air force, but they do have antiaircraft missiles and, as might be expected from a country that encircles a strategically vital body of water, a navy."

"A navy, huh," Williams grinned at the very idea. "Africans on boats—now that's something I gotta see!"

"They have a number of corvettes and one fast attack missile craft inherited from the Japanese Jieitai."

"Seriously? Sheesh!" said Williams.

I, on the other hand, could barely keep my mind on the briefing.

All I could think of was Lucia Sukrova's face. The black streaks of eyeliner running down her cheeks as she turned away from me. She would be able to give me the punishment that I needed, surely.

Unlike our usual HALO Intruder Pods, the contraption I was now inside was designed for naval warfare. Its job was to pierce the surface of the water like a torpedo, entering at as shallow an angle as possible so as to best absorb the shock of impact, and then use its external flesh to swim toward the target like a bizarre mermaid. Like their land-based counterparts, these aquatic Pods contained virtually no mechanical parts, so they were virtually undetectable to underwater sensors that relied primarily on sonar. After all, the Pod was basically made up of the same stuff as aquatic mammals, the only real difference being that it carried a passenger inside it.

The only worry was whether the troops who had fired the antiaircraft missile at the Seaweed had spotted me. I didn't imagine they had any missiles capable of shooting down a small, fast-falling vehicle like mine midair, but I definitely didn't want them to be waiting for me when I hit the water below.

"Estimated contact with water in five seconds' time."

The Pod spoke to me.

"Three, two, one."

I heard a splash, and the Pod entered the water. Having said that, the angle of incidence was less than thirty degrees, low enough to soften the impact so that I barely felt it. The optimally streamlined shape of the Pod meant that the viscosity of the water exerted only the slightest bit of resistance, leaving the Pod to gently decelerate in its own time.

Once the Pod sensed that its speed had dropped enough, it bent its tail like a dolphin and deployed its fins that had hitherto been retracted inside its body. It started swimming. It was quiet below the surface of Lake Victoria, the silence only occasionally broken by whale song or dolphin calls. The Pod's final destination had already been programmed in; all that was left for me to do was wait and be vigilant for any irregularities. Once in a while water jets would roar overhead, pinging out active sonar, but the Pod was, for all intents and purposes, invisible to them.

Of course we were invisible. The flesh of this Pod was originally from inhabitants of this lake. The Pod was just returning to its natural habitat in a slightly rearranged form.

I wondered whether Williams and the others had gotten out in time, or whether they had shared the same fate as the Flying Seaweed. Come to think of it, I wondered whether the Flying Seaweed had met any particular fate, or whether it had safely returned to base.

I was flush with anxiety. My chest pounded with worry for my comrades.

More than that, though, I worried that I would be too late as usual. That John Paul had already spread his seeds of discord among the people of Lake Victoria and had long since fled the scene, taking Lucia with him.

The impulsiveness of my decision to cut my Pod loose caught up with me. If Lucia was no longer here, then this whole mission was pointless.

The Pod swam along for about an hour before informing me that we had reached our destination. It then warned me of its impending self-disintegration, advising me to double check my diving gear. I did so—I was ready for the water. I opened the lock on the hatch, and the waters of Lake Victoria started rushing into the narrow confines of the Pod. I climbed out of the Pod and shut off its enzyme supply. Finally, I watched it drift away and disintegrate into the water.

3

The lake is here to support our lifestyle.

That was the first thing that came to mind after I reached the shore and turned back to survey the moonlit waters.

Airplane wings. Pods.

Artificial arms. Artificial fingers. Artificial legs. Industrial devices. Porters.

It was to create these things that the artificially engineered dolphins and whales were bred here, waiting for the day when they would be butchered and turned into artificial hands or shock-absorbing Meat Seats for airplanes. The shores of Lake Victoria were dotted with factories, and the poverty-stricken children of the country had three choices: become one of the factory workers who hauled the animals in and dissected them, join the armed forces, or become a whore or rent boy to service the aforementioned workers and soldiers.

European and American transport vehicles regularly flew in to pick up the processed flesh that had been carefully canned so as not to damage the precious muscle fibers. The planes would fly in, take the cargo into their giant bellies, and fly away again. Once in a while the Tanzanian or Ugandan forces would make an incursion over the border to try and reassert their fishing rights, only to be ritually repelled by the foreign-PMC-trained local army that consisted mostly of boys and girls.

Such was life in this country. There was rule of law, but in name only. In reality, the corrupt bureaucrats, in cahoots with PMCs, ruled the country. A world without effective laws meant, in one sense, a world where anything goes, a world of unregulated freedom. But the young boys and girls who grew up here couldn't afford hopes or dreams because the system robbed them of all future prospects, and then the developed countries swooped in to take the precious artificial flesh that made our own lives free and easy.

I considered the grim irony of the situation as I finished stripping off my diving gear.

I hid in a nearby thicket and waited for nearly an hour to see if Williams or any of the others would show up at the rendezvous point. Nobody did. I resigned myself to going it alone and prepared my approach to the guesthouse. Our original four-man plan was useless to me now.

The shore was too dangerous. The navy corvettes carried out regular checks with floodlights. I didn't know if there were any land mines or sensors about the place, although I figured it was safe to assume that the closer I got to the guesthouse the more interesting the obstacles would be.

I decided the best way would be through the jungle. I carefully adjusted my nanodisguise. No leaves or branches here. The cliché image of military camouflage was actually much harder to pull off than most people thought. Leaves and branches started withering the moment they fell from a tree and changed in shape and color as they did so. It was pretty difficult to make a foliage-based camouflage that blended in perfectly with the surroundings.

After I was convinced that my camouflage was as good as it was going to get, I started moving. The speed at which I moved varied according to the terrain. Jungles were, by definition, a mishmash of different types of terrain, and even when they seemed impenetrable there was always a path through them. For the trained soldier, at least.

In a jungle such as this one, full of thick shrubbery and ferns and vines, it seemed ridiculous to have to clear a path when there were animal tracks to follow—or, in some cases, trails that had been made by humans. These were the "easy" routes, and anyone without special training would usually opt for these as a matter of course.

The problem was that there were only a few of these types of paths, and the enemy knew them better than you. If you used these you were practically begging the enemy to ambush you. No, there were no shortcuts in the jungle. You had to cut a path through the thick fern forests, cross the streams without bridges, and climb the cliffs. Never take the easy option. The British SAS learned these maxims the hard way, through their bitter experiences in the Malayan jungle in the 1950s.

I advanced carefully through the thicket, covering my tracks behind me.

I was taking the long way round to flank the enemy. The best way to avoid ambushes. It took more time, but the most direct route to the enemy was often also the route directly to hell. Best to assume that the enemy would lay on normal precautions.

Jungle warfare, in other words, was a delicate and complicated affair, not unlike a game of chess.

This was real freedom. The freedom to try and determine the safest route for myself.

It might seem at first glance that there was more freedom in taking the easy way, but doing that could result in a particular type of loss of freedom: death. Freedom for humans involved the ability to avoid danger. Freedom was taking into consideration all the risks and choosing the most suitable course of action.

I moved carefully, one step at a time, constantly testing the path before me. I soon came to the conclusion that it was a fairly ordinary jungle. A good balance of flora and fauna. It had evidently been untouched by the trauma that the nearby lake had experienced these last decades. Not that nature had to always be harmonious or well balanced, of course. Humans might have driven many species to extinction, but Mother Nature did at least as good a job of destroying her own. Evolution was not supposed to be harmonious. Evolution was about adaptation. Many species were born and tested by their environment, and those that were found lacking were summarily dismissed from the face of the earth. Only those who passed the test were allowed to survive.

I remembered what Lucia said about the concepts of the self and the other being products of the evolutionary process. Human consciousness and the emergent property of language were also products of adaptation by the survival of the fittest. Conscience, sin, crime, punishment—all also part of the process. Whether they were transmitted by genes or as memes, one thing was for sure—they were not products of the independent external creature we called the soul. So she had said.

"And yet," Lucia had said. "And yet genes and memes did not determine everything about a person." People were influenced by their environment, and people always had a choice. If we were blank slates, then anything was permitted, sure. But we always had a choice. We could compare and contrast and decide for ourselves what was important, what our values were, whom we loved, what we ought to love.

The birds flying overhead amid the jungle canopy didn't have that choice. They weren't free to choose. People used the phrase "as free as a bird," but birds weren't free, they only had one course of action available to them. That which was dictated to them by their genes.

True freedom meant to have a choice. To be able to take a possibility and make it your own.

That was why I needed to be punished, I said to myself as I pushed my way through the complex ecosystem of the jungle on Lake Victoria's shores. I hadn't been able to voluntarily accept the responsibility for pulling the plug on my mother. I needed to be punished for the choices I had made. No. For the choices that I had *not* made.

The mission I was on now was an assassination mission, and the orders had come from the National Military Establishment. As per usual. Up until now I had never thought too deeply about our missions or our orders. But Alex had taken personal responsibility for his crimes, his sin. Because there was no one around him who would punish him: no person, no God. Alex had been honest about his reality, whereas my eyes had been closed. I had told myself that I was killing for my country, killing for the greater good of the world. But it had never been my choice. I had never made the autonomous decision to kill. That's why issues such as sin and crime and punishment had never even entered my mind.

This time was different, though. There was no one from HQ or the Pentagon telling me what to do. This was my decision. I had come here, of my own free will, to kill John Paul.

I could see the lights of the guesthouse in the distance. It was a traditional colonial-style building, two stories high, with an atrium courtyard.

It was surrounded by a neatly trimmed lawn and patrolled by Lake Victoria soldiers.

There was one advantage to the fact that Williams and the others were no longer with me. It meant that I could do whatever the hell I wanted. I didn't need to worry about coordinating with the others, and I could act far more boldly than I would have been able to do in a group.

There was a full moon in the sky and it was dazzlingly bright. High visibility, nothing doing. I upped my nanocoating camouflage to the max. It couldn't quite turn me into the Invisible Man, but provided I stayed flat on the ground, I would be able to creep in pretty close without anyone being able to distinguish me from my surroundings.

I inched forward from the jungle clearing toward the guesthouse. The only thing that would really throw a wrench in the works at this point would be trained war dogs. Fortunately, I saw no signs of any.

The world's developed nations supported an independent Lake Victoria state because they wanted to secure a stable supply of artificial flesh. It was much easier to deal with one country than it was with three.

Maybe "supported" wasn't even strong enough a word. The war of independence wasn't so much an organic grassroots movement that had eventually borne fruit as it was a plan that had been devised and executed. The shores of Lake Victoria were by a long way the richest regions of Kenya, Uganda, or Tanzania—naturally, because the artificial flesh industry was far more profitable than anything else the countries had to offer the world. The businessmen who grew rich from the lake found themselves increasingly averse to their respective governments squeezing them for taxes as bribes all the time. They made their dissatisfaction known by grumbling to their European bankers, and in return they were met with gentle, seductive insinuations that they might just be better off if they decided to get together and go it alone, without their so-called rulers or countries squeezing them dry.

When the US waged her wars in the Middle East, she had hardly been able to just come out with it and say "I'm doing this for the oil" even if it was true. Any modern-day national army needed at least a pretext for war before it could be mobilized. But here in Africa, causes that were fashionable elsewhere in the world—justice, stability, basic human rights—were not quite so indispensable. Scratch the surface and the medieval mindset of conquest and plunder was still very much alive.

Anyone who knew the region well, then, was hardly surprised that all it took was a cold appeal to their greed before the wealthy inhabitants of Lake Victoria declared independence.

In terms of game theory, betrayal was still the dominant paradigm in this part of the world. In the early stages of any game theory simulation, the betrayers would always get an early advantage over the cooperators. On an individual level, the decision to betray the other players would yield short-term gains. Of course, after a number of iterations and after additional complexities were introduced, the cooperators would always gain the upper hand in the long run. But on this continent, life was still simple. The game had not yet evolved that far.

No, it had, but then the ethical code had somehow been reset, returned to its primordial stages, and the game had yet to regain its former complexity.

I finally made it across the lawn and merged into one of the guesthouse walls. I traversed the passageway that led to the inner courtyard and entered the guesthouse. The atrium courtyard acted as a conduit between the rooms all around it. Its centerpiece was a small fountain surrounded by palm trees.

I walked boldly toward the centerpiece, nanocamouflage on full blast, to scope out the corridors. Occasionally one of the guards passed through the courtyard in the course of his patrols, but even when he passed within a meter of me he showed no sign of noticing me.

"Good evening, Madam Paul." I went for my knife reflexively when one of the soldiers started speaking. But I immediately realized that he wasn't speaking to me, but rather someone behind me on the second floor.

"Good evening, Mugabe."

A voice I knew well.

A voice that had told me about the Holocaust. A voice that had lectured me about the inevitability of the evolutionary development of the conscience. A voice permeated with regret about her past.

Lucia Sukrova.

"How are you today, madam?"

"Well, thank you. I'm starting to get used to this place. Although it is still difficult for me whenever I see the hardships of the people on the outside..."

"Try not to let it bother you too much, madam. We are all so grateful to you both for taking the trouble to come all the way from America to help us improve our living standards."

"I hope we *will* be able to help."

"Has your husband—forgive me—has the deputy minister for culture retired for the evening yet?" the soldier asked.

It seemed that the story here was that John Paul and Lucia were a married couple. Of course, it was always possible that they actually had married since arriving here.

"No. He rarely sleeps. He's hard at work in his room."

"I do so admire his dedication to his work, madam. I hope one day to become a fine politician just like him."

"I think he's just an insomniac, really."

"But your husband is doing so much for us. When I listen to the radio speeches he writes, my heart is lifted up. He makes me feel that if only we could all pull together we could raise this country out of poverty and get rid of AIDS once and for all. He makes me believe that the fish will come back soon. That we can carry on exporting meat to make money and at the same time live off the fish that used to swim in the lake. He makes me believe that we can have it all again. That the girls who work and sleep in the factories will soon be able to go to school instead, and that children won't have to scavenge anymore through scrap heaps of offal and bones just to find enough to eat. He makes me believe in his dream that tomorrow will be a better day than today. Any person who can write speeches like that must be a fine human being, madam."

There was silence. Lucia had nothing to say in response to the soldier's words.

Sorry. Actually, my husband is here to make you hate each other.

Sorry. Actually, the only dream that my husband has is the dream that your skulls will be added to those scrap heaps of offal and bones.

I imagined those thoughts running through Lucia's head.

Dost thou, peasant scum, truly believe we come here to spread peace? Nay, villein, we command thee to fight for our own amusement!

But no. In all probability, Lucia was still oblivious to what John Paul was doing.

"That's...very touching. Very touching of you to say so. Good night, Mugabe."

"Good night, madam."

I watched Lucia retire into her room. The central room.

I waited for the soldier to continue his patrol and checked that he had left the building before dashing up the stairs. The soles of my boots automatically adapted to the flooring, helping me make a silent ascent. I felt like a ghost. These noise-canceling boots made you forget the fact that you had two feet planted firmly on the ground.

The door was open. I readied my gun and charged inside.

But Lucia was nowhere to be seen.

There was only moonlight, scattered and diffuse, shining in through the windows.

I quickly scouted the empty room. There was a desk, and it looked like someone had been working at it until a moment ago. There was a paper notebook and what looked like some sort of manuscript, and a fountain pen. The manuscript was titled *The Federation*, and on closer inspection it looked like a handwritten draft of a presidential speech. John Paul evidently did his writing longhand.

The notebook next to the manuscript was filled with code and strange words, far removed from ordinary English. It was evidently some sort of shorthand key that described the characteristics of certain words—their gender and connotations, looked like—logic symbols that described word and sentence orders and patterns of incidence. The linguistic jargon and code were all crammed densely together, and I couldn't imagine ever being able to truly understand what was written there.

Then I heard the sound of a safety lock unclicking behind my back.

"Hello again, assassin."

I spun around.

It was John Paul, smiling sadly and holding a pistol to my face.

4

"I thought that my rescue force might have killed you," John Paul said.

We were standing in a reverse snapshot of our first face-to-face encounter in Prague. This time I had my back to the bright moonlight and John Paul's face was bleached white by it. His expression was the same though—very sane, very sad. He was holding an antique, a Browning semiautomatic. A gun without an ID. A throwback to a time when anybody could use any gun to kill anybody else.

"They almost did."

"Ho-hum. Shame." John Paul pulled up a nearby chair and sat down, keeping the gun trained on me all the while. "Anyway. You showed up in time for once, eh? I've only just begun planting the seeds of discord throughout the Lake Victoria Shores Industrial Federation."

I looked into the eyes of this man who was now sitting before me in a rattan chair. His eyes were so calm and so still. Even though this unassuming middle-aged man was confronting a skilled assassin such as myself, he managed to exude an aura of quiet dignity that put me in my place.

It occurred to me that a religious fanatic who imagined himself to be the Messiah would probably also have this kind of assured charisma. The difference was that John Paul exhibited none of the trappings that came with a Messiah complex. No wild flash in his eyes. No trace of pride or hubris. None of the affected kindness.

"Why are you still doing this?" I asked. "Is this some kind of experiment to see how many people you can kill?"

John Paul paused for a moment and then looked down at the muzzle of his gun. It was as though he couldn't quite work out how it came to pass that he was holding this weapon of murder in his hand.

"I finished experimenting years ago. Do you perhaps think that I'm some sort of madman who is just itching to see how strong my powers are?"

John Paul's eyes stayed fixed on the cold, shiny Browning. Was he digesting the reality that he held in his hands a real weapon of murder, an actual object that could directly cause the death of another human being?

"I'm guessing you've never held a gun before," I said.

John Paul looked up. "You're right. Tonight is the first time I've actually held one myself. No matter how deep I was in a war zone, I never touched one, and I always stayed away from them."

"Yeah, why would you bother when you already have the power to massacre thousands without ever having to get your hands dirty?"

John Paul shook his head and chuckled. "It's not *my* power." He stood up. His voice sounded tired. "The language of genocide was always there in the human mind. It's a presetting, a default. I just discovered it, that's all. If you could even call it a discovery. I'm not that different from the first anatomists who 'discovered' and classified human organs."

"I doubt Einstein felt that way when he discovered the atomic bomb," I said.

"Cruelty is an inherent characteristic of the human brain. How is that so hard to understand? You don't need my grammar of genocide to see that people are intrinsically capable of great brutality. Murder. Robbery. Rape." John Paul used his free hand to gesture toward the hand that held the gun. "See? I'm getting ready to kill you even as we speak."

"What about primitive societies, or isolated societies that haven't even come into contact with the modern world? They're peaceful, aren't they?"

"No. That's a lie spread last century by scientists—or social activists, really—who had a political agenda. The truth is that these so-called noble savages can be just as vicious as us. More so, in some cases. They covet and steal and rape and kill just like we do. Margaret Mead's tropical Samoan paradise was debunked with the most cursory of follow-up research. She was, as they say, not even wrong. But one thing is for sure—plenty of rape and murder have gone down in Samoa over the years."

"And wars?"

"Of course! Why not? Why should the civilized world have a monopoly on war? There are tribes in obscure corners of the

Amazon rainforest that have never seen a white man and yet are happy to fight, plunder, kill, and rape. It seems to be a basic evolutionary need, passed down from generation to generation."

"But people can make a choice," I declared calmly. "I carry my sin around with me. You can choose to accept the responsibility for your choices. Saying that murder or rape or theft is just human nature is not the same as saying that any of these things are ever justified."

"Absolutely. I agree with you." John Paul smiled.

Well, that was anticlimactic. "What?"

"If the impulse to pillage and rape and murder derives from basic survival instinct, then so too do sympathy, love, and self-sacrifice. Our brains have evolved to contain a multitude of conflicting emotional modules, each one derived from a basic survival instinct. Some of these are redundant, and others have become positively counterproductive. A sweet tooth, to give you a trivial example. Great for when you have to compete for food, as it helps you absorb nutrients quickly. Not so great when you live in a world of superabundance and you're trying to stave off obesity and diabetes."

"So you're saying that there's nothing wrong with the modules that turn us into murderers and rapists—they're basically just *outdated*?" I asked, incredulous.

"Hm. I'm not sure if that's a fair way of putting it. 'Outdated.' That's a subjective concept. Orthogonal to the current social mores of the so-called advanced nations, perhaps. Anyhow, like it or not, the grammar of genocide is also one of these modules."

"What do you mean?"

John Paul looked past me, out through the window, at the night vista of the shores of Lake Victoria, where countless families were suffering in poverty, starving, selling their bodies, doing whatever they needed to do to get by.

"Okay. Imagine there's a drought. We're talking pre-agricultural times. Well, people have already learned by this time that by forming a group and cooperating with other people, you stand a better chance of survival in the long run than by betraying the others and just taking what you wanted. Maybe this was due to evolution and genetics, maybe due to memes, but either way, altruism or love, or whatever you want to call it, emerged as adaptive behavior designed to help preserve the self. So what happens when you have an unexpected outside shock such as a drought, and there is no longer enough food and water to go around? Does the entire community perish along with its evolution and altruism?"

I thought I understood what John Paul was trying to say. "So the grammar of genocide was just a way of adapting to food shortages?" I said.

"That's right." John Paul nodded. "The grammar of genocide is a vestigial module from a time when humans were not yet able to regulate their food supply. When other animals want to exert influence over their entire group, they use pheromones or scent to pass on their message and influence the group. But the nose was a relatively weak sensory organ, at least in humans. The best way to spread influence over a large group of individuals became language. If a person wanted to communicate with an entire group, rather than one to one, language was the only way to do it."

Acts of enlightened cruelty.

Mass murder for the sake of survival.

I shuddered. However primitive a group of people was, if they could communicate and show altruistic tendencies within their group, it became impossible to deny that they were in their own way a fully fledged society. The grammar of genocide didn't result from people becoming increasingly aggressive on an individual basis. I thought back to what John Paul had told me during our previous encounters—that the Jews in Nazi Germany also spoke using the grammar of genocide. No. This definitely wasn't a module that affected people at an individual level. It was a module that started functioning only on a structural level after it had been transmitted to a given number of people within a group. Their value judgments were bent in a certain direction. *There's a genocide brewing. There's a massacre on the horizon.* The mood was set. And then once that society passed a certain threshold, those people who had a conscience-related module suppressed by the grammar of genocide would start taking matters into their own hands and engage in all sorts of atrocities.

But then I remembered Williams's story about the lemmings. Individuals didn't tend to evolve in ways that caused them to act against their own self-interest. The phenomenon of lemming mass suicide was virtually unheard of in real life.

"The grammar of genocide isn't some sort of self-destructive curse." John Paul smiled. "Because, after the killings, the population is back down to a manageable number. An adequate food supply is once again ensured. Equilibrium is reached. The group's will to preemptively forgive the act of genocide and to collectively mask their consciences as they do so is a great *advantage* in the evolutionary stakes, not a disadvantage. It's hardly surprising that this characteristic gets passed down to the next generation—it's the ultimate example of a successful adaptive mechanism toward one's environment."

"So what! There's an ancient adaptive mechanism left in the human mind that can spur humans on to kill each other on a grand scale? Big deal! How the hell does that justify your going from one impoverished country to another killing people? What is it that you even *want*? To prove that people are basically evil?"

"No. It's all because of me." A woman's voice. The owner of the voice must have been hiding, but she was now out in the open, and her slender white arm now pointed an old German Luger directly at John Paul's head.

Lucia Sukrova.

She started walking toward us, guided by the moonlight.

John Paul's gaze remained fixed on me—or rather the scene behind me. The moon's iridescence made Lucia's face look as cold as a corpse's. As beautiful as a corpse's.

"When your wife died, when Sarajevo disappeared, you couldn't forgive yourself for being in bed with me at the time. You couldn't forgive yourself for betraying your wife and daughter." Lucia pressed the muzzle of her gun into the back of John Paul's head. She was crying. Her white cheeks were shiny with tears.

"That's why you had to convince yourself... that betrayal and violence... that there is an inescapable human instinct to hurt other people. You've been proving how black and twisted human nature is just so that you could escape from your own guilt and despair. And you've killed so many people in the process—"

"No, Lucia. You're wrong. I haven't done all this to try and prove anything."

"Then why?"

"I discovered an ancient function of the brain. But at the same time I know full well that love is just as powerful an instinct—no, more powerful, really—than brutality. It's a basic biological function. I may have discovered a genocidal organ, but it hasn't shaken my basic faith in the fundamental goodness of humanity. Not one bit."

At this point I realized something really weird. There wasn't even the smallest cloud of despair hanging over John Paul. His gaze remained true and untroubled. He was as lucid, as calm, and as sane as ever. How could this be?

I took a step toward him, ignoring the gun in his hand. "So let me get this straight. If you're not killing all these people out of despair, what other possible reason could there be?"

The pause seemed to stretch out to infinity.

And then the Lord of Genocide answered:

"To protect the people I love."

5

When did patriotism become the primary motive for war?

The kamikaze pilots who smashed their own planes into aircraft carriers in order to protect their mothers and sisters. The French Resistance fighters who died trying to regain their country. The U-boat crew who suffered a briny death in order to shield their fatherland from invasion.

To fight for the greater good. Before the birth of the nation-state, that motive would have been right at the bottom of the list, if it featured at all. People fought in wars to advance their own interests or to make money. War was a specialist subject. Even if a soldier felt allegiance with the group that he was fighting alongside, it would never have occurred to him to think on the scale of "for the sake of all the people in my country." Citizens did go to war, almost always in the form of a mercenary transaction: pay me this much, and I'll lend you my arms for this length of time. Patriotism never even entered the picture until after the establishment of the national army. How could it? The concept of a standing army, a body of loyal troops that could be called upon at a moment's notice, simply didn't exist. Take the British fleet that against all odds miraculously managed to break the invincible Spanish Armada. It was a historic battle that changed the course of history forever by establishing British naval supremacy—and yet over half of the ships that fought that battle were souped-up merchant frigates, armed just for the occasion. Since time immemorial, war meant hiring mercenary forces as and when you needed them.

In other words, the very psychology of sacrificing yourself for your country was an extremely recent development. Taking a historic perspective, PMCs and independent contractors were actually the norm, and national armies such as the US or British armed forces were the aberrations. It was only recently that the business of war changed to become what we now know as modern warfare.

Ordinary citizens only started going to war out of patriotism after war became *theirs*—in other words, after they started feeling that the country was governed in their own interests. The exact form didn't matter; it could be a representative democracy as in America, or a popular form of limited constitutional monarchy, as in Britain. The people were happy with their leaders and the leaders had taken them to war, so the people were happy with the war. It was their war. And if it *was* their war, well then, it was the most natural thing in the world that they should take responsibility for it. Dress that responsibility up with fancy ribbons and voilà: patriotism.

You fought to protect someone. Your father or your mother or your sister.

Fundamentally it was an act of self-sacrifice. An act of neighborly love. An act of altruism, admittedly within certain preset parameters. Accordingly, war was fought out of love. The so-called mutually exclusive desires to love other people and kill other people had, on the battlefield at least, managed to reconcile with each other.

This was what John Paul was talking about right now.

I love therefore I kill.

"When I lost my wife and daughter in the nuclear blast I made a decision. That I would never let that sort of thing happen again. That I'd had my fill of sorrow."

"But you're the one causing all the sorrow!" Lucia bit down on her lip. "You led all those people to their deaths—you've spread sorrow across the world!"

"True, but it's a sorrow that people choose not to notice."

For the briefest of moments I thought that I detected a flash of despair in John Paul's words. "What do you mean?" I asked.

"People see only what they want to see. People don't care about the tragedies that happen elsewhere in the world. If you spend too much time worrying about them, you just end up overwhelmed by a sense of your own helplessness. Or possibly it's a case of people actually being helpless to do anything about it, so they can't be bothered to take an interest. It's pretty pathetic, but it's still my world. It's where I grew up. People go to Starbucks and shop online at Amazon and live their lives seeing just what they want to see. It's decadent and wasteful and shallow, but I love that world nonetheless, and I care deeply for the people who inhabit it. What is civilization? Conscience is a brittle and fragile thing. Civilization generally involves working toward the happiness of other people in your world. But we're not there yet. No one yet has seriously taken it upon themselves to rid the world of all its sorrows."

A world of CNN clips. The ubiquitous Domino's Pizza. Movies streamed straight to your house, the first fifteen minutes free. Metahistories that only go skin deep. That's about as far as our ethics of our civilization went.

"The people of my world seem to have become obsessed with personal identification and surveillance, even though these are almost completely ineffective as antiterrorist measures. When terrorism is born out of hopelessness and despair, traceability is no deterrent. Why should a suicide bomber care whether or not he's going to be identified after the event?"

"Yes, Lucius often used to say things like that," Lucia said.

"And so I considered the situation," John Paul said. "Rather than wait until they start hating us, why not make them hate each other? We don't have to let them kill us. We can focus their energies so that they only kill people within their own worlds. We can keep our world separate from theirs. A world of hatred and death for them, and a world of peace for us."

Find a country teetering on the edge, a country jealous of our wealth and leisure. A country that hated us.

A country that was starting to realize that their own misery and poverty was a byproduct of our freedom. That the corollary of our economic imperialism was their economic servitude.

And then, just before they got around to actually doing something about it, find a way to enter that country and introduce the grammar of genocide.

Once the resultant civil war kicked off, the country would no longer have the will or the capacity to turn its anger outward. Once the genocide began, there was no room left for thinking about killing people in *other* countries; you were too busy killing people in your own. The seething rage that had been about to spill over into the outside world in the form of terrorist attacks would now be contained, neutralized. John Paul had been sowing the seeds of destruction as a preventative measure against terrorism. His genocidal world tour was a preemptive strike against those who might one day seek to attack his world.

"I get them to kill each other. I'm not letting them lay a finger on my world ever again. The deep structure of the grammar is always the same, but it needs to be rendered differently for each language, according to the syntax. This makes it very easy to control. Each time my target existed in a distinct linguistic milieu. As long as you don't need to use English to spread your message, it's a pretty straightforward task to adjust the parameters every time you want to introduce the grammar to a new territory."

"Do you honestly believe that what you're doing is *fighting terrorism*?" I asked.

"The statistics speak for themselves. Look at the data released by your own, the US State Department—all in the public domain, of course. The fact was that the incidence of terrorist attacks was increasing exponentially, even as we busied ourselves by submitting to a biometric surveillance state. It was only after I started planting genocide around the world that incidences of terrorism in the US truly started falling. And now, there is none.

Mission accomplished. Of course, there is a trade-off, and the price we pay is the sharp increase in civil wars, ethnic conflicts, and massacres in Third World countries."

John Paul lifted his head and closed his eyes as if to congratulate himself on a job well done.

"I'm not saying for a moment that what I'm doing is right or fair. I'm just doing what I can to protect that which I want to protect," he said.

"Please. John. Put down your gun." There was nothing frail or weak about Lucia's tone of voice now. "Do it now or I'll shoot. You know I can, and you know I will."

"Of course. That would be your way of taking responsibility for your own sins." John Paul said as he pointed the Browning away from me. It only just occurred to me how long he had been talking —pretty impressive considering he had a gun shoved into the back of his head for most of it. What a bizarre situation. I walked over to him and plucked the gun from his hand.

"Mr. Bishop...What is your real name?" Lucia asked. I looked up at her face. Her eyes were clear. She knew exactly what she had to do. She was focused. I'd never once seen her with eyes like this when we were together in Prague.

"Clavis Shepherd. Captain. US Armed Forces, Intelligence."

"Clavis. Please arrest this person." Lucia's voice was composed and clear. "Please arrest him and take him back to America. You need to bring the story of the grammar of genocide to trial. People need to know. People have a responsibility to find out. If your people truly want to be free and truly want to live in a free country, they need to take responsibility for that freedom. They need to accept the burdens that come with the freedom of being able to make choices."

"Lucia, I'm afraid Clavis has orders to kill me." John Paul smiled wistfully. "He is, after all, an assassin."

I came here this night determined to kill this man. It was my own will. For once I wasn't interested in what the NME wanted, or asked, or ordered. I just wanted to put an end to all the atrocities with my own hands, for my own sake.

And now Lucia, the only person in the world who could administer the punishment that I needed, was asking me to arrest

John Paul and deliver him to justice instead of killing him as I had planned. As I had promised myself.

"This man's research was highly classified," I said. "There's no public record of it. The same goes for all of our missions to date. There's no corroborating evidence. Given that, do you really think that people will believe that this one man is the source of all the massacres and atrocities that have been occurring throughout the world?"

"I don't know. Maybe not. Maybe the jury will laugh the case out of court. But if you kill him now, if he's killed before anyone has the opportunity to learn the truth, and everything is just brushed under the carpet, then as far as I'm concerned all the people who ever died in those massacres that he caused might as well have been killed by our hand. We'd be ignoring all the corpses just so that we can selfishly grab a little peace and quiet for ourselves. That would be unforgivable."

Corpses.

Our world was built on top of corpses.

And it was filled with people who stood on a foundation of corpses and never suspected a thing.

But Lucia and I knew. That was the difference. We were past the point of no return. We couldn't go on cashing in on the misery of others.

"Fine. Let's take your John Paul with us and go," I said.

Bzz. A sound. Lucia's forehead expanded into a giant marshmallow. I stood there dumbly for a moment. *Oh, a hollow-point bullet.* I felt bizarrely calm. Lucia's forehead burst like a ripe tomato. I was standing right in front of her, so some of her blood and brain matter splattered across my face.

Lucia's left eye had been blown clean out of its socket; there was now a gaping hole where it used to be. What brain tissue she still had started oozing out through the new opening in her face. Lucia's body shifted and toppled over, carried forward by the energy of the blast. She slumped over John Paul's shoulders. Where she had been standing I could now see Williams, who was brandishing a handgun with a silencer attached.

"Lucia—"

She had lost half her head. A sight I'd seen numerous times

before. It was a common enough way to go in battle. To have part of your face blown away by a bullet.

I screamed. No, I tried to scream, but no sound emerged. My mouth was wide open, but only my anguish came out. I pointed my rifle at Williams and fired.

Williams charged at me, right into my line of fire. He couldn't stay where he was in the corridor—the guards would be here any second to investigate the sound of the gunshot.

"Clavis! Calm down! Our orders were to kill on sight!"

"She wasn't the target! You didn't need to kill her! You didn't need to kill anybody!"

Williams had run into the bathroom. I could hear voices in the distance, outside the door. I shoved John Paul away from Williams's line of fire and tossed him back his Browning.

"Use this to protect yourself," I said. John Paul nodded in silent assent.

This was a small room. Once Williams came out of the bathroom it would be a close-range battle. A bloodbath. Well, the guards would get here first anyway.

"Why did you kill her?" I shouted.

"For Monita and my baby." Williams's voice was calm but forceful. "So that they don't have to know what a shithole this world is. My baby doesn't need to know that our world is teetering on the edge of the abyss. All she needs is the opportunity to grow up at her own pace, in our own world. Got that, Clavis? I'm prepared to protect my world. I'm going to defend the world where you can order a jalapeño pizza and pay for it by thumbprint. I'll fight to the death for my family's right to eat as many Big Macs as they like and then throw away whatever they can't eat."

I heard the sound of footsteps converging outside the door. The worst-case scenario now would be a three-way shootout involving myself, Williams, and the guards. And we were heading straight in that direction.

"Lucia didn't need to die. And now you do. You have to die here," I said.

"Clavis, buddy, calm down. We have to work together now, remember? You and me. The way it always is. The guards are coming. Cooperate with me, like we always do? Whaddaya say, buddy?"

"Sure, I'll cooperate with you, *buddy*. I'll cooperate with your corpse. After I've killed you."

"Oh, for fuck's sake, Clavis. Look! Those were our orders, okay! Shoot to kill. You just weren't told about them, that's all. And I can see why now. Well, *I* was briefed to kill both Lucia Sukrova and John Paul. We have to wrap this case up once and for all. It comes straight from the top."

"Why?"

The guards finally started amassing by the doorway, so I fired a suppressing volley, full automatic, in their direction. One of them took a hit to the shoulder and spun around before collapsing to the floor.

"Dude, think about it. Think of the scandal if it ever got out that DARPA funded the research that led to international genocide. And think how bad it'd be for morale if John Paul told the world his story. Specially all the stuff about the surveillance crap that we do being basically useless. How there's no correlation between traceability and the fall in terrorism. Think how people would feel!"

"But there *is* no correlation, you idiot!"

"So what are you gonna do, huh?" Now Williams was shouting too. "Turn back time? The people *want* increased security measures, don't forget! Not just the government and industry, ordinary citizens too. People are *happy* to sacrifice a few freedoms in exchange for a safer society. So tell me, Clavis, what are you gonna do? Dismantle the entire surveillance infrastructure? InfoSec is a huge industry, you know that. Money's still being poured into it from all angles. It gives jobs to tens of thousands of people, if not more. And it's part of the system now. So call me an idiot if you want, Clavis, but just tell me this. *What are you gonna do?*"

With that, Williams chucked a grenade out of the bathroom and through the door that led to the second floor corridor. There was an explosion beyond the doorway, then screams and dust.

I turned to Williams again. "But it's all bullshit! It's all pointless! We don't *need* all that security!"

"It might be bullshit, Clavis, but it's *our* bullshit. And the horse is already out of the barn on this one. We're committed. The whole economy's committed."

We had reached an impasse of sorts. But at this rate I would be out of bullets in no time.

I grabbed hold of John Paul's arm, chucked a grenade over my shoulder, and jumped with John Paul through the moonlit window to the ground below. We landed on the lawn in a messy heap but scrambled to our feet and made a dash for the shore.

There was an explosion behind us. The grenade had just exploded. It had almost been a reflex action. I hadn't even stopped to think what would happen to Williams. Not that I cared anymore.

The guards fired their AKs at us, but they were all terrible shots and a little too far away. The nanocamouflage probably helped some too. John Paul had no protective gear, so as much as possible I covered his back as we ran away.

I realized that John Paul's shoulders were covered in Lucia's blood and chunks of brain. I realized we had left her body behind. My chest wanted to explode. There was nothing we could have done in that situation to bring her with us. We had done the right thing. Logically speaking. But none of these facts helped to numb the gut-wrenching soul-pain I was feeling. I ran with John Paul, and before I knew it there were tears streaming down my face.

"Are you crying for her?" John Paul asked.

"I just left her there. Her corpse."

"Surely you've seen plenty of corpses in your time."

The girl whose head was exposed to the heavens.

The boy whose guts spilled from his ruptured belly.

The women and children doused in gasoline and left to burn in the giant hole in the ground.

Up until now I'd always thought of corpses as *things*. When a person died, he or she became an *it*. An object. And as Lucia had lost half her face and what was left of her soft brains was now dripping out of her eye socket, she was surely a perfect example of how a person could turn into an object in the twinkling of an eye.

And yet she wasn't just a thing. I refused to see her as just a thing. She was still Lucia Sukrova, even dead. She wasn't just a mass of flesh. She might have been a corpse, but she was *Lucia's* corpse.

"Of course I've seen corpses before," I said. "But this time it's just so personal. When the person is important to you, they can't become just a corpse."

I gritted my teeth and we pushed on. John Paul and I made it into the jungle.

It wasn't easy moving through the jungle with John Paul. He might have been familiar enough with war zones, but he was still a civilian. It required quite a bit of skill to be able to maneuver through this sort of terrain. Jungles weren't designed for late-night leisurely strolls.

To make matters worse, John Paul had also sprained his right ankle when he jumped from the second-floor window. It wasn't that far to the Tanzanian border where our recovery team should be waiting, but there was a limit to how fast we could move when his leg was like this.

"There's no way I can hand you back to the Lake Victoria Shores Industrial Federation," I said, my eyes on the path in front of us. "If you were to go back you'd just start singing your song of genocide again, I know."

"I'm not interested in going back," John Paul muttered. The confidence he had back at the guesthouse had now all but disappeared. "Lucia said that I should explain what I had done to the world. She wanted me to tell the world just how shaky a foundation their 'peace' rests on, I guess. Well, I will stand trial, and I may be sentenced to death. Or perhaps I'll just be dismissed as a lunatic and laughed out of court. Whatever happens, I'll accept it, because that's what Lucia wanted. It'll be my way of apologizing to her, however pathetic and inadequate the gesture. I was the one who brought her into all this. I had only intended to stop in Prague long enough to get a fake ID, but then I found I wanted to see her face again for old times' sake. That was all…"

I listened to John Paul's story without saying anything. I just hacked through the jungle with my machete.

"I betrayed my wife and child and now I've also killed the woman I once loved."

"What about all the people who died in the massacres you caused? Don't they count at all? That's quite a solipsistic sense of guilt you have, don't you think?" I was feeling pretty cynical by now. "Don't forget that there's a staggering number of corpses behind you at all times."

"No, of course not." John Paul nodded. "I know. It's something I've carried with me from the very first time I used the grammar of genocide."

I realized that, in talking to John Paul, I was telling him to do as I said and not as I did. I was telling John Paul not to forget about all the corpses, and yet I had no idea what to do about the burden I carried with me. All of my sins, not just my matricide. The sin of killing people without having chosen to kill them myself. The sin of dodging my responsibility. I wanted closure. From Lucia's mouth. Redemption—or condemnation.

But Lucia had died. And there was no one left in this world who could either punish me or forgive me.

This was hell, right here, right now. I was trapped in a hell called myself. "*Hell is here, Captain Shepherd*" was what Alex had said. And he had been right. I was in the deepest pit of hell. I had come here to be punished and, at the end of the punishment, find a glimmer of hope, the possibility that I could be redeemed. That was why I had come to Africa. But shortly after I arrived, the prospect of punishment and forgiveness slipped away forever; it disappeared, broken.

Maybe this *was* my punishment. To be doomed to walk the earth till the end of my days, weighed down by the burden of corpses.

"I want to ask you something," I said. "Now that Lucia's dead, do you regret what you did? Laying the groundwork for so many people to die?"

Now that he had lost Lucia, I wondered whether John Paul felt any sort of solidarity with the people who had died, or the people who had lost loved ones.

John Paul shook his head. "No. Not at all. I have no regrets on that front, at least. I put two sets of lives in the scales. The lives of the people in our world on one side, and on the other side were the lives of hostile people who lived in poverty and hatred and cast a shadow over our happiness. I went into this thing eyes wide open and made a completely sober and rational decision. I even had a good idea of how many people would die in the process. Once you know what you are capable of doing, it becomes impossible to escape from your own potential."

"And what will you do next?" I asked.

"Well, I was originally planning to continue bearing the burden all on my own. But if we get to the stage where, per Lucia's wishes, the world learns of what I've done, then I suppose the choice will be theirs. They'll have to make the call as to whether they want to keep their world without terrorism, even if it means building it atop of a pile of corpses."

"And you think that'll make you feel better? If you hand the baton on to someone else? Will that excuse your crimes?"

"By no means. You can never escape from your own decisions. They are with you always."

We walked on without rest.

All things considered, and taking a long-term historical perspective, the world was probably becoming a better place over time. The world did occasionally fall into the clutches of chaos and regressed, but broadly speaking the story of humanity was a story of progress. Relativism only gets you so far. There always comes a point where you *can* say that one culture has more sophisticated or enlightened values than another, and this *can* be a good thing in absolute terms. The story of civilization is the story of the battle of human conscience against the instinct to murder or rape or steal or betray, and how even against the harsh backdrop of the world, the conscience is still moving inexorably in the direction of altruism and love for family and friends and neighbors.

But we still have a long way to go before we can accurately describe ourselves as moral actors. As ethical beings.

For humans can turn our eyes from all sorts of things.

John Paul limped along behind me, desperately trying to keep pace. He was panting hard.

Now he asked me a question. "What about you? What will you do after this? Will you go back to assassinating people? To making the world a better place?"

"I've never been fighting to make the world a better place. I just did what I was ordered to do because they were my orders."

"And is that all going to change now?"

"I don't know," I said honestly. "But what I do know is that I'm starting to see things a lot more clearly than before. At least I think I am."

The jungle ended. Suddenly.

There was a clear sky that stretched out forever. Dawn was breaking, and a white horizon unfurled before us.

There was a Jeep parked up in the distance. It was still a little too far away to confirm with the naked eye, but it looked like there were two soldiers waiting there. According to our pre-mission briefing, these guys should be deployed from the Tanzanian army, here to help us.

I took a deep breath, and then John Paul and I started walking across the flat, grassy savanna.

A hollow, dry explosion echoed all around.

One of the soldiers in the distance was pointing a gun in our direction. I spun around. There was a small hole in John Paul's forehead and he was lying on the ground.

"Welcome back, Captain Shepherd, sir! And congratulations on your successful mission." One of our sergeants was there to welcome me—a black man, no doubt chosen for this mission because the color of his skin helped him blend in with the local African soldiers.

"What happened to Williams...?" I asked absentmindedly.

"Killed in action, sir. According to a wireless transmission intercepted by an NSA team, sir."

I was overcome by a fatigue that seemed to penetrate every last nook and cranny of my body. I felt like a lump of wax. As soon as I climbed into the Jeep and sat down I was assaulted by drowsiness. Williams, Lucia, John Paul. All were now distant, half-forgotten memories. The emotions that I thought I had felt and the insight that I thought I had gained—all seemed so unreal now. It was as if I could only remember the whole journey in a series of blurry low-resolution snapshots.

"Let's get out of here."

The Jeep started rolling. Moving gently toward the white horizon in the distance. For a moment I imagined that this Tanzanian savanna was the only place in the world that was real, that it stretched across the whole world, and that the Prague and the Paris and the Washington and the Georgetown that I knew were all just a bad dream—a nightmare called civilization.

Somewhere behind us in the vast savanna was John Paul's final resting place. There his corpse would decay gently under the African sun. His sun-bleached body would be preserved for some time to come, and in this respect he was just like Mom, whom I'd had embalmed so that she would never rot away. John Paul, though, would eventually be able to return to the soil. Maybe the thought of that would have made him happy.

Epilogue

This is my story. That's what I'm going to say once I've finished it.

I left the Forces. There was no one alive left to stop me. After returning from that last mission in Africa I felt that something inside me was missing. It took me a while to realize this for myself, and in the meantime many of my colleagues suggested various forms of counseling.

I brushed all the well-meaning suggestions aside. After my return to America I found that people were speaking in ways I found too fast and slippery. I found myself unable to fully participate in conversations. It was too difficult to join in, so I just stopped speaking to people.

One day, while I was holed up hermitlike in my house, doing nothing, I received an ID and a password in the post.

The envelope was embossed with an expensive-looking InfoSec company logo. It was the company my mother had subscribed to.

The envelope was addressed to me.

The sealed letter explained that, per the terms of the Fourth

Amendment to the Personal Information Protection Law, when a person dies intestate and without specific instructions for the disposal of their subscription information assets, all accounts are embargoed for three years, and then all of the intestate party's accounts are passed onto their next of kin as designated at the time of the opening of the account. As such, and the embargo now having passed, I was now the official owner of the information account of one Ms. Elyssia Shepherd (deceased).

In this society of ours, where everything is recorded and stored for posterity, you occasionally encounter this sort of blast from the past. It was a bit like being in a traffic accident—it's not exactly a rare occurrence, but no one expects it to happen to them. I was no exception.

I didn't believe that there would be anything my mother would have particularly wanted to share with me though. I was her next of kin by default; my father had already departed this world when she set up the account, and so I, her son and only child, was the default choice.

The sealed letter provided me with two potential pitfalls.

The first was my mother's memories in and of themselves.

The second was the fact that, when I had to choose between my mother living or dying, I never put in a request to consult the memories.

When it had been medically determined that my mother was in a no man's land between life and death and in a place that no living person would ever hope to experience or imagine, I could have put in an official request to the InfoSec company for permission to read her Life Graph. Both the law and the InfoSec company were able to grant special dispensation for a concerned third party to do so when the subscriber was unconscious or medically incapacitated.

I never put in the request. I just chose for my mother to die without reading her Life Graph.

I wonder why I had been afraid of reading my mother's memories back then? I can't remember exactly why anymore. All I remember is that I was vaguely frightened and that I didn't want to.

What about now? Was I still afraid? I probably was. After experiencing the deaths of Lucia Sukrova and John Paul, however, it was now a different type of fear.

The afternoon after the letter arrived was terrifyingly silent. I felt that people were watching over me to see if I would use the account to read my mother's online memories. When I say people I meant the dead, of course.

After fifteen minutes of hesitation, I accessed my mother's account and commanded the Life Graph to compile her biography for me.

John Paul had passed me a notebook back in the jungle. I flicked through it to skim its contents, but it was full of obscure academic jargon too difficult for me to understand.

But there was one thing in the notebook that was to prove useful later on. The user name and password of an email account.

An interesting development was that the press somehow found out the true reason for the former senate majority leader's abrupt withdrawal from public life. I never discovered where the leak came from. An investigative committee was formed and Congressional hearings were held. Even as the whole affair was dragged out into the media, the former senator seemed unrepentant. He made a bold declaration—that we in the US of A always needed the spectacle of war. At any given time, we needed a war to be happening somewhere in the world. And above all, we needed the tragedy of war to be happening somewhere *else*, in some place where it couldn't affect us directly. He explained that he had come to this realization some time ago, and that only by being a witness to these sorts of wars could people truly self-actualize and become aware of the potential of their own selves.

This wasn't the old-fashioned theory that all people in a country needed a common enemy so that they could pull together as a unified nation. No. It was about wars happening overseas, somewhere, vaguely, and being able to pick up on the rustles and murmurs, like background music in a shopping mall. That was what we needed for the twenty-first century, the former senator explained. And John Paul had been the man for the job—he had been able to ensure a steady supply of war.

As a former member of the Special Forces, and as a former member of an elite top-secret assassination unit that performed the government's dirty work, I was given a huge amount of face time at his hearing and given ample opportunity to tell my stories again and again, just the way I wanted to. Because of my revelations, Washington was plunged into the greatest scandal yet of the twenty-first century, possibly one of the biggest of all time. Of course, my actions violated the State Secrets Protection Act, which was why it came to pass that the US Armed Forces Intelligence Captain Clavis Shepherd was indicted.

In the end, though, the long arm of the law never did get around to dealing with me. There was rioting across the nation by that stage, and the powers that be found that they had far bigger fish to fry. Various state National Guards found themselves opening fire on ordinary citizens, and in turn their armories were being swept away by insurgents who were arming themselves to the teeth to fight back.

Finally, I settled down to read the Life Graph, under the beady eyes of my ever-vigilant spectral companions.

My mother's life, as regurgitated by computer software.

The story of the pair of eyes that constantly watched over me.

So why was there was no room for me in this story?

Traces of my mother's gaze. The feeling that I was constantly being watched. These were my childhood memories. And it seemed that they were betrayed. If my mother's biography according to the Life Graph was anything to go by, I barely featured at all in her life.

I wasn't completely absent, of course. The important events and landmarks were all there, but with minimal detail. Almost as though I were an afterthought. The person who really came to life in my mother's memory was my father. Overwhelmingly. The man who had blown his brains out and suddenly disappeared from my mother's life. And yet he had not disappeared at all. Not from her memories.

Mom wasn't looking at me. She had never been looking at me.

I could now say with confidence that the person who'd scrubbed my father's splattered brains off the walls after he shot himself was my mother.

Everybody's life story is interwoven with sections of other people's stories. My story contained elements of Mom's story, of Williams's story, of the stories of Lucia Sukrova and John Paul. But Mom's story barely mentioned me at all.

But...

I tried to work out what had actually happened in my past then. That constant presence, the gaze that I always felt on the back of my collar. It had to have been real. It had to have been. Even after all these years I could still remember, vividly, the goose bumps I used to feel when I met my mother's gaze from the most exquisite of angles, such as from that little slip of space between the kitchen and the hallway to the bathroom. We were like two snipers targeting one another, discovering the spine-tingling coincidence that the other was looking at you through their scope at the very same instant that you had found them with yours.

And yet the record that was supposed to confirm that this constant gaze I'd felt upon me was indeed a mother's love was curiously, bafflingly, bewilderingly absent.

So what the hell was *it?*

If I thought that I was empty after that last mission, well, I hadn't seen anything yet. Because *now* I was empty. *Now* I was hollow. *Now* there was a gnawing void inside me.

And John Paul's notebook filled that void. It was a perfect fit. Maybe it was even the case that the notebook sensed the void in me and picked *me* out.

So I'm feeling pretty satisfied because I'd been able to squeeze in plenty of appropriate grammatical forms into the news clip I'm now watching. The email account that John Paul left me contained a text editor that could generate a grammar of genocide for the English language.

John Paul had used this to imbue all kinds of words with the tincture of death. He had disseminated those words around the world. Well, that was then. This was now. I'm weaving my own tale of genocide.

John Paul's grammar was, in a way, like sheet music. As an homage, I decided to make my version as close to music as I could.

So I chanted it and I recited it. The sound. The rhythm. I prayed, deliberately, intensely: *I want you to start killing each other. Just like so many people outside America have already killed each other.* All the while I thought how nice it would be if someone noticed what I was doing, noticed the simple, functional evidence that this was a prayer, a song.

My words started to take shape, and gradually they penetrated the fabric of American discourse. My words, my songs, my images, my tone of voice, all started seeping into the collective psyche of the people who watched or listened to or had any interest whatsoever in my Congressional hearing. Even if a person merely accessed the Congressional Record after the fact, there was enough latent deep structure embedded into my transcribed speeches for my grammatical tune to kick in inside their minds.

In no time at all the original scandal stopped being an issue. I rammed home the grammar of genocide into this country, the USA, a country that previously never even showed the slightest of omens that a civil war might be brewing. I was a puppet master, a god riding the crest of an unstoppable mechanical force, ruthlessly, relentlessly changing the course of the lives of mere mortals. It was a smooth process, almost automatic.

There have already been plenty of casualties all across the country. And we haven't even really started yet. The handful of news networks that are still going report that the country is on the brink of an all-out civil war. There haven't yet been any large-scale massacres that you could properly call genocide though. Not yet. But soon. Soon enough.

The seemingly eternal Starbucks and the once-ubiquitous Domino's Pizza have disappeared. I knew this was going to happen, of course, so I'd stocked up on supplies big-time. The other day I had to shoot a burglar who was after my hoard. His corpse is still in my hallway. I wonder what I should do with it. The deep structure of genocide has spread across the whole of America, quickly and easily, using English as its vector.

See? There *was* another way to eliminate the risk of terrorist attacks on the good old US of A after all. Who's going to bother with us now? We've stopped trading internationally, the import and export markets have utterly collapsed. No country is going to have cause to be jealous of us or hate us for our economic imperialism anymore.

You see, I decided to take the burden of sin upon my own shoulders. I decided I was going to punish myself. So I took America, dangerous America, the bane of the rest of the world, and I cast her into the abyss. In order to save all other countries, I gritted my teeth and made up my mind to plunge my country into a Hobbesian *bellum omnium contra omnes*.

It was a tough decision. But I've decided to accept responsibility for it. Just as John Paul accepted responsibility for the lives of people from all the rest of the world.

Outside, somewhere in the distance, I can hear an FN Minimi firing on full automatic.

Oh, hurry up and kill them already so we can get some peace. I'm trying to enjoy my pizza here!

No, it's still firing on full. The noise is starting to bother me.

But then I think about how everywhere else in the world is quieter now. That makes me feel a little better.

Keikaku (Project) Itoh was born in Tokyo in 1974. He graduated from Musashino Art University. In 2007, he debuted with *Gyakusatsu Kikan* (*Genocidal Organ*) and took first prize in the Best SF of 2007 in *SF Magazine*. His novel *Harmony* won both the Seiun and Japan SF awards, and its English-language edition won the Philip K. Dick Award Special Citation. He is also the author of *Metal Gear Solid: Guns of the Patriots*, a Japanese-language novel based on the popular video game series. All three of his novels are available in English from Haikasoru. After a long battle with cancer, Itoh passed away in March 2009.

HAIKASORU

THE FUTURE IS JAPANESE

INCREDIBLE SCIENCE FICTION BY PROJECT ITOH

HARMONY

In the future, Utopia has finally been achieved thanks to medical nanotechnology and a powerful ethic of social welfare and mutual consideration. This perfect world isn't that perfect though, and three young girls stand up to totalitarian kindness and super-medicine by attempting suicide via starvation. It doesn't work, but one of the girls—Tuan Kirie—grows up to be a member of the World Health Organization. As a crisis threatens the harmony of the new world, Tuan rediscovers another member of her suicide pact, and together they must help save the planet...from itself. Winner of the Special Citation of the Philip K. Dick award!

METAL GEAR SOLID: GUNS OF THE PATRIOTS

From the legendary video game franchise! Solid Snake is a soldier and part of a worldwide nanotechnology network known as the Sons of the Patriots System. Time is running out for Snake as, thanks to the deadly FOXDIE virus, he has been transformed into a walking biological weapon. Not only is the clock ticking for Snake, but for the world itself. Snake turns to the SOP for help, only to find that it has been hacked by his old enemy Liquid Ocelot—and whoever controls the SOP System controls the world.

THE FUTURE IS JAPANESE, EDITED BY HAIKASORU

A web browser that threatens to conquer the world. The longest, loneliest railroad on Earth. A North Korean nuke hitting Tokyo, a hollow asteroid full of automated rice paddies, and a specialist in breaking up "virtual" marriages. And yes, giant robots. These thirteen stories from and about the Land of the Rising Sun run the gamut from fantasy to cyberpunk, and will leave you knowing that the future is Japanese! *Featuring the military SF novella "The Indifference Engine" by Project Itoh!*

WWW.HAIKASORU.COM